PRAISE FOR GREG KEYES

THE REIGN OF THE DEPARTED

"Keyes is a master of world building and of quirky characters who grow into their relationships in unexpected ways. Fans of his Age of Unreason and his Kingdoms of Thorn and Bone fantasy series will want to get in on the ground floor of the High and Faraway series." — *Booklist*

"I liked a lot of what Keyes was doing in the novel, in terms of the story itself, the characters, and laying the groundwork for a multi-book narrative. The world where Errol awakens in his new body has a lived-in feel, a world with history and mythology of its own. . . . the story reminded me of Kate Elliott's Crown of Stars." — *SFFWorld*

"Starts in the realm of normalcy and quickly descends into the favorably bizarre and surprising . . . there was not one character that was uninteresting. The world building is epic. A magical realm that mirrors earth while residing under a curse was not only inventive but enthralling."
— *Koeur's Book Reviews*, 4.4/5 Stars

THE BRIAR KING

"A wonderful tale . . . It crackles with suspense and excitement from start to finish." — Terry Brooks

"The characters in *The Briar King* absolutely brim with life . . . Keyes hooked me from the first page and I'll now be eagerly anticipating sitting down with each future volume of The Kingdoms of Thorn and Bone series."
— Charles de Lir'

"A thrill ride to the end, with plenty of treachery, revelation, and even a few bombshell surprises."
—*Monroe News-Star* (LA)

THE AGE OF UNREASON
"Features the classic elements of science fiction: high-tech gadgetry, world-threatening superpower conflict, a quest to save the world, and a teen hero who's smarter than most of the adults . . . Powerful." —*USA Today*

"Seems likely to establish Keyes as one of the more significant and original new fantasy writers to appear in recent years." —*Science Fiction Chronicle*

KINGDOMS OF THE CURSED

THE HIGH AND FARAWAY BOOK TWO

KINGDOMS
OF THE CURSED

THE HIGH AND FARAWAY BOOK TWO

GREG KEYES

NIGHT SHADE BOOKS
NEW YORK

Night Shade books may be purchased in bulk at special discounts for sales promotion, corporate gifts, fund-raising, or educational purposes. Special editions can also be created to specifications. For details, contact the Special Sales Department, Night Shade Books, 307 West 36th Street, 11th Floor, New York, NY 10018 or info@skyhorsepublishing.com.

Night Shade Books® is a registered trademark of Skyhorse Publishing, Inc.®, a Delaware corporation.

Visit our website at www.nightshadebooks.com.

10 9 8 7 6 5 4 3 2 1

Library of Congress Cataloging-in-Publication Data

Names: Keyes, J. Gregory, 1963- author.
Title: Kingdoms of the cursed / Greg Keyes.
Description: New York : Night Shade Books, [2019] | Series: The high and faraway ; book 2
Identifiers: LCCN 2019004693 | ISBN 9781597809955 (pbk. : alk. paper)
Subjects: | GSAFD: Fantasy fiction.
Classification: LCC PS3561.E79 K56 2019 | DDC 813/.54--dc23
LC record available at https://lccn.loc.gov/2019004693

Cover illustration by Micah Epstein
Cover design by Claudia Noble

Printed in the United States of America

For Hyla Lacefield

Dear Diary,

I've been dead for more than thirty years.

I'm laughing, because the last time I wrote in a diary, it was the day before I died. It was something about a cute boy, but I don't remember his name.

Anyways, I spent most of that "dead" time luring men to their doom at the bottom of a forest pool. I loved to play with their bones. But then Aster and Errol woke me up and put flesh and skin back on me.

They didn't do it to be nice. Aster is a witch. She's from another place called the Kingdoms of the High and Faraway, a place where miracles are commonplace. It's separated from the normal world—where I was born—by a border called the Pale. It's hard to get to from here. There are hundreds, maybe thousands of kingdoms, each weirder and more magical than the last. Castles of gold, cities of glass, seas with tides but no water, boats of silver, howling dark monsters in deep, black swamps. Curses and spells. Everyone born there has a light in them called *elumiris*. Another word for soul, I guess. When they die, they're born again in another Kingdom, sometimes higher and further away, sometimes nearer to the Pale, depending how bright they shine inside.

Aster's father brought her to the town of Sowashee, where I'm from. It's in the normal world, which she calls the Reign of the Departed. It turns out my world is where souls go when they're all worn out. When they don't have enough spark to be born again in the Kingdoms, they're born here, live their very last life, and then disappear forever.

Aster's dad is a witch (warlock?), too, and a really strong one. He brought her to the Reign to protect her from something, though he never told her what. But he was sick. He couldn't remember things for very long, and he couldn't learn new things. He thought Aster was still a little girl, even though she's seventeen. He was trapped in his house, and Aster was afraid he would get out.

She had an idea how to cure him. There was this stuff called the "water of health," but to find it she needed help from three guides — the Mostly Dead, the Completely Dead, and a giant. The Completely Dead was me. But to catch me, she needed someone Mostly Dead, and that was Errol. Errol was someone she knew from school. He'd tried to kill himself and ended up in a coma. Aster took his soul and put it into this sort of wooden Pinocchio/Tin Man body she'd made of odds and ends. When he came to find me, I tried to kill him, like I did the others, but he didn't drown. Then Aster put my skin back on and all, and they dragged me off on an adventure to find the third guide, the giant.

Before we could start, though, two people showed up at Aster's house. One was her teacher, Mr. Watkins, and the other was the school counselor, Delia Fincher. They were checking up on her, but her dad turned them into smoke and put them in a liquor bottle.

Diary, that was not the strangest thing that happened, not even that day.

Since she needed someone to watch her father while she was gone, Aster got her dad to fetch Mrs. Fincher back out of the bottle. Then she put a necklace on her that kept control of her, and the school counselor had to follow any instructions Aster gave her.

After a little dust up or two, we went off through the Pale, me leading the way to the High and Faraway, because I could see the path they couldn't. But someone was following us; a guy who called himself the Sherriff. Seems like doing what she did, Aster had broken some rules that he reckoned she needed to be punished for. And as for Errol and me—well, we weren't supposed to exist at all, to the Sherriff's way of thinking.

In that first Kingdom, right at the border, we got a new friend—a woman named Dusk, just a little older than Aster. She said she would help us find the giant Aster was looking for. We also learned about the curse; all of the grownups in the High and Faraway had turned into monsters or just . . . gone away.

The kids had to learn to fend for themselves.

The Sherriff was still following us. He deputized some bad boys and brought them along. We didn't know that at the time. We also didn't know Aster's father had sent her teacher, Mr. Watkins, after her, and put a spell on him that let him sense which direction she was in and forced him to follow her. He took up with the Sherriff.

The deeper we got into the Kingdoms, the more powerful Aster's witchery grew. But I got stronger, too. I could feel the creeks and rivers and deeps, talk to the creatures of the water. Do things. And sometimes, I still got hungry, like when I was a *nov*. And sometimes I wanted to be one again.

We made a new friend named Billy Noname. Nobody knew where he'd come from, least of all him. But Aster started getting sweet on him right away.

And yes, I was taking a fancy to Errol. Me, the living dead, him a walking puppet. The perfect couple.

Except Errol also had doe-eyes for Dusk. When I figured that out, I went off to sulk, and the Sherriff caught me. And the teacher, David, was there. When I touched David, I suddenly knew—he was the guy who murdered me all those years ago. Surprised? Me too. But back then he'd had a different name, and a different face. Now he had his sights set on Aster.

Diary, they buried me head-down in a rocky shaft. Errol found me and pulled me out, and off we went again, until we came to the Mountain of the Winds and some folks who allowed they had a giant problem.

Boy, did they. It was huge, and we didn't have a chance against it. Until Billy turned into a giant, too. See, Billy was the giant we were looking for. He had shrunk down, years before— for a vacation, sort of—and had forgotten what he was.

After that, he put us in his palm and walked off into the High and Faraway, until we came to a golden castle. He shrunk back down, and we found the water of health, a dose for each of us.

That's when Dusk turned on us, froze Aster and Billy with her magic sword, cut off one of Errol's legs, and sliced my neck clean through. Then she took all of the water of health and left us there.

I hate to use profanity, but Dusk really is a—well, it rhymes with witch.

What she didn't know was that Aster had already given me my share of the water of health. Errol used half of it to stick my head back on. Aster and Billy unthawed, just in time for us to fight the Sherriff and his boys. And David.

I took care of David. Unfortunately, the thing in him, the dark soul—it didn't stay down. It wandered off.

Aster killed the Sherriff. But Errol—they broke him to pieces. His soul slipped back to his dying body in Sowashee.

I didn't like Aster at first, but by then she was growing on me. I didn't envy her the choice she had to make.

Billy could take us home, but if he stayed a giant that long, he would forget her, and stay a giant. And by that point Aster was in love with him. If she used the half-potion she had left, she could restore his memory. Or she could save it for her father.

Or she could heal Errol.

She picked Errol. And when he got to her house, we found her father was gone anyway. Dusk had come along, pretended to be Aster, and whisked him away.

And me? The water of health did more than just sew my head back on. During the day, I'm alive now. Heartbeat and all. Of course, at night, all of that stops again. But I'm better than I was.

Now I'm off to plot with Aster. We've got to get Errol out of the hospital, find her father, and cut off a certain person's damn head.

Until later, dear diary, I am yours,
Veronica Hale.

PART ONE

PLACES KNOWN
AND STRANGE

ONE
A KISS THROUGH THE BARS

That hot July night, in the grey hours before dawn, Errol's dead girlfriend came for a visit. She swam up Gallinger Creek and into the storm drains beneath Sowashee, under the wall around Laurel Grove Hospital, emerged from the old cistern near the orchard, slipped past the bored night watchmen, and scaled the century-old wrought-iron downspout to the ledge beneath his second-story window. The sash was propped open with a stick, but iron bars prevented her entering his room. Fortunately, there was space for her to press her face through. Her kiss was cool and wet, and tasted slightly of algae, minnows, and crawfish. He brushed a leaf from her long hair which—even wet and in the dark—still had a golden glint.

For a while Errol was conscious only of her lips, her luminous, half-lidded eyes, the night symphony of frogs and insects, the sultry atmosphere redolent of mimosa and woodbine enveloping them.

"I hate I'm all soaking wet," Veronica confided, after they finally parted long enough to talk. "It's hard for a girl to look her best after a swim. But I can't figure out any other way of getting in here without being seen."

"I don't mind," Errol said. "You were soaking wet the first time we met, remember?"

"Well, I do remember, Errol, if you must know. And naked. And I think I may have tried to drown you."

"Not the greatest first date," Errol admitted.

Her eyes dropped a little.

"Hey, I'm kidding," he said.

"It's just . . . you're all normal now," she said. "A regular boy. And I'm still . . ."

"Doesn't matter," he said. "Not to me anyway. I hope it doesn't matter to you."

"You're sweet," she said. She kissed him again.

"How much longer do you have to stay in this . . . place?" she asked, when they parted once more.

"Until I can convince them I'm not going to try and off myself again, I guess," he said.

"That shouldn't take long," she said.

"Yeah," he said. "You would think."

Suicide, as it turned out, was not without consequences.

Of course, the doctors called it "attempted suicide" because technically he had never quite been dead. But Errol knew better. He had seen death coming for him, and if it weren't for a good friend and a literal miracle, he wouldn't be alive today. Nor would he be an unwilling resident of the Laurel Grove State Hospital, a dumping ground for the mentally ill, drunks, drug addicts, and depressed teens.

His mom liked the place because it didn't cost her anything and because it took him off her hands. In his lower moments, he thought it would have probably been easier for her if he had gone ahead and died. But despite what most everyone thought, he had no intention of dying anytime soon, not if he had a choice in the matter.

"So what are you and Aster up to?" he asked.

Veronica hesitated. She squeezed his hand.

"It's kind of a mess," she said. "What with Aster's father disappearing and that teacher, Ms. Fincher."

"And Mr. Watkins," Errol said.

Veronica's small brow creased and a nasty little smile spread her lips.

"Yeah," she said. "That guy."

Mr. Watkins had been an English teacher at Sowashee High. He had also been the vessel occupied by an evil spirit who had a thing for raping and murdering girls before stealing their souls. In an earlier incarnation—thirty years before—he had been Veronica's neighbor. He had killed her, but hadn't managed the raping and soul-stealing part.

Errol squeezed her hand. "Sorry," he said. "I didn't mean to bring that up. It's only—have the police found anything? How is Aster explaining all this?"

"I'm not quite sure," Veronica said. She glanced away, as if looking at something behind him, but he knew there wasn't anything back there but a blank, beige wall.

"What?" he said.

"The police sort of took her off yesterday," she said. "She hasn't been back."

"Oh," he said. "That's not good."

"I know," Veronica said. "She was working on a plan of some kind to get us all back to the Kingdoms, rescue her dad, kill Dusk, find Billy—all that stuff." She smiled. "We were gonna break you out, if they hadn't let you go by then. But now . . ."

She shrugged.

"Do you know where they took her?"

She shook her head. "They were in a car," she said. "I couldn't keep up. And besides, she told me to stay hidden."

"Yes!" he said. "Definitely stay hidden. The police—no one—should know about you."

"Too late for that," she said. "They're looking for me already. I heard them asking Aster about me. I guess somebody noticed me at the hospital."

"That's bad," Errol said.

Veronica had been dead for decades. If anyone figured out who she was—and that for some reason she only appeared to be sixteen or so—it could lead to further questions. Like why her heart didn't beat at night. He imagined her being hauled off to a lab somewhere, never to be seen again. He didn't care for the image.

"You shouldn't even be here now," he said. "It's too risky."

"Oh, hardly," she said. "They're not so much worried about people getting in here as they are about people sneaking out. Who breaks into a loony bin?"

"Yeah, that's a good point," Errol said.

"Not that I think you are loony, dear Errol," she said.

"Thanks," he said. "We need Aster, though. I need to get out of here."

Veronica caught his gaze and held it.

"Errol," she said. "You don't need Aster or the Kingdoms. You're cured. You don't have to go back."

"What does that have to do with it?" he said. "Veronica, you were better off there. We both know that. You came back here for me. And Aster, she gave up Billy to save my life, and I know she loved him. So maybe I am cured, but I have lots of reasons to go back there. And anyway, what do I have here?"

"You don't have to fight everybody's battles for them, Errol," she said.

"Maybe I don't have to," he said. "But I want to."

"We might be able to go back, just the two of us," Veronica said.

"Maybe," he said. "But I'm not half-dead anymore, and you're not exactly what you were. Without Aster, we'd have no idea what we were walking into. Anyway—"

"I know," she said. "We can't abandon her. I was thinking aloud." Veronica patted his hand. "Always Errol, aren't you," she said. "That's what I love about you."

Veronica didn't have a heartbeat, but he did, and he felt it go funny.

"What?" he said.

"Don't get all weird," she said. "I love you, that's all."

"Oh."

Veronica wasn't the first girl who had told him that, but that first girl had been lying. That was a big piece of what had nearly killed him.

"It's okay," she said, softly. She looked behind her, at the sky. Her smile faded a little. "It's almost dawn. I better swim out of here before I start breathing again." She stroked his face with the tips of her fingers. "I wish I could come here in the day," she said. "And kiss you with warm lips."

"Warm enough for me," he said, and leaned through the bars.

"Oh, Errol, you old sweet talker," she said.

He remembered the first time they had kissed. Their first *real* kiss, lying beneath the stars in a distant and exceedingly strange land. It had been an unexpected moment of confused delight during a difficult, disorienting situation. At the time, his soul had been confined in a body of wood, steel, and ivory; he hadn't even had lips—but he had felt hers, all the way to his timber toes.

It was even better now that he was in the flesh. Now if only she had a pulse . . .

He knew he should tell her he loved her too. But as he fought his way toward saying it, Veronica reluctantly pulled away.

"I'll come back tomorrow night," she said.

"Be careful," he said, feeling like a coward, but also a little relieved. It was too hard. He could tell her next time.

"You know me," she said.

"Yes," he said. "That's why I want you to be careful."

After Veronica left, Errol couldn't sleep. It was oppressively hot, and the mosquitos were fierce, but he was used to that. His thoughts lingered on Veronica; kissing her, the nearness of her face to his, the remembered feel of holding her against him.

Did Veronica really love him? Did she know what that meant? When they'd first met, she had been a kind of monster — a *nov*, the spirit of a drowned virgin. She had lured countless men to watery deaths in a forest pool for three decades, her earthly life forgotten. She had tried to do the same to him, but thanks to the fact that automatons didn't breathe, she had failed. Aster had restored her soul and her human memories. Now, thanks to the water of health they had found in the Kingdoms, she was alive by the light of the sun, although at night her heart and breath stopped again. In the Kingdoms, she had been scary powerful and sometimes hardly seemed human at all.

So when she told Errol she loved him, what did that mean?

And there was the other thing nagging at him, the problem of Aster. He had been known her since third grade.

And Aster was crucial. It was Aster who had taken his soul when his body lay in a coma and placed it in what she called her "automaton." Aster who had known where to look for Veronica and how to bring her back to almost-life. Aster who knew how to reach the Kingdoms, where miracles happened with alarming frequency. She had needed Veronica and him to reach the Kingdoms, to find the water of health, and cure her father's insanity. But when they returned, she had found her father was gone, kidnapped by a woman they once believed to be their friend.

If something bad happened to Aster, he might someday get out of Laurel Grove, but he would still be stuck here, in Sowashee, in the world of his birth, the world that had taken his father and nearly killed him, too. A world that someone had once told him was the last stop for souls on their way to oblivion.

"Did you see that new girl?" Robbie McElroy asked, as he cut back weeds with his hoe. Robbie was brown-haired, reed-thin, and highly talkative. He had some problems with drugs which had landed him in Laurel Grove. He was sixteen, a year younger than Errol.

"No," he said.

"She weren't no crow-bait," Robbie said. "I wouldn't mind gettin' up with that, you know? Hey-howdy!"

"Yeah," Errol said, only half paying attention, concentrating on the row of beans he was weeding. Laurel Grove had gardens, a dairy farm, and orchards thanks to the "idle hands" philosophy of its founders. Errol didn't mind, although physically he was still very weak. While he was off having adventures in the Kingdoms, his body had been lying in a coma for close to three months.

Robbie kept on going about the girl, but Errol wasn't really listening until he said something about her talking funny. Then he perked up.

"What do you mean, she talked funny?" he asked.

"She had a goofy accent," Robbie said. "Like maybe she's from Sweden or some place. You know, like *yurgen, burgen, glurben*."

Errol stopped hoeing and sat down for a moment, listening to the whirr of cicadas and feeling the sweat run down his face. "What did she look like, this girl?" he asked.

"I done told you, man," Robbie said. "Sort of red-headed, you know. And a funny mark on her head, like a star."

"What was her name?"

"Didn't catch it," Robbie said. He grinned. "I think I'll call her Honey Baby."

"Was her name Aster?" Errol asked.

"Man, what did I just tell you?"

But it had to be. Who else in Sowashee would have a star-shaped birthmark on her forehead? Aster hadn't had that when he first met her—her father had hidden it with some sort of spell. But when they were in the Kingdoms, the spell had come off. When he last saw her, she had smeared make-up over it, but you could still see it if you knew where to look.

Did they think Aster was crazy? Probably, if she tried to explain a tenth of what had happened to them. He had been very careful not to say anything at all about what he had been doing while in his coma; if he did, he would be in here for the rest of his life. What was Aster thinking?

He had to figure out some way to see her. The women stayed on the other side of the campus, but there was a social hour coming up when they could mingle, assuming she wasn't in a hard-case room strapped into a straitjacket. They would have to watch what they said to one another. But now, at least, he knew where she was. And with Veronica's help, they ought to be able to come up with an escape plan.

He picked up his hoe and went back to work, mind spinning out possibilities. It felt good to have a problem to work on.

D r. Reynolds barely looked up from whatever he was reading when Errol came in. He gestured for him to take a seat in the brown, cracked leather chair in front of his desk.

After a few moments, Dr. Reynolds peered at Errol over his wire-rimmed glasses.

"How are you today, Errol?" he asked.

"I'm doing okay, sir," Errol said.

"I'm glad to hear it." He took his glasses off and cleaned them on his blue button-down shirt. He was frowning, which Errol did not take to be a good sign.

"Ah, Errol," the doctor finally said. "We admitted a young lady yesterday. She has asked repeatedly to see you. Are you aware of this?"

Errol didn't see any reason to lie.

"Robbie McElroy mentioned her, sir."

"This young lady. Would you say you're good friends?"

"Yes, sir," he said. "I guess I would."

"Would you mind telling me *how* you know her?"

"Well—from school," Errol said. "I've known her forever. Since third grade. I mean, look, she may be acting a little weird right now, but she's really okay."

Now the doctor was staring at him with an even stranger expression.

"School," he said. "You mean your school?"

"Yes, sir," Errol said.

Doctor Reynolds paused again, then tapped his intercom button.

"Carol," he said. "Have Sam and Mason bring the young lady from 139."

Then he looked back up at Errol. "Errol, when you were asleep—in your coma—did you have any dreams? Do you remember anything?"

Crap. What had Aster told them?

"No, sir," he lied. "I don't remember anything. Just, you know—passing out, and then waking up. It was the biggest mistake of my life, sir."

"Yes, so you've said," Reynolds replied. "But I'm curious. The doctors say two young ladies were present when you awoke. One was your friend, Aster. The other, however, no one seems to have known. Nor has anyone seen her since. Little blond girl."

"I'm not sure who you're talking about, sir," he said. "It was all hazy."

"One of the nurses saw you kissing her," he said.

"Oh," Errol said. "Yeah. Her."

"Would you like to change your story?"

"It was some friend of Aster's, Dr. Reynolds," he said. "I think maybe her mom works at the Dew Drop Inn. I guess I was just so happy to be alive I had to kiss somebody. But I don't know her name, or anything."

"Are you aware that Aster's father has gone missing?" he said. "Along with one of your teachers and the school guidance counselor?"

"No, sir," he said.

"No." He picked up a pencil and ticked it against his desk.

"Your friend Aster is in a bit of trouble," he said. "If you know anything about this, you aren't helping her by holding back."

"Dr. Reynolds, I was in a coma, remember?"

Reynolds nodded.

At that moment there was a rap on the door.

"Bring her in," Dr. Reynolds said.

Errol turned as the door swung open, wondering exactly what Aster's game was, how he was supposed to react. Sam and Mason were there, two of the biggest, toughest orderlies in the place. Between them stood a girl with auburn hair and a star on her forehead.

But it wasn't Aster.

"Holy crap," he said. "Dusk!"

TWO
ᗰERRY-GO-ROUND

When the earliest light of the sun sorted through the trees, Veronica took her first breath in many hours. It was morning dew, honeysuckle, cut grass, and the faint gassy stink of a papermill. She sat on the banks of the creek, letting her clothes dry, watching water-skaters dimple the stream, listening to cicadas whirr as the day grew warmer. It was a nice place she'd found — a gorge nestled amongst the streets and houses of the town, a little wild spot in the city.

She hadn't known such a place existed in Sowashee — in fact she didn't know much about town at all — or if she ever had, she had forgotten. She had grown up in the county, and in her time since returning to the world, she had stayed mostly with Aster, who also lived outside of town. When the police took Aster, they went toward Sowashee, south on 292, so she had hitched a ride in after dark in the back of a battered pick-up. She had been planning the trip anyway, to see Errol, but Aster wouldn't let her go, so she had decided to kill two birds with one stone — see her boyfriend and find out where the police station was. She found both on a map she took from Aster's bedroom, but decided Errol had priority. She found Laurel Grove without much trouble. After leaving the hospital, she had let the creek guide her, and it had brought her here.

Upstream, some boys were stirring the remains of a campfire back to life and checking the trotlines for the morning's catch. They hadn't noticed her, but the two boys skinny-dipping in a deep pool in the stream did pay mind to the little group of girls who came down the steep slope a few moments later, dashing from the water in search of clothes.

It reminded her of the place she had spent so many years, but with no Creek Man to lord over her. She nursed a brief, fond memory of her cache of bones, nestled down in the muck. She eyed the boys a little differently now, but none of them suited; they weren't old enough, and what cruelty she smelled on them was of the ordinary sort, common to most children—nothing that deserved special treatment.

She turned her mind from that. She was different now, wasn't she? Reformed. A *nov* no longer.

"Hey."

She looked up, a little startled. It wasn't easy to sneak up on her, but someone had, a curly-haired girl who looked about ten or eleven dressed in rolled-up jeans and yellow shirt.

"Hey yourself," Veronica said.

"I ain't never seen you before," the girl said.

"I've never been here before," she said. "What's this place called?"

"Massey Canyon," the girl said.

"It's nice."

"You from around here?"

"No," Veronica said. "I'm from out of town."

The girl nodded. She seemed like she was about to say something else, but instead she focused off past Veronica's shoulder. Veronica turned to see why.

He was tall, sixteen or seventeen. He wore long pants but no shirt. His stomach was flat, his arms thin but corded with muscle, and his black hair hung almost to his waist. He had big, dark eyes and an olive complexion. For lack of a better word, he was beautiful.

He didn't look exactly like he belonged with the other kids, who shied away from him a bit.

And he was staring at her in a way that made her belly go all light.

"Who is that?" she asked the girl.

"That's the Gypsy," she said. "He comes down here sometimes."

The Gypsy waded into the water and took a few steps toward them.

"You," he called.

"Yeah?" she said.

"Come here, please."

Part of her wanted to, but the fine hairs on the back of her neck pricked up. Something wasn't right. He wasn't a Creek Man, but he was *something*, and despite her earlier nostalgia, she really did not want to end up captive in some in-between place again.

"What's the quickest way out of here?" she asked the girl.

She grinned. "You sure?"

"Yes," Veronica said.

"Come on, then."

The girl ran along the bank about twenty feet before starting up the side of the gorge along a well-worn rut in the red clay using tree roots as handholds. Veronica followed, fighting down a weird mixture of panic and longing.

She spared a glance back down to see if he was following her, but he was just standing in the creek, watching her leave.

"What's your name?" he called out.

She didn't answer. By that time, she had reached level ground. The girl had gotten ahead of her and was running; Veronica followed the flashes of yellow through the trees. A moment later, she burst from the woods onto grass.

She realized she was in someone's backyard, and that the someone was there. She was old, with more grey than brown in her hair, hanging up laundry. The girl in the yellow shirt was no place to be seen.

"What are you doing?" the woman demanded. "Girl, you gave me a fright."

"I'm sorry ma'am," Veronica said. "I guess I got lost."

The woman was looking her up and down, now, seeing the jeans and T-shirt she had borrowed from Aster, still wet and dirty from the creek.

"Looks like you've been lost for a couple of days. Where did you come from?"

"Down there," Veronica said. She looked back nervously, but no one had followed her.

The woman frowned. "Down where?" she asked. "Ain't nothing down there, at least not anymore. Used to be Massey's Canyon, but they filled that in before you were born."

She paused and clipped a shirt to the line.

"I'll go on," Veronica said. "I didn't mean to disturb you."

But the woman fastened her with her gaze.

"You know, I was just thinking about Massey's Canyon. Daydreaming, really. We used to have quite a time down there when I was a kid, especially in the summers. Kids now don't have it good like we did back then. We used to leave at dawn and not come home until the sun went down, and nobody worried about us. Sometimes we camped and spent the whole night. Now I guess it's just too dangerous to let your kids run around like that. It's a pity."

Veronica thought back to that day at the falls, her new tennis shoes, the neighbor she had trusted.

"I bet it was dangerous back then, too," Veronica said. "People just didn't notice as much."

"You might be right," the woman said. "Anyway, bless you. Have fun and stay out of trouble."

"I'll do my best," Veronica said.

When Errol had last seen Dusk, she had been clad in armor and carrying a sword; now she wore the loose, light green pants and smock most of the patients dressed in when they were indoors. But no matter the costume change, Errol wasn't likely to forget the woman who had decapitated his girlfriend and chopped off one of his legs.

Dusk smiled. "Errol?" She said. "Is that really you?"

He realized he'd gotten out of his chair and was backing up.

"*Valyeme*," Dusk said. Something about her changed—the set of her shoulders, the way her clothes hung on her body.

"Doctor—" he started.

He didn't get much further before Dusk started moving, fast. She punched Sam in the throat and kicked Mason right in the propers. Then she grabbed a nearby chair and smashed it over Mason's head before delivering an uppercut to Sam's chin that sent him sprawling on his back.

"Oh my God!" Dr. Reynolds sputtered, as Dusk sprinted toward him. He fumbled at his desk drawer, but whatever was in there he never got out. Dusk dropped him with an elbow and then kicked him a couple of times after he fell. She bent over and came up with a chain of keys.

"Let's go, Errol," she said. "We have things to do, you and I."

"Are you out of your mind?" he said.

She took hold of his arm. Her fingers felt like they were

made from steel, and she dragged him a few steps, as if he didn't weigh much at all, before he started digging in. He knew Dusk was tough, and a great fighter, but she had never seemed this strong before.

His brain had been chewing at the word she'd said. *Valyeme.* May I have strength.

As he struggled against her, she turned.

"Errol," she said. "*Sekedi.*"

She let go, and he watched her walk away. Then, suddenly, one of his legs moved. His body shifted forward. His other leg jerked along.

Sekedi. Follow.

So, he did. He didn't want to, but he did.

She didn't go straight out of the building, but went instead into the wing where temporaries were held. She broke down a door in the interview room and a moment later came out with the padded clothes she usually wore under her armor.

"Turn around, Errol," she said.

It wasn't a spell, like the command to follow, but he did it anyway. But then he turned back around, quickly.

He had been hoping she would start by taking off her pants. Then her legs would be half tied-up when he jumped her. Unfortunately, she had begun with her shirt. She hadn't turned away from him, and it was pulled up just enough so he could see her belly. He jumped anyway.

He hardly saw the blow coming. It didn't knock him out, but it sure knocked him down. His vision whited out and his ears rang.

"I am sorry," he heard her say. "I hit you too hard. That body of yours is very weak. Not like the one you had before. Please do not fight me."

He came up slowly to his hands and knees. By then she had on the gambeson and padded leggings. He noticed they were different from her last outfit, newer-looking, with different patterns.

"New outfit," he said. "Where's your armor?"

"I hid it," she said. Then she laughed.

"What?" he asked.

"I didn't want to attract attention," she said. "I did anyway."

She started walking again, and his body followed, dizzy head, weak knees, and all.

Alberto was at the front door. He was nearly as big as Sam, and he had a night stick.

"Don't fight her, man," Errol warned.

But of course Alberto did, although it didn't last long. As he stepped over the guard's prone body, Errol hoped Alberto was okay. He had always been decent to Errol, and most of the other inmates liked him.

Moments later, they were through the gate, and Laurel Grove Hospital was behind him. He heard sirens in the distance.

"Constables," she muttered. "In strange chariots. Yes?"

"You've met them before, I guess," Errol said.

"Yes," she replied. "I was not prepared last time. They subdued me."

"This time they'll shoot you," he said.

"As with arrows?"

"Bullets," he said. "You remember bullets?"

She smiled slightly. "Yes," she said. "I remember you saved my life after I was shot with one." Her mouth quirked to the side.

"I think we shall avoid the bullets," she said, and started running. Then he was running, too.

They tore across a couple of yards, over a fence, crossed a couple of streets, and ran into Threefoot Park.

Errol had grown up in the country, about twenty miles outside of Sowashee, but he had an aunt who lived in town, near the park. In summer he had spent a lot of time there — taking swimming lessons in the public pool, catching soft-shelled turtles under the footbridges over the creek, watching fireworks on the Fourth of July. But the best, the coolest thing about Threefoot Park was the carousel.

His father had told him it had been built in the eighteen-nineties, and that it had been designed by a strange old guy from far away. That it was magic.

It had been magic to him. It was housed in a big white building that reminded him of a circus tent and always smelled like cotton candy. The carousel took up most of the building; horses hovered over its wooden deck on gilded poles, horses of all kinds — Appaloosas, bays, black stallions — but there were also tigers, lions, antelopes with twisting horns, giraffes, stags — all manner of beasts, all posed as if about to pounce or take flight.

After a bit of violence to one of the windows, he and Dusk stood in front of the carousel. But now it was dark, the animals in shadow.

"Come along," she said.

She led him past the empty ticket booth and onto the platform, then swung herself up on one of the horses. He had always liked riding the tigers and had started toward them when she called him back.

"Get up behind me," she said.

He was still compelled, so he did as she said. The animals were large, not kid-sized like some he had ridden in carnivals, but it was still uncomfortable sharing the rigid saddle with her. That was offset somewhat by ... well, sharing the saddle with her. Dusk was beautiful, and at one point — before she chopped his leg off — he'd had kind of a thing for her. Now he was pressed against her. She was warm, nearly hot, and he couldn't help liking it, even though he knew he shouldn't.

She was the enemy.

"Put your arms around my waist," she said. "But take no liberties."

"Okay, I won't," he said, trying to cram as much sarcasm as he could into the words. "But listen, would you mind telling me what's going on?"

"Later," she said. Then she said a word or two he didn't catch, and the platform beneath them suddenly lurched into motion. Lights came on all over the carousel, and music started up as the calliope chuffed to life, whistling out a familiar melody, its little mechanical drum beating in time.

The calliope hadn't worked in years. The park had substituted a tape player. But now the ancient machine was going full blast, as it hadn't since he was five or six. He remembered riding the tiger, his dad standing by him, grinning, holding onto the pole as it went up and down, his mother ahead on the gazelle, laughing.

They had been happy then, hadn't they? Before his dad got sick. He believed they had been.

He was shaken out of his reverie as the pace picked up; the music, the spin of the deck. He was sure it was going faster than he had ever known it to, way quicker than it was supposed to go.

Yet it continued to speed up, until he started to get sick and dizzy. He realized he had a death-grip on Dusk because the ride was trying to fling him off.

Then they *did* fly off—the wooden horse, Dusk, him—the whole package. He closed his eyes, bracing for impact, but instead felt his belly go light. Wind streamed against his face, and the smell of cotton candy was gone.

He opened his eyes, but closed them again immediately when he saw the rapidly receding ground below them. Then he cracked them again, cautiously.

Here we go again, he thought.

Because they were not in Sowashee anymore.

Things had changed in the years Veronica had been dead. The clothes were odd and sometimes just weird. Nobody wore real hats, although she saw the occasional cap. There were a lot more cars and they were all ugly. Everything was brighter and tackier and moved too fast.

But downtown Sowashee was a lot like she remembered it. Most of the buildings had been built long before her birth, and although they looked more worn and rundown, they still retained a certain dignity and — in many cases — mystery. The Obelisk Theater still looked like something out of *The Arabian Nights*. Twin sphinxes in Egyptian headdress still flanked the steps of a building she had no name for but knew had something to go with Shriners and their fez hats. The Trevis Building — the tallest and only skyscraper in town — was still embellished with fantastical motifs that seemed at once sort of Biblical and utterly exotic.

She had a little money from Aster, so she ate lunch at a diner — meatloaf, mashed potatoes, and butter beans, followed by apple pie and ice cream.

Food was one of her favorite things about being alive.

As it grew dark, she made her way back toward Laurel Grove. She climbed up into the branches of a magnolia to watch the sunset.

When the light began to fade, and her heart stopped, she went to see Errol again.

THREE
JAIL BREAK

Well. Ms. Kostyena."

Aster glanced up from her doodling to regard the woman in the rumpled gray suit who had just come through the door of the interrogation room.

"I don't know you," Aster said.

"No, we've never met. My name is Lisa Pierce. I'm your lawyer."

"Nice to meet you," Aster said. She wrote the name on the already heavily marked paper in front of her in a script she'd learned from her father's books. "I was wondering if you would ever show up."

"I've had a busy day," Pierce said, taking the chair across the table from her. "Not enough public defenders to go around."

"I'm sure," Aster said. The lawyer looked young, probably no older than her mid-twenties. Her black hair was cut to her shoulders.

"You mind if I ask you a few questions?"

"I've already answered a lot of questions," Aster said. "But sure, go on."

"The police asked you questions? In here? Without me?"

"That's affirmative," Aster said.

"They shouldn't have done that. Did you ask for a lawyer right away?"

"Yep," Aster said. She didn't point out that that had been more than a day ago, and that she had spent most of the intervening time in a cell.

"Okay," Pierce said. "We'll see about that." She opened a folder and leafed through it.

"Until recently, you lived with your father, is that correct?"

"Yes," Aster said. She tore the paper from the legal pad and added it to the others.

The lawyer noticed. "Did they give you that to write a statement?"

"Probably," Aster said.

"Is that Russian you're writing in?"

Aster shrugged.

"You and your father are from Russia, right?" Ms. Pierce said.

"That's what Dad said," she replied.

The lawyer frowned, then returned to her notes.

"It says here you went missing a few months ago."

"I didn't go missing. Dad sent me to stay with relatives in Boston."

"A teacher from your school also vanished about the same time, after he and the school counselor paid a visit to your home. The counselor—Ms. Fincher—called in and requested an extended leave of absence. But nobody has seen her for months. Then you returned, and now your father is missing. Is that all correct?"

"That's what the police told me," Aster said. "What they haven't told me is exactly what I'm supposed to be charged with."

"You aren't charged with anything," Pierce said. "But you're still a minor. Your father is missing, along with two other people last seen headed toward your house on the day you – went out of town. I think they're concerned about you."

"Concerned?"

"There are rumors that your father was involved in the Russian mafia. That he came here to hide out."

"I see," Aster said. "So I'm here for my own protection?"

"I think the police see it that way, yes. Is there some other way to see it?"

"Sure," Aster said. "My father is a sorcerer. He's under a curse, and he can't remember anything for more than about fifteen minutes. He still thinks I'm nine. I went off to another world to try and find a cure for him. While I was gone, someone came here, tricked him into believing she was me, and took him away. I guess he took Ms. Fincher with him. Mr. Watkins, the teacher, he was a sort of spook who liked to do nasty things with young girls that wound up with them dead, and he basically got what was coming to him, so he won't be back no matter what. Does that cover it?"

The lawyer frowned. "There's no need to be sarcastic, young lady. I'm sure you're scared, and you're just acting out, but I'm here to help you."

Aster leaned forward.

"Can I tell you a secret?" she asked.

"What?"

"I don't need your help. And you didn't close the door all the way."

She picked up the last piece of paper. "Lisa Pierce," she read.

"What – "

That was as much as she got out. The paper flew out of Aster's hands and stuck to Ms. Pierce's face. Aster quickly read the names on the other sheets, standing up as they, too, sailed off. She hurried past the eight employees of the sheriff's office, including the sheriff, who were all now — like Ms. Pierce — grasping at their faces, their shouts of surprise and panic muffled by the yellow legal-pad pages plastered across their features. She stopped only to collect her backpack from the receptionist and then was out the front in the heat of the evening.

She nearly ran headlong into Veronica.

"This saves me some trouble," Veronica said. "I was coming to bust you out."

"I told you to keep out of sight," Aster said.

"You did," Veronica acknowledged. "But Errol is gone, and I thought we'd best go look for him."

"Gone?" Aster said. "What do you mean, gone?"

Veronica looked over her shoulder at the sheriff's office. The commotion inside was getting louder.

"Maybe I should tell you later?"

"Follow me," Aster said.

Veronica did explain, on the way. How she had seen Errol the night before, but when she went tonight he hadn't been there. How she had snooped around and heard one of the guards joking about how some girl on PCP or something had beaten up three guards and a psychiatrist before busting out of the place, taking Errol with her. A crazy girl with a star on her forehead.

"I thought it might be you," Veronica said.

"Not me," Aster said. "Dusk. Or another relative of mine, maybe."

"There was more about it in the paper today," Veronica said. "It said there was also a break-in at the carousel in Threefoot Park. That's close to Laurel Grove, and the police think there's a connection."

By that time, they were across town and it was well past midnight. Police cars were on the prowl, but it was a simple matter to hide in the shadows and do a Whimsy of Secreting.

"The carousel," Aster said. "That might be a way through the Pale – to the Marchlands."

"You mean, like where you found me," Veronica said.

"Yes. There are lots of ways into the Marchlands, if you have the power. But most of them are dead-ends or go off to pointless places. The trick is finding one that goes through to the Kingdoms."

"You think Dusk kidnapped Errol and spirited him off to the Kingdoms?"

"It might not have been Dusk," Aster cautioned. "If she and I have the same birthmark, there are probably others. Maybe everybody from wherever I'm from has one."

"But why would they want Errol?"

"I don't know," Aster said. "But I'm going to find out."

FOUR
THE GYPSY

The door to the carousel was padlocked and decorated with yellow police tape, neither of which presented Aster with much of an obstacle. The alarm that went off was much more of a concern, so she tried to size the situation up quickly. She could feel the itch of magic on her skin.

One of the animals was missing—one of the horses, she thought. And beyond the empty space, in the shadows near the calliope, something glimmered, something familiar.

She bent and picked it up. It was an iridescent orb of silver about the size of a large marble.

"What's that?" Veronica asked.

"It's mine," Aster said. "Remember when Errol and I came to get you from the *vadras*? He chased us, and I threw this at him. It slowed him down."

"Some of that is a little fuzzy for me," Veronica said. "After all, I had just gotten my skin back. It was all a little confusing."

"I thought it was gone for good. And now here it is."

"What a wild coincidence."

"Or not a coincidence at all," Aster said. "A message. Whoever took Errol wants us to follow them."

"Sounds dangerous," Veronica said. "Let's go."

"Right," Aster said.

"But, um — how?" Veronica asked.

Aster turned back to the merry-go-round.

"I think we ride it," she said.

"I remember this thing," Veronica said. "Mom and Dad brought me here — well, I guess it was a long time ago. It's hardly changed."

"That's the point," Aster said. "Pick an animal. Quickly."

She ran through the Whimsies she knew, trying to figure out which one might work, and settled on the most obvious.

"*Geiyese*," she said, the Whimsy of Brief Life.

Nothing happened.

She heard sirens in the distance. Veronica was sitting up on one of the tigers, looking pleased and not at all concerned.

It struck her, then. It wasn't life the carousel needed.

"*Zemeryese*," she said. Suddenly all of the lights came on, and the music started blaring.

Not life, but remembrance.

She swung up onto the nearest beast, a giraffe, as the carousel picked up speed. Through the door, blue lights of police cars were flashing, but Aster knew it didn't matter anymore.

Veronica woke to find herself riding a tiger. The last she remembered, the merry-go-round had been whirling wildly, and she had laughed, and then she had become very, very sleepy, closed her eyes for a moment . . .

Also, the tiger had been made of wood. Now it was not. Its fur was stiff and warm; powerful muscles pulled beneath the beast's skin as it padded along, very quietly, apparently unaware it had an entrée on its back. The stars were out and a sliver of moon, so she could see they were on a dirt street with houses on either side.

And something big and dark was walking right beside her.

"Aster?" she asked.

"Is that her name?" someone said.

Now that she was looking at him directly, she could make him out, and even in the dark she knew him and his long, black hair. Up close, his eyes looked huge, and dark only as a starry night was dark. He had high, strong cheekbones and an enigmatic smile. He was no longer shirtless but dressed in an old-fashioned looking suit—black pants, jacket and vest, white shirt, no tie.

He, too, was riding a tiger.

"What have you done with Aster?" she asked.

"She's well," the boy said. "I wanted to talk to you alone."

"Who are you?" she asked.

"Shandor Mingo King Michaels," the boy said.

"That's a lot of name," she said.

"I'm a lot of fellow," he replied. "May I ask—again—what you go by?"

"Since you ask more politely this time," she said. "I'm called Veronica. Veronica Hale. What's on your mind, Mr. Michaels?"

"Why, *you* are, Miss Hale," he said.

"Well, I am *so* flattered," she said. "But I really would like to know where my friend is."

"Soon enough," Shandor said. "Look, we're almost there."

Veronica saw the street ended ahead, and a vast field opened up beyond, where what looked like a circus was camped, complete with wagons, tents, and bonfires.

Shandor's tiger took the lead, and soon they approached a huge tent, red-and-black-striped. There the tigers settled on their haunches. Shandor dismounted and held out his hand for her.

She took it and was surprised by what felt like a little shock of cold.

Inside, the tent was rather opulent, if dimly lit by candles and a few lanterns. Shandor gestured for her to sit on some pillows. Once she was settled, he sat down cross-legged across from her.

"I would offer you refreshment," he said, "but we both know you don't need it."

"On the contrary," she said. "I would love some lemonade."

Shandor raised an eyebrow then shrugged.

"Fetch her some," he said.

A girl she hadn't seen stirred from some cushions nearby and padded off into the darkness.

"There's no need to pretend," Shandor said. "I know what you are."

"I'm glad someone does," she replied. "So what, pray tell, am I?"

"A goddess."

"Oh."

"Not what you were expecting?" he asked.

"No," she replied. "I've been called lots of things, but never that."

What she had been called most often was *nov*, which Aster defined as the undead spirit of a dead virgin. Most everyone else who used the word said it like it made their mouths feel dirty. She sort of got that—after all, she had spent decades, dead-but-not-dead, luring men to watery deaths. Now, thanks to a half-dose of a magic potion, she was alive in the daylight, at least. She wasn't even sure Aster had a name for something like that. If she did, she'd kept it to herself.

"You've never met anyone who could truly appreciate you," Shandor said. "Not until now."

"You're making me all embarrassed," Veronica said. "I fear I may become faint from all of this sugar talk. But maybe you can just skip along to the part where you tell me what you want."

"To the point," Shandor said. "I approve. So I will also be brief. I want you to become my queen."

FIVE
⛔OON

E rrol wasn't sure how long they flew. Most of the time they
were in the clouds: sometimes cottony, gently glowing mists
with glimpses of blue sky—at others, black tempests slashed
with terrifying coils of lightning surrounded them. Most often it
was monotonous grades of white and grey. Only seldom did he
see anything beneath—glimpses of a sparkling sea, a vast green
jungle, a gloomy marsh dissected by a thousand grey streams.
He nearly fell asleep a dozen times, but each time his grip on
Dusk loosened—and he began to fall—he woke.

The clouds broke apart, became cottony puffballs, and eventually cleared entirely. The sun stood at noon and was so bright
that most of the sky was the color of butter, although it faded
to a pale blue at the horizons. It reminded him of a day at the
beach in the middle of the summer.

The landscape resembled a beach, too, but without an ocean.
Hills and plains of yellow sand rolled off in all directions. He
was reminded of pictures he had seen of the Sahara Desert.

They flew on, and after a time Dusk's weird mount began
to descend toward a snaky green line in the sand. As they drew
nearer, he saw it was a canyon cut through chalky white stone.

They flew down through the feathery tops of incredibly tall, slender trees that resembled palms, landing near a shallow stream verged by reeds.

On their side of the stream, a few yards away, he saw what looked like the mouth of a cave, mostly concealed by fernlike bushes.

Dusk swung down, and Errol followed right behind her, incredibly happy to have earth beneath his feet again.

Dusk leaned the wooden horse against a tree. She knelt by the stream and splashed some water in her face.

"Refresh yourself," she said. "The water is fresh, and good to drink."

He wanted to refuse, to get right into it, but he realized he was parched. The water was good, cold and clean and slightly minerally and nothing like the chlorinated tap water at Laurel Grove.

When he stood back up, she was regarding him with an amused smile.

"What?" he asked.

"It's still strange, seeing you like this," she said.

"Yeah," he said. Until now, Dusk had known him only as the automaton Aster had built to contain his soul. "How did you know it was me?"

"I told you once that appearances were unimportant," she said. "I know you, Errol. I would know you whatever form you wore."

"That sounds nice," he said. "Like you never cut off my leg."

"You did have a choice, Errol," Dusk said. "You could have chosen me, but you chose *her* instead. There are consequences, you know. And yet, I did not slay you as I might have."

"Yeah," Errol said. "Thanks a whole bunch for not killing me."

"I do not apologize for my actions," Dusk said. "I do not act without reason, and at the time I followed the course of action I deemed necessary."

"And I guess if I really understood it all, I would forgive you?"

Dusk shrugged. "Probably not," she said. "You had your own priorities. They were not the same as mine. We fought, you lost. It is the way of things."

Errol wanted to respond to that, but there was something so brutally honest about it that he found it was hard to sustain his anger.

"So why am I here?" he asked.

"Because things did not go as I planned," she said. "I find I have need of help."

"And what makes you think I would help you? Like you said, you have your priorities, and I have mine."

"Exactly," Dusk said. "When I first met you, we shared a goal. And we worked so well together. Against the Snatchwitch. In the battles against the Sheriff and the giant. We were excellent companions, whatever our differences later. Right now, I believe our purposes align again. I traveled a long way under that assumption, anyway. You should at least hear me out."

He didn't want to. She was evil and couldn't be trusted, he knew that.

But she was beautiful, and fierce, and . . .

He could almost hear Aster muttering in his ear, about how stupid women made him. How he was such a sucker for a pretty face. And it was true. Of course it was true, and he had Veronica, anyway.

But he was also here, wherever this was, with no idea how to get back, how to find Veronica or Aster or anyone else. He was at Dusk's mercy, and in this puny body, without magic on his side, she absolutely had the upper hand.

"Sure," he said. "I guess I can hear you out. This is about Aster's father, right? After you left us, you went to get him."

She smiled. "It was you who told me about him, remember? About his affliction, his inability to remember."

"Yeah," Errol said. "I remember."

"I thought I could convince him I was Aster," she said. "I believed with him on my side, I could set things right."

"But it didn't work?"

"It did, at first. But then things went wrong. Badly wrong. So —" She broke off as if she had heard something.

"No," she sighed. "They were more alert than I hoped."

"What's going on?"

"There isn't any time," she said. "Someone is coming for me."

"Then let's run. Get back on the horse —"

"There's no time," she said. "They will catch us both. With you still free I have a chance."

She ran over to the wooden horse and said her magic word. For a moment he thought she was going to fly off and leave him, but instead she flew it into the cave. She emerged a moment later.

"Hide in the cave," she said. "Wait until they are gone — until you are very sure they are gone — before coming out. Do you understand?"

"Then what?"

She smiled. "If I don't return it means they caught me. They will take me to the glass pyramid. Be very careful. I don't know all of the measures they might take. Stay alive. Be smart."

"Wait —"

"No time," she said. "I trust you Errol. I trust you will help me. Now, go into the cave. When you come to the glass pyramid, bring the things you will find there."

He glanced at the cave. It was shallow and dropped off quickly in the back, really more of a rock shelter.

"This won't hide me," he said.

"It will," she said. Then, suddenly, she leaned in and kissed him. It felt like the most pleasant punch in the gut he's ever experienced.

Then she pushed him in.

"*Skiuyes*," he heard her say, and the light from outside suddenly dimmed, as if he was seeing everything through tinted glass. She smiled briefly and then turned her back. As she walked away, he saw her footprints in the sand — and his — smooth away.

He heard distant hoofbeats — followed by more, many more, along with the baying of hounds, and stranger cries that might have been human or animal but to Errol sounded not quite like anything he had ever heard before.

He didn't move; he tried not to even breathe too loudly.

After a time, things quieted down and he started to feel a little antsy. He took a look around and saw some bundles near the back of the cave he hadn't noticed before.

One contained Dusk's armor, carefully wrapped in soft cloth. He was about to open the other when he heard a faint sound.

He froze when he saw someone was at the cave entrance.

It looked like a boy, a young one, maybe no more than ten. Maybe it was, but something about it gave Errol the creeps right away. Maybe it was that he almost looked like he was made of gold; his skin, his curly hair, even his eyes were all of nearly the same metallic shade. He wore a white sash and a sort of short skirt, and not much else, but he had a quiver of arrows on his back, and a short but powerful looking bow in his hand. He reminded Errol of a Valentine's Day cupid gone bad.

At first, Errol thought the boy was looking right at him, but then he saw the weirdly colored eyes weren't quite focused.

This time, Errol did hold his breath.

Bad Cupid reached his free hand toward the cave. He seemed to encounter something. But then he shook his head, shrugged, and moved on.

Errol didn't take any more chances. He sat motionless in the back of the cave staring out its mouth for a long time, until he was as sure as he could be that there was no longer anyone out there.

Finally, he turned his attention to the second bundle.

This one contained armor, too—a chest plate, greaves, whatever you called the pieces that went on the arms—but unlike Dusk's, it wasn't made of metal but of wood. Along with the armor was a sword, also made of wood. He reached for that.

It was warm to the touch, and he felt sudden disorientation, as if his hand had become longer, heavier.

More curious than ever, he studied the weapon, noticing that the grip was made of bone, or at least inlaid with it, a peculiar design that looked familiar, like a little man . . .

Then he understood and dropped it with a grunt.

"Holy crap," he said.

The sword and armor were made out of—him. From the wooden body that had once housed his soul.

He stared at it, trying to put it all together. Dusk must have gone back to the old castle, looking for him, the place where they'd found the water of health. Where she had betrayed them. She hadn't found him, but she had found—this. The thing that *had* been him.

As he watched, a little tendril sprouted from the sword where he had touched it, reaching toward him, like he was the sun . . .

"Oh, no thank you," he yelped, scrambling out of the cave, through the bushes and all the way to the edge of the stream.

If he put it on, what would it do? Grow onto him?

He had no intention of finding out.

Belatedly, he realized he was exposed to whoever might still be hunting for him, but it had been a while since he had heard anything, and being out in the open felt better than being in the cave with — that.

He splashed some water on his face, then tried to make sense of things. Horse hoofs had marked up the sand, along with bare footprints, dog tracks, and the impressions of several pairs of boots. At least they wouldn't be hard to follow if that was the plan. But was it?

The glass pyramid, Dusk had said. She was counting on him. The question was, did he care?

Maybe he did, and maybe he didn't. But at the moment, he didn't have any other plan. He could try to go back the way they had come, but that was a very long trip, and he knew enough about the Kingdoms to know that simply going in more-or-less the right direction wasn't guaranteed to get you where you wanted to go.

So he would look for this pyramid, and Dusk. When he found her, he could always change his mind, if that seemed like the thing to do.

Something was nagging at him, and after a few minutes he figured out what it was.

He had been in the cave for hours.

But the sun hadn't moved at all. It was still straight up, right in the middle of the sky.

He broke a reed and planted it in the silt near the creek, turning it so it cast no shadow.

He counted slowly to a thousand, and it still didn't cast a shadow.

The sun wasn't moving.

"Well, that's not right," he muttered.

But what else was new?

Reluctantly, he went back in the cave.

Could he make the horse fly? It was worth a try, he decided. He dragged it out of the cave and took a seat on it.

"Okay," he said. "Let's go. Fly."

Nothing happened.

When Dusk had started the thing, it had still been on the carousel. He tried to remember exactly what had happened. She had used a word, in her language. He'd understood it, because Aster had once magically given him understanding of their speech so he could understand her father. What had Dusk said?

"Not *fly*," he said. "Remember."

The horse shifted a little beneath him.

"Remember," he said. But that wasn't exactly right. The way Dusk and Aster said things when they were doing spells wasn't exactly like when they were just talking. He forced himself to think about the actual sounds he was saying, to skip the shortcut his brain was doing in translating it. When he thought "remember" — like he was asking or suggesting someone to think back — it came out as *zemerese*. If he *told* someone to "remember," it came out a *zemeredi*.

But Dusk hadn't said either of those. There had been a little syllable in the middle of the word.

"*Zemeryese*," he said.

The horse shifted upright and lifted slightly off the ground.

"Okay," he said. "Great."

The next thing he knew, he was flying through the air, but not on the horse. As he slammed into the sand, he saw his erstwhile mount arc into the distance, finally vanishing is it dropped below the line of sight allowed by the canyon walls.

"Well, crap," Errol muttered. "I guess it's walking, then."

He got up, hoping nothing was broken or sprained. He went back into the cave.

After a moment's assessment, he decided he could carry one set of armor, but not both. That worked out, because he didn't want anything to do with what was plainly supposed to be *his* set. He bundled up Dusk's stuff, arranged it best he could to carry on his shoulders, and set off following the tracks.

SIX

OPTIONS

Y our queen?" Veronica said. "Why sir, does that make you a king?"

"My mother is a queen and my father is a king," Shandor said.

"Then doesn't that make you a prince or something?" She asked.

"They are buried nearby," he said. "Hence my yearly pilgrimage to this place."

"You said your mother *is* queen, not was," Veronica said.

"Such distinctions have little relevance here, in my kingdom," he said. "I should think you would understand that."

"That's true," Veronica said. "We're in-between, right? Not across the Pale but not in the Kingdoms either."

"Yes," Shandor said.

"Then no thank you," Veronica replied. "I spent way too long here already. Looking back on it, it was not time well spent."

He smiled. "Because you were not queen," he said. "That can really make a difference, you know. Having power. Having someone who appreciates you—not for what you were, or might be, but for exactly what you are. Beautiful, independent, powerful, a woman to be reckoned with. A goddess. I hardly know you and I adore you already, Veronica."

She stared at him, searching for some sign that he was having her on, but he sounded sincere. No one had ever quite looked at her the way Shandor did. She had been viewed through the gaze of lust, horror, disgust, pity, friendship—maybe love, although her last meeting with Errol had left her in doubt about that. Shandor seemed to see everything anyone else had ever seen, and more—and he appeared to like it all, together, completely.

"Goddess," she repeated.

"A dark goddess," he murmured. His voice was almost hypnotic. "A goddess of death, of the gateway to oblivion. When the mighty fall from the High and Faraway, it is here they land, before passing into the Reign of the Departed. My realm is not so vast as the Kingdoms, I grant you. But it has many charms. You are neither of the Kingdoms nor of the Ghost Country, Veronica. You are like me, both quick and dead. Immortal. Above life and death, right and wrong, good and bad. Be my queen, and I will love you as no other ever can."

With every word he spoke, she wanted to shut her ears and hear no more; for every word he spoke she wanted a hundred more. Everything he said made sense. Before, she had been the Creek Man's slave. But in the Kingdoms, she had felt her potential, the power she might have. She loved Errol, but he expected so much of her. So did Aster. She did not tell them the truth about the urges she had at night, the hungers that came upon her, the deeds she imagined.

Shandor already knew, and not only did not care, but shared those predilections. He only expected her to be herself, and for her to let him love her. Here, she could behave as she wanted, and no one would try to make her feel bad about it.

What was wrong with that?

Maybe nothing. Maybe everything. She didn't know. But she did know something was holding her back, just as something had held her back in the Kingdoms, every time she was on the verge of losing herself to her power.

And there was something else. Shandor was perceptive enough, and earnest. But he was also smug and self-satisfied. She could tell from the look on his face he believed it was impossible for her to refuse him. And that was hard to abide. He did not know her as well as he thought he did.

"That's a very kind offer," she told him. "I'm sure it's very flattering, and some other girl would eat it up. But not me. I must say no."

Shandor leaned forward.

"You must understand, I am very determined. Since the moment I saw you by the creek, my yearning for you has been constant."

"That's, wow—a whole day," she said.

He leaned back. "You will see," he said. "There is no hurry."

"Great," she said. "But in the meantime, I have things to do, parties to attend, and so on. So, if you could point me toward my friend Aster, that would be lovely."

He regarded her silently for a long time, long enough that she began to wonder if she would be able to kill him if it came to that. He had suggested he was like her, but in what way, exactly?

Finally, he turned to the girl who had returned to her place at the edge of the candlelight.

"Take her to her friend," she said.

The girl came, took her hand, and lead her from the tent.

"You don't mind your boyfriend gettin' all flirty with strangers?" she asked, once they were outside.

"He is my brother," the girl replied, leading her through the encamped caravan. "He has no mate. He has never courted one before. Only you."

"I bet that's what you tell all the girls," she said.

Shandor's sister didn't reply. A few moments later they came to a black, horse-drawn carriage, complete with two horses.

Aster was inside, apparently asleep. Veronica leaned close, until she could feel her life pulsing.

"That's it?" she said to the girl.

"My brother bids you take the carriage," she said. "Tell the horses where you want to go."

"Tell your brother he is very kind," Veronica said.

The girl nodded. "You've made a mistake, you know," she said.

"If so, it's really not the first," Veronica said. She opened the door to the carriage and nudged Aster.

"Wake up, Sleepy," she said.

Aster stirred, but her eyes didn't open.

"Some kind of spell on her?" she asked.

"Yes," the girl said. "It will dissipate by sunrise."

"Okay," Veronica said. She climbed in and shut the door.

"Horses," she said. "Take us out of here. Take us to Errol."

The beasts shifted restlessly but did not move.

"You must name a place," Shandor's sister said. "Or at least a direction. They know much, these horses, but not the location of every person in the Kingdoms."

"Oh," she said. "Okay, then. Horses, take us out of here, into the nearest Kingdom."

The carriage lurched into motion. Soon they were on the open road, beneath the stars, the lights of the camp and the town dwindling behind them.

A ster woke to unfamiliar motion. She found she was resting against the wooden frame of an open window. The dark trunks of gigantic trees passed by beyond, the deep orange light of the rising sun occasionally visible through them. Between the trees and the sunrise were more trees, morass, and occasional open water. A gigantic grey heron raised up its neck and turned its head to watch them pass by.

She remembered riding on the carousel, the change in motion as they moved in-between — then nothing, or at least very little.

She turned her head, slowly. The window was in a carriage with two seats upholstered in earth-toned paisley fabric. She was in one — Veronica lay on the other. She leaned out of her window and saw the vehicle was drawn by two horses but saw no driver. Through the other window were more trees and swamp.

Since nothing dramatic or terrifying seemed to be happening, she took a moment to open her backpack and check her possessions. Everything seemed to be there, including the little silver orb she'd found at the merry-go-round.

That settled, she nudged Veronica with her toe. When that didn't get results, she pushed a bit harder.

Veronica cracked her eyes open.

"Beauty rest," she mumbled.

"Just — what's going on?"

Veronica closed her eyes again.

"We got waylaid by a cute guy named Shandor," she murmured. "He offered to make me his queen and fulfill my *e-ver-y* wish. I told him to scat because I've got a boyfriend. He wept and pleaded, I very was strong — no sir, mister! Then he gave us this carriage. I told it to take us into the nearest Kingdom. The end. Now let me sleep."

"Oh," Aster said. "I see. So now we're . . . ?"

"On a road in the middle of a big swamp," Veronica said. "Unless we aren't anymore. Now you know everything. Tell the horses where to find Errol, if you know, or to go somewhere we can ask someone if you don't. Good night."

"It's morning."

Veronica rolled over so she was facing the back of the seat.

Aster started to nudge her again and thought better of it. She wasn't happy about being out of it; whoever this Shandor was, he must have been waiting for them, and he must be awfully powerful. But he must have also let them go, unless the carriage was taking them to a destination of his choosing. Veronica didn't appear all that worried about it, and Aster was sure Veronica would fill in the details later.

One thing she felt in her bones: they were well beyond the Pale, and no longer in the Marches. They were in the Kingdoms again. She not only remembered her Whimsies, Adjurations, and Decrees, but also a number of Recondite Utterances, which she could never recall until there was enough elumiris present to pronounce them.

But the Kingdoms were fantastically large. They might be headed in absolutely the wrong directions.

She took out the sphere again.

"*Pendi*," she told it.

It stirred and warmed in her palm. It rolled toward her middle finger, hesitated a moment, then moved back and over to her pointer, to her pinky, and again to her thumb.

The sphere came to her from her mother; there were other spheres, and they were supposed to be able to seek each other out. Unless she knew the names of the others, there was no way to make hers seek a specific one.

So, she had four choices. Any of them or none of them might bring her to Errol. She was assuming that whoever had left hers at the carousel had one, too—that it was a deliberate challenge for her to follow.

But that might not be true. The sphere might as easily be meant to mislead her to some distant doom.

She glanced back at Veronica for a moment. She was still asleep.

There was something else she could try now that they were in this deep.

She spoke a few soft words and lifted the sphere to her right eye, closing the left. She felt a slight push, and suddenly she was staring out from a height over a lush garden, waterfalls, a winding river, a city of pyramids.

At her command, the scene changed. A mountain, riddled with caves beneath a nighttime sky. Next, a seashore, seen from a height, and what was either a rising or a setting sun.

Then an arch of stone, and beyond it ruddy light. She felt a sort of tingle and, in her vision, turned to see a man on a throne of brass. He wore a robe and crown of gold and copper.

It was her father.

"There," she whispered to the globe. "What is that place?"

And the globe, in its way, told her a name.

"Horses," she said. "Take us to Ghartas Essenas."

The horses tilted their heads to look back at her. A few moments later, they reached a crossroads, and the carriage turned northeast, leaving the swamp, moving uphill through a forest thick with brambles.

SEVEN
A FUNERAL SCENT

With no sun to tell the time, Errol couldn't be sure how long he'd been walking, but some time had passed. The armor was heavy, and his body still had a long way to go before it was recovered from months in a coma, so he had to stop frequently.

When last he had been in the Kingdoms, in the body Aster built for him, he had been tireless and strong. A hero. He had marched for days, carried heavy loads, battled monsters. Now he knew that if it came up he wouldn't be able to fight his way out of a wet paper bag.

Now and again he wondered if he shouldn't go back and get the wooden armor. Just from touching it, he knew it would make him stronger—maybe as powerful as he'd been before, maybe even more so. That would be great, if he was sure he would be able to take it off, which was anything but a given. The idea of being stuck in a wooden body again didn't appeal to him.

So he didn't turn back.

As long as he was following the wash, things weren't too terribly bad. He could douse himself in the cool water and rest beneath the shade of the tall, reedy trees. Along with her armor,

Dusk had packed some food – dried fruit, hard bread, nuts that resembled hickory nuts but were sweeter.

But eventually, the tracks left the wash and traveled off across the desert sands.

He stopped to rest, which turned into a short nap. Then he filled Dusk's waterskin as best he could from the shallow stream and set off along the trail. Soon the hospitable canyon with its shade and water was far from sight.

In very short order, the unmoving sun became more of a nuisance than ever. He was still in the green shirt and pants of a Laurel Grove "inpatient," which was fortunate in that they were light cotton – but it was very hot. He resisted the urge to take the shirt off. His dark skin didn't burn easily, but he knew in this perpetual high noon he would blister like cheese toast under a broiler. His exposed arms were already starting to hurt.

He had to rest more often, but rather than restoring him, each time it was more difficult to get back up. He began to wonder if he could make it back to the wash if he wanted too, but he stubbornly pressed on. The horsemen had to be going somewhere, and wherever that was would have water, he reasoned, and hopefully shade.

His eyes began to hurt from the glare, and since there was nothing but sand, he kept them closed about half the time, opening them often enough to make sure he was still following the trail. When he felt a breath of wind on his face, he thought he was imagining it. But as he came over the next dune, a welcome sight greeted him. The horizon was grey, with darker streaks angling toward the ground, and blue-white flickers of light in the anvil-shaped thunderheads high above.

Rain was coming his way. Water. Coolness.

But as it drew nearer, his elation began to fade, because the wind was picking up, and he saw the approaching storm was driving a wall of yellow before it. A sandstorm.

The only thing he knew about sandstorms was what he had read, but he knew they were bad in lots of ways. People got buried in them, for instance.

At the very least, the tracks he was following would be blown away, or washed off by the rain. Then what would he do?

Running was obviously no use, so he continued forward, keeping an eye out for shelter, any shelter, as the wall of sand darkened more and more of the sky.

He came over the top of a dune and stumbled going down the other side, sliding and tumbling until he reached the little valley before the next mound of sand. He wondered if he should stay there; would the dunes shelter him from the storm, or help to bury him?

The latter seemed more likely, so he hitched his pack back up and was preparing to scale the dune when he heard someone shouting. It sounded like it came from off to his right.

He broke into a slow jog but wasn't able to maintain it for long. The call came again, louder this time, and he was able to make out the word "help" rather clearly.

The wind was stronger now, and the smell of the coming rain intense.

A few hundred paces or so later, he turned a bend between the dunes and saw a little boy, maybe eight, crouched against some rocks. When the boy saw him, he shouted again.

"Help, please!"

"I'm coming," Errol shouted.

The boy was even younger than he had first thought. He was dark skinned, swathed in yellow robes, and he looked both exhausted and terrified.

"What's the matter?" Errol asked.

"Please," the boy said. "I can't walk. An asp bit my foot, and it hurts too much."

Errol saw the boy's foot was indeed swollen and a nasty purple color.

Errol dropped the armor bundle and quickly retied it so he could drag it by a line on his waist. Then he picked the boy up. He was light, very light, but still almost too heavy for Errol to manage in his current state.

"Do you live nearby?" he asked. "Is there some shelter? We're about to be in for it."

"Yes," the boy said. "Not too far, that way. Thank you, thank you, sir."

"Hang on," Errol said.

The wind was moaning now, and the sky no longer visible. Dust devils kicked grit up along the valley floor, and thunder crashed in the distance.

He followed the boy's pointing finger as the storm found them; the sand felt like tiny sparks, striking his exposed skin. It began to sting his eyes and cake around his nose and mouth. In minutes, he could hardly see.

"There!" The boy shouted.

Errol thought the boy was just pointing at a dune, but then he realized there was some sort of structure there, built of stone nearly the same color as the sand and mostly covered by it. The boy was gesturing at a dark hole that led into it.

A blast of wind knocked him from his feet. He struggled to get back up, but then the dune shifted and sand came pouring down over his legs, trapping him.

The kid was still free, though.

"I'm sorry!" Errol yelled. "I don't think I can get you there. Can you crawl the rest of the way?"

"It's okay," the kid said. He stood up and grabbed Errol by

the hand. His grip was so strong, Errol yelped in pain. Then the boy started pulling him. He yelled again as it felt like his arm was going to dislocate, but then he came free of the sand, still towing the armor. He couldn't see anything at all anymore, or even open his eyes for more than a few seconds.

He felt himself drawn along, and after a bit the wind dropped away, and the air was still.

Very still, and very dark. The boy was still dragging him — no longer over sand, but across smooth stone.

"Hey," Errol said, spitting dust out of his mouth.

He realized it was growing lighter. It wasn't daylight, or firelight, a but a sort of blue-green radiance.

Eventually it was bright enough to see that the boy was taller than he had been.

"Let go!" Errol shouted, beginning to struggle. He tore at the fingers with his free hand, but they felt like wire.

They entered a room lit by what appeared to be glowing sapphires arranged on the ceiling in the form of constellations, and now the thing pulling him let him go and faced him.

His mouth was far too wide, and he grinned, so Errol could see it was full of triangular teeth, like those of a shark. His eyes were mostly white, with little black pinheads in the centers. His fingers were very long, with nasty, sharp nails.

Errol started to scramble to his feet, but the thing moved quickly, grabbing him by the neck with both hands, stopping his breath instantly. He fought, but it was useless. It was so strong, and he was so weak . . .

"Release him," a soft of voice said.

The monster frowned. "But lady, I am hungry."

"Release him, I said. This one is not for you."

But it didn't; if anything, it tightened its grip.

"Release!" The voice shouted.

And finally, it did. Errol collapsed to the stone floor, gasping for air.

"It isn't fair," the thing said. "He should be mine."

"I sent you after him, remember?" the voice said. "He is not for you."

Errol's head was still spinning, but he was able to sit up.

"I tried to help you," he told the thing.

"That is your failing," the creature said. "If your weakness was jewels, I would have promised you treasure."

"He cannot help what he is," the other voice said. "No more than you can help what you are."

Errol rose unsteadily to stand.

"Where are you?" he asked.

"Back here. You may approach."

By now, Errol had had a bit of time to absorb his surroundings. The bejeweled ceiling was vaulted, the rest of the chamber rather squared off. In the center of it was something that looked suspiciously like a person-shaped box without a lid. Beyond that, against the far wall, was a stylized statue of a woman with wings, painted in what would probably be bright colors if the light was better.

The voice came from the base of the statue, which he now saw was actually a chair or throne, of some sort.

Seated there, in shadow, was a woman. Her hair fell in dark ringlets, and her eyes were black mirrors, reflecting the blue light from the ceiling. She wore a sleeveless white gown with complicated figures stitched along the hem. Her features were delicate, even fine, but not childlike.

Something about her felt enormously familiar.

He approached a bit closer, near enough to smell cloves, attar, and lilies.

She smelled like a funeral.

"I'm Errol Greyson," he said.

"Yes," she replied.

"Are you — do you know anyone named Jezebel?"

She smiled, showing teeth like pearls.

"I don't know that name," she said. "But you have traveled far, have you not? Perhaps a distant cousin."

"So the curse . . ." he trailed off.

"Of course," she said. "The curse is everywhere. It has broken things. The Kingdoms are shattered. Do you think you can put them back together again?"

"I'm not even sure what you're talking about," he said. "What I know is that when I was here before, everywhere I went, something had happened to the adults. They had either become monsters or just kind of disappeared."

"That is so," the woman said. "We are mostly removed from the world, yes. Mostly. The nature of our recusal varies from place to place and by the quality of our birth."

"So are you — dead?"

"Life. Death. Here the difference is less than where you are from, Errol."

"Yeah," he said. "I know." He glanced nervously at the toothy monster. "Is he going to eat me?"

"He is not," she said. "But he did reveal your nature to me. Your courage and your compassion are admirable. So I will help you, if you wish."

"I . . . yeah, that would be great."

On his first trip into the Kingdoms, he'd met a monster called the Snatchwitch, a kind of cannibal ogre. But she also had another nature, which she showed only one day a week, on Sunday — and then, she had been very helpful. So had her sister Jezebel, who also was a monster most of the time. If this woman was like them, how long did he have before she went full zombie on him or whatever? Or was she something else entirely? The whole place had sort of an ancient Egyptian vibe, which was not reassuring.

She lifted a hand from her lap, and he saw she was holding a feather.

"The storm will soon be over," she said. "This will show you the way."

"To Dusk? To the glass pyramid?"

She nodded. "But you must go further," she said. "Five Kingdoms that once were one, must be one again. You must help bring them together, together at the Isle of the Othersun."

Five Kingdoms? Othersun? Did she think he knew what she was talking about?

"I don't understand all of this," Errol said. "My friend, Aster, or maybe Dusk . . ."

"Yes," the woman said. "You are not the key. You are the companion. But the companion is essential. You must help her bring our skies back together, restore the fundaments of the Earth. Else I might as well have let the ghul eat you."

"Let me eat him anyway," the toothy creature said. "Look how weak he is. He will accomplish nothing. Your gift will be lost, and all hope vanish."

"Hope is very dim as it is," the woman said. "We cannot wait for a more perfect companion."

She closed her eyes for a moment, and suddenly appeared larger, somehow, even though her dimensions were the same. He felt very cold, as if immersed in ice water, and strange, distant music began somewhere.

"Take it," the woman said.

Errol walked over, getting colder with each step.

She thrust the feather toward him. He thought maybe it was a hawk's feather.

"Take it," she said. "Hurry. The storm is over. You must go."

Up close, he could smell the decay. Her face, although beautiful, did not look natural, almost as if it was made of porcelain. Beneath her clothing, he saw something shift, like the body concealed there was not human at all.

"Go!" she barked.

Errol grabbed the feather and ran. The armor bundle, still tied to his waist, hampered him, but he kept going in the direction of the door, determined not to look behind him. Once outside, he didn't stop. The sand was wet; steam rising from it, and the air was stifling. The sun was visible again, glaring down — if anything, with more heat and fury than before.

After a few hundred paces, his limbs failed him again, and he collapsed. Looking back the way he had come, he no longer saw anything but the desert.

But in his fingers, the feather quivered. It lifted up on a breeze that was not there and began to drift away from him.

"Okay," he said, doggedly pushing himself back to his feet. "Let's hope this isn't me losing my mind."

EIGHT
VESPER

When Veronica woke, it had grown colder, and since it was daylight, it bothered her. Aster noticed and fished a hooded sweatshirt out of her backpack. It was ugly, but it took the chill off.

She looked outside, and saw a plain of tall, thick-bladed grass.

"Where are we?" she asked.

"I don't know," Aster said.

"Then where are we going?"

"Ghartas Essenas," Aster said.

"That's a mouthful," Veronica said.

Aster nodded, but she didn't smile. She had that look, the one that Veronica had come to know meant she was hiding something.

"That's where Errol is?"

Aster shrugged. "I hope so."

"But you don't know."

"He could be," Aster said.

Veronica let that sink in for a second.

"You're not trying to find Errol, are you?" she said. "You're going after something else."

"We'll find Errol, Veronica," Aster said.

"But not now, right? Or anytime soon. What are we doing, Aster?"

Aster sighed, then looked out the window.

"We're going to my father," she said. "Errol might be there, too. You know how things work in this place. It isn't like back there, where things just happen. Thousands of years of wishes, and designs, and curses — that's like gravity and magnetism in the Kingdoms. Part of how things are."

"Sure," Veronica said. "I get that. What I don't get is why you didn't let me in on your decision."

"You were asleep."

"Not that asleep. If you'd told me something important had to be decided, I would have roused. Especially if it had to do with Errol."

Aster shrugged.

"I thought we were supposed to have each other's backs," Veronica said.

"That's unfair," Aster said. "I saved him, didn't I? I could have had Billy, but I saved Errol instead."

"I'm not talking about Errol," Veronica said. "You act like I don't exist. Like I don't matter. I thought — "

Before she could finish, she realized she didn't know *what* she thought. That she and Aster were friends? Aster had more-or-less raised her from the dead — not to do her a favor, but so she could perform a service. That service was long done, now. She didn't owe Aster anything, and Aster didn't owe her anything. That's the way it was, wasn't it? The way it really was.

"Veronica," Aster said. "He's my *father*. He sacrificed every-thing for me, do you know that? I failed him once, I can't fail him again. Not for you. Not even for Errol."

"Do you really think it will be so simple? You just said it doesn't work like that here. What if we need Errol to save you father? Did you think of that?"

"Errol ran off," Aster snapped. "Somebody came for him — maybe Dusk, maybe some other cousin of mine. I don't know. But he went with her. He left you and me and my father hanging out to dry, don't you get it?"

"Errol would never do anything like that," Veronica said. "He's so loyal, it's almost a disease."

"You think you know him," Aster said. "You don't. He's abandoned me before. More than once. He's completely capable of that, especially if a pretty girl is involved. The quicker you figure that out, the better."

Aster had become red in the face.

"Holy crow, Aster," Veronica said. "You're jealous."

"Don't be stupid," Aster said.

"No," she said. "I see it now. I haven't been thinking. You had to pick me. I was the only *nov* anywhere near you. You didn't have any other choices. But Errol, you wanted him. Not just so he could help you, but because —"

"Shut up," Aster said.

"No," Veronica said. "You need to —"

"*Keidi!*" Aster said.

Veronica suddenly felt her throat seize up. After a moment, she stopped trying to speak, and nursed her outrage, instead.

Aster breathed another word, and she felt the catch in her throat vanish.

"I'm sorry," she said. "I shouldn't have done that."

"This is my carriage," Veronica said. "It was given to me. Get out."

Aster opened her mouth to speak, but Veronica never got to hear what she was going to say. The carriage door swung open, and Aster, wide-eyed, got up and stepped out. She muttered several words under her breath, but nothing obvious happened.

"Veronica," she said. "Wait. I shouldn't have done that. I should have talked to you first."

"You got that right," Veronica said. "Horses, take me to Errol."
She grabbed Aster's backpack and heaved it out the door.

"Please," Aster said. "Veronica . . ."

Then the door slammed.

The horses, however, weren't moving.

"Oh, yeah," Veronica said. She glanced back at Aster, watching her through the window. Did she have any idea where Errol was?

Probably. But she would never tell her now, even if she was willing to ask, which she wasn't. She knew someone else whom might know—and if they didn't they could probably find out.

"The Mountain of the Winds," she told the horses. "On the shores of the Hollow Sea."

The carriage jerked into motion. Veronica leaned back in the seat, ignoring Aster's cries behind her.

A ster began to form a Recondite Utterance, but never said the words. Destroying the carriage wouldn't help her, even if she could. It certainly wouldn't win Veronica back.

But standing on the road wouldn't do her any good, either.

She had made her decision. She had made *this*. So she would deal with it.

She picked up the pack and continued on.

She hadn't walked far before the wind picked up, and it grew even cooler. The sun touched the horizon, first a red inferno, but soon fading to ginger. Above, where they sky had already darkened to a velvety cobalt, the evening star shone, and on the eastern horizon, the moon began to rise, pallid and enormous.

She stopped to stare at it for a moment, transfixed. She had never seen the moon appear so large, even though it was only a crescent. Despite its majesty, its light appeared somehow sickly, the scars and craters on its distant surface sharper and deeper than usual, as if seen through a telescope.

She walked on, glancing at the moon once in a while. After a time, she realized it wasn't rising anymore, but was fixed just peeking over the edge of the world. Nor had the sun entirely vanished; a burnt orange sliver of it remained, and the western horizon still blushed faintly in its light.

Now her feet whisked through fallen leaves. The fields on the side of the road were yellowed, and haystacks rose in steep mounds. Beyond the fields the trees wore leaves of gold, bronze, and copper.

Her light jacket didn't keep the chill out, and she began regretting giving Veronica the sweatshirt, but all she could do was continue, hoping soon she would reach a town or at least shelter. She said a Whimsy to warm her feet, which helped for a little while. But by then, she realized she had another problem.

Wolves. At first they were merely shadows in the ruddy light, weaving through the trees that had now crept closer to the road. But soon they grew bolder, venturing near enough for her to make out their shapes and eyes, to see that they were bigger than she had ever imagined wolves should be.

She spoke a Decree of Light, hoping to frighten them away. For a moment the air above her shone brighter than the sun, and the wolves scrambled back, growling low in their throats. But almost immediately the force of her spell weakened, and the brilliant illumination dulled to match that of the faded sun, which was not enough to keep the wolves a bay. They began what appeared to be a little game. Several would run in front of her, while more crept up behind. But it was a sport whose goal was to see her eaten — and soon, she knew, one would make a try for her.

Again, a Recondite Utterance came to her tongue, and this time she spoke it almost without meaning to — like a sneeze.

The air near her rippled out and away from her, and she saw the shapes of the wolves bend, as if through hot air rising off pavement, although there was no heat. The ripples swept the beasts from their feet and hurled them away in every direction, so that all of them vanished from sight into the deeps of the forest.

Her legs went weak; one of them bent, and she fell down on one knee. She felt her heart racing in her chest, and her head ached.

She heard he shush of leather shoes through leaves, but she was too spent to do anything about it. Someone took hold of her and lifted her in a carry. She was aware of others around.

"Hurry," someone said. "They will return." Then, to her, "Don't struggle. We are friends."

I n the little house in the woods, by the light of the small fire in the stone hearth, Aster studied the faces of her rescuers. The one who had carried her was big, rather flat-faced, but was amiable enough. His name was, fittingly enough, Oak. Of the three others, two had flaxen hair, and looked like they might be twins. Their names, Sharp and Quick, underscored that probability. The final member of the quartet, Copper, was a small fellow with a shrewd gaze and hair that had likely given him his name. All were dressed in layers of homespun and rough felt that had seen better days.

She noticed Oak kept staring at her.

Quick noticed, too.

"Don't be rude, Oak," he said.

"But she's a girl, i'n't she?" The big fellow said. "Dressed like a boy, sort of . . ."

He trailed off as the others glared at him. Aster realized that under her jacket she was still dressed in the jeans and T-shirt she'd had on when the police came to her house.

"I'm a girl," she said. "What of it?"

Instead of answering, Quick changed the subject.

"Nice trick with the wolves," he said. "I don't suppose you can teach it?"

"I don't know," Aster said. "I've never tried."

"Do y'think—" Quick began, then stopped and looked at his brothers. They nodded.

Quick moved to the back of the small dwelling and lifted a blanket that lay on the bed. She had noticed it before, and the lumps underneath, and assumed they were pillows.

They weren't. A man and woman lay there. Neither looked all that old; both were clad in homespun and felt. They were also both made of stone. To Aster, it looked like granite, with flecks of mica in it.

"They turned to stone?"

"Yeah," Quick said. "All of 'em. The growed-ups."

"That's the curse," Aster said. "I don't know how to fix that."

Oak shrugged. "Worth asking, I guess."

"I'm trying to figure it out," Aster said. "It's like this everywhere. My father is cursed, too. I'm sorry. I wish I could help, after all you've done for me."

"We've got to help each other," Copper said. "Especially these days, with Scratch on the throne."

"Scratch?"

"A nickname, is all," Sharp said. "You know who he means."

"I don't," Aster said. "I'm from far away."

"Oh," Quick said. "Very far away, it must be. Well, Scratch, he showed up a bit ago, and things has been nasty since."

"And he's *old*," Oak said. "Old, but not stone like the other growed-ups. It seemed all right, at first, like the olders had waked up and things were going to be okay. But then it got bad."

"How?" Aster asked.

"He wanted the girls," Copper said. "Every girl over eight. First, he put out the word, and some went because of that, because he was growed-up. But those that didn't—he sent his riders out, and they brought them in. That's what's got Oak all confused—girls is in short supply, hereabouts. And, uh—you're a girl."

"And he'll want you, too," Sharp said. "Soon as he knows about you, he'll want you. The wolves may have already told him. Or the birds."

"She looks like her," Oak said. "The star on her head. She looks like the regent."

"The regent," Aster said. "Is her name Dusk?"

"Oh," Oak said. "You know her then."

"Yes," Aster said. "Where can I find her?"

"Her?" Copper said. "Why, she's long gone. They say she's the one brought Scratch here, but none has seen her. Some say she's killed, others that he put her in the dungeon. Others claim she escaped."

What was going on? Was Scratch her father? Dusk had released him from his self-imposed prison, and all the evidence pointed to the fact that Dusk meant to impersonate *her*, his daughter. Her father was cursed so that he couldn't remember anything for more than a few moments, but he could recall everything that had happened before about eight years ago, perfectly. To him, Aster was still nine years old, and she and Dusk looked similar enough that he might believe her subterfuge. Armed with Aster's diary and the notes Aster had written to her father over the years, she'd had a good chance to pull it off.

If Scratch was her father, something had gone wrong. He must have turned on Dusk for some reason. Maybe he sensed the truth, or she made a mistake. Either way, that might be good news. It also meant it was most likely Dusk who had broken Errol out of Laurel Grove. Having failed with her father, she was up to something else, and probably not anything good.

But what was her father doing, rounding up girls? Was he looking for her?

Probably. But he was confused. He didn't know what she looked like now. Maybe he wasn't even sure what age she was. But where Dusk had failed, she was certain she could succeed — she, after all, was really his daughter.

"I'm grateful for your help," she said. "But I should not stay here any longer. I'm worried I'm putting you in danger."

"We're in danger anyway," Oak said.

"Hush, you pile of shakes," Quick snapped. "Keep that gob of yours closed up."

Chagrined, Oak looked down at his feet.

"This Scratch, where can I find him?" she asked.

"Oh, I don't think you want to find him, miss," Copper said.

"But I do," Aster said. "I think I know him. And I think I can help."

"What do you mean, help? Get the girls back or lift the curse?"

"Maybe both," Aster said.

"It's not smart," Quick said. "What if you're wrong?"

"It's a chance I have to take," Aster replied.

"At least have something to eat with us first," Copper said.

"That would be nice," Aster replied.

The meal was humble — curds and cracked wheat boiled together — but she was hungry. Afterwards, they offered to loan her some clothes, so she could "kit up like a fellow." The jeans would draw attention, and even though she didn't have a lot, bosom-wise, her T-shirt didn't hide what she did have all that well. She told them she didn't need a disguise, and hoped it was true. She figured the quickest way to her father — given what they had told her — was to be recognized as a girl. So she asked if they had any girls' clothes she could use.

After a moment of dubious silence, Copper left the room and returned with a simple, long-sleeved dress made of felt, with vines and roses embroidered on the cuffs and hem.

"My sister's," he said. "It ought to fit."

The sun, moon, and evening star were still where she had left them when she exited the house and continued on. She heard wolves howling in the distance, but they did not approach. But an hour or so into her walk, the sky filled up with birds with narrow, scythe-like wings that reminded her of chimney swifts. They flocked in clouds above her head, never settling, but darting and weaving almost like bats.

And soon, not entirely unexpectedly, she saw a rider coming her way.

He was tall and slender and he had a six-pointed star on his forehead. He wore a great cloak of felt patterned with horses, wolves, griffins, and stars and beneath that, brass colored armor. He rode a dappled horse.

"Well," he said. "You're not who I expected."

"Who were you expecting?" she asked.

He shrugged. "No one of consequence. Instead I find you."

He leaned forward, his expression almost one of amazement. "Who are you?" he asked. "I felt your utterance a league away. The nightjars are singing of it. The trees still tremble. You have the mark of the highborn on your forehead, but I don't know you. Are you a cousin of mine?"

"I don't give my name to just anyone," she said. "I'm sure you understand."

He wagged a finger at her. "You are only making me more curious, you know. But keep your little secret, if you wish. There will be time, unless he executes you right away, which I suppose is a possibility."

"He won't," she said.

"Confidence," he said. "That is so — umm, endearing, I guess."

He dismounted, put one foot out, and bowed.

"My name is Gloam," he said. "Allow me to accompany you to the castle."

"Do I have a choice?" she asked.

"That's a fascinating question," he said. "Right to the heart of it, eh? Do we have choice, or are we constrained by fate? I've read several books on the subject, but none satisfied." He stroked his chin. "I assumed you wanted to go to the castle. It is where this road goes."

"I could be lost," she replied.

"If so, you are now found," he said. "So let us go to the castle, and not become all theoretical about 'choice,' if you please."

"Fine," Aster said. "Lead the way."

NINE

THE GLASS PYRAMID

E rrol followed the feather across the sands to cascading shelves of bleached white stone, and eventually to an over-look above a broad, meandering river. The watercourse ran off to his left into what at first glance appeared to be a canyon slic-ing through a mountain range, but the planes and angles were all too regular, and after a moment he realized that he was look-ing at pyramids.

He had seen photographs of pyramids before. He had gone through a phase as a kid when he was really into them, and the fabulous tombs they protected. But usually, there were one, maybe two or three of the big stone structures within sight of each other—at most a handful. Here he was looking at dozens and dozens of them. Some were shaped like those from Egypt— four-sided, with big, broad bases. But others were incredibly steep, almost towers, often clustered together and leaning in odd directions, as if they had grown out of the yellow sand like bunching plants. The city itself ascended in steps, and he guessed if he saw it from above it he would be able to see it was one vary large stepped pyramid with smaller—but still huge— structures built on its various tiers. None of the buildings looked weathered, and many of them were capped with glass spheres, shining like little suns beneath the perpetual noon-day sky.

In the distance, one building rose above the others. He couldn't see all of it, because there were other structures in front of it, but it looked like the bottom two-thirds of the massive construction was of the same ochre stone as everything else.

The top third, however, was transparent. The rays from the sun fell through it, spilling rainbow light on the buildings below.

The glass pyramid, Dusk had said. At least finding it wasn't going to be all that hard.

Getting up it, however, looked to be a bear.

The feather settled on the ground, its job done. He cooled himself in the shallows of the river before advancing along its bank toward the city.

He found whole villages of mud huts, but he didn't see a soul, not even children. The scale of the place was even more impressive up close; even the smallest of the buildings towered over him, and the glass pyramid itself was truly gargantuan.

The river came down through the city in a series of waterfalls, flanked by grand staircases of gold-flecked stone.

When Errol finally reached the base of the glass pyramid — the part that was made of stone — he found some people. Or at least what was left of them — armor, swords, lances — and, of course, bones. Along with the human remains were what appeared to be the corpses of quite a few horses, as well. It was difficult to sort out how many had died, because none of them was — together. Something had torn them all limb-from-limb and scattered the remains fairly evenly around the base of the pyramid.

To Errol, none of that looked good at all. He backed away from the place, and climbed stairs up onto the terrace of another building, trying to figure out what was going on. He guessed that they had either all fallen or been thrown down the sides of the pyramid. That would explain the dead part. But what had torn them apart and picked the meat from their bones?

At home, he might have expected dogs or buzzards. Here it could be anything. Lions. Dragons. King Kong. He had no way of knowing; the stone of the plaza didn't take tracks very well, so no clue there. Maybe Dusk knew, and had expected him to be able to beat whatever-it-was with the nifty armor and sword she'd left him, but he hadn't brought that along, had he?

Studying the pyramid further, he saw the glass part didn't come to a perfect point; at the very top, it flattened off, forming a terrace that went all the way around the actual pointed top. He thought he saw a door, although it was difficult since the glass reflected everything around it. Here and there he could make out shadows that suggested things inside of the building, and if it ever got dark, he imagined he would be able to see inside clearly — if they had light in there. But the sun still showed no sign of moving.

After a time, when no flesh-eating monsters appeared, Errol got bored and went back down to the street. He tiptoed among the remains at the base of the pyramid until he found a nice-looking knife. With that, he cut some of the cord he'd been dragging Dusk's armor with and made himself a belt to shove the knife into. Then he hid the bundle under a shield with three lions on it.

The stone base of the pyramid proved harder to climb than he'd expected. The angle was fairly steep, and although the stones weren't mortared, the spaces between them were usually too thin to get a finger into. Still, the stone itself had enough texture for him to cling to.

Not so the glass. He put one hand on it and knew he wasn't going any further. Maybe if he had fingers like a tree frog or a gecko, or suction cups or something.

He climbed down. Maybe he could find something to make suction cups with. It was a long shot, but some of these guys had clearly made it a little higher before falling. They must have had *some* sort of special equipment.

He wasn't sure how long he'd been searching when he heard the clatter of someone riding up on a horse.

He started for cover, but the horseman had already seen him.

The rider was clad head-to-foot in armor. He lifted off his conical helmet, so Errol could see his face. He had dark features and light brown eyes; his hair was curlier than Errol's and cut short.

"You there," he shouted. "Are you ghul or human?"

"Human," Errol said. "Just a guy."

"Are you a native of this place?"

"No," Errol said, warily.

"Ah," he said. "Then have you come to essay the mountain?"

Errol glanced at the pyramid.

"You mean that?" he asked. "I guess I was thinking about it. But it's really slick."

"You seek the princess, then?" the boy said.

Was he talking about Dusk? But she hadn't been here that long. Not long enough for all of these guys to have tried, failed, and become bones.

"I don't know if she's a princess," he said. "But I have a friend up there."

Dusk wasn't his friend, but he didn't feel like explaining.

"What about you?"

"I am Kamet, the Bull of the East, from fabled Damey. And I have come for the princess."

"Okay," Errol said. "Look, maybe if we work together —"

"There is only one princess, my friend," Kamet said. "Luck go with you, but I must make this attempt alone."

With that, he settled the helmet back on his head, then rode back down one of the avenues leading to the pyramid.

Errol ran back up the steps for a better view. Maybe Kamet knew something he didn't.

Kamet turned his horse and began to gallop toward the pyramid. The horse, a long, lean white beast, stretched out its legs and started to pick up speed, but even so, Errol was having a little trouble believing what the knight was trying until they hit the base of the pyramid and started up it. Blue and white sparks struck from the horse's hooves, and unbelievably, rider and mount raced up the stone slope. They even appeared to be gaining speed.

By the time they reached the glass, Errol had begun to suspend his disbelief, so when the horse set hoof to the slick glass and continued on anyway, he shrugged and sighed.

All he'd needed was a magic horse. That made sense.

Kamet and his steed slowed a little about halfway up the glass section, but it was clear that they were probably going to make it. What did that mean? If Dusk was the "princess" and Kamet sprang her, what was *he* supposed to do?

Kamet had nearly reached the summit when a shadow in the corner of his eye caught Errol's attention.

It was a bird, a big bird, but he wasn't clear exactly how big it was until it slammed into Kamet and his horse with its claws. He watched in horror as mount and rider were knocked clear of the pyramid and tumbled through the air, looking like toy figurines at this distance.

They hit the slopes of the pyramid about halfway down and bounced several times before slamming into the pavement amongst the other corpses.

Errol jumped forward, hoping he might be able to help, pretty sure he couldn't.

But the bird wasn't done. It came swooping down and landed, plucking up the knight with its claws and flying back up to the top of the glass pyramid. There it settled and began pecking at what was left of Kamet.

Errol sat down, feeling sick. When the bird was done, it cast down the knight's armor and bones, picked up the horse, and repeated the whole exercise.

His horror faded to despair, but that in turn gave way to anger. Kamet should have made it. He had everything in his favor. But the whole thing was rigged. Try to climb, slip, fall, die, and the bird ate you. Show up with a magic horse or whatever, and the bird killed you before you could reach the top. No one was meant to survive. It was completely unfair.

But then, why should it be fair?

Kamet had acted like it was a test of some kind, one that could be failed, but which could also be passed. But if that was the case, the test wasn't the mountain.

It was the bird.

He had an idea, then, but it was a bad one. A really, really bad one.

He tried to think of a better idea, but eventually realized it was the only plan he was going to come up with. If Aster were here, he was sure she would see fifty ways in. Veronica could probably swim under the river and get in that way.

But they weren't here; it was just him, with his stupid idea.

"It's worth a shot," he murmured to himself.

After a while, the bird flew off, vanishing into the silent city. Errol waited a few more minutes, then went back down to the graveyard below the pyramid. With so much to choose from, he figured he ought to be able to find some armor that fit him.

TEN

THE MOUNTAIN OF THE WINDS

V eronica slept, and when she woke the carriage was still bumping along. It was morning, and the sun was balanced on the eastern horizon. To her right, forested hills rolled down to the road. To her left gaped the Hollow Sea.

From here it looked like the most enormous canyon in the world, so wide the other rim wasn't visible, so deep it appeared bottomless. Despite its name, there was no water to be seen. But once she had sailed the Hollow Sea on a silver boat, along with Errol, Aster, and Dusk. Where the boat traveled, water appeared before them and vanished in their wake. But more than that, she could *feel* the water there, or the ghost of it at least. Indeed, it called to her, and part of her wanted to leave the carriage, leap into the void, discover what lay beneath the mist that obscured it depths.

But she resisted, because she had to find Errol.

Or did she? Aster's comments bothered her more than she was willing to admit, at least to Aster. Once before, she thought Errol had chosen Dusk over her, and it had nearly been the end of her. But he'd come back for her, made her believe that he cared about her, that they weren't just two freaks, clinging to each other because no one else would have them.

And yet, he hadn't been able to say he loved her, even when she said it first. Maybe especially because she said it first.

And now Errol was off with Dusk, the woman who had chopped off Veronica's head, while another fellow had called her a goddess, of all things, and offered to make her a queen.

She wasn't used to thinking about such things, and she didn't like it. She had spent so long thinking only of prey, of feeding, of sleeping on her bed of bones. Uncomplicated things. Simple needs, easily dealt with. She sometimes wished things could be like that again.

Except that she wanted to find him. And her. In fact, she realized, it was possible she wanted to find Dusk even more than Errol.

Because Dusk had no business breathing. Whether Errol had gone with the other woman willingly or not made no difference at all when it came to that little matter.

She shifted in her seat and felt something hard against her bottom. Searching with her hand, she found a little silver sphere, about the size of a shooter marble, the one Aster had found back at the carousel.

"Keepsies," she said.

S he knew she was getting close when she saw that all the trees were leaning away from the direction she was going, as if a great wind or an explosion had pushed them all over.

The light began to dim, and she realized her breath was coming shorter and shorter—which was weird, because the sun had only risen an hour or two before.

She looked east and saw the sun had not only not risen any further in the sky, but it had begun to sink again.

"Well," she said aloud. "That's weird."

Soon it was dark, and she was dead again.

Without a clock or a properly behaving sun, it was hard to say how long it was before she reached the Mountain of the Winds.

It wasn't a mountain so much as a large hill that rose in tiers. The rocky, top part of it was riddled with doors and windows that appeared to have been carved by natural forces, and she knew from experience that there were caverns beneath it. Aster had brought them here, searching for a giant, and they had found a lot more than they bargained on.

By the looks of things, the same was true this visit. To make matters worse, a slight reddish glow was beginning in the east, and with that strange dawn she felt her heart strike a beat. Her blood was moving; her powers weakened, right when she might need them.

When she'd been here before, the plain around the castle had been empty. But now it was filled with campfires, tents, and people. It looked to Veronica like an army camp.

"Horses," she said. "I think we'd better go someplace else."

But she's hardly got the words out when she realized they were already surrounded both by people on foot and horseback.

A boy about her age stepped up to the window.

"Come on out of the carriage, miss," he said.

She stared at him for a moment.

"I'm just passing through," she said. "There's no need to bother me."

"We're supposed to stop everyone," he said. He sounded a little apologetic, but firm.

"Horses," she said.

But she saw the beasts were held fast by at least half-a-dozen armored figures.

"Miss," the boy said. This time his voice was rougher.

"I'm coming out," she said. "No need to be unpleasant."

The Hollow Sea was only about a hundred yards away, and she knew there were things there that could help her. If it was night. But it wasn't; everything now had the rosy glow of morning. If they cut her or stabbed her as she was, she would bleed.

But if things continued as she had observed, the sun would soon go back down. Then things would be different. She only had to wait.

"May I ask where we're going?" she asked.

"The princess will want to see you," the boy said.

"Well," she said. "I'm always happy to meet a princess."

She slipped the little sphere into her pocket and stepped out of the carriage.

The last time Veronica had visited the castle, she had reached it by air. This time she was conducted up a long, narrow staircase carved into the stone. Six of the soldiers escorted her though the high, airy halls, until they came at last to the princess.

She had hoped the princess would turn out to be either Mistral or the Brume, both of whom had lived here when last she came.

Instead, when the woman in the robes turned to greet her, she saw Dusk.

But only for an instant. Their faces were similar, but not identical. This woman was paler and a little rounder of face, and the star glittering on her forehead was silver, with only five points. Her eyes were almost white, with huge black pupils. Her hair was so black it looked like it had shoe polish in it.

"The Princess Nocturn," one of the soldiers said.

The woman smiled.

"You thought you knew me, didn't you?" she said. "I saw it on your face."

"I was just surprised by how pretty you are," Veronica said.

She was pretty, and dressed well, in a long black gown and a wide-sleeved robe embroidered in silver stars and comets that fanned out in a train behind her.

"Or perhaps you were sent by one of my sisters," the princess replied. "Or a brother. We all resemble very closely. You were sent, perhaps, to assassinate me?"

"Nope," Veronica said. "Just going about my business. I'd be way gone from these parts if your guys hadn't held me up."

"Your name?"

"Veronica Hale," she said.

"An odd name," Nocturn said.

"I'm named after my great aunt," she said. "Crazy old lady, but I always liked her."

She realized as she said it that it was true. She had forgotten her Geegant, but now she could see her face clearly in her mind's eye. The old lady had been full of stories of her travels in China and South America and all sorts of other places. Always full of jokes. She had never married. The consensus in the family was that most of her adventures were imaginary, although they allowed she had gone missing for a few years at a time here and there.

"So you remember your elders," Nocturn said.

"I guess so," Veronica replied. "Don't you?"

"Yes," she said. "But the memories are diminishing. The curse is growing stronger."

"Sorry to hear that," Veronica said.

Nocturn shrugged. "There is enough to deal with without growing sentimental," she said. "Or wasting time. You say you're merely a traveler, with no interest in my affairs?"

"Yes," Veronica said.

"And you were not sent by one of my siblings?"

"Don't even know them."

"Or by Him?"

"I don't know anyone name 'Him,'" either," Veronica said.

"The Abomination," Nocturn said. "The Elder. Scratch."

"I thought the old people were out of the picture."

"They were, and are, for the most part. But my sister brought Him, and it has changed things. Do you truly not know of this?"

"I'm not from around here," she said.

"He took my throne," she said. "He destroyed half of my army. I barely escaped with my life. I came to this place because I heard my sister had been here. Despite everything, I hope to make an alliance with her. So if you were sent by Dusk—or Dawn, or any of them—there is no reason to fear me. I stand ready for alliance."

"Sorry," Veronica said.

Nocturn nodded. "Very well," she said. "Brume?"

Veronica felt a chill, a wave of cold, wet air, and saw a little girl had entered the room. She was dressed in a dirty pink dress, and her green-black hair hung in a tangled mass.

Well, hell, she thought. This was a bad twist.

"Do you know this one?" Nocturn asked.

"She was here with Dusk," the Brume said. "That was ages back."

Nocturn nodded. "Thank you, Brume," she said. "You may return to your play."

"Thank you, princess," the Brume said.

Nocturn returned her gaze to Veronica.

"Now do you have anything to say, now that I've exposed you as a liar?"

"Your sister is a bitch," Veronica said. "I see the family resemblance."

"And yet you lied to protect her. Curious."

"Not her," Veronica said. "I honestly don't give tiniest damn about her. She tried to kill me."

"One of her other companions, then? I'm told there was a wooden boy, and another girl with a star on her brow. And a giant, in human guise? What became of them? Are they still with my sister?"

"I don't know," Veronica said.

"Maybe you've forgotten," Nocturn said, granting her a smile that would have been at home on a pageant queen. "Maybe with the correct prompting, you'll remember."

She waved her hand and the soldiers grabbed hold of Veronica.

"Hey!" she yelped. But Nocturn was already walking away.

They took her deep into the living rock, to a little chamber with no windows and only one door closed by an irregular but apparently sturdy iron door. Like every room in the place, her cell might have been worn into its shape by wind or water rather than by human hands and tools. It wasn't tiny, but it was small, far too small for her liking. She had once been buried head-down in a stone shaft no wider than her shoulders and since then, she had — issues — with tight spaces.

But it got worse. They put shackles on her arms and legs, passed the chains through holes bored in the stone in such a way that she could not sit down. She could hang by her arms, with her knees almost touching the floor, but that hurt.

She couldn't help it. She screamed, and once the first one tore out of her throat, more screams came from deeper inside of her.

The boys locked the door and left.

She yanked at the chains, she pounded her heels on the floor, and she screamed some more.

Meanwhile her heart slowed and stopped. The blood in her veins ceased coursing, her lungs stopped inflating.

At the same time, her senses grew, which only made her panic worsen. But then she closed her eyes, and let her nighttime senses go, and she seemed to leave the shackles and the little cell behind. She heard the guards talking, far away, sensed the pulse of their lives, each following a slightly different cadence. She smelled the water below the stone floor and felt it like a distant skin. She searched for voices, for snakes and crawfish or any number of much stranger aquatic creatures which might be bent to her will. But she found the waters beneath the castle to be oddly silent, as if everything was asleep.

The lock on her door rattled, and a boy stepped in.

He looked like a boy, at least, perhaps nine years old. He had strange green eyes that were a little unfocused, a shock of snow-white hair. With him was a girl a few years older, and several guards now stood in the hall outside.

"Hey," the boy said.

"Hi," Veronica replied. "Nice day, wouldn't you say? I'd offer you some iced tea, but, you know." She rattled her chains.

The boy came closer and pulled a little knife from his belt. He held it up so she could see.

"Got some questions to ask you," he said.

She was trying to think of something to say when he quite casually brought the knife up to her cheek and cut it. For a second, she couldn't believe he had really done it. And it hurt, awfully, which was also new. Back when she had been dead all day, a little cut wouldn't have bothered her.

"Look at that," the boy said to the girl. "She don't bleed."

"Why would that be?" the girl asked.

"Reckon she's dead already," the boy said. "Or half dead." He grinned. "But you can feel it, can't you?"

"Don't," Veronica said.

But the boy grinned.

"I'll bet I can cut you quite a lot before you can't talk anymore. This ought to be real interesting."

SUNDERED KINGDOMS

ONE
OUBLIETTE

G loam chattered near constantly as he led Aster past fallow fields and pastures carpeted in flowers like feathery purple wands, deep orange starbursts, tiny white bells clustered on tall stalks. Occasionally they encountered what looked like statues, carrying packs of firewood, shepherd's crooks, or frozen in the act of walking. Gloam spoke chiefly of philosophy, which she found boring and useless and soon stopped paying attention to him.

He stopped for a moment when they broke from the fields and forest and stood on a hilltop overlooking a broad, open valley with a river snaking through the heart of it. On one side of the water lay a small village. Across and beyond it, a fortress.

The fortress was a massive block of stone, taller than it was wide with conical towers projecting from either side off its top; it made Aster think of some large, catlike monster crouched on a hill, with its ears up. From the center of the wall facing her, a waterfall plunged hundreds of feet into the river. The stone, probably white or light grey, appeared bloody in the perpetual sunset. The whole view was framed by the sliver of sun and bright evening star on her left horizon and the crescent moon frozen on her right.

"Quite a sight, eh?" Gloam said.

"Yes," Aster agreed.

"The proportions, they say, are based on an ancient geometry, consonant to certain properties of the fundament," he began, rapidly becoming even less intelligible and engaging. Again, she stopped paying attention as best she could.

The town was small and neat, and to all appearances almost deserted. The few people she saw were young and mostly male. The handful of girls she noticed all looked to be below the age of nine. The figures of stone adults were everywhere; some had been pushed over, others hung with garlands of woven flowers. A few had been painted, perhaps to make them look more life-like, but the affect was — in her eyes — macabre.

"Where are the girls?" she asked Gloam as innocently as possible. "I don't see any."

"Ah ha," he said. "You noticed what? I'm sure I don't know what you mean."

But his face lost its cheerful aspect, and he was quiet for the rest of the ride.

A drawbridge spanned the narrows of the river, and beyond that an enormous arch divided the waterfall near its base, so the torrent parted above their heads and cascaded on either side of them. Beyond the arch lay a gate, which opened as they approached. The gatehouse guards watched them enter with diffidence; giving lackluster responses to Gloam's apparently enthusiastic greetings and well-wishing. They took his horse and began unsaddling it.

Beyond the gatehouse lay a rather impressive garden, made all the more interesting by the small river flowing through it, which welled from an enormous fountain in a pond near the other end of the yard. Ornate footbridges crossed the water in three places before it poured into an outlet, presumably to join the river below. Red and gold swans swam about the fountain, and tall white cranes stalked in the shallows. The trees — chestnut, maple, weeping willow, oak, ash, and many others — all were cloaked in various shades of yellow and orange.

From her new vantage she saw that there were four of the horn-shaped towers, one at each corner of the largely hollow keep.

Gloam led her into one of those towers. Up close they were gigantic, like small skyscrapers. The lowest floor of the one they entered was one vast room. A long black carpet formed a path across a floor of polished red marble, ending in front of a throne. Carved of some dark wood, its back curled up like the trunk and branches of a tree with spreading limbs and its legs resembled roots. Blue-white gems winked like stars on a clear night from where they were embedded in the branches.

On the throne sat her father, his red hair flowing down his shoulders, clean and brushed, from beneath a golden crown which bristled with little spikes pointing skyward. His robe was bright yellow figured with black and red sunbursts, bordered in dark red on the hem and wide cuffs. His feet were clad in black leather buskins.

One either side of the throne stood four boys in armor.

"Dad!" she said, starting forward.

Two boys from each side moved quickly to block her way.

"Let me go!" she shouted. "Dad, tell them to let me go."

But then she realized, from the blank look in his eye that he didn't recognize her. Of course he didn't. It was the same look she had gotten used to for eight years. His last memory of her was when she had been nine, not seventeen.

"It's me, Dad," she said. "Aster."

Her father took a deep breath and let it out. On the good side of things, he looked to be sober; he had spent most of the last four years drunk.

"And what is your name, daughter?" he asked.

"Aster," she replied. "Aster Kostyena."

He smiled, but she knew that smile, and understood it did not mean he was even remotely happy.

"You are the second young woman making that claim," he said. "That last one was a fraud, and when I catch her, she will pay dearly for her deception."

"Right," Aster said. "That was Dusk. She must have tried to convince you she was me . . ." she trailed off.

"Wait," she said. "You remember that? You remember her trying to trick you? But that must have happened days ago, weeks, maybe. You usually forget in minutes."

"She also claimed my memory was impaired," her father said. "That I could not remember anything for more than half a clock-strike, that in my mind, my daughter was still a little girl."

He nodded at the boys holding her.

"Let her come forward."

They released her, and she took a few steps.

"Stop," he said, when she was very near.

"Try to remember," she said. "Remember how you carried me, when I was hurt? You got a silver ship, and we sailed across the Hollow Sea. A dragon tried to kill us. I know you remember all of that."

Their gazes met, and for an instant she thought she saw recognition there, the light of realization dawning.

"Do you know how I knew Dusk was a fraud?" he asked, softly.

"How?" she asked.

"Because I have never had a daughter named Aster," he said. "I have never had a daughter named anything at all."

For a moment, she was struck speechless. In the back of her mind, she had known she would have to convince him of who she was. But she was good at that, from years of experience, and because he remembered her as a little girl, and because he loved her. That made him willing to be convinced.

But she saw no love in the look he gave her now, and everything in her gut told her he was telling the truth. This man did not remember her at all, at any age. There was no ladder she could erect to bring him from her childhood to the present.

"It's the curse," she said. "It must have gotten worse since you got here."

"Again, you mimic your predecessor," her father said. "Before you go on, let me assure you I have never been to the Reign of the Departed, much less lived there for years."

"No, that's not true," she said. "You did. We did. The curse is real."

"Yes, it's real," he said. "And I, like all the others past childhood was caught in it, oblivious. Yet now I am free of it, while the others are not. Fate has chosen me, or perhaps I chose myself somehow. I concede I do not know what Dusk—or you—hope to accomplish with this rather complicated piece of theater. Will you tell me? And who is behind this? She would not explain. Perhaps you shall."

Aster knew she was crying, now. She made no attempt to hide it.

"I'm just trying to get you back," she said. "Fix you, restore your memory. I want my dad back. That's all I've ever wanted. I love you."

"She's really very good," another voice cut in.

She hadn't noticed him enter. He was dressed all in black, all the way down to his boots. His hair was black and grey, and longer than the last time she had seen it, when it was cropped very short. Now it had begun to curl, a little. His eyes were glacier blue.

"I know you," she said. "You tried to kill me."

"Is my chancellor also your father?" her father asked. "Or an uncle? Or your mother?"

"No," she said. "This guy chased me and my friends all over the place. Killed a bunch of people. Everybody called him the Sheriff."

"I, of course, have never met this young woman," the Sheriff said.

"Naturally not," her father said. He stood up. "That's enough of this, for now," he said.

"I will escort her to the docks," the Sheriff said. "A ship is leaving soon."

"No! I want to know who is behind this. Put her in the oubliette and make certain she cannot escape. But do her no harm. Yet. That will come later, and at my hand, if she does not answer me."

"Sire, word is she is a sorceress."

Her father nodded. He said a word that obliterated itself even as she heard it. Pain fanned out within her to every extreme of her body, then faded into a sort of fuzziness, as if she was wrapped in layers of invisible gauze.

"The oubliette is made to render sorcery moot," her father said. "That will keep her quiescent until you reach it."

"Yes, sire," the Sheriff said.

O nce they were alone, in the corridor, Aster tried to bespell the Sheriff, but whatever her father had done left her unable to recall any of the magic she knew.

"Is it only you who've come back or is your whole little gang?" the Sheriff asked.

"You *do* know me," Aster said.

"Oh, yes," he said. "You were the brightest girl in my class. How could I forget? To be honest — and I feel I am now able to be honest, Aster — I was, in the past, somewhat obsessed with you. I told you that eventually you would meet someone who valued you for your true qualities. I just didn't tell you I was standing right in front of you."

The voice was still the Sheriff's, but it somehow didn't sound like him. The Sheriff had been spare with words, always to the point. He didn't talk like this.

Brightest girl in his class?

"Mr. Watkins?"

"Do I smell as sweet?" he asked.

A rose by any other name would smell as sweet. A Shakespeare reference—*Romeo and Juliet*. As impossible as it seemed, it had to be Mr. Watkins, her English teacher from Sowashee High. And according to Veronica, Mr. Watkins hadn't been exactly what he appeared to be, either.

"I was David Watkins," he confirmed. "Or, better said, Mr. Watkins was a name I went by for a time, a face, a life. I believed it myself, until you and your father finally set me free. And Veronica, she did her part, too, I suppose. She had good intentions—she tried to kill me, if you can believe it. But I do not die, I merely move on. And this time I did not have to move far. Aster, where is the Kingdom of Silver?"

"What do you mean?"

"Dusk had two of the Kingdoms when she left here, but they were separated. I believe she left one for you, to bring you here. Your father saw you with one, in a carriage, a short time ago. Where did you hide it?"

"I don't know what you're talking about," Aster lied.

"It doesn't matter," he said. "I can use your father's orb to find it again. It's time I relieved him of it anyway—before he gets suspicious. This is another black mark in your ledger, I'm afraid. But don't worry. The questioning will no doubt hurt—all the more because it will be your dear father torturing you. Ah, the tragedy. For that I'm sorry, but right now I must have your father's trust. Once he is done with you, I'll help you escape."

"Escape? Why?"

"Oh," he said. "You misunderstand me. I mean to help you escape that body of yours. Then you and I can truly be together, for all time, the way we were destined to be."

That he meant it was very clear, and it made her almost physically ill.

"You may have changed your face somehow," she said. "But you're still insane."

"'I was walking among the fires of Hell, delighted with the enjoyments of Genius; which to Angels look like torment and insanity,'" he said. "That's William Blake, remember? Junior Lit?"

"Now you're proving my point," Aster said.

The oubliette was not a cell, as she had expected, although it was two floors beneath the castle. It was a suite of rooms, furnished with bed and chairs, tables with playing cards and chessboards. Mr. Watkins—or whatever he was, ushered her in.

"Soon," he said, and closed the door.

She looked around the room, trying to recall where she was and how she had gotten there. She ran her finger over the cards and toyed with the chess pieces.

She felt good. Not happy, but she knew she had once been very worried, and now she wasn't. The bed was soft, and comfortable, and next to it stood a full-length mirror. It showed her a young woman with reddish-brown hair and peculiar birthmark, like a star, on her forehead.

"Who are you, I wonder?" she murmured.

I t took a great deal of willpower to watch Aster step into the oubliette and close the door behind her. He had been first searching and then waiting for her for what seemed like eternity.

To have her so near, completely in his power, and be forced to restrain himself was almost intolerable.

But as he shrugged off David Watkins and his mortal limitations, he was beginning to remember what eternity really was, and what it could be. After ages imprisoned in the rough clay vessels that inhabited the Reign of the Departed, he was determined that from here on he would have immortality on his own terms. That meant patience. For the time being, it meant keeping control of Kostye and maintaining his trust. If Aster suddenly vanished now, it might raise suspicions. The curse was strange and fickle, and he didn't understand everything about it. If some shock or turn of events brought Kostye's memories of his daughter back, that would be an immense setback.

Besides, he had other girls now, many others who had light to give him. His collection would never be complete without Aster, but for now he could be satisfied by sheer quantity. Quality would come to him in time.

But there was the matter of the Kingdom of Silver. He needed that.

He found Kostye in dream, as he often was, drowsing in his quarters. It was no matter to take the sorcerer's orb; he would miss it if it was gone for long, but what he meant to do wouldn't take long. He followed the steps up into the highest room in the tower, carrying the rose-colored sphere in his palm.

Kostye had seen Aster with the Silver Kingdom not long ago — less than a day, he guessed, if days still existed. She must have hidden it or given it to someone else before entering the fortress. That meant it shouldn't be far.

As he placed the sphere against his eye, he felt the faint tickle down in the bottom of him that was Vilken, the man he had first known as the Sheriff, whose body he now inhabited. There wasn't much left of the fellow, but what was there was useful. Memories of his former life, for instance, especially the years when he and Kostye had been friends — or at least partners in crime. The many decades before the falling out, and the curse. Before Vilken's exile in the Reign of the Departed.

And the magic — the Whimsies, the Recondite Utterances, the Names. Those were very useful indeed.

But of *himself*, the Sheriff had lost almost everything. Not quite enough to be reborn in some other Kingdom, but too much to cause him trouble in this body they shared.

The sphere became his eye, peering into the places where the other Kingdoms were. He saw pyramids under a bright sun, an island bathed in morning light, a cavernous hall of stone.

At last he saw her, the one who possessed the Silver Kingdom. He sighed in delight.

It was the other he had missed. The girl with the golden hair and the white tennis shoes.

Everything was coming together, now, all fortune bending toward him.

It was about time.

With a smile on his face, he began preparing for the journey.

TWO

LOTUS

E rrol soon regretted his choice to lie in the sun rather than the small sliver of available shade. But he was trying to get noticed, not hide, and it had seemed the obvious choice at the time. Now he dared not move. But even lying still, the armor he had salvaged was beyond hot, it was stifling.

What must it be like to walk wearing this stuff, ride—fight, for Pete's sake?

He'd never had trouble respecting Dusk. She was smart, courageous, and one hell of a fighter. But now his regard for her went up another notch because she wore her armor almost all of the time. She looked a little weird without it.

And of course, she was also deceptive and a bit murderous, both marks against her, and double points because she had betrayed him personally and tried to kill his girlfriend.

He wondered what Veronica would think if she saw him right now, if she knew what he was doing. How mad would she be? How betrayed would she feel?

He remembered the last time he'd seen her, her face so close to his, telling him she loved him.

And he hadn't been able to answer. Why? He remembered when he thought she was dead—really dead, dead for good. It had felt like something was torn out of him, like he wanted to die himself. How could he feel like that and not be able to tell her?

What was he doing? How would he explain this?

He would explain that it wasn't about Dusk, or any feelings he had for her. It was about doing the right thing. Doing what he said he would do. That was important.

Except—hadn't Dusk sort of kidnapped him? Had he really promised her anything, or it was it just him accepting her assumptions about him?

He heard a horn in the distance, a bright, high note, and a few moments later it sounded again, closer. He dared not move to see what it was. He heard it once more, far in the distance, moving away from him. Hours crawled by.

He was fairly sure his blood was near boiling when the shadow fell on him. For an instant, he didn't know what it meant, even though he'd been waiting for it. But then he understood.

Okay, here we go, he thought.

So many ways this could go wrong.

The bird hit him with such force that it knocked the wind out of him, and when he got it back it was all he could do to stay limp and not scream. But by then, he was also in the air, clutched in the creature's gigantic claws, its wings beating ponderously above him. He cracked his eyes and saw the mortuary plaza shrinking below him, the shining surface of the glass pyramid coming into view.

As he had hoped, the bird thought he was dead, just another piece of carrion that had tumbled to the bricks after an unsuccessful attempt to climb up the pyramid. He'd put the armor on to avoid being cut up and run through by the monster's talons as much as to fit the profile of a failed rescuer. But what if it dropped him now, to make sure he was deceased? It would be like tossing a box turtle off of a sixteen-story building. He could almost imagine the impact, but he bet he wouldn't feel it. Not for long.

The bird accelerated, sending his blood rushing to his head, then slowed. Below him he saw the terrace at the top of the pyramid. It was smaller than he'd thought, maybe only about ten feet wide.

He was hot and scared and angry, and it didn't bear thinking on. He was tired of waiting.

He drew the knife from his belt, leaned up, and cut at the bird's leg as hard as he could.

To his chagrin, the blade only went in about an inch, but by the bird's reaction, you would think he'd cut the whole foot off. It screamed so loudly it hurt his ears and let him go, so he fell the final ten feet and hit the pyramid with the sound of a half-ton of buckets dropped from a housetop. The impact hurt more than was reasonable, and then he was struggling against the weight of the armor to get back on his feet. Frantically eyeballing his surroundings, he saw the bird had flown back up, but he knew that was temporary. He'd seen it in action; it would get some altitude and dive, and if it hit him, he was done. Even if he stabbed it somewhere vital and killed it, its momentum would still knock him to his doom.

By the time he got back on his feet, it was on its way back. He looked around frantically, but there was no place to go except the other side of the smaller pyramid standing up from the middle of the terrace. That was better than nothing.

The bird saw what he was up to and changed its angle. It was no use. If he waited until the last second, maybe he could throw himself to the side, and the monstrous raptor would slam into the pyramid . . .

Then he realized that there was a door in the glass. He hadn't seen it a first, but now he noticed a rectangular hole in the reflection of the sky. He clanged toward it, trying not to look back, seeing the mirrored image of the bird of prey grow larger with impossible speed.

It hit him as he got through the door, clipping him with one claw. The sound was hideous, like fingernails on a blackboard but much, much worse — especially considering that *he* was the blackboard. The pain that jagged through him was surreal as he went tumbling head over heels and slammed into the glass.

But at least he was inside. He lay there for a moment, dizzy, spots dancing before his eyes.

When he opened them, everything looked red. He tried push himself up, but the glass was incredibly slippery. With red stuff.

"What?" he managed. He heard someone gasp.

What he saw first was a tree, growing right in the middle of the pyramid-top, its branches spreading to fill the sharply-peaked ceiling.

Beyond the tree, a girl was watching him; her mouth formed a little "o". He wondered what she looked so shocked about.

Then he passed out.

W hen he opened his eyes again, it was to a throbbing pain in his side. He was lying on a pile of large, brightly colored pillows piled on the floor. The air was thickly perfumed, reminding him of pine rosin, cinnamon, and honeysuckle.

"You're feeling better, I hope."

He looked over and saw the girl. She was kneeling on a cushion in front of very low, slanted desk, forming beautiful, curving characters on paper with an old-fashioned ink pen, the kind you dipped in a well.

She was maybe twelve or thirteen, with black hair and a sepia brown complexion and her eyes were made up with a lot of black eyeliner. She wore a diaphanous saffron robe over a white silk tunic embroidered with flowery yellow and blue patterns and loose turquoise pantaloons that gathered at her ankles.

"I was bleeding," he said.

"Oh, yes," she replied. "A lot." She turned to face him, smiling, and he saw she had a pale gold eight-pointed star on her forehead.

"I think you're okay now, though," she said.

He looked himself over and realized he was no longer in his armor. Or his clothes. Instead he wore something like a long white-and-blue striped nightshirt. He didn't see any blood.

"How did I get out of my clothes?" he asked.

"They were a real mess," she said.

"Yes but . . ." he trailed off, feeling his face burn.

"Oh," she said. She blushed, too.

"No, of course not," she said. "Djinn changed you. I didn't even look." She frowned, as if entertaining the thought made her progressively angrier. "Of course, I didn't look."

"Oh," Errol said. "But the bleeding . . ."

"The tree," she said. She inclined her head upward and, at first, he didn't know what he was looking at. Then he realized it was a tangle of roots, suspended in water. He guessed he was about three stories beneath the entrance level to the pyramid, and most of that was a water tank. But there must be a staircase or something, winding around the outside of it. A little searching with his gaze and he found where it came out, and another staircase continuing down.

The room he was in now was draped with translucent, colored cloth, making it look a little like the inside of a tent, but the floor was bare except for the pillows. The glass was so clear, I looked like he was about to fall a few hundred feet any minute.

"It's got these magic pomegranates," the girl went on. "You can never tell exactly what they're going to do, but it usually has to do with what you need, and you needed to stop bleeding."

She had turned away from him and was again writing in her elegant hand.

"I'm Errol," he said.

"My name is Lotus," she said. "But you probably knew that."

No," he said. "I didn't."

She stopped writing. "Truly? You went through all of that, and you didn't even know my name? When we are married, I hope you're going to be a tad more attentive."

"Married?" he said. "I—ah—think we've gotten our wires crossed, here. I didn't exactly come up here to rescue you."

"No?"

"I was kind of looking for someone else."

She frowned slightly and digested that for a moment.

"Do you mean to say you don't want to marry me?"

"Well, you seem—uh—very nice, and I guess you saved my life—"

"There's no question about that," she said. "You should see the mess Djinn had to clean up."

"Okay. But the thing is, I kind of have a girlfriend—"

"You are otherwise betrothed?"

"Uh, we're not engaged," he said. "And you, aren't you too young to marry?"

Her brow now creased dangerously. "Are you saying I'm not a woman?" she said. "Are you calling me some kind of little girl? Are you implying I am not desirable enough to be a wife?"

"No?" he said.

"My mother, grace her, was married and with child by the age I am now."

"Look," he said, feeling it all getting out of control. "I'm just—I didn't come here to marry you. I'm not even thinking about marriage to anyone right now. Or anytime soon."

She lifted her chin. "I am an honorable woman, sir," she said. "I hope you do not think—"

"Or that either," he said.

She appeared to relax a little. "You really don't want to marry me?" she said.

"I don't, no," he said.

She closed her eyes and sighed. "Thank goodness," she said. "For I've no desire to marry either. As much as I wish to be free of this place, I do not desire that. This was all my father's idea, you know. He arranged with my uncle for me to be 'kidnapped' and brought here. He thought a man willing to travel far and risk death for me would be worthwhile."

"That sounds a little—wasteful," he said, thinking about all of the corpses down below.

"Yes," she said. "I think he may have been trying to sway me, frankly. That after one or two of the poor fellows died my heart would soften, and I would warm up to the idea of marriage. But then the curse came, and the spell on me and this pyramid became quite permanent. Until now. And I would have married you, the magic knows that. But I'm awfully glad I don't have to."

"Cool," Errol said.

"Is your betrothed here, too? Have you come to rescue her?"

"No," he said. "There's another woman here, a little older than me. Her name is Dusk—"

"Oh," Lotus said. "Her."

"You've seen her, then?"

Lotus dipped her pen in an inkwell and wrote a few more characters.

"Out of curiosity, while you scale glass mountains to rescue women you are *not* planning to marry, where is this woman you love?"

"That," Errol said, "is complicated."

Lotus smiled.

"I'll wager it isn't," she said.

"Dusk is here," Errol pressed. "Do you know where I can find her?"

"Whether you marry me or not, Errol, you've broken the spell that traps me here. I am now free to return home. If you wish, I will take you with me. If you stay here, I'm afraid things will go badly for you. Cousin Hawk is not a fair-tempered man."

As she said this, she rolled up the papers on her desk and put them into a leather tube.

"I have to find Dusk first," he said. "Maybe you could help me—"

"Hush," she said, rolling her eyes. She rose and padded to some baskets in the corner and returned with an armful of clothing.

"If you intend to stay, best put these on. They can see you though the floor and walls, but if you have my clothes on, they might think you're me, at least for a little while. And they mostly ignore me, so that's good for you."

"I don't think they'll fit," he said.

"Not the pantaloons, maybe," she allowed. "But see, this shirt and robe, the shawl—that should do the trick. The top of the shawl can wrap around your face—I wear it like that sometimes. Just don't get too close to anyone. You're pretty, but not as pretty as me."

"It's worth a try," he said. "Could you, uh—turn around?"

"I can do better than that," she said. "Djinn. I'm ready."

He felt a sudden gust of wind, followed by a stronger one. Lotus stood straight, holding her tube, and began to pirouette and twirl, her feet leaving the ground as the breeze became a cyclone so strong it now forced him back.

"I heard the horn earlier," Lotus said. "That means they went hunting. There should only be a few servants around. Good luck."

Then the wind rushed away from him. He watched through the glass walls as she flew up the stairs, through the floors above, and out the door he had entered through. In a moment, she was a tiny speck, receding in the lapis sky.

As she suggested, he put on her clothes.

The inside walls of the pyramid were transparent, but that didn't mean he could see everywhere. The angles created countless opportunities for reflections and rainbows, so while looking down through the floor he caught glimpsed of things below, they weren't always clear. Furthermore, couches, beds, ornate rugs, pools of water, and potted plants also obscured perfect vision. From what he could tell, it looked as if much of the lower levels were gardens of some kind.

It was a big place, so he figured he had better get started.

He soon found that Lotus had given him good advice. Now and then he saw someone through a wall, floor or ceiling. Some saw him too, but never gave him much more than a glance as he descended deeper and deeper into the place.

He'd been right about the gardens. The lowest level was basically an arboretum, with a ceiling high enough to accommodate trees of respectable size. He didn't recognize a lot of them, but some were familiar enough – apples, pears, and figs. He had never seen a real olive tree, but he saw fruit he was pretty sure were olives.

He was hungry, and thought about eating some of the fruit, but that was probably dangerous in a place like this. What the magical pomegranate had given him, one of these figs might as easily take away. Or worse. His hunger could wait.

Dusk was still nowhere to be seen, and by coming all the way down through the glass structure, he was certain he would have at least seen where they might have hidden her.

He had now reached the stone part of the pyramid, and after a bit of searching found stairs that continued down.

He didn't see any torches, and soon he knew he would be feeling his way through the dark. But as the light behind him faded, a faint blue glow beckoned him onward. He thought it might be gems, like those in the tomb in the desert, then he saw it was a faint mist, moving ahead of him.

Once he thought he saw a face in the mist, but when he tried to focus on it, it vanished.

The passages were much tighter here than in the glass portion. He passed several chambers, some fairly large, all decorated like rooms that someone ought to live in—chairs, beds, rugs, water basins—but while he didn't see anyone in any of them, they all had one thing in common—each had a large sarcophagus in the center.

He passed them by.

Finally, after what might have been hours, he heard someone singing—or rather, humming—a wordless melody.

After a few turns, he found Dusk.

She was in one of the furnished rooms, although hers was lit by a crystal vase on one of the tables. She was clothed rather like Lotus had been, which struck him as strange, somehow even stranger than she had appeared in Laurel Grove greens. It made her look soft, which he absolutely knew she wasn't.

"Errol," she said. "There you are. You look quite fetching in that outfit."

She didn't appear surprised at all, and his reaction must have shown on his face.

"I was expecting you," she said. "I never doubted that you would come for me."

"Okay," he said. "Uh—yeah, here I am. So—let's go."

But Dusk was frowning a little.

"Where is your armor?" she asked.

"Dusk," he said, "thanks, but no thanks. I didn't have a good feeling about it."

"Then how did you get in?" she asked.

"You, know," he said, "I managed it. Without the creepy armor."

She looked impressed. "You are resourceful," she said. "You found the princess, I assume?"

"Sure," he said.

"Looking forward to your wedding?"

"Yeah," he said. "Very funny. You could have warned me. About a lot of things."

"It's no matter," she said. "Lotus and her Djinn await us, I suppose?"

"Well—no. They left."

"She can't leave without you," Dusk said. "Not unless you—"

She stopped, closed her eyes, and sat down.

"You released her, didn't you?" she said. "From your marriage."

"Well, yeah," he said. "I wasn't going to marry her. I don't even know her."

"You wouldn't have had to go through with it," Dusk said angrily. "You were just to agree to it. Then she would have had to consider any requests you had."

"Look, if you expect me to lie to someone, you need to give me a heads-up. We had a long flight here on that hobby-horse, and you could have filled me in on all of this."

"I didn't know they would be waiting," she said. "I thought we would have more time. And I hoped things would go differently. Being a prisoner does not suit me, and I expected to avoid it completely."

"Whatever, I'm here—let's go. Hawk and his posse are out hunting, or something."

Dusk sighed. "Do you notice anything about my room?" she asked.

"Nice bed," he said.

"The door," she said.

"What about it?"

"There isn't one," she said. "No lock, no chains, nothing to keep me from walking out of here. So why haven't I?"

He shrugged. A bad taste was developing in his mouth.

"Because we'll never escape them, even if they are out for the moment," she replied. "Not on foot. We needed Lotus. I was counting on Lotus." She looked crestfallen for a moment, but then brightened.

"Or the horse," she said. "Did you bring the horse?"

"The wooden carousel horse?" he said. "Yeah, I carried that thing all the way here. Got it right here in my pocket."

"You remember that it can fly, yes, Errol?"

"Yeah. It did, too. But it decided to throw me, first."

"Oh," she said. "That's unfortunate."

"Look, I brought *your* armor. It was as much as I could carry."

"Truly?" she said. "You brought my armor?" She smiled, finally. "Oh, Errol. That's worth something. Where is it?"

"I hid it outside."

"Outside?"

"Of the pyramid."

"How do you propose we descend the pyramid?" she asked.

"I have an idea," he said. "It's not a *great* idea, but it's all I've got. Come on, I'll tell you on the way."

"A moment," she said. "I came here to steal something. "

THREE

THE DAY QUEEN, AT REST

Aster was playing cards when something peculiar happened. A part of the wall — which appeared quite solid — suddenly wasn't there. Instead, there was a rectangular hole, shaped something like a door. Beyond the opening stood a woman in a red dress, with red-rimmed glasses.

"Aster," the woman said. "Come here!"

"Do you mean me?" she asked.

She realized she was holding something and looked to see what it was. She found it to be a playing card, with a knight on a horse, reared up.

"Aster!" Someone said. She turned, and saw a woman, standing in a doorway.

"Keep your eyes on me," the woman said. "Walk here."

As she rose, she bumped against the table. She was trying to remember what she was doing when she heard someone call her. It was a woman, wearing glasses, motioning toward her frantically. She was already standing, so she started walking that way, to see what the matter was.

She blinked her eyes, wondering what was happening. About two feet away, a strange woman with brown hair and a red dress was yelling at her. Had she done something wrong?

She started to back up, but the woman darted forward, grabbed her arm, and yanked her through a hole in the wall.

Almost instantly, she felt dizzy and sick, and doubled over, vomiting. The woman kept her grip on her arm. She gasped, trying to keep everything from spinning.

The woman was looking down at Aster, and she suddenly recognized her. It was Ms. Fincher, her high school guidance counselor.

"What . . . ?" she got out, before another wave of dizziness overtook her.

"I'm sorry," Ms. Fincher said. "We have to go, or we'll both get caught."

She heard a sliding sound, then a thump. Then they were in near darkness.

"Ms. Fincher?" she said.

"Oh, thank goodness," Ms. Fincher said. "You know me. Come along, quickly. Can you — can you make some light, or something?"

"Oh," Aster said. "I can try."

To her great relief, she could now remember her spells, so she said a firefly Whimsy, and a mote of light appeared; she could see the woman's face.

Ms. Fincher was a small woman, slight of frame. Pretty, with brown hair cut short, but longer than Aster remembered it. She looked strange in her red gown, as if dressed up for some sort of theatrical production. She knew she wouldn't have had that reaction to anyone else dressed that way here, where it was perfectly natural and expected.

But Fincher was not from here. Aster had only ever seen her in suits — usually skirt and jacket — once in jeans at some kind of fundraiser.

"Thank you," Ms. Fincher said. "That will help."

"Ms. Fincher. What's going on?"

"I'm saving you, hopefully," she said.

"Wait. My father—"

"I came here with your father, remember? With Dusk. She used the necklace you put on me to command me."

"You're not wearing it, anymore."

"No," she said. "Watch out, there are stairs ahead."

"What happened to Dusk?" she asked.

"I think she escaped," Fincher said. "Otherwise, Kostye wouldn't have been so angry."

"And the other guy—"

"Do you know him? The chancellor? Do you know who he is? What he is?"

"I don't know *what* he is," Aster said. "But he's bad. He killed my friend Veronica. He wants to kill me. To take my soul, even though I know that sounds kind of crazy."

"I might have thought that once," Ms. Fincher said. "But not now. I've seen things . . ."

She stopped and turned around.

"Obviously, Aster, you know a lot more about this—world— than I do. Do you know how to return home?"

Aster considered the question. Ms. Fincher knew that she, Errol, and the others had entered the Kingdoms. She did not know that she had returned from them, did she? Furthermore, Aster hadn't been able to return to Sowashee on her own the last time; Billy had done that, in his giant form. This time she'd arrived in a carriage provided by some guy—yet another guy— who had the hots for Veronica. If she put her mind to it, she could, given time, probably find her way back to the Reign of the Departed. But she didn't know how to do it right now, nor did she have any interest in doing so, not without her father.

"I don't know how to go back there," she said. "My father does, or at least did."

"Yes, I've tried talking him into it," she said. "The problem is, he not only has no desire to go back, he doesn't remember ever having been there."

"Yes," Aster said. "I gathered that."

"I'm sorry. It must be hard to know he doesn't remember you at all. Coming here has changed him. His condition. In fact, I guess it's reversed. He remembers everything since arriving here, and he remembers events of many, many years ago. But not his time on Earth. Or you, obviously."

"I need to see him again." Aster said.

"It won't go any better, Aster. It will be worse." She sighed.

"I wish we could have talked about all of this — before."

"Yeah," Aster said. "'Hi, Ms. Fincher, I'm here for my counseling session. My dad is a sorcerer from another world. He brought me here to protect me from some terrible evil, but a curse of some kind is affecting his memory.' That would have worked out great, right? Dad in an institution, me in some kind of halfway house or whatever."

Ms. Fincher nodded. "I suppose you're right. Still, once I was involved, you might have filled me in. As it is, I've been having to learn as I go, which is . . . difficult. Can you tell me what you know about the curse?"

"Only that it affected adults, everybody over a certain age, and that the deeper into the Kingdoms you go, the stronger it seems to be. At the outskirts, just past the Pale, the grown-ups have turned into monsters, but one day a week they're human again. But when we got farther in, they had become trees and stones and so forth."

Ms. Fincher nodded. "I'm sure you've seen what happened here."

"Yes," Aster said.

"And the sun? The seasons?"

"What do you mean?"

"Surely you've noticed. It's always sunset, and it's always autumn."

Aster shrugged. "Maybe some kingdoms are like that."

"No," Ms. Fincher said. "This happened after I arrived. When I first got here, there was still day and night. Whatever this curse is, I think it's getting worse. Like your father."

"Pulling things apart," Aster said. "Breaking the day into pieces, the year into pieces, as it split old from young."

"That's what I've been thinking," Ms. Fincher said.

"I can't believe you're not more freaked out about this," Aster said.

"I'm completely freaked out," Ms. Fincher said. "But I'm also rational. If I can't trust what I see, hear, and feel, then I've gone insane. And I refuse to believe I've lost my mind. The question is, is there any remedy? Your father talks about putting things right, but he doesn't know what happened, either. Do you have any clue?"

"I've been told it can be fixed," Aster said. "But I don't know how."

"I was hoping . . ." Ms. Fincher said, but then she shrugged. "Someone told me there was a way. A way to save you and break the curse. I'm taking you to her. But I don't know — I don't know who to trust, Aster."

She studied the counselor's face.

She didn't know who to trust either, including herself. One voice insisted that if she could see her father one more time, she could make him understand. He would come around, and everything would be okay.

But that wasn't really how things worked. She knew that by now. She had magic words to call whirlwinds and lightning, but the words to make her father better didn't exist — or if they did, she didn't know them yet. Ms. Fincher was right — if she went back, things would go like they had before, only this time Ms. Fincher would probably get caught, too, and then she wouldn't have anyone to lure her out of the oubliette.

"If you know someone who thinks they know how to end the curse, then by all means, take me to them," she said.

The counselor smiled grimly.

"I can't take you any further myself," she said. "If I don't get back soon, they'll figure out I helped you escape."

"Why not come with me, then?" Aster asked. "My father used to be bad—very bad. He talked about it sometimes when he was drunk. He says he was a monster. He says he changed for love. He means he changed for my mother. And since she died, he tried to stay good, to be like she would want him to be. To protect me and raise me. But if he doesn't think I'm real anymore, or worse, if he doesn't remember Mom—"

"I know," Ms. Fincher said. "That's what has happened. Right now, your father is capable of awful things. The chancellor knows that and it feeds his worst instincts. He's like the devil on your father's shoulder."

"And you're like his angel?"

"I'm not an angel. But I'm the best he has. Aster, whatever good your mother's love may have woken in him—it was already there. She just helped him find it. He's not a lost cause. But without my influence, I fear what might become of him. And what he might do."

"That makes you dangerous to the chancellor," she said. "What if he decides to get rid of you? He's done way worse."

"Right now he doesn't dare," she said. "Your father likes me. But if he suspects I betrayed him . . ." she shrugged.

"Likes you?" Aster said, her mind retracing the last part of the conversation. "Likes you how?"

She looked embarrassed.

"I'm as confused about that as anyone," Ms. Fincher said. "Just—don't worry about it for now. Look out for yourself. These steps will take you to an underground stream. You may have to swim, but I'm told on the left side it's usually shallow enough to wade. You'll know when to get out. You'll be in a cave, and a friend will meet you there and help you to safety. Her name is Eve."

Aster nodded. "Okay," she said. "You stay safe, too."

"I'll do my best."

Aster started down into the darkness.

She smelled the stream before she heard it and heard it before she saw it by the light of her mote. The tunnel she was in dropped down on the left side—where, as promised, the water only came up to about her knees. That was still a nuisance, because the dress Oak and his brothers had given her quickly became soaked and heavy, dragging at her feet. As she went along, the water became deeper. Finally, up ahead, she saw what looked like a shore or bank, and an empty space beyond.

She stepped a little more quickly; the water was freezing, and she was eager to be out of it.

Her next step encountered no bottom, and before she could do more than gasp, she plunged into the river face-first.

Aster lay wet on the stone river bank, luxuriating in and regretting memory.

Ever since her dad developed his problem, Aster had lived in fear of inheriting it—of not knowing who she was, where she came from, what was happening. She had read books on dementia, Alzheimer's, and retrograde amnesia.

In the oubliette, those fears had been completely realized.

The horrible thing was, it hadn't been so bad. She had experienced each moment of existence as if it was the first, sort of like when she had been very young, when a shiny green beetle or a water-skeeter could hold her attention for hours. Without memory, there could be no regret, no could-have-beens, and no anxiety about the future.

All that was back now since Ms. Fincher had rescued her. The stairs, the freezing water, and finally strong hands pulling her from the underground river.

She sat up in the dim light, searching for her rescuer and trying to get her bearings, but she had little to help her along, even after she called up another tiny light. She was in a cave with a ceiling so low she had to stoop. The river flowed on one side and beyond it was stone, but every other direction ended in space and darkness.

"Welcome, cousin," a soft voice said.

Aster nearly jumped out of her skin, and for a moment she still didn't know where the voice had come from. Then she saw her, sitting cross-legged a few feet away on a blanket, a little picnic basket in front of her.

Her hair and face might have been carved from a single piece of chalk. Her eyes were like two dark holes, and between and above them gleamed a silver star. Her gown was silvery and diaphanous, finer than any silk she had ever seen.

"Eve?" Aster asked.

"That is my name," she said. "You know my blood. Gloam is my nephew, Dusk my niece. My brother was king here, but he died long before the curse. The queen—took another husband, not a very good one. He also was gone before the curse. And you and I, I suspect, are also kin. You reek of our family. But I do not know you. And that is curious."

"Wait," said Aster. "If you're Dusk's aunt, why aren't you stone, or asleep, or whatever, like the other adults?"

"Dusk is a little older than me," she said. "I am the youngest of my siblings."

"And how do you know Delia Fincher?"

"When the curse arrived, I should have taken my brother's place and become queen. But my niece, Nocturn, seized power and tried to imprison me. I escaped her and found this place to hide. Whether it was here before the curse or not, I do not know. As you may be aware, things have changed. Nocturn had only the vaguest notion I was here; when Kostye and the Chancellor drove her out, they had none at all. But there are many places from which I can observe them, and I have been watching them closely. And with them, Delia. In her I saw someone who could help us. I met with her, several times. And when I saw you, I knew it was time to act. You are the one we've been waiting for."

"Who is we?"

"You will meet her soon," Eve said.

"I would like to meet her now," Aster said.

"Time is pressing," Eve agreed. "But you must eat and drink. Replenish yourself. Then we will go to see her."

On the little blanket, Eve fed her apples, grapes, raisins, figs, walnuts, and chestnuts. For drink, she had cold water scented with mint and rosemary. Aster realized how long it had been since she had eaten, and how good things could taste in the Kingdoms. Apples in the Reign of the Departed, for instance, were big, but they were also watery and grainy, sometimes sweet but with little else in the way of flavor. These apples were small, more yellow than red, and tasted like rose petals and lemon, but most of all like *apple*. The grapes were a little shrunken and wrinkled, on their way to becoming raisins or wine, sweet and musky, with thick, chewy skins. The walnuts tasted like a rain in the forest smelled.

When she had eaten, Eve suggested a nap, but Aster was ready to move on, and the other girl finally agreed that it was time.

"Which way?" Aster asked.

"It's right over here," Eve replied.

Aster turned to look that way, and she felt a sharp pain in her neck, like a wasp sting, but worse. She slapped her hand to the spot, and opened her mouth to shout, but her mouth kept opening, folding back over her head, swallowing her. Eve said something, but her words came from another place, far away, in a language she did not know.

Down another rabbit hole, she thought.

Aster dreamed of a harp the size of the sky, strummed softly by zephyrs, plucked by the swells of evening winds, hushed by the rain. She felt the lowest notes only in her bones, and the highest behind her eyes, more color than sound. When light came, it was at the far end of a tunnel, fraying at the outlines, refracted by what appeared to be tiny jewels scattered about.

As her eyesight adjusted she realized she was looking up through an immense field of webbing, and the lights were beads of water collected where the threads met. She was at the bottom of a deep pit, staring up through layers of spider web, but she gradually came to understand that she was hanging in the center of the web, and the web wasn't round, but spherical, stretching out away from her in every direction. Here and there she saw darker blobs, like insects encased in silk. Except they weren't shaped like insects; they looked more like human mummies. The nearest, only a few feet away, had something golden and gleaming poking through, like the top of a crown.

Aster.

The voice did not come through her ears; she felt it in the webs that held her captured and suspended. Inside the silk encasing the crowned figure, a faint, golden glow began, like sunlight. She made out the luminous shape of a woman.

I thought you would never come, the voice said. *It seems so long. But you have come at last to end the curse.*

"Who are you?" she asked.

The Day Queen, my subjects called me, she said. *Elbendé, The Swan, my name at birth. Bright Sky, my husband named me, and Light of Love. My children called me Mother. You must listen — my time is short. Darkness enfolds me, and only fitfully and in dreams may I wake. The curse is of your father's making. Even he cannot undo it. But you can.*

"How?" Aster asked.

Your mother gave you something. Do you remember?

"My little silver sphere," she said.

There are five of them, the Day Queen said. *Find them.*

"But I lost my orb," she said. "I don't know where it is."

It was given to you. You have the power to seek it — you always have. You have seen where two others are.

"One is here," she said. "My father has it. Another is in some place with pyramids. I think I left mine in the carriage, so Veronica has it. But what about the fourth and fifth?"

The light from within the cobwebs dimmed visibly.

"Wait," Aster said. "That's not enough. Where is the place with the pyramids? Once I have all the orbs, what do I do?"

Your heart will learn, the Day Queen said. *When you find your heart. But first you must survive the cost of coming here . . .*

Then the light was gone, and only shadow in its place.

The web, still for a moment, suddenly shook. Looking around wildly, Aster saw a darkness blotting out the little lights of the dewdrops, moving toward her.

FOUR
WINTER NIGHT

Veronica tried to pull her hand away when the boy took her wrist, but he was strong. Too strong.

"If I cut off a finger," he wondered, "Will it grow back?"

"What's your name, sugar?" Veronica asked him, trying to get him to look her in the eyes, rather than studying things to sever.

"That's not important," the boy said.

"That's a funny name," Veronica said. "I like it."

His gaze flicked up, then, and she caught it and held it. Beneath her skin, she felt a deep, powerful stir.

The boy felt it, too. His pupils grew wider and darker, and he came even nearer.

"What are you about?" he asked.

"Don't be afraid of me, honey-pot," she said.

"I'm not . . ." He didn't finish. He grabbed her behind the head and started kissing her. It was violent and awful and she knew it so well. But that was okay. Because as he kissed her, she began to feed. He struggled for half a second, then sighed and gave in.

They always gave in.

She'd forgotten how good it was. Like an ice-cold Coke on

a hot summer day. Like pressing a splinter from an abscess and seeing the puss spurt out. Like crushing the life out of a tick.

It made her tingle all over. It made her feel *big*.

"Hey," the girl said. "What are you doing? Stop it!"

She wasn't finished with the boy, but she didn't have time, not with the girl coming at her like that.

She pulled back.

"She's trying to keep us apart," Veronica told the boy. "She wants me for herself."

The girl had grabbed him by the shoulder, which only helped make Veronica's case. The boy growled like an animal and spun on his companion. He slammed his knife hand into her and she shrieked, falling to the floor and scrambling backward as he followed. They both vanished from view — her crawling, him walking with cold purpose.

A moment later, the boy was back, a dreadful grimace on his face. He kissed her again, and she finished him, taking all he had until his lips tasted of dust and marrow.

She didn't feel at all bad about it.

But she was still chained. She couldn't reach the boy's knife, and even though she felt stronger — much stronger — it wasn't enough to snap her bonds. She knew there were guards not far away, she didn't have much time.

She felt suddenly very cold. Moisture beaded on her face like sweat — or more like the condensation on a glass of iced tea.

She spotted one of the guards at the door, his sword drawn. His skin had a distinct blue shade to it, and he looked surprised.

Then he toppled forward, landing on the boy with the knife.

Behind him stood the Brume, staring at Veronica with big eyes.

"You've been naughty," the Brume said.

"So naughty," Veronica agreed. "But then so have you. Where are Haydevil and Mistral?"

"Why don't we find out?" the Brume said. She lifted her hand, and Veronica saw she held a ring of keys.

She heard shouting as the Brume unchained her. Echoing in the tunnels, it was hard to say how far away.

"Is there a way out?" Veronica asked.

"For us there is," the girl replied.

Veronica followed the Brume through the twisting corridors, trending generally in a downward direction. She felt the water, tantalizingly near, but never quite close enough to touch.

From the sounds of things, her escape had been discovered. The Brume had probably frozen every guard on the way to her, as she had once frozen Billy and Errol. But from what she'd seen, Nocturn had plenty more soldiers to send.

Veronica was starting to worry the Brume was lost, when they finally entered a room that sloped down to a small pool of water.

"This comes out somewhere?" Veronica said.

"Somewhere," the Brume confirmed.

"You first, then," Veronica said.

"I like water," the Brume said.

"Me too," Veronica said. The hammering of boots on stone was quite close, now.

"But I can't swim," the girl said.

"Oh, for —" she grabbed the Brume by the wrist and pulled her into the water.

She kicked hard, pulling the girl down with her. Veronica felt the Brume struggle for breath, then her pulse began to slow, and the blood in her veins came nearly to a stop. Her hand became quite cold.

The water, too, quickly grew chilly. Veronica didn't mind. Her eyesight was almost useless, but every other sense was so alive it didn't matter.

The tunnel was tight at first, but then it widened and turned so they were no longer going straight down, but out, away from the Mountain of the Winds. The water was almost still, but not quite, as if she was in the veins of a sleeping titan, whose heart beat in time with years instead of seconds. To say the water had purpose was probably overstating things, but it was going somewhere, as all water did. Even glaciers moved, even the stagnant water of a salt lake rose into the air to find clouds.

The Brume tugged at her, suggesting she had a more pressing direction in mind. Veronica, beginning to lose herself in the vast underwater labyrinth, tried to concentrate on those cues, to keep herself in her own present, her own mission, rather than succumbing to the ancient resolve of the netherflood.

All too soon, her sense of time became more acute as, somewhere above, the sun rose and her lungs suddenly felt the need for air. She began to kick more frantically, trying to sense some place where air might be — just a pocket of it, enough for a single breath. She squeezed frantically at the Brume's hand, trying to somehow signal her of the danger.

She swam blindly upward, hoping against hope that there was a surface she could not feel, but now the Brume tugged even harder at her hand, down.

In a panic, she tried to let go, but realized their hands were frozen together. Worse, she felt cold creeping up her arm, obliterating all feeling. Then it reached her lungs, and they froze, still aching for air.

Everything slowed and she didn't feel much at all. Together, she and the Brume drifted down, very gently.

She remembered her last day as a normal, mortal girl, strands of sun falling through the leaves of the forest, dappling the waters below the falls. She remembered the man. She remembered dying.

She remembered kissing Errol beneath the stars.

She remembered being buried head-first in the earth, and many other things.

She remembered it all without fear or anger or passion of any sort, as if she was watching the movie of someone else's life. She wanted nothing, needed nothing.

It was a good place to end.

But it did not end. After a long time, the darkness gave way to light—not bright like the sun, but tiny, diffuse sparks, like a Christmas tree seen through tears. Fuzzy.

Then the lights sharpened into pinpoints, and she realized her face was no longer in the water. The lights were stars accompanied by a tremendous full moon. White forms drifted in the water all around her, which she gradually came to comprehend were chunks of ice, bobbing in the water like she and the Brume were, still half frozen themselves.

As her awareness sharpened, she realized they were drifting down a river edged by dark, evergreen forest. When she thawed enough to move her limbs, she lethargically stroked toward the water's edge. Eventually, they were on the bank.

To her delight, the forest floor was covered in a few inches of snow. She barely remembered snow—it didn't fall often where she was from, and when it did there usually wasn't much and it didn't stay long. But once, when she was about six or seven, it had snowed for two days. Her dad had made snow ice cream by mixing it with milk and sugar. She'd thought it was the best thing she had ever tasted. Then her whole family had gone out front to make a snow man. The next day everything started to melt, but the snow man hung in there, long after the slush on the ground was gone, shrinking, becoming more and more pitiful, until she wished they'd never made him at all, so he wouldn't have to suffer.

Make her sad.

Once or twice the stream she shared with the Creek Man had frozen over. She had bumped against the ice, and once found a man looking through it at her. Then he had cracked the ice with his fist, and the real fun began . . .

She clenched her fingers in the white powder, trying to make a snowball, to remember more about the ice cream and less about the man in the creek.

She knew what she'd done to the boy with the knife. She hadn't had a choice. Errol would understand that.

But she had also enjoyed it, which he would probably *not* understand. She didn't want to understand it either. Or think about it.

She realized this place felt all too familiar. Like the in-between, like they were almost out of the Kingdoms again.

She also felt like someone was watching her.

"Come on Brume," she said. "We should get going."

But the girl didn't respond. Veronica wondered if she was dead, then she saw she was breathing. Most likely, she was just worn out.

Veronica didn't know where she was going, but she wasn't going to wait for the girl to come around. She felt like something was about to bite her or fall on her head, but she couldn't see it, and wouldn't see it until it was too late.

She was feeling strong. It was night here, and she had . . . fed, recently. Carrying the girl wouldn't be difficult.

She lifted the Brume over one shoulder. She closed her eyes and slowly turned until everything felt the brightest, and started walking that way.

The snow was as fine as dust and lifted up like little clouds around her feet as she walked along. The ground underneath felt hard, very hard. The trees were tall, and all were covered in dark green needles. Not pines, maybe fir trees, or spruce. Nothing that grew where she was from, so they must be far from there. If she found the Pale and went through, where would she be? Alaska? Siberia?

But she didn't want to go through the Pale, she wanted to go back into the Kingdoms.

It wasn't long before she came to a bend of the river which had formed a kidney-shaped pond. It was frozen solid. She was dithering about whether to walk on the icy surface or go around it when she noticed something from the corner of her eye.

It was a girl, a little younger than her. She had long black hair and almond-shaped eyes. She wasn't wearing anything, and her skin appeared almost to glow in the moonlight.

"Hello, sister," the girl said.

"I'm not your sister," Veronica said, although she knew exactly what the girl meant. Because it wasn't a girl. Not anymore.

"You're like me," the girl said.

"I *was* like you," Veronica said. "What's your name?"

"I don't remember. I've been here a long time. I have treasures."

"I know you do," Veronica said.

Again, she remembered her snowman, shrunken and sad in the sunlight.

"I wish I could help you," she said. "I can't."

"I don't want your help," the girl — the *nov* — said. "But stay here. Talk to me."

"Why?"

Then she knew. The treetops were bending, although she felt no wind. Owls called alarms in the distance.

"Who is that?" she asked. "Who is coming? A Creek Man?" She tried to remember Aster's word for it.

"A *vadras*?"

The *nov* laughed, a lovely sound, like chimes.

Veronica started to run. She slipped to one knee on the ice, and slowed to a walk, but once on the other side of the small lake, with the earth supporting her, she went as fast as she could. Behind her, she heard the *nov*, still laughing.

Now there was a wind moaning in the trees. She ran harder still, trying to get as far away from the water as possible.

She'd been held in thrall by a *vadras* for decades. They were old, and they were cruel, and like *nov*s they lived on the death of others—but they were not pretty. A desperate man wading through a stream might catch his ankle on a snag or be pulled under in a flood or be struck by a water moccasin or collapse of fever on the bank. But a *vadras* could never entice a man to simply walk into the water and inhale.

A *nov* could. So Creek Men liked to have *nov*s around.

She wasn't doing that again. Whatever she did, she wasn't going to be anyone's slave.

She scrambled up a low hill and to her relief found that the land continued to rise ahead. The river and its marsh were behind her now, and so was *he*. If he caught her, she would fight. She was different now. She wasn't sure what she was, but she knew she wasn't a *nov* anymore.

She scrambled up the next rise, where the trees thinned out into a white meadow. For the next few steps she heard only the crunch of snow beneath her shoes.

Her head was down, so she saw his boots first. Dark, oiled leather, laced in front. Black leggings stuffed into them.

She looked up.

It wasn't a Creek Man. It never had been.

His shirt was also black, and a heavy cloak of grey wool hung from one shoulder. A broad-brimmed hat was pulled so it covered part of his face. Not enough. Not those eyes, the same blue as the Sterno flame her mom used to warm her chafing dish.

"Sheriff," she said, involuntarily taking a step back.

"Hello, Veronica," he said.

The Sheriff had chased her and the others across the Kingdoms, when last they had been here. He had caught her and buried her alive—in the desert with no water to give her strength, no ponds, rivers, or streams to call to for help. The best she had been able to do was summon dragonflies from a tiny wash, far away.

It had been enough, but only because Errol had come after her, and had the persistence to find her. To see dragonflies where they ought not to be. Otherwise she would still be there.

She wanted to run, but her feet seemed frozen to the snow.

The Sheriff smiled—which looked wrong—then he laughed, which was even less in character from what she remembered of him. She felt a deeper chill in her already almost-frozen blood.

"Oh, it is so good to see you," he said. "Few escape me, when I lay my mind to them. Even fewer escape me twice."

She was shivering now, not from the cold. She didn't know what he meant. The Sheriff had only held her captive once . . .

He took the four steps between them and laid his hand on her cheek.

"The first time I saw you, you couldn't have been more than four or five," he said. "Your little arms were so thin. You were missing two teeth. But I recognized the light in you, so pretty and bright. But I knew that wasn't the time. I can be patient. I knew the light would grow as you did, become brighter as your body began bending into a woman's shape. I also knew that almost immediately after that it would start to fade. The life would drain out of your eyes, and you would abandon yourself to some savage who could never understand what he was desecrating. You would drain yourself into five or six brats, diminishing all the while, so that by the time you finally died you would hardly even notice. I was only trying to save you from that. And I did, at least for a time."

She knew him then.

"You aren't the Sheriff anymore," she said.

"Part of him is here, still. His power. His knowledge. I remember more about his life than he did. But what remains of him serves me now."

"I killed you," she said. But even as she said it, she knew it wasn't true. She had killed the body—the teacher, David Watkins. But the thing inside of him—that hadn't stayed down.

"You did me a favor," he said. "Usually when the meat I'm staying in dies, I must wait to be born again and spend years helpless, unable to do what I must. But you dug me out of David, and the Sheriff was there, broken but still alive, waiting for me. Now I can repay you."

"That's okay," she said, finally finding the power to back up. "That's fine."

"You are already mine," he said. "I was cheated for years, but no longer. I will keep you as you should be: perfect, ageless, never to fade like a flower past its time."

Veronica's fear was starting to dwindle. She had killed his other body. She could kill this one. Drag him back down to the water, beneath the frozen surface . . .

"No," he said.

It wasn't merely a word. It stabbed into her brain, and her limbs seized up. She stumbled back as her arms lost feeling. The Brume shifted on her back, put her off balance, and she fell onto the snowy ground.

From down there, he looked very tall. Impossibly tall.

He stooped toward her. His grin reminded her of a skull.

FIVE

A VERY BAD CUPID

S ometimes, Errol thought, he had a limited imagination. He had known they would fall fast, but he hadn't been able to picture *how* fast, how his stomach would feel like it was trying to float out of his mouth, how all the blood would fill his head like a water balloon.

Technically, they weren't falling, but sliding—not that he could see the difference as they reached an estimated one million miles an hour. The silk curtains he and Dusk lay on reduced the already minor friction of the glass to almost zero.

It wasn't this part that worried him, though, but what was coming. When friction came back.

There was no seam where the glass met the stone, but he felt the change instantly. When his feet hit the new surface they caught a little, even lubricated, as it were, by the sheer fabric. His upper body, still on the glass, tried to speed around his feet by flipping him over; his hands and face left the pyramid, but with a yelp he was able to slam back against it.

Then they were on the stone, and resistance was uniform again. They were still going down fast, really fast. The difference was that the silk was starting to feel hot on his bare skin.

Just as he thought it was about to catch fire, they crashed into the base of the pyramid.

He lay there, wondering if his legs were broken. They certainly hurt enough, as did his lungs and his gut.

Dusk sat up before he did, coughing.

"Well, that was a bad idea," Errol said. "Although it was also kind of awesome."

"Amazing," Dusk said. She was smiling. "Shall we do it again?"

"Maybe some other time," Errol. For now we probably ought to—"

"Yes," Dusk said. Her face fell. "Yes," she said. "We should try. You remember where my armor is?"

"Yes," he said.

They retrieved the armor from beneath the shield with the lions, but she didn't put it on. Instead they began to run, and when their energy was spent, to walk. It felt like forever before the city was behind them, but once it was out of sight, Errol began to think they were safe. That they had a chance.

He was wrong. They'd not even made it back to the wash when he heard horns in the distance.

Dusk pushed on a few more moments, then bowed her head.

"It was a good try, Errol," she said. "Now you must leave me."

"No," he said. "Not this time."

"Yes," she said. "They will not kill me, at least not right away. But they will kill you. Flee, Errol. You've done enough."

"Let's run together. They haven't caught us yet."

"Errol," she sighed. She stepped close and took his hand. She leaned up and kissed him very lightly on the cheek.

"Take this," she said. She pressed something into his hand. It felt like a marble.

"*Éidi*," she whispered, pointing.

At first he didn't get it. But then his feet started moving—away from her.

"Dusk!" he shouted.

She was already running the other direction. She quickly vanished over a dune and was out of sight.

He tried to retake control of his legs, but it was no good. He heard the horns again, still far away. Then, a bit later, he heard the sound coming closer.

He glanced behind him and saw them, raising a cloud of dust, clearly coming his way.

Had Dusk been trying to save him, or had she sent him off as a decoy? The good feeling he'd started to have about her was quickly evaporating. When was he going to learn? When would he stop being such a chump?

The magical compunction was starting to wear off. He was tired and he was angry and he'd had enough. He knew he couldn't outrun them, so he stopped, turned to face them, and waited. He looked to see what Dusk had given him; a little golden ball. He contemplated it for a moment, then knelt and buried it in the sand near a withered stick of a bush.

The leader rode a white horse and wore armor that flashed in the sun. Several other horsemen rode with him, but he was also accompanied by a handful of figures on foot. When they got a little nearer, he recognized the golden cupid-things. They ran in advance of the horses, incredibly fast, almost like hounds. They reached him first, and circled him, staring at him with those weird, metallic eyes.

The horsemen arrived a few minutes later. To his dismay, he saw Dusk was with them, tied hand and foot and slung across the saddle horn of the leader.

The first time Errol had seen Dusk, she had been in armor, and he had assumed her to be male. It was dumb assumption, and he had become much more careful since then. This armored character had fine features and high cheekbones — not unlike Dusk — and a shock of blond hair. His — her? — skin was dark, almost black. Could be a man or woman and the armor wasn't much help. He or she had a forehead mark too, a little golden dot with a bunch of swirlies radiating out from it, like a kid's drawing of the sun.

"My name is Errol," he said, standing as tall as he could. "Who are you supposed to be?"

"I'm not supposed to be anyone," the rider said. "I am Hawk."

"That's great," Errol said. "You've got my friend there. How about you give her back?"

Hawk looked amused.

"Your friend, my sister. Who has more right to her?"

"No one has a 'right' to her," Errol said. "You've got her tied up. Untie her and — wait, did you say 'sister'?"

"Yes," Hawk said. "That makes me her brother. Is that too complicated for you?"

"No," Errol said. "But how can you treat your own sister like that?"

"I have several sisters," Hawk replied. "Some I like, some I do not. Dusk is not presently in good favor with me."

"Oh, uh-huh," Errol said. "I guess I can understand that. She cut off my leg once. But still, I need you to let her go."

Hawk stared at him for a moment like he was something gross he'd found on his shoe. Then he shrugged.

"I was curious," he said. "I wondered who she might have tricked into becoming her ally. I am curious no longer."

"I'll fight you," Errol said.

"I'm sorry, what?"

"Fight you. For her."

"You're joking, I assume?" Hawk said.

"Not a bit, you cowardly jerk."

"You have no sword. No armor."

"Don't need 'em to take down a creep like you," Errol said.

Hawk glanced around him, then shrugged. He dismounted and began taking off his armor. Then he removed the padding underneath, until he wore only a white loincloth. Stripped down he looked like a bodybuilder.

"My man will blow the horn as a signal for us to begin," Hawk said. "Agreed?"

"Just let's do this," Errol said.

Hawk nodded. The horn blew.

The other boy moved so fast Errol almost didn't have time to respond at all. He caught the first punch on his forearm; the next hit him hard in the chest and sent him staggering back. Hawk kept on coming. Errol set his feet and swung, but his opponent ducked and popped him in the chin. He tasted blood and again retreated.

Errol feinted with his left and followed through with his right. Hawk blocked him and returned a cuff on the side of his jaw. Errol saw spots, but not so many he couldn't see the other guy winding up to finish him off.

Ignoring the punch coming his way, he let fly at Hawk's chin. He connected so hard it felt like his fist was broken. Then his head seemed to explode.

The next thing he knew he was lying in the sand, staring up at the blond-headed boy, who was wiping blood from his nose.

"Okay," Errol said. "You give up yet?"

Hawk turned and walked away. As Errol tried to get back to his feet, he saw two of the cupid-things helping the other boy back into his armor.

"We fought," Hawk said. "You did well. But you lost."

"Just—let her go," Errol said.

"Sorry," Hawk said. "No."

"I'll find you," Errol said. "I'll come again."

"I know you would," Hawk said, as he mounted his horse. One of the golden boys stepped forward, lifting his bow.

By that time, Errol had managed to stand.

The arrow knocked him back down again.

He lay there, staring up at the sky and at the feathered stick in his chest. He dimly heard the horses start off.

The bright sky began to darken, as if night was finally falling. But the sun was still where it had always been.

Finally, something blocked out the sun itself. A human shape. A woman.

"No," he said. "No."

Her face was in shadow; he could not see it. And he knew if he did see it, he was done. It was over. She had come for him again, and this time . . .

"Hush," the woman said.

That was a surprise. He had seen Death coming before, but never heard her speak.

Renewed pain shocked through him. He felt dizzy and, at last, the light of the endless day went away.

The light returned, but gently, along with a familiar sweet-sour taste on his tongue.

He remembered the pain, then, and sat up, clawing at the arrow in his chest. But it was no longer there.

Lotus sat a few feet away, cross-legged. She had a pillow on her lap with a board and paper on it and was busy with her ink pen.

"You should finish that," she said. "You were a lot closer to dead, this time."

She nodded at the red fruit lying next to him on the blanket. He and Lotus were in the shade of a large palm next to a stream. Not far away, the broken towers and eroded walls of some ancient city lay half-buried in the sand.

He picked up the pomegranate and began plucking out the seeds, which looked like garnets and tasted like heaven. With each bite, he felt a little better. He remembered a long time ago, when his father had brought him a pomegranate and showed him how to eat it. It wasn't simple, like eating a grape. It took patience, and a little problem solving to sort through the bitter white membranes that kept the seeds in their neat layers. It took time, but it was worth it. You could spend an entire lazy summer afternoon reading comic books and eating a pomegranate.

"That's the last one," Lotus said. "Try not to get killed again."

"I thought you'd left," he said.

"I started feeling bad for you. I knew there was no way you could escape them, not without Djinn. I even told you so."

"You didn't tell me you could also rescue Dusk," he said.

"No," she said. "I didn't. I don't like her. But then I felt bad, so I came back to look for you. I saw Hawk hunting and followed him to you. I think you ought to be grateful, rather than nit-picking."

"You're right," he said. "I'm sorry. Things haven't been going my way lately." He picked out a few more seeds.

"I guess you saw they caught Dusk, too," he said.

"I know what you're thinking," Lotus said. "And the answer is no. We could have helped her just after you set me free, especially as Hawk was away. If my Djinn and I go back now, we risk being captured, and that won't do."

"I have to go back," he said.

"I figured that," Lotus replied. "So I sent Djinn for some things. But consider, for a moment. Must you return for her? You can go with me and help me rule my kingdom. Or I could take you home, back to this girl you say you love. Dusk and Hawk are my cousins; since the curse came, and our parents became . . . less . . . they and their other siblings have done nothing but quarrel and fight for supremacy. What is that to you?"

He thought about that for a moment as he ate more of the fruit.

"I don't know," he said. "Maybe nothing. But I feel responsible."

"I don't see why," she replied. "Look, there is Djinn."

He followed her gaze and saw a dust-devil moving across the sand toward them.

"Did you, what, find him in a bottle?"

She looked puzzled, obviously not getting the reference.

"No," she said. "He was my bodyguard, before. My dearest friend and protector. When the curse came, most of the adults went into the tombs. Others became ghuls or peris or ifreets. He became a djinn—I think so he could continue to protect me, although he does not remember our lives before. Even to say his real name causes him pain, so I do not speak it."

"Oh," Errol said, at a loss for words.

The whirlwind arrived, then flattened out and dissipated. Before it was entirely gone, he thought he saw a bearded face outlined in the drifting dust. But if it had ever been there, it was quickly gone.

On the sand stood the wooden horse from the carousel— and the pack containing his armor.

He felt a little chill creep up his spine.

"I am going home soon," Lotus said. "What is your choice?"

"Thank you," he said. "Thanks for saving my life twice, and thanks for the offer. You're probably right, I'm being stupid. But I think Dusk needs me. Brother or not, I have a bad feeling about that guy."

"Finish the pomegranate," Lotus said. "Then Djinn will bring us some water and sturdier repast. You might as well die on a full stomach."

SIX
THE WATCHTOWER

S tand away from her," a familiar voice said.

The thing in the Sheriff's body turned, slightly. Veronica couldn't move, but she could see him from the corner of her eye, standing between her and the sheriff.

Shandor.

"You're being foolish," the Sheriff said.

"This is the March," Shandor said. "My domain. She is under my protection."

"The Marches are large," the Sheriff said. "And this is not your portion of it. Even here you are no match for me."

"Come, then," Shandor said. "We will discover if that is true. Together."

She heard a snick and, straining her neck, she saw he was holding a long, curved sword. He glanced at her.

"Go," he said. "Get the girl away from here." He nodded upslope. "That way."

Instantly, she could move again. She scrambled up. The Brume moaned.

"What's happening?" the girl asked.

"Come with me," Veronica said. "Run."

She pulled the girl to her feet. Behind her, she heard a sound, like an animal snarling, and the air suddenly felt like a balloon stretched to the point of exploding.

"Run!" she repeated.

When she looked back, it was hard to see anything; the wind had started again, picking up the snow and whirling it about. All she could make out were two shadows, coming together.

She thought then, that she ought to go back. To help Shandor.

But the wind redoubled, and suddenly others were there: a boy with flaming red hair and a slight young woman with long black braids.

The boy grabbed her wrist, and the girl the Brume's. In an instant they were in the air, flying like the wind itself.

She knew them. The redhead was Haydevil, and the girl Mistral, brother and sister to the Brume.

Peat marsh and forest, meadow and taiga flew by beneath them. Veronica saw less and less green and more snow until there was nothing but white, and at last mountains of ice, splendid and blue beneath the persistent moon. The stars were clear and cold, the Milky Way so bright it almost outshone the cratered satellite.

The weirdest and most wonderful of all was the crackling, shifting curtain of colors that hung above the northern horizon. She didn't know what it was, or how it came to be, but she knew she had never seen it back in the world of her birth. It had to be a product of magic, of the Kingdoms.

At last, they reached a pinnacle in the mountains more regular than the surrounding crags. Like the Mountain of the Winds, it was riddled with caves and tunnels. Soon, they were inside, where it was more stone than ice, in a great hall before a roaring fire.

Veronica did not feel cold; in the eternal night of this place, her heart had stayed quiet in her chest, and her lungs remained as deflated as balloons three days after the party. But she did find the joints of her limbs were stiff, and the heat helped thaw them so she didn't move like a old woman. She wondered what would happen if she were outside on her own. Would she freeze solid, like a block of ice, still aware but unable to move, speak, or act? Or would she merely become very slow, as she had when the Brume worked her spell on her?

She didn't know. There was so much about herself she didn't know. She did recognize that if everything else was the same, but the sun was out, she would be dead now. Not almost dead or mostly dead, but well and truly dead.

Haydevil and Mistral were fussing over the Brume. Eventually they let their sister be and came over to Veronica.

"You're lucky I can hear a pin drop a thousand miles away," Haydevil said. "Else you surely would have perished back there, along with my awful, monstrous excuse for a sister."

"Did you—do you know what happened? Between the Sheriff and Shandor?" Veronica asked.

"Eh—was that his name?" Haydevil asked. "Creature of the Pale, him. Brave to go against the Raggeman. Must have the sweets for you."

"Do you know?" she pressed.

"We don't know how he fared," Mistral said. "We knew who you were. We didn't know if he was friend or foe, but he was delaying the Raggeman, so we let him."

"Veronica was looking for you guys, anyway," the Brume said.

"We know that, goblin-girl," Haydevil snapped.

"True," Mistral said. "But we don't know why. What is your quest, Veronica? Why did you seek us out?"

"I'm trying to find Errol," she said. "From what you said last time we met, I figured you guys got around. A lot. I thought you might have seen him, or something. Please." She looked down. "Now that I say it out loud, it sounds stupid, I know. Everything is so big here. But Aster and I had a fight, and I didn't know what else to do. And I know you guys, and you kind of owe us a favor."

"Eh—favor?" Haydevil said.

"Your mom," he said. "The apple orchard? We solved your little giant problem."

"He wasn't little," the Brume said. "He was really big."

"They know what I mean," Veronica said.

"It is true," Mistral said. "We do owe you a kindness."

"We're hardly in a position to help anyone," Haydevil protested. "Driven out of our castle, exiled here. And now the Raggeman knows we're here, so we'll have to find another place to hide. And anyway, no, we don't know where your stick man is—we've been far too busy, as you see."

"Hush, Haydevil," Mistral said. "We must help her. Certainly we must. We may not know where Errol is, but we know someone who might, don't we?"

"Do we?" Haydevil said.

Mistral glared at him. Haydevil folded his arms.

"But it's so far," he said.

"We're going to have to leave anyway," Mistral said. The Raggeman is on his way here."

"What? Are you sure?"

"I hear him," Mistral said. "As would you, I suppose, if he were a pin dropping."

Haydevil's mouth fell almost comically open.

Veronica felt oddly hollow. If the Sheriff—Raggedy Man? Whatever he was now—was on the way here, did that mean he had beaten Shandor? Was the Gypsy dead? Or had the Sheriff simply broken away from the fight to come after her?

Whatever happened, she hoped Shandor was okay. He seemed to be a decent guy. Maybe she didn't want to be his queen, or whatever, but he had some good qualities.

"How?" Haydevil asked, incredulous. "How is he following us?" Then he frowned and pointed at Veronica.

"Wait," he said. "How did he find *you*?"

"I'm sure I don't know," Veronica said. "He was just — there."

"We came the under way," the Brume said. "It would have been hard to track us."

"She must be calling him, somehow," Mistral said.

"I most certainly am not," Veronica said.

"No," Mistral said. "Not on purpose. But do you have something — a charm, an amulet, a ring — something he might be able to sense from far away?"

"I don't think so," Veronica said. "I —"

Then she remembered. She reached into her pocket and pulled put the silver sphere.

Haydevil made a funny noise. Mistral's eyes grew wide.

"The Silver Kingdom," Mistral said. "That would do it."

"That would absolutely do it," Haydevil said.

"This means we have to leave now," Mistral said. "We cannot wait. He will find us in moments."

"He'll follow us," Haydevil said. "If we have this thing."

"Then we won't have it," Mistral said. "I will take it and lead him off the trail. You take Veronica to the Watchtower."

Haydevil stared at the sphere. "I want to see it," he said. "Before you take it away. I've never seen one of those."

Veronica handed the sphere toward him.

"What is it?" she asked. "Aster had it —"

She stopped when she saw the look of pure glee steal over Haydevil's face.

"Devil!" Mistral cried. "No!"

"Nice try, sister," he said. He turned once, twice, and spun so fast he was only a blur of color before he shot off through the tunnels.

Mistral started after him but had only gone a few feet before she turned back.

"You may well regret that," she said. "But there is no time or sense in going after him, now. Come. Let's go to the Watchtower."

She took Veronica and the Brume by each of their hands and they were once again airborne, the mountain of ice dwindling behind them.

The world had run out of green. Below them now, Veronica only saw shades of white. The stars were more interesting; they grew brighter with each passing breath, and when she closed her eyes the larger ones left red spots, like the sun. The rainbow curtain drew nearer, too, and now she could hear it. It sounded like the crinkling of a hard candy wrapper or something tearing. It began as the thinnest whisper.

But it got louder, like someone turning up a radio tuned to static, almost but not quite on a station. At times she thought she caught part of a word or the rising tone of a question, an exclamation. The volume continued to grow, and now there were hundreds of voices trying to be heard. Just as she was almost able to understand some of it, just as it all was about to become clear — like the tuner finally finding a station — it started getting worse again, and quieter. The entire sky was alive with colors, but as the sound faded, so did the light. Soon the curtain was far behind them.

Veronica felt in her bones that they passed through some sort of border, just as they had when crossing the Pale into the Kingdoms. If so, where were they now?

The stars, still bright, grew even brighter. She remembered a night, which now seemed long ago, when she and Errol had

laid on their backs in tall grass, and he had explained the constellations to her. That night, that moment, his voice, his presence, had changed her, or at least shown her the possibility for
change. She knew lust well: the hunger of a man for a woman's body, her own desire for the blackest part of a soul. But of
love she had never known very much, and most of what she
had known she had either forgotten or had been twisted by her
years as a *nov*.

Love was peculiar, and it was terrifying. It required more
than lust. Love wasn't conquest or submission, it was connection, kinship that went beyond mere blood, acceptance — vul-
nerability. She wasn't even sure it was something you could
look for, but more something that found you.

It had found her that night. She hadn't wanted it; she'd told
herself she was playing a sort of game, that she would have a
laugh at Errol's expense when it was all over. If he'd a had a different reaction, that might have been how things went. Instead,
she had changed.

She missed him. And she missed Aster, too, despite their
quarrel. They were the closest thing to family she still had.

Ahead of them, a shadow blotted out the stars. Soon, however, it was more than shadow, for the starlight gleamed on
snowy slopes and broke into pale rainbows where it struck the
beveled faces of glaciers. Veronica had never imagined a mountain so large; it was like an entire world, unto itself. She wondered if it was even rooted in the Earth — or if instead it was
simply floating in the sky, like the moon.

Mistral took them still higher, and the mountain kept rising,
until even the ice no longer clung to the stone, for they were
now higher than any cloud, beyond the kiss of sleet and snow.
From there on it was only bare rock, cold and grey in the light
of the stars.

Even after that, it was a long time before they finally reached the summit.

The mountain did not come to a perfect point, but instead split to form a valley. In the center of the valley a lay a nearly round pool.

They settled on the moon-colored stone of the valley rim, several hundred feet from the water.

It didn't feel cold at all, but it was very still. So still, that Veronica realized the only motion besides the three of them was that of the stars. They moved very slowly of course, but most peculiar was *how* they moved. Rather than arcing across the sky from east to west, they appeared to be revolving around the mountain, with one star straight above that did not move at all.

"The Watchtower," Mistral said. "From here, with keen eyes, one might see anything in the Kingdoms."

"Is that why we're here?" Veronica said. "To look for Errol? Do you have binoculars or something?"

"I will look," Mistral said. "But I fear you are right—there is too much to see, and too little time. They say wisdom can be found in the pool below—if you dare."

"If I dare?"

"Some who have looked in the pool have never returned. Others have, but were driven mad. If you want to know where Errol is, though, you must try."

"Well," Veronica said. "I guess I will, then."

The pool was like a perfect mirror, the Milky Way reflected in a blaze upon its surface. And there was her own image, in shadow, but her eyes glowing faintly green. She paused, for a moment, thinking how inhuman she looked, how strange. What did others see when they saw her? What did Errol see?

Or Shandor?

She reached to touch the reflection of her hand and ripples distorted her image. Her mouth seemed to widen and fill with teeth, her hair to squirm like serpents.

Then there were only wavelets.

"Oh," she said. She stood there for a moment, wondering what she was supposed to do. She stood like that for maybe two seconds.

Then a hand darted from the water, grabbed her arm, and pulled her in.

SEVEN
DELIA'S CHOICE

D elia liked the garden. She had always wanted one, ever since she was a little girl. And if someone had bothered to ask that little girl what sort of garden she'd wanted, she would have described something much like this — not the large garden in the central keep, but this much smaller courtyard, hidden away in a less-traveled part of the castle, with high walls and a small fountain in the center. Creepers with white and purple blooms climbing the stone; maples, weeping willows, gingkoes, and chestnuts with golden foliage spreading their limbs from terraced beds, and spider lilies crowding around their roots. Spider lilies were her favorite flower. At home they didn't last long. Here, they bloomed each day.

It would be nice to have some honeysuckle, violets, peach blossoms, magnolia, roses. But those were in other gardens, where spring and summer held sway or at least passed through. Perhaps one day she would see them again, but until then, this would do.

She'd tried to have a garden behind the house she'd shared with Scott. She'd bought bulbs, a hoe, a trowel — even a hat. He'd gently made fun of her about it, referring to her as "Candide" or "Mrs. McGregor". Over time she came to realize that the gentleness was an illusion, just contempt dressed up in fine words, poetry, and literary allusions. He thought he was better than her, smarter than her, better bred than her, and for a long time she believed it too.

Even now, it was her first reflex—to blame herself for him leaving, even though she ought to know better.

But Scott's new, younger wife had a garden. Delia had seen him helping her in it, along with their beautiful little girl. Confronted with that, she remembered the things her mother had told her when she was little—about not setting her sights too high, how she wasn't pretty enough to pull off the fairy tale, how she needed to keep her mouth shut—preferably in smile form—and be prepared to weather disappointment, because God knows that was all *she* had ever known.

She wondered, sometimes, if her mother had ever realized that complaining to your only child about how your entire life and everything in it was at best third-rate could possibly affect that girl's self-esteem. That telling a six-year-old to expect a disappointing life might set a self-fulfilling prophecy in motion.

Probably. And just as likely, she wouldn't have cared.

Another reason Delia liked the garden was that almost no one ever came to it but her. In the years since her marriage dissolved, she had come to value her solitude. The reading chair on her porch, the tub with lion's feet, her kitchen table set with a very simple meal and almost no mess to clean up.

But now someone was here. And not any someone.

Him. Kostye Dvesene.

She had first met him as Aster's father, years before, an enigmatic man with a strange accent and a mysterious, possibly dangerous past. She had found him surprisingly handsome

despite his red hair, which she did not think suited men very
well. Kostye pulled it off, somehow. He had flirted with her,
which she liked just enough to feel bad about it, because she'd
still been married, then. She had decided, on reflection, that
he hadn't been serious, but had merely been trying to get into
her good graces so she would admit his daughter to the school
without all the necessary paperwork.

After that, she hadn't seen much of him. If he showed up at
all for conferences, he often seemed a little out of it. Eventually
he stopped coming entirely. Aster did well in school, but Delia
began to suspect her home life wasn't good. When she'd gone
to his house to confront him, she'd gotten far more than she had
bargained for.

And now she was here, in some other world, staring across
the garden at him.

He didn't look happy. Did he suspect something? Did he
suspect *her*?

"Hello," she said. "It's a nice surprise, seeing you here.
What's the matter?"

"The girl. The one who claimed to by my daughter. She
disappeared."

Play dumb, Delia. She realized how much her own inner voice
sounded like her mother. How had she never noticed that before?

"Dusk, you mean? But that was weeks ago."

He raised an eyebrow. "No," he said. "There was another,
just now."

"That's unusual," Delia said. "Not to mention suspicious."

"Yes," he said, putting his hands behind his back and meeting her gaze directly. "It is."

"What?" Delia said. "Why are you looking at me? Wasn't I
the one who told you Dusk wasn't your daughter, once you got
that damned necklace off me?"

"You did. But I've lately been reminded that you also insisted that although Dusk was not my real daughter, I did have one."

She's hoped he had forgotten that, as he had forgotten many things in their early days here. She had tried to convince him of the truth, but she now saw that as pointless and even dangerous. Especially since the chancellor, Vilken, arrived. That had changed everything.

So, she lied.

"I was wrong," Delia said. "I assumed that if Dusk was pretending be your daughter, you must have one."

"You also said we all once lived in the Reign of the Departed. This girl made the same claim."

Delia stood up and frowned at him. "Are you accusing me of something?" she said. "If so, please get to the point."

"Do you know anything about this girl?"

"I don't," she said.

"Did you help her escape the oubliette?"

Something caught in her chest, and panic threatened to climb out of her throat and sit on her shoulders, but it was too late to admit to anything now. Her mother had always said that once you started a lie, you were married to it, and if you divorced it you would end up with nothing, or worse.

Her mother hadn't been wrong about everything.

"I not only did not," she huffed, "I've no idea what you are talking about."

"Don't you?" he was frowning dangerously, now. "I'm told otherwise."

"By who?" she asked. "Vilken?"

His glower deepened.

"I am not new to power," he said. "Or to the court. Or intrigue. You speak against him, he speaks against you — it is how things are. Each of you wishes to sway me. Do you flatter yourself to think you can control one such as I?"

"I'm not trying to control anyone," she said. "When you ask for my opinion, I give it. That's all."

"You once said that the curse has robbed me of my memories," he said. "You did claim I had a daughter. I remember that."

"I told you —" she began.

"I know what you said," he replied. "But this plot involving my imaginary daughter . . . It baffles me. Yet it keeps coming up."

"A lot of things baffle me," Delia said. "Why do you collect every girl over the age of eight and send them off with Vilken?"

"I have my reasons."

"Then you should be able to explain them," she said. "I think you do not have any reason at all. I think this comes from *him*. You are doing his bidding."

"The Chancellor believes it is necessary to end the curse."

"Really? Has he explained how that works? How it will end the curse? Because I see no rhyme or reason in it. Unless he doesn't need *every* girl — maybe he only needs one — one particular girl. But to find her, he must search through all of the others."

"Why?"

"Now you're asking for a reason?" she said. "I don't know. There is one person who knows the answers to these questions, and it is not me. Ask him."

"He is traveling," Kostye said.

"Wait," Delia said. "When did he leave?"

"A short time ago."

"Before the girl showed up? The one claiming to be your daughter?"

"No," he said. "After."

"I see. And who took the girl to the oubliette?"

He didn't answer.

"I see," she said. "You have the nerve to come here and accuse me, when the truth is as plain as an old maid?"

"I accused you of nothing," he said.

"That is a lie," she said. "You absolutely came here to accuse me."

He stepped forward. It was a simple motion but had so much potential violence in it that she took an involuntary step back.

"You dare speak to me like that? Who do you think you are?"

She was frightened. She had seen him set an army on fire, break the back of a demon with horns, summon a storm that would make a hurricane slink off in shame.

But she was also furious.

"You know," she said, "I can't even count the number of times I've been asked that, one way or another. Who do I think I am? And what they mean, these men — and it *is* always men — is who am I in terms of who *they* are. Am I a plaything, a girlfriend, a woman who doesn't know her place, a girl talking out of turn? An enemy or a friend, a ring on your finger or a rope around your neck? Who do I think I am? I'll tell you who I am. I'm Delia Fincher, and I don't give a good goddamn who I am or aren't to you. So just — the hell with you."

She was preparing to walk defiantly away when he suddenly turned inside-out, his head and feet folding through his belly and coming out as wings from his back, a face full of teeth erupting from his chest as he exploded into something far larger with claws and fire and smoke. A talon wrapped roughly around her arm and another around her waist. Then the courtyard was receding below them, the castle itself shrinking with incredible speed.

She tried to scream — she may have — but if she did, she could not hear it. The roar of the wind was deafening.

Delia closed her eyes and tried to pretend she was on a roller coaster, that it was all perfectly safe, that he would not drop her to her doom.

It took her a little while to understand that they had stopped, because her inner ears kept spinning, telling her she was falling even though she could feel the stone beneath her.

She cracked open her eyes.

They were on a mountaintop, surrounded by more mountains. Valleys swamped by shadow lay below and all around. The sun was still a bloody stain on the horizon. Kostye stood before her without a stitch of clothing on. He was panting and his eyes were wild, as if he was watching a battle of some sort. Then his gaze focused on her.

"Something is missing," he said. "Before the curse came. Something happened. I don't know what. I don't know, and it drags at me. Sometimes, I feel trapped, but I cannot see the snare."

"You scared the hell out of me so you could tell me that?"

"I—I am sorry," he said. "The rage, it overcomes me sometimes. I was born with it. It is part of me. The rage. It is the source of my power."

"That's really too bad," Delia said.

"You know I have enemies," he said. "Many enemies who would destroy me. I cannot be passive. If I leave them be, they will come to me, and bring my doom. So you understand, if one of my enemies is already here, near to me—"

"You're going to drop me off of a mountain, is that it?

"No," he said. "Look around you."

"Yes," she said. "I might find it beautiful under other circumstances."

"The Kingdoms are many," he said. "And they are wondrous. And they are ill, infected by this curse. I believe there is a reason that only the three of us have somehow escaped its grasp. You, Vilken, me. It may be that he has . . . needs that do not pertain to my goal. As you enjoy your garden and your books, the chancellor enjoys—other things that have nothing to do with me or my designs."

"Oh my God," Delia said. "What is he doing with those girls? What is happening to them?"

"That isn't your concern," he said.

"Vilken, then. Who is he to you? Why do you trust him at all?"

"I have known him for a long time," he said. "We were young together, fought together." He looked troubled. "He has changed, I admit. His face is familiar, but I do not always know him. Time is an anvil, Delia. We are shaped on it, we are broken on it. It may be Vilken took the girl. It may be that he wanted me to think you did it instead. I see that now. I have been lied to before, and no great harm came of it. A lie or two is acceptable. Betrayal is not. I will sort this out. If the chancellor has betrayed me, he will regret it. Very much."

But Delia also heard what he didn't say. That if he learned *she* had betrayed him, the same applied to her. Rage or not, that was part of the reason he'd brought her up here like this. To show her what he could do if he wanted. Any time.

"You said you do not care what you are to me," he went on. "I understand your anger. I admire you, Delia. But I need to know you're on my side."

"That depends on whether you're on mine," she said. "Are you?"

He stepped closer, and the hair on the back of her neck stood on end. Something in her belly caught fire.

Then he kissed her. It was rough; his hands clapped to the back of her head, and she felt fear that nearly matched her lust. But after a second, he grew gentler, although his breath was quick and hot.

He hadn't answered her question, and what was now happening was certainly no answer—just because a man was on you didn't mean he was with you, her mother always said.

But she had her desires, her needs, and answers could wait.

EIGHT

THE SILVER KINGDOM

T he web shook more violently. In the dim light, Aster could make out few details of what was coming, but it was big, bigger than a school bus, and many-legged.

But she didn't think it was a spider.

That would have been bad enough, a black widow the size of a semi, but something about its shape, the deranged kinetics of its stride—this was the nightmare some shadowy fragment had been spalled from to create spiders.

She struggled against the web's threads, but they held her fast. Panic tried to take her senses, but she fought it down. Even if she could move, she would never escape the thing, she knew that. There had to be another way out.

How had she gotten here?

She didn't know. She'd felt the sting in her neck—then she was here.

It was almost on her now. In the shadows, she saw faint clusters of gleaming spheres, hundreds of them, like the black caviar her father liked . . .

Several Utterances came to mind, but all seemed like bad jokes in the face of this thing.

What was it the Day Queen had said? About surviving the cost of coming here?

She understood then, or at least she thought she did. She couldn't fight it, any more than you could fight a dream. Instead, you would wake. This place wasn't merely her dream, it was a nightmare the universe itself was having. It took more than pinch on the arm to wake from.

She pronounced a Recondite Utterance, and vomited light. Beams shown from her eyes as the world unfolded, tearing her as it did so, shredding her bone and sinew and then pulling it all back together again.

The web disappeared. She was lying on a stone floor, the echo of a noise like thunder repeating itself in the depths of the cave. Gradually the sound faded, replaced by the burbling of the underground river

Eve sprawled on the floor nearby, struggling feebly; she looked as if she had been thrown there. Her lips were red, and a spray of red droplets covered her face like freckles.

Instinctively, Aster slapped her hand to her neck, which still stung. It felt wet, and when she looked, she saw her hand was covered in blood. She felt very weak.

"What did you do to me?" she said.

"It's hard," Eve said. "It took all of my strength to send you there. It was only fair to take some back." As she said this, Eve climbed slowly to her feet.

What was she, some sort of vampire? But Aster kept remembering the thing in the web. Not a vampire, something weirder, and worse. The Day Queen had been warning her, she saw that now.

"It's okay," Eve said.

But Aster saw the hunger in her eyes, in the way her hands yearned toward her.

"It really isn't," Aster said. She fought to her feet, tried to sprint to the river, but she was so weak she stumbled and fell after a few steps. The water was only about twenty feet away, but even that seemed too far. She struggled back to her feet.

"No," Eve shouted. "Don't. You won't survive."

Maybe not, but Aster knew she wouldn't survive if she stayed. Whatever Eve's original intentions, she now had a hunger that would not be satisfied with a few drops of blood. At least in the river, Aster had a chance. She took a breath and ran. She heard Eve coming close behind.

Aster knew what she had to do, and she did it. She was much deeper in the Kingdoms now and needed no fetish to accomplish it.

Eza azmi lassas.

She jumped, and the cold, black water took her in. She exploded; then came back together, but not the same.

She had transformed once before, with the aid of a feather from her father's things. She had become a raven, and she had very nearly remained one; if it hadn't been for Billy, she probably would have.

Now she was one with the swift water; she heard sound in her bones and smelled with her skin and saw nothing at all. The river fell, and fell further, and even her skill at swimming was no match for it. All she could do was thrash her fins, and hope she wasn't smashed to death on the way down.

There came a moment of terrific speed and pressure and absolute confusion, then, at last a blush of light filtering down through the grey-silver surface above her. She flicked her tail, trying to find a quieter place where the water wasn't moving so quickly, where she could take time to feed.

No, a stubborn thing persisted in her. *Not to feed.*

She imagined leaping from the water but knew deep down only death lay in that. As much as she knew she should, it seemed strange, impossible, suicidal to leave the life-giving stream. How much easier it would be to stay in the river, or to have remained in oubliette?

No. She recalled herself.

Then she was struggling toward the surface, her lungs aching, the water already numbing her fingers and toes.

Her strength was nearly spent when she pulled up onto the mossy bank. In the distance, her father's fortress was shadow against a coral sky. She had assumed the underground river was a branch of the one that cascaded in a waterfall down the front of the castle, and that it would eventually rejoin the river she had seen flowing seaward. If she had been wrong—if it had emptied into some deep, sterile aquifer—she would probably have remained a fish long enough to die of starvation.

But she hadn't been wrong.

She sat on the bank, shivering.

Find the orbs? She needed at least one to find the others. And vague visions aside, there was only one she knew the location of—the one her father had.

Which meant going back into the castle. This time she couldn't simply walk in—that hadn't worked out so well. No, this was going to require a little thought.

Veronica had been right. It had been a mistake coming here before going after Errol. Whatever Errol was up to, he would almost certainly have helped her. And she would still have Veronica, too. Now she was alone.

And cold. And naked. Probably, she thought, the first order of business ought to be to find some clothes.

Quick's eyes widened when he answered the door, but he almost instantly averted them.

"I'm sorry," she said. "You were kind to me before. I didn't—"

"Come in, fast," he said. "Oak, bring a blanket. And keep your eyes shut."

"You're being peculiar," she heard Oak say.

But a moment later, she was safely wrapped in a rough woolen blanket.

Sharp came through the entry door behind her to join them.

"Where's Copper?" she asked.

"Scratch got her," Sharp said.

"Her?"

"Yeah. We cut her hair and dressed her like a boy. Worked for a while, didn' it?" He sounded like he was working at being cheerful, but he looked miserable.

"Wait," Quick said. "You got away, didn' you? Or were you never caught?"

"I got away," she said.

"Can you tell us where the girls are?" Quick asked.

"I don't know," she said. "I was never with the other girls."

She heard an odd snuffling sound and saw Oak had turned away to hide the fact that he was crying.

Aster's jaw tightened.

Nothing had ever been simple. Once she had been focused on a single goal—curing her father. Every complication had been either an aid or an impediment to that objective.

She had failed, and now things were completely muddled. The curse might have been bad, but it wasn't her fault. Her father being here was. If she hadn't entered the Kingdoms, she wouldn't have met Dusk, and if she hadn't allowed Dusk to tag along on her little quest, the warrior-woman would never have learned the information she needed to bring all of this to pass.

It now went way beyond trying to cure her father, if there even was a cure for what he was now. Now she had wrongs of her own making to consider.

"I promise you," she said. "All of you. I will find Copper and the others. Somehow I will set them free. Do you understand?"

"Who are you?" Sharp asked. "Who are you to make such promises to us?"

"I am Aster," she said. "Aster Kostyena. I will do what I say."

The name didn't appear to mean anything to them, but her tone did.

"Oak, go get her another of Copper's dresses," Quick said.

The three boys stepped outside to give her some privacy.

This dress was much plainer than the last, just a grey wool shift. She realized that on her last visit, Copper had probably given her her very best clothes.

She wasn't quite finished adjusting the dress when the door burst open.

"Apologies," Quick said. "But a whole bunch of Scratch's divlings are coming up the road. You'd best go out the back and be quick."

"Oh." But she hesitated.

"They won't hurt us unless they find you here," he said.

"Right," she said.

She dodged out the back door, which, it turned out, led into a pen containing a chicken coop. Several offended hens squawked and flapped as she passed through. Then she was in the yard proper and running.

For a few minutes, she thought she'd been lucky. Then she heard hounds start to bay, and voices shouting behind her. They didn't sound . . . normal.

Call the Silver Kingdom.

She wasn't sure if it was her own thought; if it felt like that of an intruder. Nevertheless she did it, feeling the magic roil around her. She thought hard about the orb and her first memory of it: the feel as it touched her skin and its weight pressed in her hand, a soft, lilting voice . . .

She'd been fishing a few times, so she knew what it felt when something took the hook. This felt a little like that. She yanked.

A sudden concussion of air—*whump!*—flung her to the ground. Something more solid crashed into her. She scrambled up, as the other fellow did, too, shaking his red tresses as if stunned.

"Haydevil!" she shouted.

"Eh, that's—what?" he said.

"Never mind," she said. "Get me out of here. Get me out of here now!"

She glanced behind her, and saw the dogs through the trees, rust-red mastiffs with gigantic eyes. Behind them he saw vague forms that didn't look exactly like people. She remembered the boys who had served the Sheriff before, how they had devolved into creatures both less and more than human.

"No need to yell," Haydevil, taking her arm and whirling into the air.

"Where are we going?" he asked.

"You have something with you? A little sphere?"

"The Silver Kingdom?" he said. "I have it."

Her father's castle was a distant monster, crouching by the sea.

"Let me see it," she said. "Then I'll tell you."

NINE
ᴡOODEΠ HORSE

E rrol sat, staring at the bundle. Lotus was back to her writing; she spoke without looking up.

"Why are you afraid of the armor?" she asked.

His first instinct was to deny his fear of it. A man wasn't
supposed to be afraid, right?

But what was the point? The truth was easier.

"Because I'm worried I won't be able to take it off," he said.

She nodded her head a little. "I know what it's like to lack
choice," she said. "Being in the pyramid wasn't my choice.
Watching men die to win me—I had nothing to say about that.
And if it had been someone other than you, I would have had
to marry him and be his sweet little poppet—no choice. So I
understand."

"Yeah," Errol said. "I guess you do. The thing is, it's starting to look like I don't have a choice after all. If I go after Dusk
again, and I don't wear the armor, I'll get creamed again. But
this time it'll be permanent."

"How do you know the armor will help?"

"I don't for sure," he said. "But you know what? I'm tired of
being weak. I'm sick of everyone else having to take up my slack."

He started to unroll the bundle.

"Wait," Lotus said. She put her pen down, stood, came over and sat cross-legged in front of him.

"First of all," she said, "you got here, through the desert, without the armor."

"I had a little help with that," he said, and told the story of the lady in the cave.

"You showed compassion," she said. "You thought you were saving a child. That's why she helped you."

"Maybe," Errol said.

"Okay, but what about this, then? Maybe a hundred guys died trying to get to me. You made it. Without the armor. Without anything special."

"I would have died if you hadn't saved me," he said.

"But nobody else got even that far," she said. "Those other fellows, they had armor, magical horses—some of them had claws on their hands and feet, talking ropes, all kinds of things. They all failed. Errol, you made it because you *aren't* strong, at least not physically. But you have a solid mind, a stout heart, and a good soul. Maybe you don't need the armor."

He looked back at the half-unrolled parcel. Then, with a sigh, he trundled it back up and tied it.

"Thanks," he said.

"You're welcome," she said.

"But if you didn't think I needed it, why did you bring it to me?" he asked.

"Djinn and I assumed it was yours. What we really thought you might want is the horse."

Errol glanced over at the wooden steed.

"Where was it?" Errol asked.

"In the desert," she said. "About halfway between the city and where your armor was."

He remembered the trajectory of the horse when last he'd tried to ride it. Maybe it couldn't go all that far on its own.

He had tried to ride it once, with disastrous results.

There was no way around it—he was going to have to try again.

He spent a moment finding the little gold sphere Dusk had given him before he'd been shot; it was still there, buried near the little stick. He tied the bundle of his armor around his shoulders, making a crude backpack. Then, feeling a little stupid, he walked over to the horse and pulled it upright. It was as heavy as he remembered.

He sat on it, trying to use his legs to balance.

"Okay," he said. "Let's try this again. Let's go get Dusk."

"Wait," Lotus said. She got up, stood on tiptoe, and kissed him on the cheek.

"Just so you know," she said. "I think it probably wouldn't have been terrible being married to you."

"Thanks," Errol said. He picked up the reins of the wooden horse and said the magic word.

The horse bucked violently, hurling him through the air to plow face-first into the sand.

But it didn't fly away this time.

"Excellent start," Lotus said.

H is next try, he managed to stay on for two or three loud yelps; by the fourth he felt he was making progress. During one of his recoveries, he had a glance at what Lotus was working on. It looked suspiciously unlike writing, and more like a drawing of a cartoon character being thrown from a horse.

Finally, he sat on the thing, and it did nothing at all. He waited, bracing himself. Nothing.

He snapped the reins. Nothing happened.

He leaned forward. The horse shot up so fast he nearly lost his grip.

After a few moments, he found controlling the horse was easy enough, now that it was cooperating. He'd done some riding, western style, and the wooden steed responded to the reins and shifts in the carved saddle pretty much as he expected. The big difference was in the flying. If he went too hard on the reins his mount didn't just turn, but also started a barrel roll. Leaning forward and back worked for up and down, respectively. If he'd had time, he might have spent a few days learning to control the thing, but he felt like he'd probably put this off as long as he ought to already.

When he first sighted the pyramid city from the air, he was lost in awe for a moment. It was bigger and more dazzling than he'd thought it was.

Then he noticed a lessening of the sun, although there were no clouds.

He banked hard to the right; the bird cut through the air where they would have been.

"Jesus," he muttered. "This thing again." He watched it spread it wings, brake, and begin climbing again "Okay," he told the horse. "If that thing hits us, we're done. Hurry."

To his surprise, the horse flew a little faster. He urged it toward the top of the pyramid, but he knew the bird would get at least one more try at them.

It climbed until it was a speck, then came down like a thunderbolt.

"Wait," he said, more to himself than the horse. "Hang on. If we veer too soon, it might still hit us."

He barely had the sentence out of his mouth when the horse suddenly rolled hard to the right. He let go of the reins and wrapped his arms around the wooden neck, clamping his legs as hard as he could as the whole world suddenly spun around him. The horse turned upward and sped straight toward the descending raptor.

"No, no, no," he told the horse. "Terrible idea. Really bad."

For answer, the wooden steed doubled its speed.

Any second now, he thought. Any second, it'll turn . . .

The bird thought so too. It figured out it wasn't going to happen about the same moment Errol did, because it screeched in harmony with his scream.

In that last split second, the bird tried to avoid them, but it was too late for that. The horse slammed head first into one of its wings. The impact was so great, Errol lost his grip on the neck and slid back. He clinched his legs even harder around the horse's saddle — or, really, the part of the horse shaped like a saddle. Then he had that weightless, belly-tickling feeling you got when jumping off of something high or ramping your bike over Fisher Creek.

Except that it kept going; the horse tumbled, uncontrolled.

Errol was able to clamber back up and clamp his arms around the neck; he grabbed the reins right at the bit and yanked.

For a heartbeat, the horse didn't respond; then he felt his weight come back, increasing as the magical carving fought its former capitulation to gravity. Black spots appeared in his vision.

Then they were rising again, almost level with the ground. The glass pyramid was straight ahead, and Errol saw the bird folded awkwardly against it, slowly sliding down the side. He felt like hollering in victory, but it took everything he had just to hold on. Anyway, he hadn't won yet.

A moment later, the horse dropped toward the terrace landing where the bird had dumped him before. Errol felt his heart beating, trying to catch up. He was ready to get off of the crazy thing, to put his feet back on solid ground.

But the horse didn't land. Instead, it whipped through the narrow door at what felt like seven hundred miles per hour.

He had an erratic, blurred view of the tree, Lotus's former rooms, and several floors of glass before he finally lost his grip somewhere above the garden, slamming into the top of a palm. It bent under his weight. Although it knocked a lot of his air out, he got a grip on the fronds, so when the tree snapped back it didn't hurl him like a catapult. The leaves tore, though, and he tumbled unceremoniously to the garden floor.

"This is not good," he mumbled, when he had enough wind back. He climbed to his feet. Everything was quiet, though, and after a moment or two he relaxed.

Where had the stupid horse gone? Back down to where Dusk had been held prisoner before? Errol didn't know what kind if spell she had put on the damned carousel pony, but it was as buggy as all get-out.

He got his bearings and was starting toward the stairs when everything suddenly wasn't quiet anymore. Someone was yelling, not that far away.

He heard a hiss, and a *thwump*! Suddenly he was staring at a golden arrow in the trunk of the tree next to him.

He ran the way the arrow had been going, trying to keep low, under cover of the trees.

Some rescue, he thought. This was worse than the last time — he hadn't even made it to Dusk.

He was near enough to the side of the pyramid that he could see the stairway he had once descended. He also saw a bunch of guys in loincloths were coming down it. He zigged and zagged off to his left, trying to remember where the way down was. Maybe he could hide in the caves underneath the place, climb into one of the sarcophagi or something.

He caught a glimpse of gold through the leaves and threw himself forward, just as another arrow whizzed by his head. He rolled back to his feet, but he hadn't made it five more steps before he saw he was surrounded by the cupid-things.

He stopped, panting. They had their arrows on their bows, but none of them looked like they were going to shoot. Probably they were waiting for Hawk to give the order, now that they had him cornered.

"Listen," he said. "I know this looks bad —"

One of the golden boys yelped and drew his bow, aiming over Errol's head. The weapon snapped, the arrow flew —

Something banged into him. Something big, with black-feathered wings. Errol smelled sulfur.

It moved fast; it turned and reared up, kicking sharp hooves at another of the bad cupids. Its eyes blazed red, and suddenly, so did its mouth, spewing flame in a semi-circle that sent his attackers scrambling back into the vegetation.

Only then did he understand what he was looking at; it was Drake, Dusk's horse as he had last seen it, bigger than any horse had a right to be, dark red and black winged — sort of half-horse, half-feathered dragon.

Dusk was mounted on the beast, holding out her hand to him.

"Come on," she said. "We don't have much time."

He didn't stop to think. He jumped up and took her hand. She pulled so hard his arm nearly came out of its socket, but then he was on the horse, wrapping his arms around Dusk's waist.

Drake jumped and beat his wings, coughing out more fire, and suddenly the now-smoking garden was dwindling below them as they flew toward the balconies above.

O nce out of the pyramid, Drake went nearly straight up, leveling out only when the pyramids below looked no larger than a collection of children's toys. Soon the city was completely out of sight, and they were winging over what appeared to be endless desert.

"I thought you were dead," she said. "I am . . . happy I was wrong. But how?" She had to shout because of the wind generated by Drake's flight.

"Lotus," he shouted in her ear. "Came back for me. Brought me some fruit."

She nodded to show she understood.

"Thank you, Errol."

"Nothing to it," he shouted back. "Where are we headed?"

"You tell me," she said. "The Kingdom of Gold. You have it."

"What?"

"The sphere I gave you."

"Oh." He fumbled in his pocket, and brought it out.

"What do I do?" he asked.

"Close your eyes," she said. "Think of Aster—and hope she found the sphere I left her."

He did as she said, trying to picture Aster, with her almost-red hair, her funny nose, a look of vexation on her face.

He wasn't sure what was supposed to happen, but nothing did.

He tried thinking of her as he'd last seen her, in the hospital, Veronica standing by her side.

Veronica. He felt a pulse of guilt at the thought of her.

In his fist, the sphere stirred, pulling his hand until it was pointing off to their left.

Dusk, glancing back, saw.

"Very well," she said. She turned Drake in that direction.

Desert gave way to mountains, and beyond the mountains green jungle and a river delta like a million half-coiled silver snakes, then a long, sandy strand, followed by a blue-green ocean. The sun had finally moved toward the west, in the direction they were traveling, although it was still far from the horizon.

Finally, they passed over a green archipelago, and Dusk circled Drake down for a landing. They dismounted on a rocky beach overseen by a jumbled forest of giant ferns and palms.

"Drake needs to rest, and eat," she said.

"I could use a break, too," Errol said, as she unsaddled the beast. When she was done, it trotted into the jungle.

The sun was still not touching the horizon, but it was quite low, and that made a huge difference. It was cool, and the wind from the sea made it more so.

"Neat trick," he said. "The wooden horse was Drake all along."

"Drake could not exist as such in the Reign of the Departed," she said. "I didn't transform him back immediately because we didn't stand a chance against Hawk and his people. I hoped if left him in wooden form, you could ride to my rescue. And you did."

"Eventually," he said.

"You did well with him. I'm glad he didn't kill you."

"Yeah," Errol said. "Me too."

"Errol," Dusk said.

"Yeah?"

For a moment, she seemed to have trouble choosing her words, which was unusual for her.

"Why?" she asked.

"Why what?"

"You came back for me. Again. After what they did to you. After what *I've* done to you."

He had seen Dusk in a lot of situations. In battle, captive, attacking him. He had even seen her mortally wounded. Even then, he had never seen her looking so . . . vulnerable. It was shocking.

"I—ah—why don't we have a little fire? I'll get some wood. I assume you can do some sort of hocus-pocus to make it burn?"

She nodded.

"Great," he said, and went to collect some sticks.

To Errol's surprise, Dusk started the fire with flint and steel rather than magic, throwing sparks into a little wad of dried fern and threads of palm bark, gently breathing them to more ardent life. She placed it in the little tent of sticks he'd built, and soon the fire was burning merrily.

Errol sat across from Dusk, who still looked thoughtful.

"You've been a better companion to me than I deserve," she said, after a little while. "If you will bear with me, I will try to explain myself. Not to excuse my actions, but so you will understand them."

"Okay," Errol said.

"When the curse came, I was ten years old. My mother was queen. Our mansion was filled with siblings, aunts, uncles, cousins, servants, and all. They became strange, distant from us, their children. Soon after, my mother vanished and within days the other adults went missing or became stone or beasts in the woodlands. We began to understand we were on our own. Like those boys we first met, yes, you and I?"

"Jobe and those guys," he said. "Yeah, I remember." He also remembered how cruel and lawless they had become, and that they had not come to a good end, any of them.

"I have two brothers and two sisters. Hawk you have met; he is eldest. There are also my sisters Nocturn and Dawn and my brother Gloam. Hawk made himself king, and we accepted that at first, for each of us had palaces and lands to spare. He gave Nocturn the north to rule, Dawn the east, Gloam the south, and me the west. I made it my quest to discover the cause of the curse, its nature, and what its ultimate affects might be. As we grew older, would we, too fade into obscurity? I had to know.

"I traveled much, to many far kingdoms. I found a few answers, and many more questions. But at the heart of it all was Kostye Dvesene, Aster's father, my — stepfather."

"Wait, wait," Errol said. "Your stepfather?"

"My father died before I was born. My mother married Kostye when I was very little. It was a political match, for the good of the Kingdoms. I did not know him, only that my mother hated him. He is the most powerful sorcerer our histories tell of, and history is steeped in his evil. Empires rose and fell at his whim. It was said he once stopped the very sun in her track across the sky.

"Not long after they married, he withdrew to a mountain fastness, deep in the wilderlands. He stayed there for many years and then — for no reason anyone can tell — he loosed the curse upon the world and fled it. He was pursued, of course. But all who confronted him perished or were caught by the curse.

"I came to believe he had escaped to the Reign of the Departed, where most magic cannot reach. It took a long time, but I was finally near to finding him when I ran across you, and Aster and Veronica."

"Yeah. You decided to tag along with us."

"To discover Aster's aims. I assumed she was on a mission for her father. When I learned she sought the water of health, I reasoned that I could use it to restore my mother, or better , find the source of the curse and use it there. First I had to wrest control of the Kingdom from Hawk, who had become somewhat deranged and declared war on the rest of us. After leaving you in the castle of gold. I went to Aster's father and convinced him I was she."

"That's what she figured," Errol said. "You took her pictures, and her diary."

"It worked at first," she said. "We returned, and my brother fled before Kostye's power. My sister Nocturn fought, but her lands were conquered. Gloam, my brother, surrendered to him. Dawn, the youngest of us, vanished. I set about trying to right things. Kostye's memory was still strange, at that time. Once, when mad with drink, he spoke of the 'island where it all began.' I went in search of it. When I returned, the chancellor, Vilken had come, and everything was changed. Vilken—I will say more of him later. The point is that when I tried to convince Kostye I was his daughter, he didn't remember having any daughter at all. He imprisoned me, but I escaped."

"What does all of this have to do with me?"

She lowered her head. "You think I am heartless," she said. "But everything I did, I thought it was best for my Kingdom. My people. When I left you, I knew I was abandoning you to your doom. I—regretted it. Later—after fleeing Kostye—I went back to see what had happened. I found you, or what was left of you, and I took the remains to certain women I knew of. They told me you yet lived, and that you might be my companion in all of this. My helper. They made the arms and armor you still carry. Then I followed Billy's trail back to you."

"Because you thought I would help."

"I did," she said. "And I was right. The weavers were right."

Errol poked at the fire. "You don't get off that easy," he said. "You could have told us. Aster would have—"

"Aster had only one goal," Dusk said. "Her father came before everything else. I could not let her cure him. If he remembered everything he was, if no one had control of him, I feared he would do terrible things."

"But that's exactly what happened, right?"

"No," she said. "It's far worse. Vilken holds his reins, now. I'm not sure how, exactly, but he is able to control him as I was not."

"Why is that so bad? Who is this Vilken guy?"

"Back in the far-off days, they say Kostye and Vilken were friends, or at least trusted peers. Something changed between them. After Kostye made the curse, Vilken and others set out after him. Vilken's companions all died. He himself forgot who he was, and became exiled in the Reign of the Departed. You know him as the Sheriff."

He let that sink in.

"Aster said she blew him off the roof. That's a long fall."

"Vilken is not frail," she said. "But he is—different now. Not the Sheriff, but perhaps not as he was before, either. Kostye has forgotten the strife between them—he remembers him as a peer."

"What does Vilken want?" Errol asked.

She shook her head. "I don't know what he actually wants, because I don't know what he *is*. He's convinced Kostye the curse can be broken by sacrifice."

"What sort of sacrifice?"

She laughed, roughly.

"A thousand worthy girls," she said.

For a moment, he couldn't find any reply to that at all.

"That's insane," he finally said.

Dusk nodded. "You see how serious it is."

"Then what the hell are we doing? What was your plan?"

"My plan was to convince Hawk to become my ally against Kostye and Vilken. Short of that, I meant to steal the Kingdom of Gold and flee. I was afraid I would fail. I needed you to come get me if I did. As you would say, you were my back-up."

"You could have explained that to me."

"I thought I would need to win you over before explaining," she said. "I thought I would have time. Once again, I was wrong."

"What now?"

"We need Aster," Dusk said. "I hoped we wouldn't, but without Hawk or Nocturn we have no hope of taking the fortress or invading Vilken's demesne, where the girls are sent."

"Fine," Errol said. "Let's go get her, then."

Dusk stood up. He rose, too, thinking she was ready to go. Instead of calling Drake, she stepped around the fire until she was right in front of him.

"You never answered my question," she said. "Why?"

Errol didn't usually know when a girl wanted him to kiss her. Usually, they had to either make the first move or send him an unmistakable signal.

"You should kiss me," Dusk said.

TEN
DEEPS

O nce before, a hand had emerged from a well to pull Veronica beneath the water — toward darkness, familiarity, becoming again what she had been for three decades. She had struggled, against it with everything in her, knowing that if she went into the well, the humanity Aster had so recently restored would be lost forever.

This time it was different. There was no sense of coercion; instead, it was as if a childhood friend had taken her hand because she wanted to bring her along and show her something amazing. As the fingers laced into hers, she realized something else.

It was her own hand, attached to another *her* beneath the waters. It wasn't a reflection, she was sure of that. The other Veronica was somehow stronger, surer of herself. She smiled as if she had a secret.

Then she pulled through her other self, and was alone, drifting downward. She began to swim.

Rather than growing darker, as she went deeper her eyesight grew clearer.

She saw fish with lamps for eyes, a thousand faintly glowing ghosts that she thought must be jellyfish, and massive, dark tentacled things at the edge of her vision. Schools of what she thought were iron-colored fish turned in complicated patterns below her— it was only as she drew nearer she saw they were shaped like long, tapering cones rather than trout.

A distinct amber glow shimmered up to her, like a fire in the water or sunlight seen looking up from the bottom of the sea. She descended past gigantic statues of women toward a pavilion of luminescent, translucent stone half hidden by a forest of leafless tree-like seaweed—at least that's what she thought it was. But as she passed through to the middle, she began to suspect they might be roots instead, from some gigantic plant above them. Which didn't make sense, because what was above them was a mountain all covered in ice.

In her experience, nothing made all that much sense, even back home, and here even less so.

Seated on a sort of raised dais she saw a woman. Or something that resembled a woman from the waist up. Below her navel, her body became like that of a snake or an eel. She smiled, and Veronica saw her teeth were mother-of-pearl, as were her eyes.

"I know of you, Veronica Hale," the woman said. "The waters beneath the world carry news of you."

"My, people gossip so," Veronica said. "I'm not such a big deal."

The woman smiled. "That remains to be seen."

"I, ah, guess I can't return the compliment. I don't know who you are."

The woman shrugged. "Do you need a name? Call me Yurena. Whatever I might have been, since the curse I am only a dream, a glimmer in deep water. I sleep more often than not, but my streams are always talking to me. And I am jealous of my knowledge. What have you come to ask?"

"If you've heard of me, maybe you've heard of my friend, Errol," she said.

"You came to the stream with the scent of him still on you, in the grey place where my eyesight fades. Yes, I know him. And I know the other, Aster. And the prince, who spoke so sweetly to you . . ."

"Is he still alive?" she blurted. "The prince? Shandor?"

She smiled. "There is a price for my knowledge, but this is my gift to you: he lives, insomuch as his sort is alive, and is well in those same terms."

That was good news, wasn't it? Shandor had been nothing but nice to her, whatever hidden motives he might have.

"Okay," Veronica said. "Errol. Can you tell me how to find Errol?"

"Are you certain?" the woman said. "You have other paths available to you, roads down which great power might lie."

"It seems like everyone is telling me stuff like that," she said. "Yes. Errol. I want to know where he is."

The woman looked skeptical but shrugged.

"I can tell you," she said. "But it will do no one any good."

"What do you mean?"

"By the time you reach him, he will be dead."

"That's not true," Veronica said. "You're messing with me."

"I withhold the truth, at times," Yurena said. "I do not lie."

It fell into her like a stone. She had worried about him, of course. She had nearly lost him once, and now he was in a mortal body, and a weak one at that.

Errol, what have you gotten yourself into?

"But he isn't dead," Veronica said.

"No. Not yet."

"But there's nothing I can do about it?"

Now the woman smiled, a slight, somewhat mocking smile.

"Okay, you can stop that right now!" Veronica exploded. "Damn you and your secrets. If I can help him, tell me how!"

"Ah. For that there is a price."

"Oh. I get it now. First you tell me he's going to die, get me all upset. That part I get for free, right? But saving him, that's what is gonna cost me, is that it?"

"I might have asked for payment before I told you anything."

"Yeah," Veronica said. "So what is it? What do you want?"

"You," Yurena said.

"How's that?"

"You give yourself in service to me for a year and a day," Yurena said. "After which you will be free, if that is your wish."

"A year and a day?" Veronica said.

She remembered being the slave of the *vadras* all too well. "Servant" didn't sound much better. A year wasn't all that long, but it wasn't so much the duration as the very idea. It made her a little sick to even consider it.

Was she considering it?

Not no, but *hell* no.

"No thanks," she said.

"Well, then," the woman said. "It has been a pleasant chat."

That seemed to be that.

"You can't tell me anything?" Veronica asked.

"If you do not find him soon, he will die, and his death will be a true death."

"Yeah, I got that part already," Veronica said. "Anyway, how can I save him if I'm working for you?"

A little smile curved Yurena's lips, which pissed her off. She knew exactly what she was doing.

"Your service will begin in fourteen days," she said. "Days as they were once reckoned, before the curse."

"How do I know you aren't lying to me?"

"As I said, I do not lie."

"Right, see, I don't know that," Veronica said. "Because I don't know *you*."

"You have a dilemma, then."

Veronica stared at Yurena, her anger growing. Could she just *take* what she wanted? She felt strong, very strong, and all of these dark, creepy types obviously thought she was something special. What was the use of saving Errol if she couldn't *be* with him?

But even as she thought it, she realized that was the *nov* in her, the creature that thought only of itself, that wanted to collect Errol as if he was one of her piles of bones, to keep him forever.

She knew someone else like that, she realized. Someone who wanted to rip the soul from her and hoard it away.

Mr. Watkins. David. The Sheriff. The Raggedy Man, or whatever Mistral called him.

This thing she was, whatever she was becoming—was *he* the end result? Would she become like him?

One thing she knew: in the years she had been a *nov*, in the first days and weeks after Aster had brought her back—she could never have even contemplated these things. The habit of pure selfishness was too strong.

Now the question occurred to her—if their places were reversed, what would Errol do?

But she knew. It made her angry, but she knew. So did Yurena.

"A year and a day," she said. "After that I'm free?"

"Yes."

"Okay, fine," she said. "I'll do it."

"He is on an island in the South Seamark," the woman said.

Veronica waited for her to finish.

"That's it?" she said, when it became clear the woman wasn't going to add anything. "Some island in place I don't even know? That's not worth a year of my time."

"You will find him," the woman said. "Before he dies. That is part of our bargain. Whether you save him—that is up to you."

She leaned forward.

"There is another thing, more important than this boy — and this I give you at no cost. You must remember it."

"What's that?"

"The maiden of the northeast wind, the daughter of the dark one. Tell her it is on the Isle of the Othersun."

"You mean Aster? Another island, or the same one where Errol is? Where?"

Then the woman turned, and her black hair fanned out over everything and began to spin around Veronica. Her body came apart, melting, becoming an amber tint in the waves, and for a moment, despite the incredible force she felt all around her, all was still.

Veronica was kneeling by the pool on the mountain, staring at her own reflection.

"Son of a bitch," she said. Had she actually been anywhere, talked with anyone?

Her own gaze mocked her.

You have a choice to make.

"You are different," she breathed, looking at her reflection. "How different?"

Once more she reached to touch the water, touch her own hand.

Light dazzled her, the golden light of long ago. She stood again on the falls, looking down at her tennis shoes — her beautiful, white, brand new shoes.

She had remembered this, many times. Her last memory before becoming a *nov*.

This time, the memory drew her further along.

As she watched, a spot of crimson appeared on one of her shoes, brilliant, small, like a ruby.

Then another, and another, and her white shoes were suddenly spattered red . . .

She opened her mouth in a soundless scream. She stretched out her hands for something she would never reach, and then, with everything she had, strained toward the water below.

And the water took her in and made her at home and the *vadras* was there to tell her to forget, to push the light far away, and with it those last moments — eventually every moment — before.

She stood on the falls again. This time, something else was waiting for her. Like the water, it had always been there, but she had never had the eyes to see it, until now.

Before, she had only seen the dark and the light. Become human again or return to be a *nov*. And after drinking the water of health, those parts of herself had teased themselves apart, like night and day, like winter and summer — like the Kingdoms themselves were pulling themselves apart.

She was tired of being torn apart. Now, in the dark eyes of her watery likeness, she saw the promise of something else.

She didn't know what it was, but unless she embraced it, she would never know.

And Errol would die.

She reached toward the water again.

ELEVEN
COLLECTION AND RECOLLECTION

D elia awoke alone on a bed that was almost the size of the house she had lived in after her parents divorced. If the sheets weren't silk, they were a decent substitute. The pillows were so fluffy they could almost float on their own. Light from a tall, narrow window fell across her — twilight, as always, but pleasant. Candles burned in sconces around the room. She rolled on the bed, enjoying the feel of the fabric against her skin.

Not for the first time, she wondered where she was, where the Kingdoms lay in the obviously more-complicated-than-she-had-ever-imagined geography of the universe. At about twelve she had discovered her mother's romance novels; her favorites had been those with historical settings. Eventually, that had led her to reading books on the Middle Ages, the Renaissance, the Elizabethan period. She learned that the romances had ignored, glossed over, or simply lied about a lot of things. Medieval castles might be neat to look at, but they were actually dreadful places to live — cold, drafty, without running water. Life was short and disease-ridden, and the chivalrous knights were more

akin to Mafia thugs than Galahad and Lancelot. And two-thou-
sand-thread-count silk sheets? Not likely.

No, she wasn't in the past. What it reminded her of was
the book one of her uncles had given her when she was quite
young — a book of fairy tales, part of a set titled by color. Some
of the stories had been difficult, but the illustrations were beautiful and amazing and made her think wonderful thoughts of
faraway places. Places very distant from where she was — where
if she wasn't exactly safe at least the dangers would be interesting — dragons and djinns instead of insults, missed meals, and
a leather belt. On reflection, it was probably that book that had
made the romance novels palatable, later on.

This place was not a fairy tale, and it was not the Middle
Ages, but something in-between. Maybe the place that the
Middle Ages wanted to be but could never accomplish, the truth
the fairy tales simplified. Sometimes she felt that the Kingdoms
must be the *real* world, and the place where she had been born
was some dull, poorly made copy, like the sorry knock-off of the
Mona Lisa you might find in a knick-knack store.

The Kingdoms were beautiful and magical and nasty and
brutish. The man whose bed she now woke in was no prince
charming or pirate with a heart of gold. She needed to keep that
clear in her mind if she was to survive.

She rose and went to the window, looked out over the village, the mountains, and the fields. In the distance, she saw
dark silhouettes against the sunset. Familiar, and yet somehow
out-of-place.

"Oh, my God," she said.

They were ships, tall ships with several masts and sails and
pennants and everything. Except they weren't in the water.
They were flying.

"I will find her, you know."

She instinctively tried to cover herself as she turned, but quickly realized how pointless it was and let her hands drop to her sides.

"Get out, please," she said. "I don't think you are supposed to be in here."

Vilken rolled his eyes. "Really, Delia," he said, waving his right hand to encompass her. "No need to be modest. You don't interest me in that way."

"I see," she said. "Too old for you, am I?"

"Yes, in fact. If I had known you earlier, before your light became so dim—"

"I'm thirty-two," Delia said.

"Now I only find you sad," he finished.

"Then you won't mind," she said. She walked over to the bed, pulled off a coverlet and pulled it around herself.

"But the girls. You don't find them sad, do you?" she said.

"I find them acceptable, most of them, and a few are outstanding. It has always been so. Why did you interfere with Aster?"

"I have no idea what you're talking about," she said.

He walked toward her. She backed up, but within a few steps found her back against the stone.

"I can find out," he said. "There isn't much shimmer in you, but I can take what you have."

His eyes were like glass. Her belly clenched, and her heart felt cold.

Then he shrugged and walked away.

"Or I can ask her," he said. "Her father put a spell on me once. Do you remember?"

"I don't."

"You were there," he said. "My face was different."

It didn't register immediately. But then she remembered, Kostye touching him, the blood on his forehead . . .

"David?" she gasped.

"I've gone by that name," he said.

"Oh my God. What happened to you? What did they do?"

"You have it backwards," he said. "David didn't know what he was, but he wanted Aster, even before the spell. After, he could always sense where Aster was. The spell is faded now, almost gone, but now that I've been near her again, I think I can make use of what remains. My only concern is what you are up to."

"I'm not up to anything," Delia said.

"Vilken."

She hadn't noticed him come in, but now she saw Kostye standing in the doorway.

"Yes, my lord?" Vilken said.

"This woman is under my protection," he said. "And you are in my room, where you were not invited."

Vilken turned and smiled. "My concern, as always, is only for you," Vilken said.

"I'm sure," Kostye replied. "I'm told you've ordered the navy out?"

"We need more girls," he said. "To heal the world, to bring your kingdom back to its former glory, we need more."

"I see," Kostye replied. "And where are you taking them, exactly?"

"To my old demesne," he said.

"That is where this shall all take place?" he said. "This healing of worlds?"

"Yes, sire. When we have enough."

"Very good," Kostye said. "Then I think we shall locate the court there for the time being, if you are agreeable."

Vilken cut his eyes ever so slightly toward Delia. He smiled.

"Certainly, my lord. You are very welcome there. I will make the arrangements."

He turned rather stiffly and left the room.

Once he was gone, Kostye came closer to her.

"Did he disturb you?" he asked.

"He meant to," she said.

"I will see to it that you needn't deal with him again," Kostye said.

"That would be a blessing," she replied.

He bent and kissed her. She thought she felt actual sparks, and after a moment's hesitation she reached her arms around him, and a few moments later the gigantic bed received them.

"What changed your mind?" she asked later, as the nightbirds warbled their throaty refrains to a night that would never come. "Why are we going to his place? I thought you didn't care about his — appetites."

"I don't," he said. "But you do. And he has become — very bold, spreading my navy and my dragons thin without my permission. Or at least, without my knowing permission."

"What do you mean?" she asked.

"I saw a document today, ordering the sailing of one of my ships. It was signed by me — there can be no doubt of it." He rubbed his forehead. "The greatest betrayal of all is to betray oneself. I know I have forgotten things because of this curse. But I have been too confident of what I remember. It is possible Vilken has found some method of manipulating me — and that I cannot abide."

He pushed up on one elbow.

He was a long, lean man, muscled like a swimmer. Most of his body was tattooed in stars, planets, stylized birds, beasts, and monsters.

"Look on my back," he said. "On my left shoulder blade. Tell me what you see."

He rolled over to present it.

"There's more than one thing," she said.

"Start from the top."

"There's kind of a black snake, coiled all around itself," she said, "And a sort of stick-figure, with arms raised."

"The snake is for Dvese, my father," he said. "The other figure marks me as his child."

"Then there is sort of an upside-down bowl with an eye inside—"

"My mother," he said.

"Then, below that there's a half-moon and a star and the stick figure again."

His breath, regular and even to that point, stopped. She thought it was probably near a full minute before it started again.

"This is true?" he said. "There are mirrors in the castle. I can see for myself."

"Why would I lie to you?" she said. "I don't even know what it means."

"You have already admitted lying to me," he said. "First you told me I had a daughter named Aster. Then you told me I did not."

"I was afraid," she said. "Because you couldn't remember. Because I was terrified of what you would do."

"Are you still?" he asked, turning back to her and brushing a lock of hair from her face.

"Yes," she said.

"I see," he replied.

"What does the tattoo mean?" she asked.

"It means 'Aster, daughter of Kostye,'" he said. "It means you were telling me the truth to begin with. Before Vilken came."

"Yes," she said.

"And that girl, the one I sent to the oubliette, that was her."

"Yes," she said.

He closed his eyes. "I still cannot remember her," he said. "Nothing. Nothing."

"I'm sorry."

His eyebrows lowered, and she felt her skin prickle.

"Did I love her?" he asked.

"I think you did," she said. "You once told me you sacrificed everything for her, that you had done terrible things to protect her and would do more if you had to."

"Did I?" he said.

"Yes."

He nodded, gently stroking her face.

"We will go to Vilken's demesne, and we will have a look for her. You will help me, yes? Help me remember?"

"Of course," Delia replied.

DRAGONS

E rrol had been enspelled before. Aster had yanked his strings with various enchantments. His first sight of Veronica had sucker-punched him with lust, love, and deepest admiration. As a Venus flytrap was to flies, a *nov* was to men. Heck, the most recent to put juju on him was standing right in front of him. Yet he knew this time, no magic was involved.

But there might as well have been. Her face was almost hot; she was small and strong and hard, and the body he had been trying to ignore now pressed against him. When Dusk had kissed him before it had been a taunt, an I-dare-you, and he had always felt that behind it there had been at least as much contempt as affection.

Not now. Her arms reached around behind his head and pulled him in deeper; he was lost in her breath, her pulse, the very aliveness of her . . .

Yeah.

He pulled back. It wasn't easy. She thought he was playing, and tried to follow.

"I—I'm sorry," he said.

"Why?" she asked. "I asked you to, after all. I was hoping you would."

"Right," he said, backing up further. "But I'm not supposed to be doing this."

"You deny you have feelings for me?" she asked.

"Look, that doesn't matter," he said.

"Of course it matters," Dusk said. "And I know the answer. I know how you look at me. And now I know how you kiss me. How you hold me so sweetly. You may think I have experience with these things, but I have very little. I have spent my life fighting and striving, not cozying to boys. Even so, I cannot be so wrong."

"Dusk, I have a girlfriend. You know that."

She frowned. She opened her mouth to speak but hesitated a moment.

"Are you — do you mean the *nov*?" she finally said.

"Veronica," he said. "Yes."

"Errol, I cut her head off." Then her eyebrows arched up. "Did you keep her head? Oh, Errol, that is — "

"No!" he said. "I gave her the water of health."

She blinked. "You had one vial between you," she said. "I took the rest. I assumed you used it on yourself, to heal your true body."

"I used half of it on Veronica," he said. "Aster used the other half on me."

"So the *nov* still walks," she said. "And once again you chose her over me."

"It's not that simple," he said. "Look, Dusk, you're right. You've always been right. I — yeah, I feel things for you. But Veronica, she . . ." he trailed off.

"Needs you?" Dusk said.

"Look, I don't want to talk about it. I shouldn't have — it shouldn't have happened. It's my fault. I — "

She suddenly didn't seem to be listening to him anymore. She whistled, loudly, then went to Drake's saddle where it lay in the sand and drew out her sword.

Crap, he thought. *Not again.*

She pointed the weapon past him, up toward the sky, where he now saw something flying toward them. He thought it might be another bird, but then he wasn't sure *what* it was. It wasn't until they landed that he recognized Aster and Haydevil.

"Aster!" he said.

Aster took a wobbling step, stared at Dusk, and lifted her chin. Errol felt his skin tingle.

"I hope I haven't interrupted anything," she said.

Dusk met her gaze, and for a terrible, dragged out moment, Errol was afraid things were going to go bad.

Dusk made a sound in the back of her throat and sheathed her weapon.

"No," she said. "Nothing important, anyway. Please, join us. We have much to discuss."

But then things went bad.

The dragon was the first sign of things going haywire, but the ship came hard on its heels.

The last dragon he'd seen had been dead, skin-and-bones, and that had certainly had its own special charm. But the thing he saw coming down out of the sky toward them now was the real deal; it punched every ticket for "dragon" in his personal inventory.

Errol had never been bothered by snakes. He would even go further and admit he liked them. This made him different from almost everyone he knew — most people in his experience either got away from a snake as fast as possible or went hunting for a hoe, stick, or shotgun to put an end to it. That was a shame, because most snakes weren't dangerous to people. Even those that were venomous didn't have it in for anyone, and they would avoid humans if they could. They weren't like ticks,

for instance, ticks could make a good meal out of biting you —
rattlesnakes had absolutely zero to gain from harming human
beings, and they knew it.

His favorite snake had always been the copperhead, and
that what this dragon reminded him of, although its scales had
a far more metallic gleam. And it had wings, beautiful wings
like lightning-laced storm clouds. The dragon was probably a
hundred feet long.

The ship looked like a pirate ship from the movies, with
three big sails and several smaller ones. What set it apart from
the run of ships Errol was familiar with was that it was several
hundred feet above the water.

"Stupid," Dusk muttered, throwing him a look. "We should
never have rested for so long."

Resting, he thought. Now there's a word for it. He glanced
at Aster, wondering what she suspected.

"We don't know they're here for us," Errol said, hopefully.

"I think it would be a great coincidence if they were here for
anyone else," Dusk said. "Drake!"

The horse-dragon trotted from the woods, and she quickly
began saddling him.

"Are you coming?" she asked Errol.

He looked at Aster and Haydevil.

"I will take her," Haydevil said. As he said it, he grabbed
Aster's hand and they whirled up into the air.

Dusk was already mounted; Errol quickly climbed up
behind her, and a moment later, Drake beat his wings and
soared upward.

The dragon was fast. It changed directions incredibly
quickly for a creature its size. As Drake fought for altitude, Errol
watched the beast attack Aster and Haydevil, coming at it from
above, moving sinuously, like a banner in the wind, forcing

the dragon down. Haydevil did his best, jinking and swerving to get around, but each move he made was countered by the titanic creature.

Aster wasn't going without a fight, though. He saw something flare as brightly as the sun, followed by a black whirlwind that dipped into the sea long enough to become a waterspout. For a moment he lost sight of the dragon in the impromptu tornado, and his heart soared.

Then he saw it come through the pocket maelstrom, its tail snapping against Haydevil and Aster sending them plummeting toward the waters.

"Dusk!" he shouted.

"I see," she snapped.

He wasn't sure if she intended to try to help the others, because before she could finish the turn, the dragon was winging toward them.

"Hold on," she said.

She sent Drake into a steep dive, straight toward the water, pulling up when they were mere feet above the waves. A glance behind showed the dragon following their every move and gaining fast.

Dusk hauled back on the reins, and their mount turned up and away, climbing with such speed that Errol felt lightheaded and more than a little dizzy. He wasn't sure where up and down were anymore. Suddenly, he was staring at a solid column of metallic scales closing around them. He heard Dusk yell and saw her cut at the monster with her sword.

The next moment they were falling.

He hit the water, hard, and at such a sharp angle he skipped once before slamming back down and into the depths.

Surrounded by bubbles, he tried to get his shell-shocked arms and legs to move, but now he was even more confused about which way was up. He didn't have very much air in his lungs, either, and he was quickly losing hope of drawing any more.

Weirdly, he felt something pulling him up, and realized it had to be the armor on his back. On land it had been somewhat heavy; albeit not as heavy as Dusk's metal gear. In the water, however, it appeared to be buoyant.

His head came out of the water, and he began heaving deep breaths, looking around wildly to see what was going on.

He saw Drake, riderless, speeding across the water—toward the dragon.

"Drake, no!"

Her voice sounded distant and thin, but it was Dusk. He saw her some twenty yards away, treading water.

In the instant before Drake struck the dragon head-on, the horse-beast belched a stream of flame. Compared to the dragon's firebreath, it looked like a cigarette lighter trying to burn a jet plane.

Then that whole half of the sky blazed into raging, scarlet flames. As the flare faded, he had a glimpse of the dragon's great body, smoke boiling from where its head had been, as it struck the sea.

Something grabbed him by the ankles. Acting out of pure instinct, he gulped a lungful of air before the water once again closed over his head.

When Aster came to, it was to the creaking of wood, disorientation, and nausea. She wanted desperately to throw up, but her empty stomach could not oblige. It was dim, but not completely dark, and she quickly realized she was in a wooden room, with irons on her hands and feet. She tried to open her mouth and felt the gag that was tied in it.

She wasn't alone. Dusk was a few feet away, similarly bound and gagged.

There were others: all girls, girls of every description. No Haydevil and no Errol. What had happened to them? Had they escaped, or been ignored by her captors?

Or — as seemed more likely — killed?

They must be in the belly of the ship, she reasoned. Her father had managed to have her followed, or possibly used an Adjuration of Prescience to foresee where she would end up — or any number of spells she wasn't aware of.

Still, something about that didn't ring quite true. Her father had wanted her questioned. He had singled her out, whether because he thought she was part of some plot or because some part of him did remember her. But here she was, with a whole shipload of captives, and her father nowhere in sight. What if it she hadn't been captured on her father's orders at all? What if this trap had been meant for Dusk, and she fell into it?

She tried to calm her mind. There were spells that could be done without speech, although at the moment she couldn't recall any that were likely to be of use. There was no telling how long the voyage would be; it could be a day or a year, for all she knew. She had to keep calm, work out what was happening and why, and find the way out.

THIRTEEN

LOVE, DEATH, AND OTHER CONFUSIONS

Errol's breath didn't last long; the rush of the water beat it out of him even before his blood demanded oxygen. He kicked desperately at the grip on his foot, but it was too strong. The salt stung his eyes and his nasal passages.

Water rushed in, and he knew it was all over. It hurt, at first, like knives in his chest, but the pained dulled then stopped. Everything became kind of peaceful. He thought he saw Veronica, and hallucinated she was kissing him, pulling him ever deeper into the water.

I'm sorry, he tried to tell her. *I didn't mean to.*

The next thing he knew, the pain was back, and he was coughing his lungs out. Everything tasted like salt and seaweed. His eyes felt swollen, and they stung like the Devil had spit in them.

"You're okay, Errol," someone said.

No, not *someone* — Veronica. He would know her voice anywhere.

He opened his smarting eyes, trying to focus, and found her sitting next to him, legs tucked beneath her. She was wearing his green shirt — her legs were bare.

They were on sandbar near the banks of a muddy-looking river winding through a forest of oak, hickory, and loblolly pine. The ocean was nowhere to be seen.

"What happened?" he groaned. "Where did you come from?"

"That's sort of a long story, Errol," she said.

"There was a ship," he said. "A dragon . . ."

"That's all way over there," she said, gesturing vaguely to her left. "and we're way over here. How do you feel?"

"Like I've been drowned," he said.

"Well, you know me," she said.

"That was you who pulled me under?"

"Yes," she said. "That was me."

He sat up. "Hey."

"Hey yourself," she said.

For a moment he didn't know what to do. Insanely, he almost blurted out what had happened, that he had kissed Dusk.

Instead, he reached for her, feeling a little weird about it. The way she was looking at him, he couldn't tell what she wanted.

But he felt like he should do something, so he leaned up to kiss her.

She hesitated, but then kissed him back. That was good, wasn't it?

Her lips were salty, like his, but he realized with a shock that they were also warm. Of course—the sun was out.

She drew back from him.

"What's that?" she asked.

"What?"

"You taste . . ." she trailed off. "Maybe I'm imagining things."

There it was, the window. His chance to be honest, to get right with his guilt. But her expression was no longer unreadable; there was a question there, and the beginning of hurt.

"Veronica?" he said.

"What is it, Errol?"

"I love you."

Her mouth opened, and he heard an intake of breath. Then she bent, slowly, and kissed him again, leisurely, sweetly, so his toes tingled and all the pain in his body faded off into nevermind.

"I love you too, dummy," she said.

He kissed her again. It was constant surprise and amazement, and although on one level he knew they ought to talk, on a more immediate level, he didn't want to stop. Each touch felt like lightning.

He pushed her gently down and lay on top of her, moving his lips down her neck, to her collarbone. She tasted like the ocean, like everything he'd ever wanted.

"Errol," she said. It was a sort of a sigh, and he took it as encouragement. Then she pushed at him a little.

"What?" he asked.

"Just—I'm not ready."

"Ready for what?"

"Errol."

"No," he said. "I wasn't going to—" he stopped, feeling a little defensive.

"Sorry," he said. "I thought you were enjoying it."

"I was," she said. "That's kind of the problem. I love you. And I'm confused. I'm feeling things I don't know how to feel. New things. So just—be patient with me."

"Yeah," he said. "No, I wasn't planning—"

"I know," she said. "They never are."

He heard the darkness behind her words and remembered what she had been. Not long after he met her, she almost drowned a guy, a man she claimed had some very nasty intentions concerning her. She could sense guys like him, she said. When she kissed them, she could feel the things they wanted to do.

And she did things to them instead.

"Hang on," he said. "Are you comparing me to those guys you drowned, back in the day? The ones trying to rape you?"

"Yes," she said softly. "I mean, no—I know you wouldn't do that, Errol. But it's all still in my head. And before, you know—before he killed me—I had hardly done anything with a boy. This life, this thing we're doing—it's all new to me."

It struck him that Dusk had said nearly the same thing, although without the being murdered, and . . .

Something else occurred to him, then.

"Veronica. Mr. Watkins—or whatever he is—did he . . ."

"He didn't rape me," she said. "But he touched me. He touched me in places that were supposed to be all mine. He was going to rape me. But I got away and I jumped. I didn't let him."

"You killed yourself?"

She shrugged. "Before I got away, he cut me with a knife." She touched her throat. "He was going to do it while I was dying. It's what he likes, to see our eyes go all black, to take all of the light out of us while he . . ."

She stopped and bit her lip. Tears formed in the corners of her eyes, but he couldn't tell if they were from grief or fury.

"I think it surprised him that I broke free up and jumped," she finished. "So he didn't get it all."

"Yeah," Errol said. That would be a surprise. He had never cut anyone's throat, but once you did, you probably figured they would go down and stay that way. He felt suddenly sick, even as he tried not to imagine it, what she had gone through . . .

"God, Veronica, I'm so sorry."

"I had forgotten," she said. "But the more I'm alive, the more I remember. Sometimes—sometimes I wish I wouldn't."

He helped her sit up. "I'm sorry," he said. "I don't want to do anything you don't, okay? Remember that."

She nodded, and looked him in the eye. It was all suddenly too intense. He realized he was angry.

"You know," he said, "before, when Jobe's boys were coming for me—I decided I didn't want to kill anybody. I shot to miss, just tried to scare them, slow them down. I still don't like the idea of hurting anybody that bad. But when I find this guy—this thing, whatever he is—it seems to me he maybe needs some killing."

"I tried to put an end to him," Veronica said. "I thought I had. But I didn't. He's stronger and worse than ever. He somehow got into the Sheriff's body, and he has his power, too. You can't go against him, Errol."

Now that there was space for it, the last second before he was dragged under came back to him—and with it, a sudden stab of guilt. Here he had been smooching it up, when . . .

"Aster," he said. "She was there, with Haydevil. She fell in the water."

"She's alive," Veronica said. "A ship fished her out of the water. I'm not sure about Haydevil."

"That's a relief," he said. "What about—" but then he stopped.

"Dusk?" she asked. "I saw the two of you on her little flying horsey."

He nodded.

"They got her, too."

"Oh," he said. "Okay. So, you—how did you find me?"

She looked down.

"I'm still trying to figure that out," she said. "I've changed, Errol. Something happened, and I'm different now. But I'm also the same."

"Different how?"

"I'm not sure," she said. "Or not completely sure. But how I got here? I came through the water."

"You mean you swam? But the sun is still up. How could you breathe?"

"That's one of the things that's different," she said. "I didn't swim exactly, anyway. Can we — I don't want to talk about this anymore. Not right now."

He had about three hundred more questions, all of them vital, but when Veronica said she didn't want to talk about something, she usually meant it.

"Okay," he said. "But you'll tell me eventually? How you got here? What's going on with you."

"I came to look for you," she said. "Maybe you should catch me up first, lover boy. Last word I had, Dusk was not one of our friends. But you two looked kind of chummy."

"She sort of kidnapped me," he said.

"Sort of? Like she sort of chopped off my head?"

"She was in Laurel Grove. She beat up a bunch of orderlies and then put a spell on me so I would follow her."

Veronica lay back on the sand.

"Go on," she said.

He told it to her, more-or-less, leaving out some fairly specific parts, and emphasizing that he believed he needed Dusk to get back home — or anywhere, for that matter. He also stressed what the woman in the sarcophagus had told him about ending the curse. He thought it put his efforts to save Dusk in a bigger context.

Veronica didn't say anything, but he could tell she wasn't completely buying it.

"The way I see it," he said, "our next move is to find out where they took Aster."

"Why?" Veronica said.

"Well—because she's our friend."

"Is she?" Veronica said. "You think if you were in trouble, she would come after you?"

"Isn't that why you're here?" He asked. "Didn't the two of you come here to save me, or whatever?"

"Yes," she said. "And now you're saved."

"But now Aster and Dusk are in trouble. We can't abandon them."

"Errol, they've both abandoned you in the past. Once we got to the Kingdoms, Aster went to find her father instead of you. And Dusk—you don't need a reminder about her, do you? I came here for you. Only you, Errol. We're finally together. You say you love me—let's go *be* together. Without all the rest of this. Just you and me."

It wasn't the first time Veronica had suggested something like this. He'd thought she was getting better, that she was beginning to understand, but maybe that was him seeing and hearing what he wanted to. Of course Aster had gone after her father. If his father was alive, and in trouble . . .

"Veronica," he said, "I do want to be with you. And it's tempting—"

"No, it isn't," she said. "You would rather go fight for them than be with me."

"Veronica, when you were in trouble, I came after you."

She sighed. "I know. It made me feel special. But I guess any ol' damsel in distress will do, so far as you're concerned."

"That's not fair."

"I know it isn't. Anyway, I'm sure that's probably one of the reasons I love you. Or one of the reasons I *should* love you." She cut her eyes away.

"Veronica—"

"Look," she said. "The sun is going down."

He looked and saw she was right; the sun had moved during their conversation and was now touching the horizon.

"Where are we?" he asked.

"I place I know," she replied. "I thought we would be safer here. Come on. I know where we can spend the night."

PART THREE

VOYAGERS

ONE
DREAD

The first time the ship came to a stop, Aster assumed they had reached their destination. She was wrong. Instead, another group of girls were herded into the hold, after which the voyage continued.

Their captors were all male, and some still appeared to be human, or mostly so. The ones in charge, though, the overseers — were more monstrous.

The Sheriff's boys had come to resemble wolves, in the end. This wasn't the case with the sailors, who tended toward reptilian traits. Their skin ranged from glossy scales to rough, bumpy, multicolored hide. Some had vertical pupils, like cats or more aptly pit vipers. The one she saw most often, who brought them food and water, had an unusually long neck and lips. His teeth were small, numerous, and sharp, and hair clung to his head in only a few patches. He had a tail.

She heard some of the other girls call them divlings, which made her wonder if they were boys that Vilken had transformed, or if they were actually some other species.

In practical terms, she figured — or at least hoped — it didn't matter.

By the sixth port, Aster had begun to think the voyage would never end. But this time, when the ship came to rest, a large gang of divlings came down into the hold and began removing the girls.

Aster had been preparing for days, but now that the moment was on her, she had to struggle to reach the right frame of mind, to still her conscious thoughts and drift toward a state almost like sleep, where familiar sounds became strange and absurd thoughts and images seemed natural, the place her books called the *marge*.

Most spells—Whimsies, Charms, Decrees, Adjurations, Utterances—required a spoken word. Even her father was not certain why, but he'd once mused it had to do with what he called the "fuzziness" of thought and the precision of speech. Without speech, the mind tended to be a chaos of impressions, possibilities, wishes, fears. Thought left to itself, unguided, was a poor tool. But speech—and writing and drawing, for that matter—required thoughts to distill into something simpler, more workmanlike and consequently more powerful. The sorceress wasn't speaking to the world, but to herself, to the *elumiris* gathered within her, which had no agenda of its own, but could only be cajoled or commanded by the mind. And that mind had to have the razor concentration usually only found in words to accomplish anything specific.

It was possible to achieve the required focus without speech or writing, but it was far more difficult to achieve the desired ends.

Sometimes powerful sorcerers, like her father, cast spells without knowing it—usually in their sleep or from the depths of madness. These were called *Fancies* or *Dreads*, depending on the outcome.

And the outcomes were . . . unpredictable, precisely because they were the product of an unguided will.

So when the boys came and began to unchain her, she was at the *marge*, gathering magic in a sort of inchoate cloud.

She let it go, and every thought in her mind melted, became the light behind eyelids, salt of sea spray, bruised pines, gulls, waves on stones . . . the slow thrumming of the tide, whale song, the long inhale and exhale of the sea caves, the arc of the stars across the sky, the stately procession of the Wanderers, the whirring of the seasons now broken into cacophony, a sound like a voice, deeper than the rumbling of the Earth's heart.

Aaaaaassssss . . .

From everything slow, something fast came, fast and hard. Darkness rushed from behind and covered her.

She heard Dusk shriek—not from pain or fear, but from fury, and opened her eyes to see the warrior woman free of her chains and striking about her with her fists. Two divlings lay in heaps against the ship's bulkhead, with enough blood to suggest they had been hurled there with terrific force. Three more beat at Dusk with wooden clubs; two were on the floor near her feet.

Aster tried to say something, but the gag was still in her mouth, so she struggled, frustrated, as two more beast-boys ran up and Dusk staggered back beneath repeated blows from their batons.

A girl of about ten or eleven dashed up behind one of the divlings and threw herself on its back. She was quickly joined by four more captives. The boys turned and dealt them blows that sent them to the boards, but in the mess, she saw Dusk wrest a baton from one of them. In two heartbeats she struck as many heads, dropping her opponents to the deck. She quickly moved in on the others, who backed away, right into a mob of girls who had already been set free. In moments, all their captors were subdued.

As Dusk knelt in front of Aster, she saw that she still had one leg iron on.

Dusk took off Aster's gag.

"Quickly," she said. "I know no spell to unbind us."

"Ah — *n'bendete!*" Aster said.

The chains fell off with a clank. So too did those of the other girls who hadn't already been unchained.

"Everyone who can find a club, pick it up," Dusk said. "The rest of you find something, anything, and get behind us."

She helped Aster to her feet.

"How did you do that?" she said.

"What?"

"You summoned something," Dusk said. "Something invisible. It crushed those two against the wall as they were unchaining me."

"I don't know," Aster said. "I'm not sure."

"Doesn't matter," Dusk said. "Are you ready to fight? Can you spell?"

"Yes," Aster said. "I think so."

"All right," Dusk said, pushing her way forward, mounting the first step of the stairs, and turning to address the rest of the girls.

"We have to hurry, before those above know something has happened. Push through the hatch, and stay behind us, but do not fail or flag. Yes?"

Aster stepped up beside her. From there, she could see most of them; in her chains she had only been able to observe those nearest her. There were probably more than a hundred, ranging in age from nine to twenty or so, although she guessed most of them were under fifteen. Some looked angry and determined, others were clearly frightened. Most just looked bewildered.

Dusk turned and started up the stairs to the hatch, and Aster went right behind her.

There were plenty of divling sailors on deck, but only a handful looked their way as they emerged from the open hatch. Beyond the ship she saw docks, white cliffs, green hills, and neat buildings of clapboard, some with thatched roofs, others covered in shingles. It was morning, with the coral sun barely peeking over the horizon through a gauze of pink and gold. The ship itself was on the water, not in the air, and had been pulled up to the dock by a stout rope wound around an immense wooden reel.

Dusk charged the nearest sailor, a fellow with wide, froglike eyes and grey-green skin.

He gawped at her for an instant before drawing his sword; it was too late. Dusk smashed his elbow with the club and had his cutlass in her hand before he hit the ground.

By that time more than half of the girls had climbed out of the hold. Dusk brandished the sword over her head, and that set something off in the girls. Whatever individual trepidations some of the might have, as a group they were suddenly of one mind, charging across the deck toward the rest of the divling boys.

This got the attention of the sailors, who drew weapons and formed into a rough line. Although the girls outnumbered them three- or four-to-one, most of them weren't armed. It was, Aster thought, going to be a slaughter.

A slaughter she had no intention of allowing to happen now that her mouth wasn't stuffed with a filthy rag.

She uttered a word, and the air between Dusk and first line of divlings took fire and rushed in a wave toward the beast-boys. The flame vanished almost as it hit them, but the hot air and shock broke their line and sent many of them sprawling to the deck. Unfazed by the fiery display, Dusk continued her charge and in moments was striking at the dazed enemy with her newly acquired weapon.

It might have ended quickly, then but more of the changed boys — some armored, all armed — came swarming up the gang-plank from the docks. Dusk and the girls — many of whom were now armed — turned to meet them. In an instant there was such a confused mess of fighting that Aster couldn't think of an Utterance that wouldn't harm the girls as much as the boys. The one thing she could so, she did: challenged the sea to rise in a wave and sweep the gangplank away, so no one else from shore could easily board — which was fortunate, as she saw more divlings arriving on the dock at each moment.

She didn't know what their chances were in the best case, but if they stayed moored, they would ultimately lose. Another plank would be thrown up or grapples or whatever, more divlings would board. For them to have any chance, they had to be unmoored.

She faced the wooden reel and sent fire scurrying along the rope that held them to the dock.

Bodies now covered the deck, and lots of blood. Many of the dead and wounded were girls, but they were pushing the divlings back.

Her gaze fastened on a girl with amber curls, lying in a pool of blood. She could tell by her eyes she would never breathe again. How many had died already? How many would die?

For a moment, the terrible reality of what was happening paralyzed her.

The rope burned through. Aster took a deep breath and con-sidered the ship. The sails were down, and even if she knew how to put them up, she knew she couldn't do it alone.

Instead she turned her effort to the sea, proclaiming an Utterance of the Deep. The ship suddenly surged away from the dock, carried by an enormous swell.

A ragged cheer went up from the girls as they drifted—not only away from the dock, but upward, lifting out of the sea so the bullets and arrows now being fired from shore were no longer able to reach them on deck, as the hull of the ship now shielded them.

Weakened from her efforts, Aster staggered and caught herself on the rail as the deck tilted a bit. She saw the crowd below, uniformed soldiers reloading their guns through the barrels, archers taking aim.

And she saw *him*, his ice-blue eyes, staring up at her. She tried to look away, to push herself back from the rail, but she couldn't; she saw his mouth moving. Her legs and arms refused her will.

"No!" she gasped, through clenched teeth. "No!"

She was too weak. Her resistance broke, his eyes drew her on, the sea rose to greet her.

What followed, Aster remembered more like a series of snapshots than a continuous sequence. The cold water, flashes of sky, being dragged up on the wooden dock, the cries of gulls and other, stranger-sounding sea birds, being bound and gagged again, a ride in a bumpy cart, shadows, darkness, stone halls.

Then hot water, and someone scrubbing at her flesh, soap that smelled of ash. She was given something to drink, mild and sweet and with a faint taste of alcohol. She spit out the first mouthful but she was thirsty. She swallowed the next several.

Time came back in the tub. Two girls were washing her; one with hair as sleek and black as a raven's feather, the other with wide cheekbones and watery-looking eyes. Both looked to be on the younger side, nine or ten.

"Where am I?" she asked.

"Oh, you can talk," the girl with the black hair said. Aster focused on her, saw she had a small nose and a long, rounded jaw.

"I can talk," Aster said. "Where am I?"

"Where we all are," the girl said.

Aster sorted back through to where her memories became unreliable.

"I fell off the ship," she said. "Where is he?"

"He?"

"The man with the blue eyes. Vilken."

"Oh, you mean the chancellor. Well if you want to see him, you're in luck. That's who we're cleaning you up for."

"I don't want to see him," Aster said.

The two girls shared a glance between themselves.

"I reckon you don't," the black-haired girl said.

"What are your names?" Aster said.

"I'm Magpie," the dark-haired on said. "This is Violet."

"My name is Aster," she said. "I need to get out of here."

"Yeah," Violet said. "Don't we all. But there's no way out, except that ship you fell off."

"You probably should've stayed on," Magpie said.

She poured some powder in the water and swirled it around. It smelled like perfume.

"There's another man," Aster said. "He has red hair—"

"You mean the king?"

"Yes."

"He doesn't come here," she said. "This is the chancellor's place."

"And where is that?" she asked.

"Don't know," Magpie said. "Us girls, we call it the Kingdom of Birds." She stood and pulled up a towel.

"Think you can stand? It will make it easier on us."

They dried her off, and dressed her in a robe woven of yellow and red silk, so it looked orange at a distance. Then they conducted her up a flight of stairs to a room of white stone, with a single window, a bed, a small writing desk, and a stand with a pitcher of water and two glasses. She went to the window, which had a crosshatch of metal bars, and looked through. She was someplace high, looking out over verdant hills, fields, copses of trees growing along streambanks. It was still morning, and it seemed likely this place, like her father's kingdom, was also stuck in time. Far in the distance, she saw what might be the sea, or else an illusion created by low clouds.

Had Dusk escaped with the ship? The girls who bathed her thought so. If she had gotten away, Aster was glad. Not so much for Dusk, with whom she had some . . . issues . . . but for the other girls. She hoped they sailed as far away from this place as they could get, so far that her father and Vilken could never find them.

Of course, their escape didn't help her at all, or the other girls here. How many had Vilken collected. Hundreds? Thousands?

She felt calm, too calm, and she began to wonder whether there had been something in the drink or the bath to blunt her anxiety. She also felt sleepy—but that might be natural. She hadn't had much real rest on the boat.

She realized Magpie and Violet were gone. She tried the door, but naturally it was locked.

Aster sat on the bed. The sheets were soft and inviting. She lay down, thinking. There ought to be a way to loosen the bars or crack the stone. She did not know any spells which would allow her to fly, but maybe if she called a wind it would slow her fall . . .

She woke, and realized she's been asleep. Someone was stroking her leg.

She sat up, violently, and backed against the headboard.

It was the Sheriff, or Mr. Watkins, or Vilken—whatever he was. He wore a robe similar to hers.

"Hey, now," he said. "No need to panic."

The horrible thing was, she still wasn't panicking. Her head and mouth felt as if they were stuffed with cotton, and her body torpid, difficult to move.

"What have you done to me?"

"I don't have quite your father's facility with word-spells," he said. "But I am knowledgeable about herbs and the grains of the earth, and such. Witchbane, if you know what that is, and a few other ingredients I retain the right to keep secret."

He reached to touch her again.

"Don't," she said.

"Aster, you gave me quite a chase," he said. "But it turned out well, in some ways, less well in others. I expected to net Dusk and Veronica since they bore the orbs. Instead I found you."

"But Dusk got away."

He shrugged. "For now. But I have her orb, and that is more than half of what I wanted. I will find her and the ship she took from me. You can be sure of that. Soon my reach will extend to furthest corners of the Kingdoms. So there's that. Veronica? I'm disappointed to have missed her again. But that is also temporary.

"On the balance, I have you, and far from your father's watchful eye. That is more than enough to put me in very high spirits. And you—you are better off, I think, than you would have been if your father had had his way with you. Since he doesn't know you're here, you need not worry about him. I cannot imagine how terrible it would be to be tortured to death by one's own father. I am so happy I can spare you that."

She tried to bolt forward, knock him aside and reach the hall beyond. But she was so slow and her limbs so heavy, that instead he caught her by the shoulders and gently forced her back down upon the bed. She finally felt a little panic, and kicked at him with her feet. He forced her legs down onto the bed and then straddled them. He smiled, slightly, but his eyes were dull stones.

"This isn't going to hurt," he said.

"Oh, no, don't," she said as he began to undo the tie on her robe. She tried to think of a spell, something that would burst him from the inside out, but she couldn't focus.

Once she was exposed, he sat down next to her again, gently stroking her here and there. Her skin did its best to crawl away from his touch. There was nothing comforting about it. It only made everything more horrible.

"You can't know how much I've wanted this," he said. "Part of it's your father's fault, you know — the curse he put on me made me obsessed with finding you. But to be fair, it was an easy sell — I'd had my eye on you for a long time. Waiting for the right time."

He leaned over to the desk and fished out a bottle of something and took a drink from it. The all too familiar smell of liquor filled the small room.

"The Reign of the Departed," he sighed. "I was stuck there for so long. Generations. I can't even remember how and when I got there. Every time I'm reborn, I lose a little something." He tapped his head. "I have Vilken's memories rattling around in here, too, making everything even messier."

He took another drink.

"Have you ever wondered why magic works so well here, but almost not at all back in the Reign? Vilken wondered about that a lot. He had some theories about it."

"Please," she said. "Mr. Watkins!"

He laughed and took another drink.

"You see, almost everything in the Reign of the Departed can be explained by physics. Life, consciousness, art, science — all the products of electrochemical processes. There's no need for magic, for the thing we call *elumiris*. Everything that happens there can be explained by gravity, magnetism, the weak and strong atomic forces, and so on. It is a world that doesn't need magic, like here, like the real world. Back there, computers and robots imitate life, you know? They can play chess and write poems and carry on conversations—but none of it ever seems quite right to a human being, because a computer isn't human—it's a bunch of circuits trying to appear human.

"Similarly, the people in the Reign of the Departed are like imitations of real people, higher people, the ones who shine with *elumiris*. They look like us, act like us—but it's all a little flat because they don't really have souls—just electrochemical processes pretending to be souls. And when they die—*pfff!* They're gone."

"And that's where I was exiled, where I was consigned to. Me—who love beauty, gorge on it, keep it safe within me—adrift in a world without beauty."

He flashed her a doting smile.

"Or at least without much. Sometimes a little flower sprouts in that barren soil—girls like Veronica. But their light is so feeble and dies long before they do. Then there are the visitors, like you. Oh, you shone so bright, even there, Aster. Even in that dead, awful place. At the time I didn't even know what I was sensing. I even felt a little bad about it, like it was inappropriate. Now I know what I am, and you know what are—so everything is fine."

"My father," she said. "He wants me alive."

"He does, but only to torture you. He doesn't remember you, and he won't."

He leaned down and kissed her belly. It felt like a spider walking on it.

"I am the cure for the curse," she said. "Only I can end it."

"I know that very well," he said. "But you see, I have no interest whatever in ending the curse. I like things just as they are. If things were perfect, I would wait, save you for a special moment, the night of my triumph—my wedding night, you could call it. But you are far, far too dangerous to keep around for that long. You slipped away from me once, and nearly escaped again. No, it must be now. I have waited long enough. I deserve this."

He pulled himself back on top of her; his weight crushed her breath away. She tried to close her legs, but he put his knee between them and pushed.

Then she saw a gleam of light, and realized he had something in his hand—a curved knife, polished to a mirror finish. She could see herself in it, her wan, terrified face.

"It won't hurt," he said. "I'm very, very good at this."

TWO
ARMOR

B y the time they came to the gypsy camp, Errol was so tired
he was stumbling more than walking. Fortunately, they
were met with hospitality, and he soon found himself resting on
pillows and blankets inside of a tent. It was hot, and the buzz of
insects and cries of owls sounded familiar to him, like he was
near home.

"How do you know these guys?" He asked Veronica, as he
lay down.

"It took some rambling about to find you," she said. "I made
some friends along the way."

"Sounds like a story," he said.

"A story for later," she replied.

"Okay," he said. He reached for her and gently pulled her
down. She kissed him, and curled against him with her head on
his chest.

"I do love you, Errol," she said.

"I believe you," he said. "I love you too."

It felt good, having her next to him. It felt right, and once
more he experienced a jab of guilt about the kiss he'd shared
with Dusk. He thought again about confessing to Veronica but

didn't see the point. It would hurt her, and for no reason. He and Dusk weren't and would never be. How could he ever trust her?

For the first time in a long time, he thought about Lisa, his old girlfriend, the one who had dumped him. In hindsight, he didn't think he had loved her at all. He'd been trying to prove something—not just to himself, but to everyone else. That he could get the girl, the hot chick everybody wanted. There were other girls he'd liked better, liked since grade school, but he didn't think his friends would consider them a catch.

Aster, for instance. They had been friends when they were young, but by high school everybody thought she was too weird, and he'd pretended to feel the same way.

He wondered where she was, if she was okay, where the ship was taking her and Dusk. But he was too tired to think about it. Tomorrow, he and Veronica would make their plans, figure this whole thing out, find Aster, beat the bad guys. They had done it before, they could do it again, if they were together, the three of them. He knew it.

He drifted off to sleep, holding Veronica.

He woke to light bleeding through the fabric of the tent, wondering what time it was. For so long, that had been a meaningless question; it felt comforting to be able to ask it again.

Then he realized Veronica was gone.

He dragged himself up, feeling good. Better than good. He found some clothes laid out for him—pants with suspenders, a white shirt, a vest, some leather shoes. Old-fashioned looking stuff, but it fit him, more-or-less.

Once he was dressed, he went out to see where Veronica had gotten off to.

In the daylight, he found everything even more familiar, the

camp itself aside. Like everyplace else beyond the Pale, there
were no adults. The young men he saw were dressed as he was.
The women wore a little more color, but they wouldn't have
stood out as all that weird back home. And the trees, the insect
sounds, the weeds pushing up through the beaten dirt of camp-
ground—all varieties he knew.

How close to home was he? Veronica had said they were
near the Pale. The first time they'd entered the Marches of the
Kingdoms, they had run into Jobe and his bunch, who didn't
look and talk that different from the people he'd grown up with.
If it hadn't been for the magic and such, he might have imagined they had wandered into some backward part of the county.
But gypsies—

He remembered something—a graveyard, in town, where
his dad once took him, to see the grave of the Gypsy Queen.
She had died somewhere nearby, and in those days a body
couldn't be preserved for long, so she'd been buried quickly in
Sowashee. When her husband died, he was buried beside her,
and every year the gypsies came around to leave presents on
their graves—beads, money, orange soda . . .

Where was he?

A girl sat nearby, tending a cookfire.

"Excuse me," he said. "There was a girl with me, ah, in the
tent . . ."

"Yes," the girl said. "She's gone."

"Gone? Gone where?"

"She went with my brother," she said.

"Where?"

"I don't know," she said. "But she left a note for you."

She pulled a folded piece of paper from her pocket.
Something was written on it, it looked like with an old-fashioned
ink pen. It was cursive, with lots of flourishes and loops.

Dear Errol, it began.

I have a few things I need to do; I don't think you will like all of them, and I have reason to believe you might not survive if you are with me. I can't have you dying on me. I thought you were dead once before, and I did not care for how that made me feel.

You may not hear from me or see me for quite some time, maybe never. I do not feel that I should explain, because knowing you, you would only get yourself into trouble on my behalf, which would make me sad, and I don't like being sad.

The gypsy camp is very near the Pale and Sowashee. The young lady who gave you this note knows how to get you home, where you will be safe.

I will understand if you do not wait for me. But please know that I will cherish what little time we got to spend together. Thinking of you has gotten me through hard times before, and I think it will again. Do know that I love you, and that I've finally realized that means I must think of you before I think of myself.

                                        I am yours,
                                            Veronica

He read it again, then folded the sheet and put it in his pocket. He felt dazed, only half-present as he questioned the girl. Where did they go? Who is your brother? Everything he could think of. The girl didn't seem to be trying to hide anything from him, but she also wasn't going out of her way to help. What she did volunteer, bit-by-bit, he didn't like. Her brother's name was Shandor-something-or-other, and he had apparently proposed marriage to Veronica.

Why hadn't she mentioned that? She was off with this gypsy king, leaving him here, where he was "safe," while Aster and Dusk were being hauled off who-knew-where.

He knew why she thought he needed protecting. And she was right.

"Which way to cross the Pale? To the Ghost Country?" he asked the girl.

She pointed down the road, to the west.

"Thanks," he said.

He went back into the tent, and unrolled the bundle he'd been carrying this whole time, the dead weight, the armor he was too chicken to wear.

He picked up one of the greaves and tried to figure out how to put it on. There were no straps or buckles. He pushed it against his shin and felt a pull that reminded him of a magnet, but it wouldn't stay. He took off his pants and tried again. This time it snapped into place, molding to the contours of his leg.

"Oh, God," he said. He tried to pull it off, but it might as well have been glued to him. As he had feared, once he put this on, it wasn't coming off again.

He stripped off his clothes and donned the rest of the armor.

Unlike the heavy metal stuff he'd worn at the glass pyramid, this armor didn't weigh much of anything. It was as if it became a part of him, to the point that if he dug a fingernail into it, he could feel it.

"Just like old times," he said, thinking of the time he'd spent with a wooden body.

He held the helmet up. It reminded him of the ones the ancient Greeks wore, with a nose guard but a space carved out for his eyes and mouth.

He was already in this far. He put it on. Then he gathered his few belongings and walked back out of the tent.

He looked west, down the road toward home.

Then he turned and walked east.

V eronica enjoyed being on a horse again. The black mare felt strong underneath her, and her gait was smooth, even while trotting.

"You've ridden before," Shandor said.

"Yes," she replied. "I've been on a horse or two."

So had he; he sat the horse in a regal fashion, back straight, shoulders square, arms relaxed, moving the reins only sparingly. It was as if the beast knew what he wanted before he did. He was born to ride.

She also had to admit he looked good doing it. His long hair spilled from beneath a brimmed hat, and he had affected another three-piece suit. The jacket on this one had a high, stiff collar and lots of buttons. He wore a sabre and a pistol, and had a rifle thrust in a holster on his saddle.

"I didn't thank you for before," she said.

"You don't have to," he said.

"But—ah—you were following me, right?"

He nodded. "I was," he said. "After my altercation with the Sheriff, I lost your trail."

"So how did you follow me through the water, through the caves under the Castle of Winds?"

"I didn't," he said. "I took a short cut. So did the Sheriff."

"You know shortcuts?"

"Some. I have a knack for them."

"I know some shortcuts, too," she confided. "But right now I don't know where to go. Do you think you can find him? The Sheriff?"

"I know where to start," Shandor said. "Although as you must know, he isn't really the Sheriff any longer."

"Yes," Veronica said. "I'm aware of that. Now he's the Raggedy Man."

"Is he?"

"I've been trying to figure out what to call him," she said. "I remembered some names from church. Beelzebub, Mammon, Moloch, scary devil names. But my friends Mistral and Haydevil called him something like Raggedy Man, and I think that fits. He's just a nasty old guy who steals things. He puts on enough airs of his own, I don't figure I need to help him out with a name from the Good Book. Even if it's a *bad* name from the Good Book."

"Names can have power," Shandor said. "And they can take power away. But it's no matter what you call him to me. He threatened you, that's all I need to know, and I will kill him for you."

For some reason, that grated on her a little.

"Like you did last time?" she said.

"I wasn't prepared for him last time," Shandor said. "This time I am."

"Yes, well, prepared or not, if you want him you're going to have to stand in line," Veronica said.

"I am at your service," Shandor said. "You are strong, but everyone needs steady companions."

They rode in silence for a few moments.

"Careful what you're thinking," she said. "Errol has saved me, too—more times than you have. He's the steadiest."

"Yet I am here, and he is not," Shandor said.

"That's because I care a lot more about him than I do about you," she shot back. "If he dies, I'll mope around for years. I can't be doing that."

"And what if I die?"

"I'll bring a flower to your grave," she said.

"A beautiful gesture."

"Nothing store-bought, mind you. A primrose or some ragweed, maybe."

He laughed. "I'll take what you offer."

"That's right, you will."

"But in time—"

"Don't start up again," she said.

He shrugged. "As I told you—I am patient. You—you are more magnificent than ever. You've changed, haven't you? You're more awake to what you are."

"I'm still little ol' me," she said. "And I've had about all the hummingbird food I can stand for the time being. Why don't you just be pretty and keep quiet?"

"I'll do what I can," Shandor said.

THREE
ECHOES

Aster felt him, as he lowered himself upon her, but most of her attention was on the knife, as she realized he wasn't merely threatening her with it.

He was going to cut her throat.

His other hand was between her legs.

She couldn't move. All she could do was watch it happen, feel it happen. And she wasn't ready.

The knife touched her throat . . .

Vilken screamed. His body jerked up and off of her as he clutched at his face, staggering backwards until he slammed into the wall.

Aster didn't know what had happened, but she knew she hadn't done it. Her brain was as dead to magic as it had been a moment before. Her limbs felt like they were made of marble. She tried to move anyway and succeeded in rolling off of the bed, landing clumsily, painfully on the floor. She crawled toward the door.

She heard him whimpering, but she didn't dare look. She needed all of her focus to move her arms and legs, to reach the door . . .

Then he was there, in front of her. His face was blanched, and one of his eyes was bleeding, but he was standing. He heaved her up by the armpits and threw her roughly back on the bed. Then he sat back down. She saw he still had the knife in his hand, but it was shaking, like an old man with palsy. With a cry, he tossed the knife away.

"Your father's curse," he said. "I thought I was done with it."

When Vilken was Mr. Watkins, her father had put a spell on him to seek her out and bring her back to him. The spell had included an inner compass that allowed Mr. Watkins to always know what direction she was in, and an obsession that made sure he would never stop trying to find her.

Obviously, it had included something else.

"Of course, you asshole," she said. "You think my father would send some guy after me — make him obsessed with me — without including an anti-raping-and-murdering clause?"

"Shut up," he said.

"You shut up," she said. "You're a disgusting clown, and I'm going to see the end of you. I swear that on my mother."

He pushed his hair back.

"You'll see no such thing," he said. "Your father's curse lost most of its force when I took this body. The part that remains — now that I'm aware of it — I'll find a way to deal with. We will take this up again, I promise you."

He rose, pulled his robe back on, picked up the knife in his still-trembling hand, and went out the door. She heard it lock, and bolts slide into place.

She picked up her robe and put it back on, still feeling as if she was living in slow motion.

Only then did she begin to cry.

And not just for herself. There were hundreds of girls on the island, and because Vilken hadn't been able to have her, he would have another. Because she lived, someone else was about to die. Maybe more than one.

There was nothing she could do until the drugs wore off. She knew he would never let that happen.

She was right. A few minutes later, the door burst open, and ten divlings came into the room—bigger, nastier, less human than any she had yet seen. They held her down and forced her to drink something bitter and black. She tried to resist it as it crept into her brain, but it was no use. Everything began to dissolve into nightmare. But she was still aware when they put her in the box and covered her with flowers.

Stop, she tried to tell them. I'm not dead.

They put the lid on anyway.

After a few hours, Errol realized he was going in circles—or, rather, the road was. He had passed the same oak several times now, he was sure, but to be positive, he marked it with the tip of his sword and continued, straight.

Half an hour later he saw the oak again, with his mark on it.

The weird thing was, he couldn't see that the road curved at all, one way or the other.

He tried going back toward the gypsy camp, but the result was the same. The road no longer had a beginning or an end, only this middle, this little section.

There was no use staying on it. The problem was that the road was surrounded by blackwater swamp, which looked to be hard going. But he couldn't keep going in circles, could he?

He found a way that looked relatively clear and started out, wading first ankle deep then dropping very quickly to above his waist. Eventually he came to a long hummock and climbed out on that, only to see a maze of lowland and swamp stretching out in every direction.

He couldn't see the road anymore, and he suspected that if he went back to find it, he probably wouldn't.

Night came, solid black and full of bugs. He climbed up into a tree and dozed fitfully, waking once to what he was sure was the sound of music – drums and voices – faint and faraway.

The dawn was slow to come, and murky when it arrived. Errol wondered if the curse was still spreading, if day and night were teasing apart even here in the marches. Would it eventually affect his world, what these people called the Ghost Country?

He didn't see how. Day and night were caused by the rotation of the Earth, and if the Earth stopped turning, one side of it would probably burn up and the other would freeze. His world wasn't magical – any miracles that happened there were strictly imported from elsewhere and had limited affect. According to Dusk, people in his world didn't even have souls. If you died in the Kingdoms, you were reincarnated. If you died in the Reign of the Departed, that was it. You were done.

But he had seen his father, or thought he had – when he was dying in his hospital bed, and the woman in white came for him, his father had appeared, and tried to protect him. He hadn't been able to, but there had been something, right? At least a wisp of something remaining of the man he loved so much?

Or maybe it had merely been his brain cells going dark. It had felt real, but so did a lot of things that weren't. Maybe Earth really was the last stop for souls that had worn out their welcome with the universe.

Anyway, that was all stuff that didn't matter right now. What was important now was getting out of the swamp. He climbed down from the tree and started slogging along again.

About midday somebody started shooting at him.

He thought he'd caught a branch or something and it had whipped him in the chest—until he realized an arrow had just skipped off his chest plate.

"Hey!" he shouted. He ducked behind a tree, which was useless, because he wasn't sure where the attack had come from.

He didn't have to worry long, because another missile whizzed by and a third hit him in the shoulder. Once again, his armor saved him from being shish-kabobbed, and now that he knew intimately how that felt, he was more grateful than ever that he'd put it on.

He had a glimpse of the shooters through the trees. They were dead white—not beige or tan or pinkish, but white like a sheet of paper, except where they were speckled—on their backs, a little like trout.

"I'm not looking for trouble!" he yelled.

His answer was another eight or so arrows. They were made of switch cane and fletched with black feathers.

"Dammit!" he grunted, and started to run, hoping they would get the message that he wasn't interested in a fight.

Of course, they might not be interested in a fight, either—given the way things fell out in this part of the Marches, they might be hunting him to present as the main course at some sort of banquet.

He had a sword, but what he knew to do with it came strictly from movies and television. Anyway, a sword didn't quite have the reach of a bow . . .

He hit water and churned through it as best he could. Something else splashed nearby, loudly. The good news was, by now he would normally be laid out from exhaustion, but with the armor he was barely breaking a sweat.

He was almost to the other bank when the water in front of him fountained up.

It was a man, and a big one. He was probably thirty years old. His front was the same frog-belly white he'd glimpsed already, but his flanks and the tops of his arms were mottled green with blue speckles. His glossy black hair was tied up in a topknot.

He shrieked in Errol's face and brandished a big wooden club. It looked sort of like a baseball bat planed flat with garfish teeth set along the thin edges.

"Look," Errol said. "I'm just trying to get out of here."

The man swung the club. Sheer reflex made Errol raise his arm, and the weapon hit him, hard, sending a numbing shocked through his arm and shoulder and knocking him sideways into the water.

When he came up, the guy was starting another swing. Not knowing what else to do, Errol drew his sword.

His arm seemed to jump up on its own, catch the descending club at an oblique angle, then cut forward, pulling him with it. The warrior dodged back, but only barely. He came back at Errol, the club singing through the air as it came down on him.

The sword stopped that, too, and this time the return cut hit the man on the arm. Blood spurted from a nasty-looking cut, and the guy fell back, dropping his club and grabbing at his wound.

Errol sloshed out of the water and started running again, but now they were everywhere, yipping and screaming. Arrows hissed and snapped all around him; one dug into the armor deep enough to hurt.

He was finally starting to tire; his lungs were burning and his legs were getting wobbly, and running wasn't getting him anywhere. He didn't want to fight these guys, but it looked like he didn't have a choice.

He stopped, put his back to a tree, and yelled.

"Come on!" he said. "Let's do it!"

For a moment, they did. He counted maybe fifteen of them starting to fan out in a circle around him. He eyed the nearest; if he could knock a couple down, maybe break through their circle . . .

They stopped coming forward. The warrior he'd cut arrived and approached a little closer, but then he, too stopped, looking past Errol.

Their eyes turned up. And up, as if watching something rise into the sky.

Every single one of them turned and ran.

"What?" Errol started. He looked behind him and saw a bunch of trees falling his way.

"Holy crap!" he yelped and took off after his erstwhile enemies.

The ground beneath his feet shivered once, twice, again. The din of shattering cypress was ridiculously loud. Looking back, he couldn't make out what it was, only that it was big, far taller than the trees. And coming fast.

His breath, on the other hand, whistled in his chest, and his whole body ached. The armor made him stronger and faster, but it didn't make him a superman. He noticed almost absently that he was oozing red where the sharp-edged club had hit him, but he didn't have time to consider the consequences of that before something came down, through the tops of the trees, breaking limbs above his head before slamming him into the ground and holding him there, pushing the breath out of him. It almost felt like a gigantic hand, but almost as soon as he had that thought, it was gone, the pressure released, and he was lying in an Errol-shaped depression in the mud, water slowly filling in around him.

He hurt. Everywhere. But everything appeared to be working. He pushed himself up with his arms, then clambered to his feet.

Above, something had cleared the canopy so he could see the sky, and behind him was a long swath cut through the forest, a lot like the path of a tornado. But whatever huge thing had been after him was no longer visible.

Then he heard a faint groan and tracked his gaze down into the undergrowth of cane and ferns.

A young man lay there, about his own age, naked as the day he was born. He looked up at Errol with a blank expression on his broad, brown face.

Errol blinked. He knew the fellow.

"Billy?" he said.

THE PATH OF BIRDS

A ster dreamed of dark forests and caves beneath the earth, of serpents and centipedes and maggots. She dreamed of her own bones, becoming clean and polished.

She dreamed that despair was the best she could hope for as she sank ever deeper into the world.

When she was about ten, she had become fascinated with dirt daubers, the wasps that build their nests from mud. She'd broken open some of their tubular nests and found them filled with spiders. The spiders appeared dead, but they didn't rot. On her next trip to the library she'd checked out a book on insects and learned that the spiders weren't deceased, but paralyzed. Eventually they would slowly be eaten by the pupae of the dirt daubers.

That was how she felt, when things were clearest; as if she was slowly being eaten — would feel every bite taken from her — and be unable to do a thing about it.

The very worst dreams were of him. He came to her in her coffin and lifted the lid, and kissed her on the lips, touched her body, wept, laughed, spoke softly to her the way one would a lover. She knew he was the worm, the offspring of the dirt dauber, slowly devouring her.

Soon, all she wanted was for the dreams to end, for absolute oblivion. She wondered if this was what Errol felt the night he tried to kill himself. She had always seen her path clearly; her father had saved her, loved her, sacrificed for her, and now it was her turn to do that in turn for him.

Yet he was fine without her. Evil, terrible—but fine. And Errol, whom she also picked to save, no longer needed her help. Veronica was on her own path.

No one needed her. No one but Vilken, and what he desired was so awful it was better not to be needed by anyone at all. She knew that one day he would come again for her—not just for a kiss or to fondle her—but for everything.

It was better not to be here when that happened. It was better that she somehow found a way to die first.

And she found it, in the magic, in the *elumiris* that still dwelt within her. Once before she had invoked the magic of dream. It was possible that she could do so again, that she could make another wish. Not to escape or kill Vilken or anything so big and showy. But she might be able to do something very small, like burst a blood vessel in her own brain. Then, at least, she could have the consolation of knowing Vilken would never have her the way he wanted.

Gradually, she gathered what *elumiris* she could, preparing to focus it through a very simple wish—the wish to die. Her fears began to fall away, the mortal reflex to fight the inevitable to dull.

Then, unexpectedly, she dreamed of birds.

Thousands of them. Millions. They filled the sky—crows and cardinals, mockingbirds and parakeets, wood ducks, humming birds with ruby throats and viridian wings, swallows, woodpeckers in scarlet headdress, grackles, blue jays, coots, peacocks fully plumed, buzzards, canaries, graceful stilt-limbed grey herons, macaws, geese, red-tailed hawks, clouds of blackbirds. They swirled and dove, flashed their wings, danced their dances, warbled, piped, cooed, and shrieked their songs. All were lifting up, rising to a form an immense flight, a flowing river of birds, a path across the heavens.

Watching them, she almost felt as if she had wings herself, as if she strained enough she might take flight and join that migration to that passage that went beyond the sky.

She heard the flap of wings, very near and in her dream she pushed against the lid of her glass coffin, and painfully, with difficulty, opened it.

The coffin lay on green grass at the crest of a hill, surrounded by apple and pear trees. To one side, the hill rolled down gently to a stream before rising again to lift up a modest mansion built of white shell. On the other, the land fell away to reveal an azure sea.

And she knew this place. She remembered lying in the sun, watching grasshoppers amongst the blades of grass, giants in their own jungle. She remembered the slightly tough, bitter skins of the apples and the nectar that lay beneath, the buttery flesh of the pears. She remembered her father, his red hair caught in the wind, looking out to sea.

And a woman, with rose-gold hair and eyes full of light . . .

She remembered it all.

Above, the last of the birds had vanished into the limitless sky.

All but one, the one that stood a few feet away, regarding her with eyes of coal and amber, her white wings tucked against her sides, her long, slender neck turned elegantly.

"Hello," Aster said to the swan. "Do I know you?"

The swan didn't answer, but she came closer, hopped up on the edge of the casket, and laid her long neck and head against Aster's breast. For a few heartbeats, she knew the most profound peace she had ever known. She stroked the white bird's head; her feathers were like silk.

"I don't know if this is real," Aster said. "But I need help. I thought I knew what I wanted, but now—can you help me?"

The bird said nothing but withdrew her head and once again stared into Aster's eyes. She raised her wings so the sun shone through them, turning them coral. Aster could see the fine bones within.

The swan clapped her wings against the air and rose up into the winds. Aster watched until the bird was a white speck on the horizon.

After the swan was gone, the sky darkened; the sun faded to a pale lemon color. Shadows grew, and from those shadows dark things began to creep. Aster held on to her memory of the birds, of the swan, as nightmare closed in on her once more.

Delia had always wondered what it would be like to sail on a tall ship, and now she knew—sort of. Kostye took her down to the docks and onto a ship that might have been at home in the Spanish Armada, with its many masts, sails, and pennants. After a bit of fussing and making ready, the ship sailed out of the harbor with the wind. The sky was full of gulls; pelicans skimmed inches above the waves, and she saw a pair if dolphins, grey backs arcing out of the water. When they were farther out, flying fish came skimming and skipping along the swells. By then she felt mildly seasick, and while she figured it was worth it, she hoped it would end soon.

It did, but not due to her adaptable constitution—rather, because the ship left the water and its waves behind, climbing into the sky.

She had ridden in a hot air balloon before, so that part was weirdly more familiar than the ocean-bound portion of their journey.

They passed through clouds for quite a long time, until ahead of them a massive thunderhead appeared, anvil shaped like most such storms, but more gigantic than any she had ever seen in the world of her birth. As the ship's angle changed she saw there was not one, but two storms, twins, with the narrowest of blue gaps between them. On either side of that sliver of light, the clouds were almost as dark as night except when lightning flared within them, fluorescing the depths of the storms orange and blue-white. It reminded her of the footage she'd seen of an air barrage of London in World War II, with artillery shells filling the sky with terrifying, deadly light.

But there was no thunder, no sound at all except the creaking of the rigging and the voices of the sailors giving each other instruction.

"What is that?" she asked. "Are we really sailing into that?"

"The Cloud Straits," Kostye told her. "It is the only approach to Vilken's demesne. The only easy one, at least."

"If that's the easy way in," Delia said, "I can do without seeing the hard way."

In the end it wasn't as terrifying as it looked. The gap between the storm clouds was bigger than it appeared, and the air there calm. Beyond the straits, the sun was rising over a grey-green sea, and a mountainous archipelago—one large island and at least a dozen more laid out in a curving strand. She felt dislocated; when last she had seen the ocean, it had been very, very far below, and until this moment she had never had any sense that the ship was descending; it had always seemed to be tilted upward, climbing. The waters felt far closer than they ought, as if the world was put together like a wedding cake and they had just sailed from one tier to another. Had the clouds hidden an immense waterfall, thousands of feet high? Or was it something weirder, more arcane? More Jack-and-the-Beanstalk?

The ship put into port near a quaint, mostly-abandoned waterfront town on a small island. As the sun in Kostye's realm was stuck at sunset, here it appeared to be permanently sunrise, the eastern ocean horizon pleasantly layered in rose, canary, and aquamarine.

From the port they went by carriage across a causeway to small, walled city with streets of cobblestone. The buildings were ornate, with domes, spires, and square towers springing asymmetrically from them and lavish, curvilinear decorations between stories and around their many windows that reminded her of vegetation, though they were more abstract than that. She thought it had a European—perhaps German— character, although she had never been to Europe.

In the center of town—in the midst of a great square— stood a castle that reminded her of the illustrations of the Tower of Babel in her children's Bible or a telescope placed with the big end on the ground.

The place might have once been cheerful, but it had a run-down feeling to it. The colors on the facades of the buildings were dirty and dull, but the more than that, almost everything was spattered in bird droppings. This was hardly a surprise, because she had never seen so many birds in one place. In one long glance, she saw everything from parrots and macaws to pigeons and ducks—perching, nesting, hopping, waddling, and excreting on every available surface. Clearly, no one was bothering to clean any of it up.

Vilken himself did not show when they arrived, but a handful of his demon-boys escorted them to their rooms in the lower reaches of the castle. Compared to Kostye's rooms, they were heavy, and dark, with only a single narrow window overlooking rolling green hills and a distant, rocky strand of coast.

"I have something for you," Kostye said, when they were alone.

He dug in to his bags and produced a garment of some sort, or at least the flimsiest excuse for one. It was so sheer that the light from the window passed through it almost unaltered.

"Oh," she said.

She'd worn a negligee on her honeymoon; she'd thought it was pretty and sexy, but Scott had hardly noticed. She'd decided that was a good sign, in a way — he liked her as she was, without any fancy packaging. A few months later, after returning from a trip to New Orleans, he had proudly presented her with "a little something" he'd picked up there. She'd put it on for him, but it didn't make her feel pretty or sexy. It was uncomfortable in every way, but the worst part about it was the way Scott treated her while she was wearing it — as if she was someone else, some-one who would routinely wear something like that. She tried to play along, but when he wanted her to wear it again, he had seen her reluctance.

"But you like lingerie!" he's said, angrily. "You wore some on our wedding night."

She tried to explain the difference, but it only made him angrier.

Now here was another, very different man presenting her with "a little something."

She took it from him. The fabric felt almost like water in her fingers. She was relieved to see that for all of its near-transpar-ency, it was a floor-length robe with a hood.

"It's pretty," she said.

"Try it on."

She hesitated. "Should I . . . ?"

"Yes," he said. "Disrobe first.

She reached for the fastenings of her dress.

"Could you turn around?" she asked.

"I have seen you unclothed," he reminded her.

"Yes," she replied. "But you either undressed me, or — I just find it weird, that's all, sort of like stripping."

He shrugged and turned around. She quickly got herself out of her dress and pulled on the robe.

It wasn't exactly normal. The hood had no opening for her face; it just pulled on, like a hold-up man's stocking mask.

Well, that was a little kinky. She wondered how it would feel to be kissed through it.

"Okay," she said.

He turned, but instead of appreciating the result, he looked past her, toward the back of the room. She turned to see what he was looking at, but there was nothing there but a wall.

"What is it?" she asked.

He smiled, slightly. "Don't you understand?" he asked.

Confused, she looked down to see if she had it on wrong and saw — nothing.

"I'm invisible," she said.

"Indeed," he replied.

A negligee that revealed nothing at all? Her mind had been completely on the wrong track.

"Why am I wearing this?" she asked.

"So that while I'm occupied with Vilken, you can search for Aster."

"Oh," she said. "Okay. I thought — never mind. Should I get started right away?"

"After," he replied. He found her shoulders by feel. She learned what it was like to be kissed through an invisible negligee.

She woke to voices nearby, and after getting her bearings, realized it was Kostye and Vilken talking. They were discussing going someplace; Vilken was saying later would be better, Kostye was insisting now was the best time. Quietly, Delia rolled out of bed.

She realized she had fallen asleep still wearing her "veil" — that was what Kostye called it. The window was dark; when she glanced outside she saw stars, so she'd been wrong about the sun. Could it have been a whole day? Had she slept that long?

After adjusting the veil to make certain she was completely covered, she padded toward the door.

The two men were in a sitting room adjoining the bedroom. Kostye was fully clothed in russet pants ticked into high leather boots, off-white linen shirt, and a long coat that didn't hide the sword he had belted on.

Vilken was bowing as she came out. He didn't look pleased.

"As you wish, sire. We shall journey to see them now."

"That is what I wish," Kostye said. He rose.

"And the Lady Delia?"

"She will not be coming," Kostye said. "These matters are between you and me, and no one else."

"Understood," Vilken said.

With that they both walked out of the room.

Delia froze for a moment, uncertain what to do. Kostye had said he would distract Vilken, and perhaps that was what he was doing. Or maybe he really didn't want her to see whatever he was going to see.

She didn't have long to make her decision, nor did she take long to make it, but followed them through the door and down the stairs, out of the castle and down a road that crossed the island to a landing and a rather large barge with a crew of six young men in Vilken's black livery. Unlike most of his retainers, these looked fully human, with no obvious aberrations. The two men went aboard, and she slipped along behind them. The young men began cranking a capstan, and a large cable pulled up from the water. With a few more turns, they were in motion.

A half-moon washed the sea and land in wan luster, but even competing with its light the stars were brilliant, more vivid than she had ever seen them. The breeze was cool and salty, and reminded her of childhood trips to the Gulf Coast—albeit without the stink of sewage and paper mills.

"Why don't they escape by swimming?" Kostye asked Vilken. "The distance isn't so great."

"The water is quite cold," he said. "One or two essayed the swim, and in so doing created cautionary tales for the others. Besides, where do they have to go? If they reach any of the other islands, they will be found and returned. After that, there is only the sea for league upon league. Besides, as you will see, they are in no discomfort here."

By the time they reached the other side, a small crowd of girls and young women had gathered to meet them. They were of many hues and complexions and dressed in a variety of styles. They were chattering among themselves, and when Kostye stepped off, several of them began tugging at the others to kneel.

"It's him," she heard a few of them whisper. "It's the king."

Neither Kostye nor Vilken paid them much mind. They followed the road toward he interior of the island.

As Delia wove her way through the girls, one of them muttered something under her breath, and another shushed her to silence.

"He can't hear me," the girl retorted.

"I just don't think you should call him that," the second girl said.

"I'll call him Scratch if I want," the first one said. She had short, red hair, and was probably no more than twelve. "I say we try the barge again."

"We've got no weapons," another girl said. "And besides, where would we go?"

"Back there, steal a ship, a real ship, and sail the hell away from here."

Delia had stopped; Kostye and Vilken were now out of sight.

"That's you dreaming again, Copper," a dark-haired young woman said.

"Look, Onyx," Copper said. "How do you think those boys feel? The chancellor has taken every girl in the kingdom. *Their* girls, the way they see it. You're pretty enough. Show 'em a smile, wiggle your hips . . ."

"Those boys know the chancellor will skin them alive if they touch us," Onyx said.

"If you think boys have that much sense when it comes to what's in their pants, you don't know much," Copper said. "One of my brothers near broke a leg trying to peek at Corlean Rye bathing in the creek."

"You always start this," Onyx said. "Why don't *you* wiggle something?"

"I've nothing to wiggle," Copper complained. "Give me another year or two."

"They might farry us," a blond girl said. "They might farry us uphill and down. But they'll never take us off the island."

"That's the point. While they go to farry, and have their pants around their ankles, we clobber 'em."

"With what?" Onyx said. "Come on, you. Let's keep you away from trouble. I want to see what Scratch is up to."

"I thought you said we oughtn't call him that," Copper said.

"I'm two years your elder, so shut your hole," Onyx replied.

With that all of the girls but Copper turned and started walking back up along the path. Copper, however, sat down on a rock and crossed her arms.

"Fine," Onyx called back. "Get yourself farried. Little good it will do anyone."

Copper mumbled something unintelligible and probably vulgar.

Delia glanced back at the barge and saw most of the boys turning away as the older girls disappeared over the bank.

Delia approached Copper and knelt down beside her.

The girl's eyes widened, and she turned with a jerk in her direction—but then her expression of surprise muted to one of relief, followed by puzzlement.

"Copper," Delia whispered.

Copper jumped. "Damn it, ghost, leave me be!" she yelped. "I've got sacks of grief to carry as it is!"

"Stop that!" Delia hissed. "I'm not a ghost, you just can't see me. I'm here to help, if I can. But if the boys know I'm here—"

Copper was reaching a hand toward her, but stopped.

"Yeah, okay," she said, looking away. Delia thought it was a rapid acceptance, even here, where miracles were commonplace. Hopefully that suggested a quick, adaptable mind.

"Let's take a walk, away from the barge."

The girl nodded.

They walked up the path a bit, and over the hill, and Delia saw the town.

Delia wasn't clear on what she had been expecting—some sort of prison or work camp maybe. What she saw was a village. The buildings and cottages had obviously been there for some time, a village like many others before the curse came and sent the adults into whatever form of limbo the Kingdom in question chose. Now it was a girl's town. The younger ones played in the streets and squares, while the older ones went about various tasks. Everything was relatively clean and neat, there were no guards to be seen, and no one she saw was in any form of pain or extremis. Indeed, they all looked healthy, well fed, even.

"What do you eat?" Delia asked.

"We eat good," Copper said. "We've got some little garden patches, but a lot of the food comes on the barge. Wheat, barley, potatoes, cheese—fruit, rock candy, wine. We fish and pick oysters, too." She frowned a little. "I think we're being fattened up, but no one believes me."

"Fattened up for what?"

"All I know is, pretty much every day, one of us gets taken off, and whoever she is, she don't come back. The boys say they've been chosen to go to an even better island. That seems dumb to me. I think he's eating them."

"Who?"

"The chancellor. Maybe Scratch, too. I don't feel like waiting around to find out."

"Why doesn't anyone believe you?"

Copper sighed. "I exaggerate. My brothers say it's one of my faults. Some think the same as I do. The problem is, life is decent here—for some, a lot better than where they come from—and there's a bunch of us, and more every day, so it's easy to figure it won't be you who's taken off, right?"

"I see," Delia said. She saw Kostye and Vilken far up ahead.

"Let's walk on," she said. "I'd like to know where those two are going."

"Sure," Copper said.

"You say some girls like it better here," Delia said.

"Sure. No boys."

"What's wrong with boys?"

"Some are fine," Copper said. "My brothers are good folk. But some, they want to mess with you, you know? Paw and push on you and such. Farry you till you're too sore to walk, if they get a chance. It got like that a lot of places, after the curse came along. Here, there's no problem like that. Sure, some of the girls get bully-like, and some are just plain mean, but they ain't gonna get you with a barny, you know?"

"Pregnant, you mean? Delia said.

Copper nodded solemnly. "That kills some girls, you know. Especially the younger ones." A look of suspicion formed on her young face.

"You're a girl, right?"

"I am," Delia said.

"How'd you get to be a ghost?"

"Like I said, I'm not a ghost," Delia said. "But I—I'm trying to help. But I need to understand some things. And I'm looking for someone. A girl named Aster."

"Oh, yeah, her," Copper said. "With the star on her head, like Gloam and the regent."

"You know Aster?"

"She was in my house. Set on walking right up to Scratch's door and knocking, she was. We told her it was a noddy idea, but she went anyways."

"Where is she now?"

"I haven't seen her," Copper said. "And I think I would have. I come to the dock every time the barge arrives. I like to meet the new ones."

By now they were through the small town, walking on rising ground of worn stone and bristly grasses. Delia feared picking up a sticker or a sandbur in her bare feet, but they apparently either did not have those here, or she was having good luck.

The breeze was cool and the veil didn't do much to warm her. Despite the situation, she felt buoyant, as carefree as she had in a long time, just a girl out for a walk at night in her bedgown. Copper reminded her a lot of Nena, a girl she'd only known for one summer—but it had been a good summer, full of harmless mischief. Mostly harmless. They had both tried cigarettes for the first time, and a little cheap wine stolen from Nena's mother. She often wondered what growing up had done to Nena, but after school started, she never saw her again.

The men walked out into a long spit of land that continued to rise until, at last, the hill crested and the ground dropped off sharply to reveal a vast seascape beyond.

Something gleamed on the horizon. Delia thought it was just another star, but then she saw it was brighter even than the moon, though much smaller. While some stars showed a little color, this light shimmer in peach, coral, brick orange. It had a halo that resembled a flower with many petals or a hand with fingers spread wide, sending rays into the darkness. Its reflection on the water formed a rippling, inconstant path from the cliff to the horizon.

She wanted to ask Copper what it was but didn't want to risk the sound. The men were too close. They were conversing in low tones, but she couldn't make out any of the words.

Then Vilken lifted something in front of him; something small, and spherical, that shone in the night.

Kostye took a step forward, but Vilken said something, too low for her to hear. Kostye stopped, dropped his head and bowed his shoulders. He reminded her of a pit bull who had been scolded. The power, the danger was still there—but momentarily leashed. Useless.

In the distance, the strange star faded and vanished.

Kostye and Vilken turned and walked back the way they had come. In the faint light, she saw a sheen on Kostye's face and realized that—as impossible as it seemed—he had been crying.

Once the men were far enough away, she asked Copper what the light was. The girl shrugged and said she didn't know, but it was pretty. It was the first time she had seen it.

Kostye and Vilken were doubtless headed back toward the barge; if she didn't hurry she would be stranded here.

"I must go," Delia told Copper. "Take care of yourself, and I'll do what I can. But it's best you don't tell anyone about me."

"I won't," Copper said. "They wouldn't believe me, anyway."

She reached over and touched Delia and laughed softly.

"You *are* real," she said. Then, groping a little, she gave Delia a hug. She was little and wiry, and it felt both awkward and nice.

"You be careful," Copper said.

"I will," Delia replied.

As Delia followed the men back onto the barge, she was already beginning to doubt that Kostye had been crying. A trick of the light and her own feelings — desires? Were probably to blame.

Or maybe fear. It was terrifying to think what might make that man weep.

Soon they were once again crossing the space between the islands.

For most of the voyage, the men were quiet, but as they neared the shore of the big island, Vilken broke the silence.

"There is the matter of the woman, Delia," he said.

"She is my amusement," Kostye replied. "She knows nothing."

"I would prefer to be very certain of that," Vilken said.

"She's harmless."

"I disagree."

Kostye's face had gone red, and she saw him tremble with what appeared to be rage. She thought he was on the verge of attacking the chancellor.

But instead he looked out at the horizon.

"Very well," he said.

FIVE
A FRIEND RETURNS

V eronica and Shandor watched the war from a distance. It was twilight and had been for some time. A few days of travel and several of Shandor's "shortcuts" had brought them back to the Kingdoms where the days and seasons had become stuck. Here, it was nearly dark, but the weather was warm and muggy, like a hot August night. Lightning bugs rose from the grass around them, as off across a bay or inlet, brighter sparks flashed, followed by a low rumble like thunder.

"So that's what cannon sound like," she said.

"It is more fearsome when you are near," Shandor said.

The fight was between a town on a little spit of land and three ships very much like the ones that had taken Aster and Dusk—and flying the same flag—a simple crescent moon on a dark blue field.

"I think this will be over, soon," she said.

"Why do you say that?" Shandor asked. "They look well-matched. The city walls are high, and strong."

"Sure," Veronica said. "But see?"

Something big was rising up against the faintly violet sky, something with wings like a bat.

"I guess he has more than one of those," she said. As she said it, flame spewed from the dragon's maw onto the parapets of the city wall. They were too far away to see much more, but as with the cannon, Veronica guessed things were probably much worse up close, right now.

They kept watching until things finally grew quiet. The dragon was no longer in evidence, and the ships stopped firing their guns.

Veronica stood up.

"I think it's time," she said.

Shandor cultivated a sense of calm and acceptance, but Veronica began to see the cracks in that on the ride to the city.

"My horses cannot cross waves," Shandor said. "But you can. I sense it in you."

"Can you?"

"You are mistress of the depths," he said.

"You make it sound kind of naughty," she said, "But yes, I could swim after them, if I thought that would work. The only trouble is, the ship that took Aster and Dusk could fly — and I definitely can't follow them in the air. Can you?"

"No," he said.

"So this is what I've chosen," she said.

"I would like to formally disagree with your choice," Shandor said.

"You can wear a tuxedo, for all I care," Veronica replied. "It won't change anything."

"You are strong-headed," he said.

"A goddess, I believe you called me," she replied. "When you made your marriage proposal, did you think I was just going to hang laundry or whatever? Is there a goddess of clothespins?"

"Whether you marry me or not, it is my wish you be what you are," he said. "But I am due an opinion, I believe. You can correct me if I'm wrong."

She regarded him for a moment. "Yes," she said. "You are due an opinion. And if you can tell me a better way to get to Raggedy Man, I'll listen."

He nodded. "That's the trouble," he said. "I can think of no better plan."

They were almost at the town. Fires were still burning, but it was mostly smoke, now. From inside, she heard a near constant babble of voices, screams, and moans.

"So you had better stay here," she said. "You've been a big help. But I'm on my own from here on out."

"I can accompany you."

"There isn't any point," she said. "They won't hurt me, but if you go in it could start a fight. A fight will call way more attention to me than I want. Or the wrong kind, anyway."

"Understood," he said. He sighed, then took her hand. "Do not fear your power, Veronica. If you are threatened, if you fear for your life, unleash it. But do not be overconfident. This thing that was the Sheriff — I have never felt power like that. Whatever he is, he is very old, and from very high and faraway. If you are pressed, retreat to the Marches. I will be there, waiting."

She squeezed his hand.

"Thanks," she said.

He raised her hand and kissed it. She felt a little jolt run up her arm, and for a moment she wondered what it would be like to kiss those pretty lips of his.

So she did.

It wasn't long, the kiss, but she felt it all the way down to her knees. When she pulled away, she felt a little guilty, but she thought she could hardly be blamed for being curious. And now she knew a few things about Shandor that she had not before, at least for certain.

Anyway, where she was going, there wouldn't be any more kissing, and odds were she wouldn't be kissing anyone else ever again. If she did survive, she still had that year of service to old what's-her-name in the well. Best not think too much about romance for the time being, and concentrate on doing what she could to end one or two people who needed it.

There were a bunch of semi-human goons at the gate. The Sheriff had bent his followers to suit his needs, and apparently the Raggedy Man was doing something similar, although the results appeared a little less—purposeful. The Sheriff had cultivated loyal hounds; the Raggedy Man's hangers-on were more a random mishmash of human and beast. Some had ape-like features and long arms, some were more bat-like, others had scales like lizards or fish. Two of them were half possum, which wasn't a good look for anyone.

Whatever they looked like, they acted like boys. They were armed with swords and spears, but two of them also had old-fashioned looking guns.

Since they were posted there to keep people from escaping the village, they didn't notice her until she was close. Then they got all excited.

"Hey, how did you get out there?" one of them said.

"I'm coming back from my cousin's house in the country," she said. "What's going on?"

Another, a crouching boy with rodent-like features, gave her a gap-toothed grin.

"You're going on a trip, is what," he said. "Don't fight and you won't get hurt."

She looked at the smoldering ruins of the town. "Wherever

we're headed, it's probably nicer than this," she said. "Besides, fighting is not my style, boys."

Despite her words, she had an abrupt urge to do just that. Escaping this handful wouldn't be a problem, and with the water so near she could easily evade pursuit. She remembered when the Sheriff's boys had caught her. They had almost raped her, and when they got her to the sheriff, things went even worse for her.

But that was then, in a high desert. This was now, a few feet from the sea. If anyone tried something nasty, they would be sorry, at least until they couldn't feel anything at all. No, this was the best way to get where she needed to be.

She went with them onto one of the ships, where they put her in irons below decks. Veronica could feel the sea all around her, and if she closed her eyes, it was almost as if she was in it, among the sharks and jellyfish, and not chained in a dark, uncomfortable place.

Soon enough, however, her earlier fears were vindicated, for the ship left the sea and rose into the sky — taking her far from the comforting, profound waters below.

B illy blinked at Errol.
    "Billy?" Billy said. His face was blank of emotion, and his pupils were so large they nearly eclipsed the rest of his eyes.

"No, you're Billy. I'm Errol. Remember?"

Billy shook his head, slowly, as if to clear it.

"I felt," he said. "I heard . . ." He looked around. "Saw her last around here . . ."

Errol saw a movement from the corner of his eye, a white shape through the undergrowth.

"Hey, Billy," he said. "We're kind of in trouble, here. Some guys are trying to kill us. Can you run?"

Billy stared at him, and his pupils shrank some.

"Little," he said.

"Yeah. You're little. So they aren't scared of you, right?"

Billy kept looking at him like he was speaking Zulu or something, but now he knew the fish guys were back.

"Come on!" he said. He grabbed Billy's hand and started running. Billy resisted for a second, then acquiesced. After a few strides, he was running faster than Errol, pulling *him* along.

An arrow zipped by, way too close for comfort. More followed. Errol was having a hard time keeping his feet under him. Billy was *strong*.

They had first met Billy in a village in the Marches. He was the adopted son on an old woman named Hattie, and no one knew where he'd come from. He traveled and fought with them until they crossed the Hollow Sea to the Mountains of the Winds, and there they'd had to fight a giant. It was a fight they would have lost if it hadn't turned out Billy was a giant too, a giant who had decided to take a little break from being a giant and ended up with amnesia.

He and Aster had sort of developed a thing. He wasn't sure how serious it was, or how far things went, but he knew Billy felt strongly about her. To save them and get them home, he'd become a giant again, and stayed that way too long—so long that he forgot about the little people he was carrying and their tiny, mortal affairs. Errol hadn't been around then, but apparently Billy the giant had struck out for the places giants liked, which were very far from everyone and everything. According to Billy himself, once he was in that state, he wasn't likely to ever give another thought to any of them, even a girl he had done a bit of making out with.

Yet here he was.

An arrow hit him in the joint of his shoulder plate and upper arm, and he felt a bright sting where the tip buried itself.

"Billy —" he started.

Billy jerked them through a canebrake, and after a minute, Errol realized something felt weird. In another moment he understood what it was — they were going uphill. After all that time in the swamps, he had almost forgotten there were such things as hills. Now they were chugging up one, through mountain laurel and hickory, steeper and steeper until the leaf litter and dirt gave way to slate. From then on they were climbing upward at a sharp angle.

Billy had long ago let go of his hand. It was all Errol could do to keep up with him. He seemed to have all but forgotten Errol existed.

Errol had been avoiding looking behind him. When he did, and saw how high they were, he felt a touch of vertigo. The swamps were a hazy green stain in the distance.

"Hold up!" Errol shouted. "I don't think they're chasing us anymore."

If Billy heard, he gave no sign. He kept clawing his way up the glossy grey stone.

"Billy!"

Then he did stop, and so did Errol as they came to the top of a ridge running off to the right and left in a series of peaks so tall they vanished into the sky. Errol spent a few seconds teetering on the edge of what he conservatively guessed to be a seven-hundred-mile drop.

Billy was standing still, staring off into space, his chest heaving.

"Billy!" Errol said. "What the hell?"

Billy considered the drop below them for a moment before reluctantly turning left and running along the ridge.

"Billy!"

"Aster!" Billy shouted. He ran even faster.

Chest aching, Errol tried to keep up.

I n human form, Billy was prone to the same weaknesses and feelings as your run-of-the-mill guy, so eventually he wore out, first leaning against a spire of rock and then slowly folding to the stone below his feet. He looked confused.

"You're exhausted, Billy," Errol said. "Take a rest."

He leaned on the stone and slid down next to the giant.

It felt like they had been going forever. The sun moved in the sky here, but Errol suspected the day was going on much longer than usual.

The view was spectacular. His experience with mountains was limited. A few vacations in the Smokies and his last trips to the Kingdoms pretty much summed it up. But in his earlier trips here, he had either flown over mountains or been walked through them by a giant. It hadn't been like this.

He had seen pictures of the Rocky Mountains. Relatively young, steep—sharp, for lack of a better term. These peaks were more like the Appalachian range with which he was familiar— old, worn, slump-shouldered mountains. Except that when they were young, they must have gone all the way to the moon, because they were still very tall. Most of those he could see the peaks of had "balds," where their rocky skeletons showed through coats of soil and vegetation. Some of those were really fantastic—twisty spires of stone more fanciful than real. Here? Who knew? They might be the remains of ancient castles or dragon nests or something far crazier.

Some—in the distance—were tall enough they were capped in snow.

And the valleys—deep and green and lovely, all around. It was a nice place to sit and catch a breath.

It seemed impossible now that he had ever wanted to kill himself. Even if he had never learned of the Kingdoms, he knew there were sights equal to this in his own world: vast continents, amazing cities, people worth knowing, liking, loving. How had he ever let things get so small? It was like his entire world had shrunk around him and become an overcoat of pain he wore. He'd come to believe there was nothing beyond it, nothing out in the vast world to wake his wonder, bring him joy, lure him toward greater things.

Even then he'd had second thoughts, but they came too late. Without Aster it would have all ended. He would never have seen this or the Hollow Sea or any of a thousand places and things that had made him more, lifted him higher.

"Errol?"

Billy was looking at him.

"Hey," he said. "You remember me."

Billy slowly shook his head. His eyes looked nearly normal.

"It takes time," he said. "Giants live a long time. But we live—slowly. And we don't feel little things. So sometimes we become little, like this, just for a while, so we can . . ."

"I remember you told us that before," Errol said.

"Yes," Billy said. "Before."

"But I also thought you said you would forget us."

Billy nodded. "Thought I would," he said. "Like I said, we forget the little things. Cool water, a breeze, the taste of food, pleasure . . ." he stopped for a moment, and his brow wrinkled.

"So?" Errol said.

He reached over and took Errol's hand.

"Turns out," he said. "Love isn't a little thing."

Errol felt a small catch in his throat.

"Love?" he said.

Billy nodded. "I didn't know what it was, I guess. But I love you and Veronica. Mostly though, I love Aster."

"Yeah," Errol said. "I figured."

He thought about releasing his hand, but Billy was still holding tight. Billy didn't know it was weird, and no one was watching. Hell, why couldn't he hold Billy's hand? He'd held his dad's hand. He'd loved it, the hard feel of that calloused palm.

Sometime before middle school, he'd started shaking it off. It wouldn't look right to his friends. But if he knew then what he knew now, he would take his Dad's hand and hold it as long and as hard as he was able.

"Are you hurt?" Billy asked.

"What?" he said. Then he realized he was crying. "No," he said. "I'm fine. How did you find me?"

"Aster found me, somehow, in my head. She was in trouble. I tried to help her, but she was so far away, and she wasn't calling hard enough. I got my hand through for a moment—then she was gone. But it made me remember. So I went back to the place where I left her last, and she wasn't there, but I felt you were nearby. I looked for you. And found you."

"You sure did," Errol said. "Just in time. But where are you headed now?"

"The place she was—the place where I put my hand. Now that I'm like this, I think I can find it. He pointed off through the mountains. Then he started to get up.

"Whoa," Errol said. "You're human again, remember. I have a little food we can split, After that we need some sleep. I want to find her, too, but we won't be able to help her if we kill ourselves."

"Okay," Billy said. "It's only—she's in trouble."

"I know," Errol said. "I know she is."

"We won't get there in time like this."

"What choice do we have?"

"I can become a giant again," he said. "For little while, if you can keep me from forgetting."

"What if it's too long?" Errol asked.

"It won't be," Billy said. "It can't be."

"Look, I'm up for it," Errol said. "I'm lost in this place."

"I'm always lost," Billy said. "Except when I'm with her."

"Okay, don't get ridiculous," Errol said. "Girls don't like guys who are *too* sappy."

"I'm not a tree," Billy said. "I don't have sap."

"That's not what I meant—" Errol began, but then he saw the little smile on Billy's face.

"Kidding," Billy said. "I remember jokes, now."

He stood up slowly.

"Are you sure about this?" Errol said.

But Billy was already growing taller, pulling him along for the ride.

S omething hit the ship hard. Veronica saw the timbers flex and as her teeth snapped together. Some of the other girls in the hold with her screamed, but many were so worn down into apathy they hardly reacted.

"What's happening?" Someone yelped.

The ship shuddered again, and this time she heard explosions above her, all strung together like a chain.

A girl with dirty brown hair and freckles raised her head.

"We're fighting again," she said. "Probably to get more girls."

"It's already full in here!" Another girl said, her voice near breaking with hysteria. "We'll suffocate!"

The next shock was a big one, tilting the ship a few inches. Veronica heard swearing above decks.

She guessed the freckled girl was probably right about them fighting. It put her in a funny situation. She didn't want any more girls in the hold, because it looked as full as it could get without stacking people on top of each other, which would probably be fatal for some, which the Raggedy Man wouldn't like. What she didn't want was for the ship to lose the fight, because that meant she would get no closer to him. If she tried to get loose and interfere, that could spoil things, too.

It was probably best to sit tight.

The cannon on both sides kept firing until there was a titanic grating noise, and the deck tilted again, this time sharply enough that a lot of the girls went rolling or flopping toward the side.

"That's another ship grappling us," Freckles said. "I think we're being boarded."

She looked toward the ladder up to the hatch, and saw the handful of boys guarding them were gone, presumably to the deck.

It wasn't exactly quiet, after that. They heard cries and screams above, but the hatch between them and freedom made them sound very far away.

Veronica turned to Freckles, who seemed to know the most about what was going on.

"Who do we think it is?" she asked.

"God knows," Freckles said. "If we're lucky, it's some ship meant to liberate us. But it could just as well be pirates."

From what Veronica could tell, they were still far above the water, so her most useful qualities were denied her. She was sure she could wile a pirate or a guardsman into releasing her, as she had done the boy in the Mountain of the Winds.

She would wait, though. No one here knew her, and if possible she wanted it to stay that way. If her plan to find the Raggedy Man this way was derailed, then that was how the cookie crumbled. At least she was probably closer to her goal.

The sounds of fighting finally subsided. A few moments later the hatch opened. The girls nearest it raised their arms and cheered.

Veronica, feigning disinterest, waited to see who they were so glad to see, wondering if she would share their sentiment.

Her heart was beating fine, these days, but almost stopped when she saw it was Dusk.

"Well, crap," she said, under her breath. She scooted back farther into the shadows, as Dusk started giving a speech about how they were being liberated, how she would set them ashore if they wished, but if anyone wanted to stay and fight, to rescue more girls bound for a horrible fate, she would welcome them to her cause. As she spoke other girls came down, armed with swords and pistols and what-have-you and began freeing everyone from their shackles and chains.

She turned her head. If someone freed her before Dusk recognized her, she had a chance. Otherwise, she had a feeling she had another decapitation coming on, and the first one hadn't been one little bit of fun.

She had to wait a long time before someone got to her. Her rescuer was older, eighteen or nineteen, broad-shouldered, with a fresh cut under her grey eyes.

"Stop. Rain, stop."

Veronica rolled her eyes. The key was in the lock, but now the girl withdrew it.

"Veronica?"

She tossed her hair back and looked up with a pseudo-smile. "See," she said. "I thought this was an exclusive cruise."

"Bring her to my cabin," Dusk said. "Keep her chained."

PART FOUR

HIDDEN HEARTS

ONE
SPIT-SHAKE

W hen the barge reached the shore, Delia considered fleeing. She could probably sneak onto an outbound ship,
steal food to survive until they reached a mainland and then . . .

Go where? Do what?

Something, an inner voice said. Anything was better hanging
around a man who she'd just heard promise to kill her. She had
always sworn she wouldn't be *that* woman, the one the police
found dead after a domestic dispute because she fooled herself into thinking he didn't mean it or she could change him or
whatever. In retrospect, she knew she had taken plenty of abuse
from Scott, but none of it had been physical. If he'd ever laid a
hand on her — or even drawn it back — that would have been it.

Or so she told herself. She had never been tested before.
Until now.

What did she have with Kostye? Sex, but nothing else that
she could be sure of. He hadn't promised or even hinted at anything deep or long-lasting. She didn't think he was in love with
her — he seemed to like her, but that was easy to fake for as short
a time as they had been together. She knew he was amoral and
at times quite ruthless.

But she didn't think he would kill her.

But then again, neither did most of the women whose husbands and boyfriends sent them to the morgue.

In this case, it was clear that killing her was not his idea. That had come from Vilken. Kostye was strong and arrogant and did not like being told what to do. Even if she was merely an amusement, as he'd said, it was hard to imagine him giving her up against his will. He had come here ostensibly to get to the bottom of things, and all of a sudden he was acting like Vilken was in charge. What had changed? Was it the light? What did it mean to him? Or was it the little sphere?

No. She wasn't going to run. She followed them back to the castle, and Kostye back to his rooms once the two men parted.

She watched him sit on the bed and clasp his hands together between his knees.

"I don't know if you're in here," he said, not looking up. "I don't want to know, so if you are present, do not speak. You are no longer under my protection. Do what you must to make yourself safe. Keep the veil—it is your only defense now."

She wanted to speak, to ask what was wrong, how she could help, but there was a certitude in his voice that warned her against it.

What had Vilken done or said to him. Did it involve Aster? Had his memory been restored?

He'd left the door open. She crept out quietly. She would search the castle. If she found Aster, maybe it would change things, and maybe it wouldn't—but it was something to do.

D usk faced Veronica across the small table. She still wore her sword but hadn't drawn it.

"You're a pirate queen, now?" Veronica asked.

"I'm no such thing," Dusk said. "These lasses and I captured one of the chancellor's ships. Since then we've made prize of two more. You know something, I assume, of the events of the world?"

"Something," Veronica said. "But I don't like to gossip."

"You know the man—the thing, really—that killed you, made you a *nov*. He survived. This was his ship before I acquired it."

"He's not the only one who killed me," Veronica said. "Or tried to."

Dusk nodded. "I don't blame you for being angry with me."

"That's awfully sweet," Veronica said.

"We were allies," Dusk said. "Companions. Sisters in arms. The four of us—you, Errol, Aster, me—we worked well together. I betrayed you. I don't ask forgiveness for that, but I will admit that I regret it. I understand one day you will want satisfaction from me. I do not flinch from that either. But right now I need you. Aster needs you. And Errol . . ."

"Holy crap," Veronica said. "Are you crying?"

"I have some bad news about Errol," she said.

"You mean the fight with the big bad dragon?"

Her eyes widened. "You know of it?"

"Yes. I was there. You can stop the crocodile tears. Errol is fine. I saw to that."

Veronica wasn't sure she fully understood the look that went across Dusk's face, and she wasn't sure she wanted to.

"Is this true? He lives?"

"As far as I know. I took him back to the Pale, so you can't get him into any more trouble."

"You're aware, then, of our travails?"

"The glass pyramid and all that? I think I'm up to speed."

"Yet you are here, without him." Her eyes narrowed. "You let Vilken's divlings take you captive, didn't you? You arranged it."

"That's a gold star for you," Veronica said. "Or another one, I guess. You know, 'cause you have one on your head. If you

think I have a score to settle with you, you can imagine what I
have planned for *him*."

"Then we do have common cause," Dusk said. "Aster is
his captive. Together we liberated this ship, but she was taken.
I intend to rescue her. I intend to slay the chancellor and put
whatever plans he has to wreck. Will you delay your revenge
on me long enough to help me with those things? Help me set
things right?"

"And if I say yes, you'll trust me? Trust the word of a dirty
nov?"

Dusk bowed her head. "If you give me your word, I will
take it."

"Fine," Veronica said. "I won't do anything nasty to you
until Aster is free and the chancellor is dead. But you have to
make me the same promise."

"And you would trust me? After what I did?"

"Sure," she said. "After that, you've got no place to go but
up, right?"

Dusk grinned wryly. "Well said."

"Shall we spit-shake on it?" Veronica asked.

"I don't know what you mean by that," Dusk said.

Veronica showed her. Dusk looked appropriately disgusted.

"Now what?" Veronica said.

"His demesne lies through the Cloud Straits," she said.
"Any ship approaching his stronghold must pass through them.
That has benefited me up until now—I've been able to capture
his ships as they approach. This is the fourth."

"You've got a regular fleet."

"Aster's father supplies Vilken with ships and sailors. He
has at least fifty more. I fear if we sail through the straits, he will
spring a trap on us."

"What is the plan?"

"My hope was that word of my resistance would spread, and that my brothers and sisters would join me in the fight. I have begun to despair of that. But you bring me new hope."

"How is that?"

Dusk didn't answer right away. Instead she withdrew a key from her pocket, bent down and released Veronica from her shackles.

"Come above with me, if you please," she said.

The crew stared at her as she came up into the light. They were chiefly girls, but it looked to her like at least a quarter of them were male.

The ship was high in the air and nearby, Veronica saw the other three ships Dusk had spoken of. Clouds surrounded them, and a glance over the rail showed only clouds below, fluffy and white.

Up ahead, however, were clouds that were neither fluffy nor white. There were almost black, except when lit from within by wriggling blue-white snakes of lightning, when they incandesced in strange shades of red.

"The Cloud Straits lie there," Dusk said. "As you can see, they are aptly named – they must be approached from the air. The sea is far too dangerous – a maze of reefs and seamounts which would be perilous enough, but there are also sea serpents of particularly ill-temper that dwell in those waters. But you, with your gifts – you might be able to find us a way through."

"Come around from the back, huh?" Veronica said. "Well, I can try. When do we start?"

"We have a bit of mending to do, after this last fight, and we must set our captives ashore someplace. Then we should proceed with all speed."

"We probably should proceed with all speed right now," Veronica said.

Dusk frowned, and followed her gaze, but the lookout in the crow's nest was already shouting. In the distance, the storm clouds flared with lightning, outlining a number of shadows in the shapes of ships—and at least two with big bat-wings.

"I don't think he's waiting for you to sail into a trap," Veronica said. "I think you already have."

With at least eight ships and two dragons encircling them, there was no question they should stay for the fight. Dusk wasted no time in ordering the retreat. In moments their ships were diving down through the clouds in a fashion Veronica thought of as very un-ship-like. At times they dropped so quickly her belly went funny.

She remembered lying on her back as a little girl, watching jet planes etch white trails though the sky, looking forward to the day that she was grown and could ride in one herself. She wondered if this was anything like being on a plane.

They broke through a final layer of cloud and the sea appeared, spackled with gold from the morning sun.

And more ships waiting for them. Dusk swore as the guns on the nearest thundered from only a few hundred feet away. She could actually see the balls coming, as if in slow motion, but it took far less than an eyeblink for them to arrive. The impact quaked through the wood of the ship and into her bones.

They returned fire even as the ship groaned into a sharp turn; Veronica smelled burning wood.

The whole left side of the sky flared yellow-white. Veronica snapped her eyes shut, but the light had already burned red streaks and blobs into her retinas.

When she opened them again she saw the dark coils and snaky body soaring back up into the clouds. One of Dusk's ships was burning. The sails were like torches, and she saw little figures, like insects with yellow wings fluttering downward toward the sea, trying in vain to fly.

The ship careened through another turn, dipping nearer the swells below. Above, the dragon burst back through the clouds.

"Take us lower," Veronica said. "Take us to the water."

"We'll be caught if we go that low," Dusk said. "We won't be able to maneuver."

The dragon belched once more on the burning ship, and this time the timbers caught.

"Looks like Raggedy Man isn't afraid to lose a few girls this time," Veronica said. "That's going to be us in about three minutes. Take us to the water."

Dusk barked a few orders at the girl at the helm, then at those working the sails. Booms swung; sheets snapped in the wind; the nose of the ship swung downward, so Veronica had to grab onto the rail. She looked up and saw the great beast making another turn, and more ships were coming through the clouds, the flare of their guns appearing as distant sparks.

The whole ship shuddered as it slammed into the water.

She closed her eyes again; the red stain of the dragon's fire remained, but now she sensed the life around her, the salt and the spray, the sleeping might of the deeps.

She leapt overboard, and the sea rose up to welcome her.

All her bones shattered; her skin scalded, blistered and split as the water boiled furiously around her. Agony was everything, and all her purpose was briefly forgotten. But as swiftly as the pain arrived it faded, replaced by a giddy elation. She surged upward, rising up in her cloak of spume. The dragon was there, almost too high.

Almost, but not quite.

The impact shocked through her, but ordinary human feeling was distant now. She felt the light of a thousand little lives wink out—slippery, swift, silvery lives—but that was her skin, not her core, her organs, her being. That was far too deep for a dragon to harm.

She wrapped the dragon up and pulled him beneath the waves. His strength was immense and ancient; a billow of flame erupted, burning even in the depths, but she held him tightly, as she had held all of those men who came willingly her to grasp, sinking toward the bottom, fathoms distant. Still he fought, the fire in him shining through like nothing she had ever seen. She felt her own strength ebbing, a balance point approaching as they both weakened. She sensed the hammer and anvil of his heart, the furnace began to falter, but by then she was starting to come apart, her mind breaking into flitting, flashing fragments seeking safety in the dark waters, trying to school away from her in to the shallows, the labyrinth of the nearby reefs.

Then something took hold of her and pulled, and she no longer had the strength to struggle.

L ight and shadow poured through her eyes, but it meant no more than the babble of voices around her, not until she began to remember, until her bones set back the way they had been and blood replaced the seawater.

She realized someone was holding her, someone familiar.

"Errol?" She murmured. How was it possible?.

"Never leave me again," he said. "Never."

"I won't," she agreed, although she knew she was lying. But she was dizzy, open, her defenses down. She'd resigned herself to never seeing him again, never feeling his embrace, but here he was. She pulled herself up on the wet deck, just in time to see a giant whose head was almost literally in the clouds snatch a ship from the air and hurl it down, as if he was a child and the sea a bathtub.

She had seen a giant before. It had coarse, simple features without anything resembling human expression. And yet she knew who it was.

"Billy," she said.

"Yep," he replied.

B illy had knocked a lot of the ships down before shrinking to human size again, but not all of them, so they fled.

Veronica led Dusk's three remaining ships through a maze of reefs, beneath thunderheads so low their tallest masts were nearly in them. After a few hours, she found them harbor at a small island where they weighed anchor.

As far as they could tell, none of Vilken's surviving ships had followed them. Flying was impossible in or beneath the oppressive, lightning-filled clouds, and the shallow seas were deadly to anyone who did not know or could not magically navigate them as his girlfriend could.

Billy was human sized again, and clothes had been found for him. Veronica had also dressed; whatever she had been doing in the water had apparently been rough on her garments. Now she wore grey sailor pants that came right below her knees and a pale blue shirt way too big for her, belted at the waist. Dusk had greeted Errol with a brief clasping of arms, and been busy since, but now that things were a little calmer, his unease grew.

He began trying to catch up with what was going on.

It wasn't easy, not with both of them there. Dusk looked more tired and worn than he had ever seen her. Veronica was – different. When Billy had first pulled her from the water, she hadn't been human, exactly, although even now his mind had difficulty trying to picture accurately what she had been. Even now, her skin had a blue-green tint to it, although that was fading. She clung to him; physically she was very near. But he felt a distance like he hadn't since they had first met. Some part of her felt very far away — a little like Billy, who was still settling back into his smaller shape.

Eventually he would ask her what she had done, what she had become, or whatever. But in private.

The good news, he guessed, was that when he and Billy showed up, the two women hadn't been trying to kill each other — but that was possibly because they had been too busy fighting flying ships and dragons.

He wondered how much chance they'd had for conversation, and what they might have shared.

He listened as Dusk laid it out. Aster's capture, her own escape, her plan to rescue Aster. But something about her determination didn't sit right.

"Why?" he asked. "I mean, I'm all for rescuing Aster. But why do you care so much?"

Dusk sighed and nodded. "Because she is necessary. Without her we cannot end the curse."

"Why didn't you go after her, then?" he asked. "Why kidnap me?"

"I didn't dare," Dusk replied. "If I had come against her — or Veronica — in the Reign of the Departed — either would have easily defeated me. I did not go into this blindly, Errol — I had information. You, also, are key and I think you know that by now. All of you are. I knew that if I brought you here, they would follow."

"And here we are," Veronica said.

"Aster," Billy said.

"Yeah," Errol said, putting his hand on the giant's shoulder. "We got this far. We'll find her."

Dusk nodded out at the sea. "If there's a way, it's out there. Veronica?"

She'd just finished speaking when something fluttered down from the sky and landed on the bowsprit.

Errol saw that it was a swan.

"I think we're in," Veronica said. "I may have to chat with a sea serpent or two, but yes."

They spent a day making repairs. Veronica, worn out, slept. Dusk was apparently avoiding him, so he sloshed ashore to answer a question he'd been dreading finding the answer to.

He found a pool of clear, fresh water fed by a stream coming down from the mountains, and there he tried to strip off his armor so he could bath.

As he feared, it wouldn't come off. It was fastened to his skin as if glued there.

He was alone, so he let his anger out, screaming at the sky, slamming himself into trees, punching the stone cliffside. Why was this the choice? To either be normal and helpless or strong and a freak? Was he never going to be free of what he had done, of trying to take his own life? Was this his punishment, for now until the end of time, to live inside a suit of armor?

But he'd known what he was doing, that there was probably no going back. If it meant his friends didn't have to take pity on him, exclude him for fear he would get hurt, it was worth it, at least for now. And maybe, someday, after this was all over, Aster or someone could figure out a way to get him out of the wood and metal that were again so much a part of him.

Meanwhile, he would suck it up.

So he bathed with the armor on, went back to the ship, and waited for it to get underway. If he was stuck in the armor, he was ready to use it.

He was ready to fight.

TWO

HIDDEN

T here had been times when Delia wished she was invisible. She had majored in psychology long enough to recognize that impulse in herself, along with the contradictory urge to be noticed and admired. She had once called it the "Look at me! Don't look at me!" syndrome.

After a few days of the actual thing, though, she was tired of invisibility. Part of that was the constant fear of being discovered. She wasn't silent, after all, and just as Copper had seemed to see her from the corner of her eye, several of the guards had somehow noticed her briefly. There was also the matter of getting food without being discovered, taking care of the business that eating and drinking inevitably led to — worst of all, finding someplace to sleep where no one could possibly trip over her. If you had a rat in your house, it was usually evident even if you never saw that rat itself — and she was much bigger than a rat.

Fortunately, the castle was also much bigger than an ordinary house. And had rats.

It took her a few days to search most of the building, narrowing her hunt down to a few rooms that were locked. These she had to stake out, waiting for someone to come and unlock them before she could see what was inside. In so doing, she discovered a small treasury, an apparently special wine cellar, and an empty room where one of the handful of female servants met to make out with one of the more human-looking guards.

Eventually, she found Aster, in a room near the top of the castle. Almost no one went beyond the fourth or fifth floor due to the climb, except for the soldiers who manned the watch from up there. But one day Vilken passed her on the sixth floor, and she followed him. He unlocked a door and entered the room where he was keeping Aster.

It wasn't large; it didn't have to be. She lay asleep in a small bed, and didn't stir when he came in. Delia watched with growing disgust as he fondled her unconscious body and murmured to her all of the things he planned to do to her once Kostye's spell was completely removed. He opened her mouth and poured a yellow liquid in. He made sure she swallowed it all, wiped her lips clean with a small rag, and kissed them. Not a little peck or a nip, but a long, lingering kiss that ended with what might have been a playful little bite if it weren't part of a pervert's assault on a drugged, sleeping girl. He kissed her neck, too, and her breast, before rising with what was clearly great reluctance.

She watched all of this from the threshold, trying not to vomit. The room was so small she feared he would notice her if she went in.

Finally, he left, closing the door behind him. She followed him down at a discreet distance, hoping to see where he put the keys, but he vanished into his room with them, locking his door behind him.

She kept careful watch after that, and the next time he went up, she did slip into the room, practically holding her breath the whole time he was there. When he left, he locked her in, as she knew he would, and she spent the next several hours trying to wake Aster—but whatever it was he gave her, it kept her asleep, and her breathing so shallow that at times Delia feared she was dead.

She woke after a brief nap, feeling something was wrong, or different, and turning, found herself nearly face-to-face with a swan perched in the narrow window. It stared at her for what seemed a long time before taking wing and gliding off toward a nearby river.

When next Vilken came, she slipped out quickly, dizzy from thirst. For the next few days she checked on the room often, hoping against hope he would leave the door unlocked.

Then, as she was lying nearby, drifting in and out of sleep, she heard something that sounded like deep drumbeats in the distance. Her weary, sleep-deprived mind took her back to a performance of the *1812 Overture* she'd once heard, with its symphonic bombast and actual cannon fire thrown in for good measure.

That's when she realized what she heard *was* cannon fire, up near the roof. Shaking off the cobwebs, she made her way up the steps.

She emerged to clouds of smoke and the smell of black powder. She was now on top of the tower of Babel, the small end of the telescope. A low wall edged the circular roof.

Divling bodies were strewn upon the stone platform, some wounded and some clearly far beyond that. Down below, she heard a clamor of alarm—horns blowing, bells ringing, cannon firing.

A ship was drawn up to the fortress wall, and as she watched, a gangplank thudded onto the castle roof and sailors began streaming down it. They were mostly girls. With a start she realized their leader was familiar—Dusk, the young woman who had dragged her along with Kostye into this bizarre land.

With her was another girl, and young man in odd-looking armor. His visor was up. He looked familiar.

After strafing the roof a couple of times with cannon fire, they invaded. Errol followed Dusk down the gangplank, trying to ignore the mess their guns had made of the boys standing guard. He hadn't fired any of the cannon himself, but he was complicit. His vow to not kill anyone was broken, at least in spirit. He pushed that down; the eggs were broken, and they couldn't be put back together. And besides, the enemy had no compunction about killing Dusk's girls. He couldn't put his feelings over their lives.

He waited impatiently as Dusk made certain the roof was secure, that the survivors were disarmed and helpless.

Veronica's back way into Vilken's demesne had been far from easy. The storm clouds hung so low above the waves it was impossible to fly. Rain and hail pounded them without mercy, and the sea tried at each turn to murder them. Through it all Veronica stood at the bow, her eyes empty of human emotion, fingers writhing on the rail like sea anemones. She was beautiful, and she was terrifying.

It must have taken days, maybe a week before they reached a break in the clouds, a hole like the eye of a hurricane, but small, barely wide enough for the ships to pass through.

It had been worth the trouble. They had arrived at the castle unnoticed until they were mere yards away, swooping down out of a dense cloudbank drifting near the fortress.

Now came the hard part—finding Aster. The castle was a single tower, rising up in tiers, but it was a big tower, and they didn't have long before the fleet he'd seen in the harbor was airborne along with dragons and whatever else Vilken had to throw their way. Surely by now, more soldiers were swarming up from below—soldiers they would probably have to wade through to get to Aster. And that was assuming she was in this building, and not someplace else. But this was the only place Dusk knew to come; if she wasn't here, they were out of luck no matter what.

They were about to start down the stairway, when Dusk — who was not easily surprised — yelped and took a quick step back, raising her sword.

A naked woman had appeared in the stairwell.

"Don't hurt me," the naked woman said. "I'm here to help."

"Delia!" Dusk said.

"Ms. Fincher!" Errol burst out. He knew he ought to avert his eyes, but the whole thing was so weird. He knew, intellectually, his school counselor was in the Kingdoms, but seeing her here, now — in her birthday suit — was hard to handle.

Ms. Fincher's eyes went round. "Errol Greyson?"

"Uh . . . yes ma'am."

"This is no time for greetings," Dusk snapped. "We've come for Aster. Do you know where she is?"

"I do," Ms. Fincher said. She pulled something around her, and most of her simply vanished, although her head was still there, and bits of her arms and legs.

"Follow me."

The door was sturdy, and it took quite a bit of effort to break it down — way more time than Errol thought they probably had. Aster was asleep, like Ms. Fincher said she would be. He went in to pick her up, but Billy shouldered roughly past and gathered her in his arms. Then they started out and back up.

As they got back out onto the stairs, he heard the inevitable clatter of counterattack coming up from below.

For Errol, it was a moment of déjà vu. He remembered another tower, another staircase he had defended. It hadn't turned out that well for him.

Dusk saw his hesitation and tugged on his arm.

"We can make it back to the ship," she said.

But up above, things weren't looking so good, either. Two of Vilken's ships had already arrived and were trading broadsides with Dusk's remaining two. He saw Billy running up the gangplank with Aster in his arms, even as the ship shuddered beneath a fusillade. The shock slammed the ship hard against the top edge of the castle wall, and then it rebounded, sending the vessel drifting away, dragging the gangplank away into open space.

Worse, another of the enemy ships had thrown out grappling hooks and was pulling itself toward the wall. At least Vilken's guys weren't firing cannon at them, but he figured that was probably because they were wanted alive.

This was going to be a hell of a fight, after all.

"I'll keep those guys from coming up the stairs," he told Dusk. "Can you and your Amazons hold those guys off until your ship manages to get back to pick us up?" He pointed to the divlings massing on the enemy ship, ready to leap onto the roof as soon as the grapples pulled it close enough.

Dusk nodded grimly. "When I call for you, come, and quickly. There will not be much time."

Looking down from her place at the bow, Veronica saw more ships rising from the harbor. They were already overwhelmed, and soon things would be much worse. She knew the Raggedy Man was down there, close to the sea. She could feel him. She had a chance; once he got up here, into the air, that chance might slip away.

Another round of artillery fire smashed into the ship. Through a blooming cloud of smoke, she saw Errol on the roof, ready to fight against every odd for her, for Aster — and yes, for

Dusk. That was who he was. She might be able to reach him, pull him out of the fight once more, but he would just come back, wouldn't he? Until he was dead, or this was all over.

Billy was on board, carrying Aster, looking dazed.

"Billy," Veronica said, but he didn't react. She slapped him in the face, not too hard. "Billy!"

"Yeah?" he murmured.

"Can you become a giant again? Can you get us out of here?"

He could probably carry them all, a ship in each hand, get them all away from here in ten big steps.

Billy looked around, his eyes still largely blank. But he nodded.

"Aster," he said.

Then he started to grow.

The ship sagged as his weight increased, but before it could flip over, he reached out with one leg and stepped onto the tower.

"Billy, wait—" she said.

He was really going up, now. He stepped down with his other foot onto a lower step of the castle. Aster was tiny in his hand.

One of his feet reach the ground, and as his head rose above the tower, he began to walk away.

"Well, hell," she said. She couldn't blame Billy. If he had time to settle into his human self, to become the thoughtful, considerate person she remembered, he would never have abandoned them. But this Billy had spent too much time moving back and forth between human and giant, and giants were simple. And what had brought him back—the single thing that truly motivated him—was Aster. He'd found her, she was in trouble—he'd gotten her the hell out of there. Good for him. She hoped it worked better than her attempt to save Errol.

Her own choices were easier now, as well. She had come here to do something, and her feelings had gotten her all muddled.

She took one more long look at Errol, as he started swinging his sword. Then she leapt overboard.

The thought of rescue, of escaping from Vilken's castle, his demesne, and all of its madness was all Delia could think about at first. By the time they'd broken into Aster's prison, the wheels in her head had inevitably begun turning, and she knew what she wanted wasn't that simple. When she reached the roof, and saw that the rescue was going south anyway, she didn't spend a lot of time thinking about what she ought to do.

She put the veil back on and ran down the stairs.

A few floors down, she ran into some of Vilken's twisted boys, but with all of the clamor it was easy to slip against the wall and let them go past. One of them bumped into her, but he kept going.

She found Kostye in the room they'd shared, slumped on the bed, a bottle of some sort of liquor in one hand. Four empties lay on the floor. He was conscious, but his eyes were fogged from the inside by alcohol.

"Well," she said. "This is familiar."

His eyes turned toward the sound of her voice.

"You," he said. And took another drink.

"Me," she said.

He rubbed his hand on his forehead. "Why did you come back?" he said. "Didn't I warn you? Weren't you there to hear?"

"Of course I was," she said, pulling the veil off. "And I heard you and Vilken on the ferry."

"Then you know you should not have returned."

"Listen," she said. "Listen to me. I don't know what he has on you. I don't know how he controls you. But I'm telling you this. Your daughter Aster is upstairs. Vilken has been keeping her unconscious, Kostye, and he's been doing things to her.

Disgusting things. He plans to do worse—he plans to murder her—but some spell of yours is stopping him. There are people upstairs right now, trying to rescue her—but they're going to fail, unless you help them."

He took another pull on the bottle.

"Come here," he said.

"Kostye . . ."

"Come here!"

He grabbed her arm and pulled her down; his grip burned her arm, and she gasped as he pulled her in for a kiss. She felt a kind of pinch, like a needle going on, but all through her body. Lights began to flash, bright, colorful, painful. She closed her eyes, but it didn't help—they were still there. She felt as if something was unwinding; she heard voices, music, thunder, wind-chimes, a child crying, her mother singing.

She tried to pull away, but it was if their flesh had fused where the touched—at the lips, where his hands gripped her arms. She began to tremble, then to shake. Her hands and feet felt like ice, and cold crept up the back of her neck.

Then he let go, and she slumped to the floor. She lay there, breathing weakly, fighting for the strength to run.

Kostye was no longer paying any attention to her. She realized she was lying near the veil and, feeling her nakedness, pulled it back on.

Perhaps a minute after, Vilken entered the room.

"You!" Kostye growled.

Vilken's eyes widened in surprise, but he reacted quickly, drawing the orb from beneath his robes and holding it toward Kostye. As before, it stopped him cold. He seemed hypnotized by it.

"What's happened?" Vilken demanded. "Why do you address me so?"

He didn't see her. The tiny globe was perched between his fingers.

She didn't know what it was, but she knew what it did.

She knew she couldn't consider too long, or she might talk herself out of it. She rose, took four steps forward, plucked the sphere from his fingers, and ran.

She didn't make it far before he roared in a voice that was louder than human.

She sped down the stairs, not certain where she was going. Away, that much was certain. As she ran, she had an idea. If she could reach the bay and cast it in, he might not find it. If he couldn't find it, maybe whatever hold Vilken had over Kostye would be ended. If so — well, at least it would stir things up.

She was within sight of the water when something seemed to pass through her, literally — it was as if a wind physically cut through her body. She accomplished three more steps before realizing she was no longer in control of her limbs — only momentum had carried her forward.

She struck the ground, banging her head so hard that for a moment everything went white.

When it was over, Vilken had her by the ankle, and she wasn't wearing the veil anymore.

"So nice to see you, Delia," he said. "I should have known he would have a hard time killing you. I should have asked to see the body. He has developed a weakness for women, I suppose."

"Let go," she gasped. The little ball was still clutched in her fist. He pulled her up and forced her fingers open.

"Thank you," he said. He set her on her feet and said a word. She found she was able to walk again, but not of her own will. She could only follow Vilken — down to where she had been headed, to where the causeway met the water. Ahead of her, at the port, more ships were lifting into the air.

Vilken glanced up. "This will all be over soon," he said. "But I'm afraid you won't be here to witness it. Jump into the water, please, and make no effort to swim. You may breathe or not breathe as you wish, but it will go quicker if you do."

She wanted a rejoinder. She wanted last words. But she wasted the moment between her next step and the fall to the water to take a deep breath. Then the water closed over her.

She sank. She opened her eyes, despite the sting. She wanted to see, to be aware as much as possible.

And she wanted to live.

But as the rippling, silvery surface grew further and further away, and her arms and legs refused to obey her panicked commands, she knew she would not.

THREE
THE CURSE

E rrol almost took a step back as the first of the boys appeared — they weren't human or at least not completely so — like the Sheriff's boys, but even weirder. This bunch wasn't so much wolf-like as just — wrong. Each one was a different mixture of lizard, baboon, hyena, and — devil, what with their horns and fangs. Their bodies, too, were distorted in all sorts of unexpected and often puke-inducing ways.

It made it easier to knock the hell out of them with his sword, but he was still set against killing them if he didn't have to — they had once been normal boys, like him, even if they had fallen in with a bad — *really* bad — crowd. As before, the weapon had a mind of its own, feinting here, jabbing there, finding clever angles of attack he would never have thought of on his own. But he was in control enough to make sure the blows came from the flat of the blade or the hilt.

The first several divlings were now piled inside the landing's threshold, which made it harder for the others to get to him. The sword hardly weighed anything. He wasn't winded at all. He felt as if he could hold this spot all day.

But from the sound of things, Dusk was having a harder time repelling the enemy trying to reach the roof by ship. He only had to defend a few square feet; the roof was wide open.

He dared not glance behind him to see exactly how bad it was. He could still hear Dusk's war cries, so she was at least still fighting. But he did see her flagship drift by, in flames.

Veronica was on that ship.

Trying not to think about that, he smacked a monkey-snake-devil and kicked him back against his comrades.

S pots dancing before her eyes, Delia couldn't take it any longer. She had to open her lungs, put something in them, even if it was seawater. What was left of her free will was gone.

Then something grabbed her and water rushed by and she was above the surface, on the stone. Air, sweeter than anything she had ever known poured into her like God, like the Holy Spirit — like life itself. Her eyes, still open, blinked away the tears of the ocean as she struggled to comprehend what had saved her.

Vilken was still there. And a demon.

The demon looked like a young girl, but her eyes were all wrong, voids into a Hell of deep water. The Marianas Trench was in those eyes, the crushing depths at the bottom of the living world. Her hair was sea-foam, her slender arms and legs pale eels wriggling before her, far longer than they should have been.

She reached for Vilken, and he shouted, once, before she closed him in those arms and yanked him into the water.

The air made Delia dizzy, and she began to push herself up when what she wanted to do was just lay there and breath.

But her body had other ideas. It was supposed to jump into the water, and that's what it meant to do. She screamed for help as she crawled back toward the water's edge.

Veronica drew the Raggedy Man down into the depths. She had been here before, and last time it had been easy. Then, he had seen only a victim who had escaped him once and that he could finally have.

This time was different. He was afraid and he was fighting.

She kissed him and felt the sickness that was older than time invade her mind, the decaying, festering core of him that always sought to be whole but which would never—could never—be complete. He was a mass of black tumors; every soul he had ever taken had become a cancer, and that's what he was: a malignancy on the universe itself, a disease not of the living, but of the forces that made life possible.

She had failed to kill it before, and she understood she couldn't kill it this time, but she could rob it of a body, of hands and feet and sexual organs. It would come back—it always came back—but for a time the world would be a better place, and she would be a little happier herself.

As they reached the bottom, the wave-shattered shells, the rotting beams, the thousand thousand tiny lives going about their business, she felt him begin to quiet, his struggles to lessen. He began to give in.

Lightning struck—everything went blue-white and her marrow turned to flame. She tried to keep hold of him, but her limbs wouldn't respond.

Shandor had been right. Once again, she had underestimated the monster. Once again, she had failed.

Delia had almost reached the water when someone stepped in front of her. She tried to push past the legs to obey the command turning in her brain, but he bent, and strong hands lifted her up, and he kissed her, and her cramped, knotted muscles relaxed all at once—her body was her own again.

"Kostye?"

He turned, quickly, and slapped his hands together. The water erupted, and Vilken with it. The chancellor crashing to the cobble stones.

He was wet and looked pale, but he still succeeded in regaining his feet. He held the orb out in front of him.

"Stop!" he shouted.

Kostye didn't stop. He moved as if he was struggling beneath an impossible burden, but he moved. Vilken didn't seem to believe it as Kostye reached out, grabbed his hand, and began to crush it.

Vilken screamed, but it wasn't merely a sound; there was a word in it, the sound of which sent a quiver of revulsion through her. Kostye screamed, too, and struck Vilken with the back of his other hand before staggering and dropping to one knee.

Vilken skipped backward, became a shadow, and vanished. Kostye stayed where he was, panting heavily. She stumbled over to him.

"Where is he?" he asked.

"He's gone," a small voice said. It was demon from the sea, but she had changed, diminished, become the blond girl she'd first seen at Kostye's house. A friend of Aster's.

"Skedaddled," the girl added.

Kostye nodded grimly. He looked up, to where more ships converged on the tower.

"Aster is there?" he said.

"When I last saw her," Delia said.

He closed his eyes, and once again turned inside out, and rose skyward on black wings.

The blond girl sat down next to her.

"I recognize you," she said. "Aster's teacher."

"Guidance counselor," Delia corrected, absently.

"I'm Veronica," the girl said. "And actually, Aster isn't up there anymore."

"Why didn't you tell him that?"

"Because my other friends are, and they could use some help."

Delia looked back up. In this state, Kostye was capable of anything.

"He might help them," she said. "But he will also be angry, and that is . . . bad. Do you know where Aster is?"

"Sort of," Veronica said. "Maybe."

"We'd better go tell him, then," Delia said. "And we had better hurry."

"Yeah. But maybe on the way up we can find you something to wear."

Delia glanced at herself. She had forgotten she was naked. But after everything that had happened, that was a small worry.

Errol felt heat like the summer sun on his back, and the faces of his opponents were suddenly lit as if by a camera flash. He saw their pupils shrink to nothing. Then even the reflected light from their faces forced him to squint. Behind him he heard screams as if a choir was being tortured to death.

When the light faded, he didn't have anyone left to fight. All of his enemies had dropped their weapons and were either backing away, holding their hands over their eyes, or had simply turned and run.

Errol spun around to see what had happened.

The sky was full of burning ships. The only one that hadn't been set aflame was Dusk's remaining vessel. The cause was easy to see: two dragons were circling the castle. As he watched, one dove toward a ship arriving from below.

The dragons were on their side, now?

Before he could parse that out, a demon settled onto the rooftop.

Dusk and her warriors were still fighting a knot of Vilken's boys, but they quickly broke when the demon started toward them. Dusk raised her sword, but the monster knocked her sprawling with a clawed fist.

Then it came for Errol.

The demon was hairless, with glossy scales like a snake, gleaming in murky rainbow colors, like a slick of oil in a swamp. It had gigantic, translucent, featherless wings. It's eyes, now bearing down on him, were oddly human.

He raised his sword, but to his surprise, the thing stopped.

"Where is Aster?" It demanded.

"She — she's not here. Billy took her."

The demon leaned in near him, then stood straight and pulled its wings around itself. A rush of hot air buffeted him back, and the demon was gone. In his place stood Aster's father in all of his naked, tattooed weirdness. He looked . . . hurt, but he had no obvious wounds.

"Who?"

"Billy," Errol said. "He's sort of her boyfriend. He's a giant."

Aster's father frowned. Behind him, one of the flaming ships slowly sank out of sight.

"Where?" he demanded.

"I don't know."

Aster's father began an answer, but suddenly stepped past Errol, toward the stairs.

"I think I do," someone said, behind him.

It was Veronica. Ms. Fincher was there, too, still naked. She ran forward and hugged Aster's father.

"You kind of took off before I could say anything," Veronica went on.

"Then tell me now," Kostye said.

"She's supposed to go someplace called The Isle of the Othersun."

Kostye's eyes widened, and he passed his hand across his face.

"I see," he said. He looked around him, studying each of them in turn.

"You are all her friends," he said.

"Yes, sir," Errol replied.

He nodded at Dusk. "What of her?"

Dusk pursed her lips but said nothing. Veronica coughed up a little laugh.

"She's good," Errol said.

Kostye swayed on his feet; Ms. Fincher got up under his arm, supporting him.

"I need rest," Kostye said. "And strong drink. Help me on board the ship. We will go together to find my daughter."

Dusk's single remaining vessel was singed, but still in one piece. Now that the enemy was cleared away, it was able to move back to the castle. Before boarding the ship, Kostye managed to find a bottle of a clear liquor, but drinking it didn't seem to strengthen him; instead he looked steadily weaker. Ms. Fincher sat beside him, holding his hand. One of Dusk's girls had fetched her a dull-yellow shift.

"You," he called Errol over.

"Yes, sir."

"You were Aster's friend. At school."

"You remember now?"

He nodded. "Yes," he said. "Vilken said he could restore me. He told me things, showed me things. But it was all from before, from the old days. That was the Kostye he wanted, the old me. He never intended that I should remember Aster or you or Delia." He glanced up apologetically at Delia. "But I became sure you were telling me the truth, Delia. So—I took memories from you. I'm sorry. But I remember now, maybe everything, maybe not. There is a price for that, and I will pay it soon."

"What do you mean?" Delia asked. "Are you hurt? Sick?"

He ignored her question. "Aster is in terrible danger," he said. "I never meant for her to come back here. But now that she is here, there are things she must know, immediately. If I am not able to tell her, you must. Do you understand?"

"Yes, sir," Errol said.

He sighed and lay back.

"Those were great and terrible times," he said. "War raged. Every kingdom fought every other. I did not care. Alone, in my demesne, I was uninterested in the affairs of men, only in power, in the mastery of sorcery. I hunted in the lower realms, I fought demons, I mastered myself.

"I was not, however, completely without obligations. My father arranged a marriage for me that many believed would end the strife, a marriage to join Heaven and Earth and the Hells below."

"There was a queen. The death of her husband was in part what began the Troubles. She was beautiful and strong and wicked in her own way. We made a good match, I thought. Our marriage brought the peace everyone desired. The Kingdoms prospered. My wife indulged my appetites, and I spent much of my time in my dark places, learning the runes that undergird creation, while she governed. She raised the children of her first husband. Between us there was no issue, which suited me."

"Wait," Errol said. "The queen wasn't Aster's mother?"

He shook his head. "No," he said. "That was another. Someone—unexpected. Someone who truly changed my heart. The queen discovered my . . . indiscretion. Her champion fell upon me as I dreamed and smote me down. I lay as dead for days, but then I rose. I went to the place where my love and I used to meet, our secret place. I found her, or what remained of her. And I found our child. For a few years, I was content in my sorrow and my happiness. I put aside thoughts of vengeance. I foreswore my power, as only he who has seen the limits and shortcomings of power can. I raised my daughter.

"Then the queen's minions, my enemies, came. Not for me. But for her. For Aster. The queen had a dream, they say, that one day Aster would bring about the end of her reign and ruin to all of the Kingdoms. They came to murder my Aster.

"I cursed them. I cursed them all, with every dark fiber of my being, with every art in my possession. Then I fled, and took her to the one place I believed none of our enemies could follow."

"You made the curse," Errol said.

He nodded. "It caught me, even in the Reign of the Departed. Now it is catching me again. In remembering I've put myself at its mercy, even as we return to where it all began."

"That's where Aster's gone? The Isle of the Othersun."

"Yes," Kostye said. "So she can end it. But if she ends it . . ." he coughed. He looked somehow older. His hair was still red— it hadn't faded or gone grey—and he was no more wrinkled, or anything. But something was leaking out of him. It was like Errol's dad, right before the cancer killed him, when it had taken everything from him but the very breath of life, reduced a strong man to a pile of rags.

He knew Aster's father was dying.

"We'll find her," he said. "We'll figure it out."

Kostye's eyes had closed. He was still breathing, but his chest rose and fell only by increments.

Errol went up on the deck of the ship. Veronica saw him and came over, saw something in his face, and without a word took him in her arms.

"I love you," he said. "I'm sorry —"

"Hush," Veronica said. "You don't need to talk so much."

Over her shoulder, he saw Dusk gazing down at them from her position at the helm. She shrugged a little before turning away.

Kostye came up a few moments later and unsteadily moved to the rail. He lifted his hand and recited something that sounded like a poem. When he was done, a light shone on the horizon. It was not the sun, or the moon, but it was bright and growing nearer.

A ster woke to a warm breeze, and the smell of flowers. For a moment, she thought she was back in nightmare, for the glade she lay in looked very much like the meadow where she had seen the birds fly, where the swan had come to her. But it didn't feel like a dream.

She sat up, and realized someone was watching her, sitting with his knees drawn up under his chin. Then she realized who it was.

"Billy?" she said. It seemed impossible. Maybe it *was* a dream.

"Aster," he said. "I found you."

He had that sort of dazed look he'd had after turning into a giant and then coming back to his smaller self. She didn't care. She had pushed her feelings about him so far down, so hard, and now it all exploded out of her. She ran to him and bowled him over, pressing her lips against his.

He didn't respond — his mouth felt sort of like a cold cut.

She drew back. "Billy?"

Then his beautiful amber eyes cleared, and he reached for her, pulled her back to him.

It was wonderful, it was impossible. And all too soon it had to end.

"Billy," she said, half-heartedly drawing away. "I have to know what's going on. What happened. How we got here."

"You called me," he said. "I was on the Far Shores, where the stars are near. Where the sea caves are big enough even for a giant to walk in. There's music in those places, made by the wind and the stone. It takes a long time to listen to. I used to listen for seasons, for years, for decades. But I didn't hear music; I heard you. You were hurt, scared, in pain. I searched for you."

He went on, in brief, clipped, sometimes confused sentences. About finding Errol, and the ship which Dusk had made hers, the battles to reach her.

"Errol and Veronica," Aster said. "They're still back there."

He shrugged. "Yeah. I wasn't thinking, you know, like a little person. I only knew I had to bring you someplace. Bring you here."

"Why here?"

"I don't know," he said.

But she did. She remembered the woman in the webs, how she had said when she found her heart, she would find the Isle of the Othersun. And here was Billy, her heart—and she felt, somehow, this was the place.

But Errol, Veronica—even Dusk, who - to hear Billy tell it, was on their side again—what had become of them? Had they been captured, or killed? Billy's account wasn't detailed enough for her to be sure.

"We may have to go back," she said. "They came to save me, I can't just let Vilken have them."

"I don't want to go back," Billy said. "If I do, I'll lose you again."

"That's what we thought the last time," she said.

"We were lucky," he said. "I know now I would have remembered you no matter what. Love would have made me remember. But it might have taken me a hundred years, or two hundred. That I remembered almost right away — "

"I made you remember," she said. "I did a Dream, a wild magic, and it found you. We're connected, Billy. We can always find each other. We have to go back."

Billy looked away, off toward the horizon. He stayed that way for a long time.

"No," he said.

"Billy — "

"We don't have to. They're coming."

He pointed by pursing his lips slightly. Then she saw it — a small dot in the sky, moving slowly toward them.

THE KINGDOM OF CORAL

I t took long enough for the others to arrive that the anticipation began to weigh upon Aster. She had abandoned Errol and betrayed Veronica. When she and Dusk last parted, it had been as mortal enemies. Even with Billy's support, she knew the reunion was going to be hard, especially since there was so much she didn't know. She felt like she had been given a chance to set things right, and instead had only made things worse in hopes of saving her father, and she hadn't even managed the trade-off.

Her concerns were nothing more than the first few drops of a coming storm when the ship landed and her father was brought down the gangplank on a stretcher.

He was pale and unconscious. They carried him into the shade of some willows and left her with him. She clasped his hand, and began to weep.

"Streya."

Her nickname, barely breathed.

"Dad?" she said. "Are you talking to me?"

His eyes were open now,

"Streya, I'm so sorry. I did it all for you. I would have done more, if I had the strength."

"I know that, Dad," she said. "What's happening? What's wrong with you?"

"The curse I made," he said. "That did all of this. It's found me at last. I made some . . . bargains. I am in debt, you might say. And I have many enemies. But so do you, Streya. So do you."

Looking into his eyes, she realized he was all there, all of him. She hadn't seen him like that since she was eight. He had finally come back to her. Despite all of her screw-ups, he was himself again.

"We can fight," she said. "I have learned much. I have spells—"

"You will fight," he sighed. "But not for me. Vilken will come. He is not—who I remember. There is a thing in him, an ancient disease—but you know that, don't you. He won't be far behind, because this is the place, and he knows it."

"What place, Dad?"

He tilted his head. "Where I met your mother. Where I came to love her. Where I met you. Where I learned what real, true love is, and what it can do. And where I made the curse. This is the place it all began, and this is the only place it can end. Vilken knows that, and he does not want it to end. He would have the curse become permanent."

He closed his eyes and let his head rest. His breaths became more ragged, spaced further apart.

"I saw her from my tower," he said. "Like a second sun, a sun that was not in the sky, but in the sea."

"My mother?"

"Do you remember her, still?"

"A little. And the house with the garden. But is it here? I don't see it."

"It's here and it isn't here," he said.

He squeezed her hand.

"There was a rumor, long ago, that I had removed my heart and placed it far away, in hiding, so that nothing could ever hurt me. Some called me *bezhmirtes*, "deathless.'"

"I've heard of that," she said. "Of hiding one's life from harm. I thought it was just a story. Is it true?"

"Things like that can be taken too literally," he said. "It was true in a way. Before I met your mother — before I met you — I believe I truly was deathless. But without a heart, how is one day, one year, one century different from another? What is the point of an endless banquet if the food has no taste? I found my heart, and became mortal. I lost it again, Streya — but only for a short time."

"You can't die," she said.

"There is no true death in the Kingdoms," he said. "I have come to believe the closest thing to a true death is immortality itself."

"Daddy, please. This was all for you. Everything I've done — "

"You're still young," he said. "There is more for you to do."

He pulled her down, so he could whisper in her ear.

"The Names," he murmured. "You are strong enough, although the peril is still great. I wish . . ." he trailed off and feebly touched the side of her face with a limp hand.

"I am proud of you," he said. "You are more than even I imagined."

In her hand, his became cold — not slowly, but all of a sudden. His eyes turned toward her one last time, and then they hollowed out.

"I love you, Streya," he said.

His lips stopped moving. And his chest. Tears blurred her vision as his hand became hard and stiff.

The earth below him began to sag with his weight and began to tug at her. She gasped and pulled back, but he was incredibly heavy now, and instead she was pulled with him.

She screamed when someone grabbed her under the arms, trying to wrench her away; she clenched her fingers on her father's, refusing to let go.

But her hand ran out of strength, and she watched her father vanish into the hole as Errol dragged her, still screaming, away. The earth closed back, grass and all, as if her father had never been there.

She turned and began beating at Errol's chest with her fists, shrieking that she hated him. Billy came and pulled her gently away, and together they walked off. They sat down on a low hill nearby. She cried while he looked out at the sea.

She realized that she had something in her hand, something that had not been there before.

S he shouldn't have said that stuff to you," Veronica told Errol, once Aster was out of sight. "If you hadn't pulled her back, she would have gone with him. She would be dead, too."

"It's true," Dusk said, folding down cross-legged to sit with them.

"It's okay," Errol said. "I know how she feels. When my father died, I stayed. I stayed until everybody was gone, even my mom. I stayed until the bulldozer started pushing the dirt in. You know, the first couple of handfuls of dirt went in at the funeral. I guess it's symbolic, or something. In the movies, it's usually some guys with shovels that finish the job. But not for my dad. It was a bulldozer. Like they were building a parking lot. It wasn't quick as what happened to Aster's dad, but it wasn't any better. The sight of red clay still makes me want to vomit. If I'd had somebody to take it out on . . ."

Veronica kissed him on the cheek.

"You did," she said. "You took it out on yourself."

Errol nodded ruefully. "Maybe. Anyway, we've got bigger problems, don't we? If this Vilken character is coming, we've got to get a plan together, and fast. I don't think the — what, thirty? Of us are going to able to handle him. Not without Aster's dad."

"You said a mouthful right there," Veronica said. "I couldn't stop him. Maybe Aster can, but I wouldn't count on it."

"We're supposed to do something," he said. "With the orbs, to end the curse. Her dad said we were in the right place."

"Yes," Dusk said. "But we don't have the orbs. Vilken has mine. Kostye had one, which Vilken presumably also has. Aster had one —"

"Which I ended up with," Veronica said. "Haydevil took it. I don't know if he still has it."

"I don't know who has the other two," Dusk said. "The point is, we don't have them, so remaining here can have no purpose. Given time, we might be able to find and acquire the orbs and learn the secrets of this place. But we will not have that time if we wait here for Vilken."

Errol sighed. "I hate to admit it," he said. "But you're right. I'll go talk to Aster. The sooner we got out of here, the better."

Aster wiped her tears and rolled the orb in her hand. It wasn't the silver one she had possessed twice before; it shimmered; pale rose, saffron, carmine, gold. It was like the first light of day, the dawn rolled up into a ball, a fire deep in the sea . . .

It pulsed in her hand and sent tingles up her fingers, into her chest.

When you find your heart, the woman had said.

When Billy showed up, she'd thought she understood those words. Now she understood she hadn't.

"The Kingdom of Coral," she sighed.

"It's pretty," Billy said. And . . . big. Inside."

"Is it," Aster said. She stood up and turned slowly, to face the way the ball was tugging her. When it stopped, she let it slip from her palm to roll on the ground.

As it rolled, it grew — baseball sized, basketball, beach ball and then very, very quickly much bigger. Its diameter expanded far faster than the distance it was traveling. In an eyeblink she was inside of it, as was Errol, a few yards away, looking astonished, and soon the whole island. The inside of the sphere was a faint pink film, retreating in every direction.

The hill, the trees, the sea were all the same, but the quality of the light was different. The sun wasn't to be seen, neither could they see the stars for the golden light that rose up before them, painting the clouds above in the colors of dawn. The horizons, on the other hand, were indigo and grey, with strange coils of cloud rising up to reflect the light on their tops, like a forest of titanic fiddlehead ferns.

It was like a sunrise in the middle of the sky.

The light came from a castle on the highest hill of the island, which had been bare of any built structure a moment before.

"The Isle of the Othersun," she said. She sank to her knees, and put her head down, not even understanding what she was feeling.

She heard birdsong, a lilting, four-note melody that repeated itself, broke with a little trill, then started again. It was no bird that lived in Sowashee, nothing she had heard on any of her journeys. But knew it from when she was a girl. And the flowers, like jasmine, but also like lavender — those were familiar, too.

She was here, at last, a place she had only barely known she missed.

But it was too late. Her father was gone.

"All for nothing," she said. "For nothing."

"Think so?" Veronica asked.

"Veronica," she said. "I'm so sorry. Errol — "

"It's okay," he said. "You don't have anything to apologize for."

She hadn't known she needed to be forgiven. Despite everything she'd said to Veronica, all of her justifications, she knew she had betrayed Errol. She had striven so long with a single purpose, told herself anything was justified so long as she achieved it. That the end justified the means.

Now that the end was no longer possible, all she was left with was the means. It made her feel dirty.

Was this how her father had felt, these last nine years? If so, how had he borne it?

"Everyone," Veronica said. "I'd like to speak to Aster alone for a few minutes."

Billy took her hand, but Aster patted it.

"It's okay," she said. "Don't go far, okay?"

"Okay," Billy said.

Once the others were at a discreet distance, Veronica sat down in front of her.

"Errol means it," she said. "He understands."

"Do you?"

Veronica shrugged. "Here is what I understand," she said. "I spent a long time not caring about anyone or anything besides where my next . . . meal was coming from. Your dad, your whole quest—never meant anything to me. He wasn't my dad, and I didn't know him. But Errol means something to me. Unfortunately, so do you. So I stuck around, you know?"

"I know," Aster said.

Veronica leaned close. Her voice dropped to a whisper.

"You know what *he* likes, don't you? You know what he does. His pleasure—his existence—is about our pain. Causing it, remembering it—but more than anything, *possessing* it. I went to a museum once. I don't remember much about it except this one exhibit—a stuffed lion. All that it had once been—all that life, that power—just a sack of skin with glass eyes. The fur was worn through in places, and its hair was falling out. I started crying, and nobody understood why. They thought it was because I knew it was dead—but that wasn't it. And now I know all about that; I used to keep the bones of the men I killed. I polished them, when algae and stuff crusted on them. I played with them, like a kid plays with blocks. When they were drowning, taking that last breath, I was already dreaming about how their bones would look in my collection.

"Ever since you brought me to life, I've had to fight against that. I've been becoming something else—not a *nov*, not human. It's like I keep coming to forks in the road. At each fork, there's a road that leads to what *he* is, and a choice that leads me—someplace else, I hope. So far, I think I've made the right choices—because of you guys.

"Your father may be gone, Aster. But the Raggedy Man is still around, and he's not going to stop. I know that because I understand him. The girls he has right now—that's only the beginning. I can't stop him by myself—I tried twice. But you, Errol—together we might be able to. And ending the curse—that's probably a good start."

Aster remembered him climbing up on her, the knife in his hand. Only her father's spell had stopped him, and now her father was gone.

"I'm scared of him," she whispered.

"Maybe," Veronica said. "But you're mad at him, too. Aster, that's the part of you that gets things done, no matter what—we need that now. We may lose anyway, but with you all whiney and sad, we don't have a chance."

"It feels like we've already had this talk," Aster said.

"Yep. Is it working this time?"

Aster shrugged, stood up, and faced the light. "I don't know," she said. "Let's find out."

On first sight Errol thought the castle was built of white stone, but as they drew nearer, he realized it more resembled a shell. It wasn't made of shells—he couldn't see anything that looked like an oyster or a clam or a conch—but it looked like a huge, weirdly shaped shell itself, a little rough and bumpy. Once they passed through the round gate, the impression was heightened, because inside the walls were smooth to the point of being glassy, and were various shades of pale pink, rising up in places to form delicate-looking, spiral towers.

The courtyard was filled with light. Bright, but never blinding. Even in the very center, from which it emanated.

A few yards in Aster stopped, and they all halted with her, waiting.

After a moment she nodded and continued on. When they got closer, Errol saw why she'd paused. She had just lost her father, after all—and now this.

Dusk had once told Errol that souls began in the highest Kingdoms and worked their way down. Some—the lucky ones—got recycled back to higher Kingdoms at some point and became part of a cycle. But some ended up in The Reign of the Departed, his world.

People on Earth knew about the Kingdoms, sort of—fairy tales, myths, religion—he figured that those were fractured memories of this place. Whether it was because the damned souls carried foggy recollections with them to their new and final lives, or because of people like him who had been over and back, he didn't know. But there was some connection, that much was clear.

As clear as the glass coffin he was staring at, and the beautiful woman inside of it.

"You're kidding," he heard Veronica breathe.

He watched Aster move up to the casket and place her hands upon it.

"Oh, God," Errol said. Because it was Aster lying there, eyes closed, arms lying at her sides.

The perception lasted only long enough for him to swear; then the differences began sorting themselves out. The woman looked a little older than Aster, maybe twenty. She and Aster shared the same high, broad cheekbones and sharply pointed chin, but there was something of Aster's future in them, too. And this woman had hair so golden in color it deserved that adjective. She was dressed in a long, shimmering, sleeveless gown the color of a primrose whose every border was embellished with flowers. An eight-pointed star gleamed on the woman's forehead.

"Is that . . . ?" he began.

"My mom," Aster said.

She didn't look dead. Her cheeks and lips appeared flushed — but of course she was also glowing.

He could see it was all too much for Aster.

"Come on," he said to the others. "Let's have a look around."

Aside from the open gate they'd come through, each of the other walls had entrances. Errol and Veronica went through the one on the north.

It was less a castle, he saw, than a mansion, and not a particularly big one, given some of the places he'd seen lately. It wasn't kept up. Flowering vines had climbed in through the windows, snaking their way on floor, walls, and ceilings, seeking the light in the courtyard. With the flowers came bees, butterflies, and aphids. Small brown lizards had in turn followed those in, and there was sign of larger, four-footed animals. Birds nested on the sills of upper windows.

They found stairs that turned upward into one of the spiral

towers, where again the scale proved deceptive. The upper story was only a few feet wide and opened to the sky through graceful ogee arches.

"It's not a real castle," Veronica said. "More like a big playhouse made to look like a castle."

"Yeah," Errol said. "I noticed that too. Which is bad, because it means it probably isn't defensible. Not that I know a lot about defending castles."

"Dusk does," Veronica said.

He blinked. "Maybe," he allowed. "Probably."

"Maybe you should go talk to her about this, then," she said.

Veronica's expression was hard to read. He felt like he was working without a net, and not for the first time. He'd thought — hoped — the kiss he'd shared with Dusk would go away, but the unspoken lie between him and Veronica kept growing.

"I'm not in love with her," he said.

"I thought we were talking about castles."

"She kissed me," he blurted. "Or I kissed her. There . . . uh . . . was a kiss."

Veronica frowned a little and looked out the window.

"I guess I knew that," she said. "You two are so weird around me. Of course, there would be lots of reasons for that, like her attempt to murder me, and all, and you being so cozy now."

"Yeah," Errol said. "There is that."

"I was planning on killing her," Veronica said. "I thought about that a good bit, I can tell you. I had a couple of different ideas about how to do it."

"Why didn't you?"

"Because I needed her to get to the Raggedy Man, and I wanted to kill him a lot worse. I also wanted to clear the rest of this up. Then I started thinking — maybe *you* need her. After this is all over, if we're any of us still in one piece."

"I don't want her," he said. "I want you."

"Well," she said. "Maybe I don't want you. Did you ever think of that?"

It felt like a gut punch. One he deserved.

"Yeah," he said. "When you abandoned me back in your boyfriend's gypsy carnival and ran off with him."

Even as it came out, he wondered what he was doing, why he would say that.

Her mouth formed a little "o", and he could tell he was about to get it, but then she sighed.

"That's right," she said. "You got it just right. Sorry, Errol."

"Hey, wait a minute," he said. "I was just mad. I don't really think—"

"You ought to," she said. "It's been great. First boyfriend since coming back to life and all that. But it's time to move on. For both of us."

"You aren't serious. Veronica, I love you," he said.

"Good for you," she said. "It's great you've learned how to say it. But right now, there are more important things to worry about than who loves who."

"Like what?" he asked.

"Like that," she replied, pointing.

Ships outlined against the dark horizon, at least half a dozen of them.

"Oh, crap," he said. "That was fast."

"Yep," Veronica said. "Come on."

But before she could go, he caught her by the arm and kissed her. To his relief, she kissed him back. But he wasn't sure it resolved anything.

"We'll talk about this later?" he said.

"If there is a later."

FIVE
THE NAMEBEARER

The light in the castle was too much for Delia; she retreated to the place where she's last seen Kostye. She did something she hadn't done in years; she prayed.

She hadn't been sure what she believed about God before she came here. It had been a conversation she'd stopped having with herself or anyone else. It wasn't that she didn't believe, exactly — she wouldn't have called herself an atheist, and even the word *agnostic* stuck in her craw, although it was probably the term that most accurately described her. She had always prided herself on seeing things as they were, not as she wanted them to be.

In this place, she had seen everything *but* God. Demons, dragons, monsters — possibly the Devil himself. She had watched her lover literally be swallowed by the earth.

If all of that was real, why not God? Maybe not like she'd been taught in Sunday School, any more than the woman in the glass casket was actually Sleeping Beauty or Snow White. But real, nevertheless. Maybe one of the details people got wrong was that God answered prayers. But it wasn't so much that she *wanted* something as she wanted to *say* something in case anyone was listening. What she wanted to say, in her halting way, was that the world was awful and terrible and wonderful and beautiful and that she was lucky to have lived in it as much as she had. And that whatever happened next, she was grateful for that.

It was worth saying. Life was short, and by the looks of things, her own race was nearly run.

Vilken's ships were arriving.

It occurred to her that everyone else was in the castle — out here, she might not even be noticed. She might be able to slip away, hide, ride it out.

But she'd had enough of hiding. If she did manage to survive, she would either eventually be captured or stuck on this island. Neither idea appealed to her that much.

If she hurried, she could be with the others before the ships arrived.

She hurried.

W e can't defend this place," Dusk said. "We have no cannon except those on the ship, no ballista or catapults. Vilken can fly over our walls and drop his divlings right on top of us."

"Can we outrun them?"

"Not too likely," she said. "But we could try. It's a slim chance, but probably the only one we have — and it gets thinner with each breath we waste on words."

"Billy?" Errol said. "Do you think — "

"No." It was Aster, her voice flat and dangerous. "Billy's tired. It takes a lot out of him to change back and forth, and he's at his limit. He's also not invulnerable. You all can leave if you want. Or you can stay here with me and end this, now."

"That sounds great," Errol said. "But Dusk says we can't defend this place, and you can see we're way outnumbered."

"We don't have to defeat all of the ships," Aster said. "Just one of them."

Dusk frowned. "Vilken's ship. You're suggesting I sail my ship right into the middle of his fleet."

"Yes."

Dusk turned her mouth a bit to the side, then tilted her head.

"Can you tell which ship he's on?"

"I believe I can," Aster replied.

"What about the dragons?" Veronica said.

"The dragons were Kostye's," Delia said. "He talked about it. He had an arrangement with them. I don't think Vilken can command them on his own."

"I don't see any dragons," Dusk said. "And even if I did— Aster, my ship is yours. Tell me where to steer it."

B y the time they were airborne, Vilken's fleet was closing in and arcing around them so they had nowhere to run.

But they were running, anyway, or pretending to, steering hard to the west. Aster didn't feel as confident as she sounded, but she was heartsick and angry, and one way or another determined to finish this. In fact, she had lied to the others; she'd thought of a way they might escape.

But she didn't want to.

She could feel Vilken—they had a connection now. His ship wasn't marked any differently from the others. The real Vilken— the man they had called the Sheriff—had been a warrior. He would be leading the charge, flying the banner, the point of the spear and all of that. Not so the thing that had taken his body and his strength. Veronica's Raggedy Man was no general, no warrior. He was a coward, a thief, a rapist, and a murderer. He would let the boys he had twisted into devils do his work, or at least the most dangerous part of it.

No, his ship was near the rear, and continued to hang back as his servants pursued them, stretching his fleet out to close off their escape.

"That closest ship is almost in range," Dusk informed her.

"How much ammunition do we have?" Aster asked.

"We have more shot than powder," she said. "Very little to waste."

"Fine," Aster said. She had thought to stretch the feint out, put up a bit of a mock battle to make things more convincing. But if they were low on powder, best they save it.

"Hold off until the last second—until right before they come in range—then turn us toward that one in back."

"Very well," Dusk said.

A moment later the warrior-woman began shouting orders, and the girls on deck and in the rigging began working furiously at the sails.

Aster closed her eyes, preparing herself.

The deeper she got into the Kingdoms, the more magic she remembered, but up until now, the most powerful spells she could recall were the Profound Recondite Utterances.

Now, in this place where she was born, something new had formed in her memory. Something her father had mentioned, with almost his last breath.

A Name.

It welled up from the light inside of her, found her tongue, and spoke itself.

E rrol was standing a few paces from Aster when her mouth opened and a sound came out like none he had ever heard. It was almost below the register of hearing, but he felt it in the atmosphere, in the wooden planks of the ship. Aster seemed suddenly bigger, and her skin was the color of ash. Her eyes were gone, replaced by blue-white slits.

"What the—"

Before he could finish, the wind came. The sails stretched full, the ship creaked and groaned, and somewhere something splintered. Aster raised up her arms, and the hurricane grew even stronger. The ship was hauling ass, jumping and skipping as if beating through waves.

Cannon barked behind them, but they were far out of range, and ahead of them, one of Vilken's ships was coming up fast, very fast.

"I think we'd better find something to hold on to," Veronica said.

"I think you're right."

Lightning slashed on all sides; the boiling, tar-black vapors of a thunderhead followed behind. Dusk screamed orders over the shrieking wind. One of the masts leaned forward crazily before the cables holding it upright snapped. With a terrible wrench the entire mast and the sails on it tore loose and hurled itself ahead of them. The other ship grew larger with breathtaking speed.

Errol kept waiting for them to start slowing down so they could board.

Then he realized that wasn't what was about to happen at all.

The broken mast slammed into the other ship. So did they, but in the moment of impact, Errol felt something wrap around him, supporting him. A cloud of flying wood splinters and broken beams parted around him, Veronica, Billy, Dusk and her crew. They were all suspended in a breath of wind as the bow of their ship crashed into the side of the other, cutting it almost in half. The deck beneath him buckled under the strain, the boards springing up as Dusk's ship cracked along her centerline.

Weight returned—along with vertigo—as both ships, turning horizontally, began to fall. But not too quickly; whatever magical force allowed them to fly in the first place hadn't entirely dissipated.

Dusk screamed like a bird of prey and charged. Errol followed, along with Dusk's warriors.

Many of the divlings had been flung from their craft at impact; others were struggling to find their equilibrium when he sprang onto the ruined deck. One of the creatures swung a nasty looking scimitar at him. He dodged to the side and whacked it hard in the jaw.

Dusk, a few feet away, had no compunctions about killing. Her sword sent blood spraying left and right.

Errol knocked another of the things down and turned to see Vilken standing a few yards away, pointing a pistol at him. He tried to turn, but there was no time; the gun puffed smoke, and something slammed into him so hard he fell to the deck. He clutched at his chest and found, not a hole, but something stuck to his armor.

It resembled a black starfish, and it was chewing him. It was also growing, quickly. Distantly, he heard the pistol fire again, and once more as he tried to beat the thing off of him with his sword, but the angle was weird, so he dropped the weapon and began prying it off with his hands. The pain, small at first, was quickly becoming agony.

Aster was a grain of sand, she was the sky. She was Savare the Namebearer, without fear or pity. She was herself, watching as from a great distance as Errol went down beneath some strange horror, and Dusk was flung back by the weapon in Vilken's hand.

It is done, Savare told her, in speech that wasn't speech. *My debt to you father is loosed.*

And with that Savare was gone, and all Aster's senses came rushing back to her body.

"Vilken!" she shouted.

He turned, and pointed his gun, but she Uttered a bolt of lightning from the storm Savare had left behind. It struck through him, and his long coat went up in a blaze. He staggered back, and she yelled in triumph; but he wasn't down yet. His blue-eyed gaze caught her, and in an instant she was back in the room in his castle, with him pulling himself on top of her, as she lay there helpless. Fear greater than any she had ever known gripped her, and she watched him as in a nightmare, striding across the broken deck toward her. One of Dusk's warriors leapt at him, and he shot her in the face, never looking away from Aster, never breaking eye contact.

Mine, his voice laid on her like gravity. *You have always been mine.*

He was a few steps away now. There was no one between him and her.

Then the ships hit the water. The impact threw Vilken from his feet, and sent Aster bouncing painfully across the deck, but the dagger of terror in her brain was withdrawn. Everything rocked as the broken vessels settled upon the waves. She saw him begin to stand, just a few feet away. He locked his gaze with her again, but this time she was ready, drawing on the deepest marrow of her nature.

"I am Aster, daughter of Kostye, daughter of Nevese," she told him. "And you will not take another step toward me."

His eyes blazed with fury; the veins on his forehead stood up. The knife trembled in his hand.

"I am Aster," she shouted, "Companion of Errol, companion of Veronica, companion of Dusk."

She felt a swell of strength as she said their names.

"You are no one," she said. "Motherless, fatherless, without companions, without love. You are nothing, and you are no one."

It stalled him, but he was ancient; he had the strength of time. Like a river that had been flowing in the same bed for ten thousand years, he had etched himself into the foundations of the world; not a strength of presence, but the hideous power of absence that nothing could fill. Against that, her mortal fury and determination could only last so long; she began to waver. He began, very slowly, to move again.

"Child," he snarled. Something snapped in her, and she staggered back.

Then something struck him from the side. She had the briefest glimpse of something huge, gray and white, a fin, a tail, a vast spray of water . . .

Then he was gone.

She realized then, that she stood in water up to her knees; the ships were sinking, fast.

As she started to collapse, Veronica was there.

"Easy," she said.

"What happened?" Aster asked.

"Some problems," Veronica said solemnly, "Are best solved by shark."

B y the time Errol ripped the thing off his armor, it was as big as he was. Its whole underside was teeth, one big star-shaped mouth flopping toward him through the water that was rapidly engulfing everything. He kicked at it, but it latched on to his foot.

Hollering, he cut at it with the edge of his sword. It was the first time he had used the sharp part of the blade, and he was pleasantly surprised at how readily it cut. It went through the monster like a hot knife through butter.

He chopped it off his leg and kept mincing it until it left him alone. He wasn't sure if it was dead or if it *could* die, but he didn't care so long as it wasn't chewing on him, anymore.

Panting, he tried to take in the situation.

They seemed to have won. The divlings were either gone or motionless, and Vilken was nowhere to be seen. Veronica was holding Aster, who looked out of it, and Dusk was being tended to by several of her sailors. She looked wounded, but how badly it was hard to tell. Her eyes were open, and she was swearing, which was hopefully a good sign.

They still had a few worries, though. In a very short time, both ships would be underwater, so they would have to swim, and fight the drag of the ships trying to pull them down. It was probably better to try and get clear now. Except for the other thing—all around them, Vilken's other ships were arriving, and soon they would have an army to deal with. Besides himself, Dusk, Veronica, and Aster, he figured there were about fifteen girls left capable of putting up a fight.

He sloshed over to Veronica.

"This is going to be rough," he said.

"Might be," she agreed.

"Look, about before—"

"Hush," Veronica said. "I might be able to get us out of this. Dusk, too. It won't be fun for you, but . . ."

Above, the sky rumbled. He thought it was still Aster's storm, but that was dissipating. He realized that some of the ships closing in on them were firing on the others.

"Why are they fighting?" he wondered aloud.

Dusk limped over, holding her side. She looked jubilant, despite her injury. "Their standards, you see? Those are not Vilken's ships."

"Whose are they, then?" he asked.

"The flag with the field of black and eight stars, that is my sister Nocturn. The golden sphere—"

"Yeah," Errol said. "I know that one. Your brother Hawk."

"And there is Dawn and Gloam," she said. "They've come after all."

"Is that good? Errol said. "I mean, Hawk did try to kill me."

"Nocturn imprisoned me and had me tortured," Veronica added.

"Those are my siblings," Dusk said. "Contentious and untrustworthy. But if they are together, it is a good sign."

"Why?"

"It means they have agreed to come together to end the curse."

"Yes," Veronica said. "But they do have a friend of ours tied up to their mast."

Errol thought Veronica's eyesight must be better than his— maybe a lot better. As the ships drew nearer, he saw she was right.

"That's Haydevil," he said.

"Huh," Veronica said. "At least we know how they found us."

SIX

FIVE KINGDOMS

I t was Hawk's ship and his creepy little gold men who fished them out of the water. When Hawk saw Errol, he grinned ruefully.

"You were a worthy foe," he said. "I hope now you can accept me as an ally."

"I'm just— your guy *shot* me," Errol said.

Hawk shrugged. "If you wish satisfaction, I understand. We can fight at your convenience. But if it's all the same to you, I think it would be better to end the curse first and fight later."

Errol nodded as if he agreed; he had a hard time believing anything Hawk said, and even more difficulty turning his back on him. Every time he caught sight of one of the bad cupids he itched to draw his sword.

It wasn't a lot better with Nocturn. He'd never met her but knowing how she had treated Veronica didn't endear him to her. As for Gloam—he had apparently been Vilken's footstool up until recently. And they had all had a bad experience with Dusk. The only one he hadn't heard anything bad about was Dawn. She was the youngest of the lot, maybe thirteen, with red hair and freckles. She was bubbly and affable.

Coming from this family, though, he was willing to bet she had her moments, too.

After they were all back on land, Hawk took his fleet back out, scouting to make certain Vilken's forces were routed and not merely regrouping.

Food and drink were unloaded from the remaining ships, and soldiers began setting up camp around the castle. Several of Dawn's retainers were—or at least claimed to be—physicians, and began tending the wounded. Aster was found to be weak, but physically sound. After a few sips of some sort of tea, she came back to weary consciousness. Errol wanted to talk to her, but Gloam was with her, falling all over himself with apologies for the part he'd played in Kostye's Kingdom. He was a very talkative fellow, and Errol wasn't in the mood for pointless chatter. He went searching for Veronica, but couldn't find her, which worried him. When last he'd seen her, she had that look in her eye he'd come to recognize, the one that meant she was up to something. But if she'd wanted him to know what it was, she would have told him. He took it as another sign that their relationship was even more seriously damaged than he thought.

He hoped she wasn't off to kill Nocturn or someone else. Everything finally seemed to be going their way, but at the same time, the peace felt very fragile. If anything happened to one of Dusk's siblings, it was all sure to come apart.

Whatever "it" was.

He decided to look in on Dusk and see how she was. Maybe she could tell him more about what was going on.

Dusk had been stripped of her armor, part of which had been dissolved by some sort of acid Vilken's weapon had discharged. She now wore a flowing robe over her bandages. Her side had been burned, and the pain had obviously been terrific, but she acted as if nothing had happened.

"What of you?" she asked him. "You were injured."

"Yes," he said. "But the armor heals itself, you know."

"But what of the man beneath? You were bleeding."

"It doesn't hurt anymore, so I guess it fixes me, too. But there really isn't any way to know."

"What do you mean?"

That sort of pissed him off. Why was she taunting him?

She saw the look.

"Errol?"

"You know I can't take it off," he said.

She blinked, looking astonished. He realized she wasn't faking it.

"Of course you can," she said. "You have only to say the words."

"Words?" he said.

"Oh. I suppose in all of the tumult I forgot to tell you," she said. "You need only say *bernas veras*."

"Real boy?" Errol translated. "Seriously?"

"You understand the reference? It was something Aster told me about, a story—"

"Yeah, I get the reference," he said. "It's just—never mind. *Bernas veras*."

The last syllable was hardly out of his mouth before the armor simply fell off of him.

"Well," Dusk said. "This is hardly proper." She turned her head away, but he caught a smile as she did so.

"Oh," he said, looking down. "Yeah. Sorry. Excuse me."

He quickly put it back on and made a mental note to ask some of the guys if he could borrow a shirt and pants.

"Thanks," he said, when he was decent again.

"You're welcome," she said.

"Listen," he said, lowering his voice. "We haven't had a chance to talk, since, you know . . ."

"There is nothing to talk about," she said. "I made a mistake, yes?"

"Well—mistake? I don't know. But it's just that—"

"You're loyal," she said, her voice rather flat. "That is your nature. I must respect that loyalty—as you must respect mine."

He immediately felt a little wary. The last time her "loyalties" had come into play, things had gone poorly for the rest of them.

He was wondering how to frame a question about that when Nocturn arrived. She looked like a spooky, dark-haired version of Dusk. He kept expecting her to smile and show vampire teeth.

"Vilken?" Dusk asked.

"His fleet is routed. As for he himself, it isn't clear. I did a Night Spinning on the matter of his demise, and it was inconclusive."

"A shark ate him," Errol said.

Nocturn looked at him as if he had entered a fancy restaurant wearing camouflage and a trucker's hat.

"For one such as he, that is hardly proof of his death," she said.

"She's right."

He hadn't seen Veronica arrive, and he now began to wonder how long she had been there, outside of the tent flap. Had she heard his conversation with Dusk?

"You don't think he's dead?" Errol said.

Veronica shrugged. "I don't know for sure. But my gut says no." She nodded at Nocturn. "You're a bitch, by the way," she said. "Just so you know."

Nocturn looked daggers at her.

"I remember you." The black-haired woman said. "You wouldn't happen to know what became of my prisoner, would you?"

"You mean Haydevil?" Veronica asked. "Oops. I sort of let him go."

Errol sighed. So that was what she had been up to. He'd hoped to free Haydevil by negotiation.

Nocturn swore something under her breath and reached for her sword. "*Nov*, that will be the last of you, I think—"

"Nocturn," Dusk snapped. "Stay your hand. Haydevil? You had him prisoner? Why didn't I hear of this?"

"He has been a thorn in my side," Nocturn said.

"You kind of moved into his house without permission," Veronica said. "I don't blame him. Anyway, he's our friend. Ask your sister."

"Yes," Dusk agreed. "He has been helpful to us in the past. Nocturn, forget this, and think instead of the task at hand."

Nocturn's expression suggested she wasn't in such a forgiving mood, but then she shrugged.

"You're right. And if on nothing else, on this the *nov* and I agree. We must act quickly. The Five Kingdoms. We must employ them immediately and end the curse."

"Kingdoms?" Errol said.

"She means the little marble-things," Veronica explained.

"Indeed," Nocturn said. "Aster unrolled the Coral Kingdom to reveal this island. We discovered the Kingdom of Silver on Haydevil, which led us to this place. I myself possess the Kingdom of Obsidian. Hawk has the Copper Kingdom. The Kingdom of Gold, I assume in is your possession, Dusk."

"It is not," Dusk said. "It was taken from me when Vilken made me captive. He must have had it. Which means—"

"Yeah," Veronica said, "On that subject."

She opened her fist. On her palm rested a gleaming sphere.

"The Kingdom of Gold!" Dusk exclaimed. "You found it!"

"Careful," Veronica said. "It has shark vomit on it."

Dusk closed her eyes and sighed in relief.

"Thank you," she said. "Without you—"

"Let's just do this, okay?" Veronica said. "I'm a little tired of all this honey-talk."

Dusk nodded. "Gather everyone in the castle," she said. "Whether Vilken survives or not, there are others who would frustrate our designs. This is best done now, while we have the means and are unopposed."

"I'll go find Ms. Fincher," Errol said. "I'll get Aster, too."

D elia entered the garden, seeking still and quiet. Her mind was unable to stop replaying the motion of the last few . . . hours? Days?

Time had so little meaning without clocks and sunsets.

She hoped to find a little solace here but found that Aster was already present. She hesitated a moment, debating whether to go in at all and was just deciding not to when Aster noticed her and beckoned for her to enter.

"This is nice," she said, at a loss for how to start a conversation that might be the very one she was dreading.

"I remember it," Aster said. "From when I was a little girl. Sometimes—back in Sowashee—sometimes I started to believe it was only a dream. Something I imagined or made up. Sometimes, after Dad got bad, I began to think maybe none of it was real. That I was crazy, like he was."

"But you weren't."

"I might have been better off if I was," she said.

"Are you all right?" Delia asked, knowing it sounded inane.

"No," Aster said. "I'm really not. Dad—you didn't know him when I was little. He loved me so much, sometimes it was hard for me to understand. But the thing I did know was that I was the only one he had. My mother was gone; he never talked about any other family. He never had friends. Only me. But I could also tell he had given up . . . a lot. But I never knew what it was. I still don't. You never understood why I wouldn't apply to colleges. Do you get it now?"

"Yes," Delia said. "You didn't have any other goals."

"That's right. I was going to fix him, and he was going to be my dad again, and we were going to live happily ever after. And if I couldn't have that—"

"Then you didn't want anything," Delia said. "I understand."

"I'm sorry I got you pulled into this," Aster said.

"Don't be," Delia said. "I would rather . . ." But she couldn't think of any way to say it that wouldn't sound trite and stupid and somehow the moment seemed to rise above something one might find on a dime-store gift card.

"Did you love him?" Aster asked.

Delia realized she was crying, but she didn't make any effort to hold it in.

"Yes," she said.

Aster was silent for a bit. "This is weird," she said.

A laugh coughed up out of Delia. "Yes," she said. "Very inappropriate."

"I think it's okay," Aster said. "I don't imagine you're going to get your old job back."

"Right," Delia said. "Probably not."

"Thank you," Aster said.

"For what?"

"For being with him. I'm glad he had someone who cared about him besides me. It makes it a little easier."

"I hope so," Delia said.

She heard a soft clearing of the throat, and saw Errol was standing at the entrance to the garden.

"Time to, you know, save the world," he said.

"We'll be right there," Aster told him.

T his would be the weirdest group photo ever, Errol thought. The
brothers and sisters and Aster, with their various forehead
birthmarks. The bad cupids and Nocturn's gaggle of bat-wan-
nabees, a boy in wooden armor, Billy looking out-of-place in
one of Gloam's dandified outfits, his high school guidance
counselor wearing a peasant dress.

All standing around a chick in a glass coffin?

Say "cheese."

But no one said much of anything. He had expected some
sort of incantation, boiling green liquid, incense. Why, he wasn't
sure; he'd seen plenty of magic by now, and none of it was like
that. On the other hand, he had never been around when something really big was being done, like taking a curse off of the
entire universe.

What happened was that Dusk opened her palm, revealing
the silver sphere. She gently rolled it onto the ground as Aster
had, with the same results; it expanded quickly, and the light
changed once again; the weird glow in the castle was gone,
replaced by a setting sun in the west. Then Nocturn rolled hers,
and night fell. Not instantaneously—the setting sun simply
very quickly finished its journey. The moon rose, full, with the
same unnerving speed.

Then it was Dawn's turn, and night became morning, with
the sun peeking up in the east.

Hawk was next, rolling out the Golden Kingdom. The sun
charged up to midday, and the earth shifted under them. Errol
realized that they were no longer in the seashell mansion but
were instead within the golden walls of a gigantic castle, with
all sort of towers and minarets climbing skyward.

And the glass coffin—it wasn't glass anymore. It wasn't the same thing for two seconds in a row. In one blink of the eye it was a body wrapped in cobwebs, in the next, the sarcophagus he had encountered outside of the city of pyramids, the woman with the porcelain face, then a sort of mermaid with a snake's body, a shining tree with golden fruit. The images shifted, went faster and faster until they became a column of rainbow light that was soon too bright to look directly at. He felt heat on his face, growing hotter.

Then the light dimmed and the heat backed off, and the images and effulgence resolved into a woman. It was not the woman they had seen in the coffin. Not Aster's mother.

She was tall, clothed in a shimmering gown of yellow-white. Like Aster's mother she was blond, but her hair was even lighter, almost true white. She wore a white crown with a hundred little points flaring out. She was beautiful, and she was also terrifying.

Hawk dropped to his knees, quickly followed by all his siblings, including Dusk.

"Majesty!" Hawk said.

Errol watched them, wondering what the hell was going on. Who was this woman? He had seen the sarcophagus in the mash of images. Was it her, the one who had saved him from the ghul, given him the feather?

"Rise children," the woman said. "You have done well. You have done very well." Her words were music; Errol had never heard a more perfect voice. To his great surprise, she took a step toward him.

"Errol," she said. "So pure of heart. My true champion."

She turned to Veronica. "And you, darkling. You found your way here. I am so proud of you."

Veronica's eyes were wide; she was trying to keep her face otherwise expressionless, but to Errol she looked troubled.

"And you, Aster," she said. "Most of all. You brought me back, when so much stood in your way. Yours is the greatest sacrifice."

"Who are you?" Aster asked.

"She is our mother," Hawk said. "The queen."

"Aster!" Ms. Fincher said, but the queen waved her hand, and she caught at her throat, unable to speak. Aster blinked and opened her mouth, but she, too was waved to silence.

"I don't understand, Mother," Dusk said. "Have we not done what was needed? Is the curse not broken?"

The queen's smile was so radiant it made Errol's legs quiver.

"The curse cannot be undone," she said. "The world you were born into will never exist again. But you and I, my children, can remake it. Better. Brighter. It can be ours."

"How?" Hawk said.

The queen pointed at Aster. "Aster is the issue of the curse. She is the very nadir of it. Her blood will change the world and heal it."

Errol got that. He didn't need to be a genius to see where this was going. He drew his sword.

"Yeah," he said. "Hell no."

"Errol," the queen said. Her voice was gentle, full of care.

"There is a place for you at my side. You need never return to the dead world from which you come. Your soul, like ours, can be eternal."

That stopped him. He remembered the white lady coming for him. The terror, the absolute certainty that when she ended him, nothing would remain. No ghost, no spirit, no soul. To live forever, to be free of the fear of facing her again, this time for real—it sounded good.

Yet, his father had been there, too, and his father should have been just as dead and gone. Maybe he was; maybe none of that had been real.

But maybe it had. And maybe it didn't matter anyway.

"There are worse things than dying," he said. "And what you're asking me to do is one of them."

He started forward, but one of Nocturn's goons seized him from behind. Billy jumped forward and knocked Gloam down before charging the queen, but three golden arrows appeared in his chest. His eyes went wide, and he dropped to his knees, looking more puzzled than anything else. Aster ran toward Billy, but Hawk grabbed her by one arm, and Nocturn by the other.

"Dusk," the queen said. Errol struggled, but he couldn't break free of the men holding him.

Hawk forced Aster to her knees and pushed her head down, exposing her neck.

"Dusk!" Errol shouted. "No!"

Dusk drew her sword. She shot Errol what he took to be an apologetic glance, before raising her weapon to cut off Aster's head.

Instead, Dusk punched Hawk in the face with the butt of her weapon, and moving very quickly indeed, slapped Nocturn on the side of the head with flat of her blade. She yelled something, and a sort of shock ran through the air. Aster gasped for breath, and shouted a word of her own.

In an instant, a whirlwind sprang up around Aster, sweeping everyone outside of its eye away, the queen included. Nocturn staggered into the wall of wind and was gone. Errol charged forward, balled up his fist, and hit Hawk with every ounce of strength he had, and he too vanished into the screaming cyclone.

Now only Aster, Dusk, Veronica, Billy, and Errol were visible, although a terrific light was growing in the direction the queen had been blown.

"Aster!" Dusk yelled. "The Kingdom of Coral! Roll it back!"

Aster, wild eyed, didn't seem to understand her. But then she opened her mouth and called, beckoning with her hand.

The wind and light died away to nothing. Dusk's siblings and their minions were scattered all about the great courtyard, but the queen still stood, looking very, very angry. She raised both of her hands and began to speak. Even then, it sounded lovely, like singing.

The world closed in around Errol and his companions. Everything distorted as if they were inside of a goldfish bowl, looking out.

Then everything stopped.

They were standing on the island, but there was no seashell castle and no golden palace. It was exactly as when they had first arrived. And in her palm, Aster held the Kingdom of Coral, again the size of a shooter marble.

She tucked it into her pocket and dropped down beside Billy. He didn't look calm, as he usually did. He looked like someone bleeding out from three arrows wounds ought to.

Aster was weeping. "I don't know how to save you," she said. "I don't have any spells for this."

"It's okay," Billy said. He looked terrified, but he reached up to touch her face. "At least I saw you again."

"Aster," Dusk said, stepping forward.

She held a small phial in her hand. Errol recognized it.

"The water of health," he said.

"I used the rest," Dusk said. "I tried to revive my mother with it. It didn't work, although it did awaken her from her deepest slumber—and I suppose, led us to these straits. But I never used the last dose."

Errol saw, then, that Dusk had her other hand pressed to her side. It was completely red, and her gown was soaked with blood.

Aster noticed, too.

"I may live," Dusk replied. "It bleeds, yes, but the blade may have missed my organs. Take it. Please. I cannot redress all I have done, but this I can do for you."

"Thank you," Aster said. She took the phial and knelt beside Billy, pouring the liquid between his parted lips. Then she pulled out the arrows. Billy screamed until he passed out.

Dusk turned her gaze to Errol and collapsed.

When he reached her side, she was still breathing, and her eyes were still open.

"My armor!" he said. "If we put it on you—"

"Only you may wear it," she said. "It is part of you." She clutched his hand. "Errol," she said. "I didn't know. I didn't know they meant to kill Aster, not until right before you did. You must believe me."

"I believe you," he said. "Why shouldn't I believe you?"

"Because I have lied to you so often," she said. "I thought my reasons were sound. I told myself I was doing what I must. Our mother promised to restore the world, to set things right. She is my mother, and I believed her. Forgive me."

"Sure," Errol said. "But you need to hang in there. You've survived a lot worse than this."

He noticed from the corner of his eye that Veronica was also kneeling down next to her.

"Apologize to *me*," Veronica said.

Dusk was noticeably weaker with each passing second. Her eyes were half closed.

"I *am* sorry, Veronica," she said. "What I did to you was unforgivable."

"Uh-huh," Veronica said. She took a deep breath. "You may not like this."

Dusk, wheezing now, lifted her hand toward Veronica.

"It is our time of reckoning," Dusk said. "I understand."

"It is," Veronica said. "So I hope *you* understand."

Dusk nodded.

"Veronica—" Errol began.

"Stay back, Errol," Dusk said. "It is what must be."

It wasn't a spell, but he nevertheless felt transfixed by the certainty in her tone.

Veronica bent, cradled Dusk's head in her hands, and kissed her. Dusk groaned, lay back, and was still.

Horrified, Errol watched Veronica rise, unable to process what she had done. What he had let her do.

Veronica let out a slow breath and turned to him.

"I have to go Errol," she said. "I can't explain."

"What are you talking about?" It wasn't what he wanted to say. But what he wanted to say, he couldn't even wrap his head around.

She smiled sadly, then kissed him, too. Her lips were very warm.

She turned, ran, and dove from the cliff. Errol chased after her in time to see one leg kick above the water. Then she was gone, except—he thought he saw something else, an ocean swell, but with something beneath it, something big.

Then, that too was gone.

SEVEN

CARGO

Errol sat on the stony shore watching the waves come in, break into foam, pull away. He knew they'd won, at least for the moment, but it didn't feel like victory. A glance back showed Aster and Billy as a single shadow, clutched together, and Ms. Fincher sitting apart. He knew he should go talk to them, try to figure out what to do next, but at the moment he couldn't stand the thought of it.

Instead, he walked up the shore. It wasn't a beach like he was used to; there was no sand, but instead water-worn, slippery stone. The tide was out, and lots of little pools had been abandoned by the sea, along with starfish, crabs, and the occasional fish. The pools shimmered in the sunlight, growing brighter by the moment.

Because in the east, the sun was rising.

And outlined against that light, a shadow.

He thought Veronica had come back. But then—by the outline of her dress—he figured it was Aster.

Then the woman turned onto the beach so the sunlight shone on the side of her face, and he saw it was neither.

In a blink, as when the Kingdoms had been unrolled, everything changed; everything he knew was in doubt.

Death had come for him before. Had he ever truly escaped her? Was he still in his hospital bed, in a coma, dreaming this? If so, this time the woman in white had chosen a more pleasing form, one he wasn't afraid of. He had been offered eternal life, and he had turned it down. He wasn't sorry, so if his time had finally come . . .

Then he saw the white dress was bloodstained, and when the sun finally lit her features, and he saw her eyes, he did not find death there.

"Dusk?" he said.

She stopped a few feet away. The surf rolled up and retreated, leaving froth on her bare feet.

"Yes," she replied.

"Is this real?"

Dusk laughed. "If it isn't, it hurts like it is."

"How can you be alive?" He asked. "Veronica . . ."

She bowed her head slightly. "Veronica healed me," she said. "It is not what I expected. *Novs* are capable only of feeding on life, not restoring it."

"What does that mean?" he asked.

"It means she is no longer a *nov*," Dusk said. "And it means she showed me mercy — more mercy than I deserved."

She stepped closer. "Mercy I shall try to be worthy of."

"I thought you were dead," he whispered.

"I am here, Errol," she said.

It was wonderful and confusing. The surf and the sunrise became as distant as the stars as he stood there, not knowing what to do, how to feel.

How long they stood that way, he didn't know. But when they broke, it was because he heard Aster shouting.

"There," Dusk said.

Something was approaching on the sea. They gathered together on the hill, waiting.

"I knew they would come after us," Dusk said. "I thought it would take longer."

"It is only one ship," Billy said.

It was on the water, not in the air, but its sails were billowed, even though the wind was still. It gleamed silver in the sunlight. As it drew near, Errol saw a familiar figure standing in the deck.

"I know that ship!" Aster exclaimed. "That's my father's ship!"

Suddenly the wind did come, a great whirl of it and an instant later, Haydevil stood before them, and there was Mistral too, and the Brume.

"No," he said. "Still our ship, you know. You traded it to us." He looked them over, clucking and shaking his head.

"You're a sorry-looking lot," he said. "What a mess."

"Haydevil!" Aster said. "You came back."

"You didn't make it easy," he complained. "All of that rolling and unrolling of Kingdoms. And our ship isn't so fancy, you know—built for water, like a sensible craft. But it does have its talents."

He smiled, but looked nervous.

"Let's, eh, be quick, shall we? I believe if we wait here for much longer, we shall have visitors of a quite unpleasant sort."

They boarded and set sail with both their triumphs and their losses as cargo, and for a long time, they let the winds take them where they would.

EPILOGUE

O nce more, he was without body, drifting. Currents tugged him this way and that, but the strongest of them was pulling him down, to the place of his former exile, the grey, diminished place where he had lived so many impoverished, frustrating lives. He had been so close—how long before he had another chance? A century? A millennium?

Longer.

He still had them, the little lights he had collected. They still shone as brightly as when he first salvaged them from their coffins of flesh. But they would not sustain him for long, not in the Reign of the Departed.

Down in the bottom of him, what was left of the Sheriff was laughing. He tried to shutter him away, overpower him with his own thoughts, but he couldn't. Still, it built his anger. It grew in him like a black star. Though he was without substance, he fought with the only things he had left. His ancient, implacable will. His fury.

It came out of him like a scream, and although there was no sound, Creation heard it, deep in its bones. He had no substance—he couldn't move a feather—but he could be heard. At least he could do that.

He began to lose himself. Terror, apprehension—thought itself vanished as he became all rage and wrath. And resistance.

Still the tide pulled him out, toward that dark shore of the universe. But he no longer cared.

Eventually, he realized some other force was tugging at him. It was slight when it began, not enough to stop his fall, but it gradually grew stronger, until finally he was at rest.

He felt himself lifted up, slowly at first, but with gathering speed. No longer down, but higher, and much farther away.

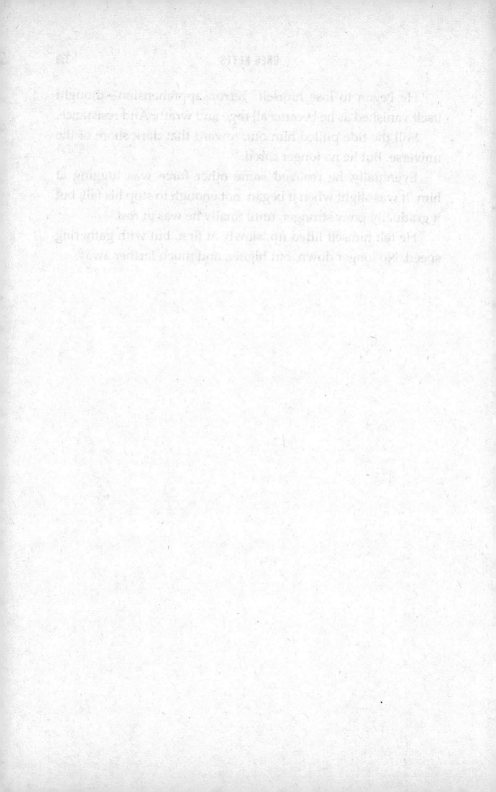

ACKNOWLEDGEMENTS

Thanks to Paula Guran for a thoughtful and thorough edit; to Micah Epstein for another wonderful painting and to Claudia Noble for turning it into an excellent cover. Appreciations to Joshua Barnaby for production, and as always to Cory Allyn for bringing these books to print.

GREG KEYES

was born April 11, 1963 in Meridian, Mississippi. When his father took a job on the Navajo Reservation in Arizona, Greg was exposed at an early age to the cultures and stories of the Native Southwest, which would continue to inform him for years to come. He earned a bachelor's degree in anthropology at Mississippi State University and a Master's degree at the University of Georgia. While pursuing his PhD at UGA, he wrote several novels, one of which—*The Waterborn*—was published, along with its sequel *The Blackgod*. He followed this with The Age of Unreason books, the epic fantasy series Kingdoms of Thorn and Bone, and novels from several franchises, including Star Wars, Babylon Five, The Elder Scrolls, and Planet of the Apes. He now lives and works in Savannah, Georgia with his wife Nell, son John Edward Arch, and daughter Dorothy Nellah Joyce.